ANDY C

OXFORD BLUES

Orphans Publishing

To John and Kay

This edition published in 2023 by Orphans Publishing
Enterprise Park, Leominster
Herefordshire HR6 0LD

www.orphanspublishing.co.uk

A Cataloguing in Publication record for this book is available from the British Library

Paperback: 978-1-903360-53-8

Printed and bound by Clays Ltd, Elcograf, S.p.A.

'If only there were evil people somewhere insidiously committing evil deeds, and it were necessary only to separate them from the rest of us and destroy them. But the line dividing good and evil cuts through the heart of every human being.'

Aleksandr Solzhenitsyn, *The Gulag Archipelago, Part IV*

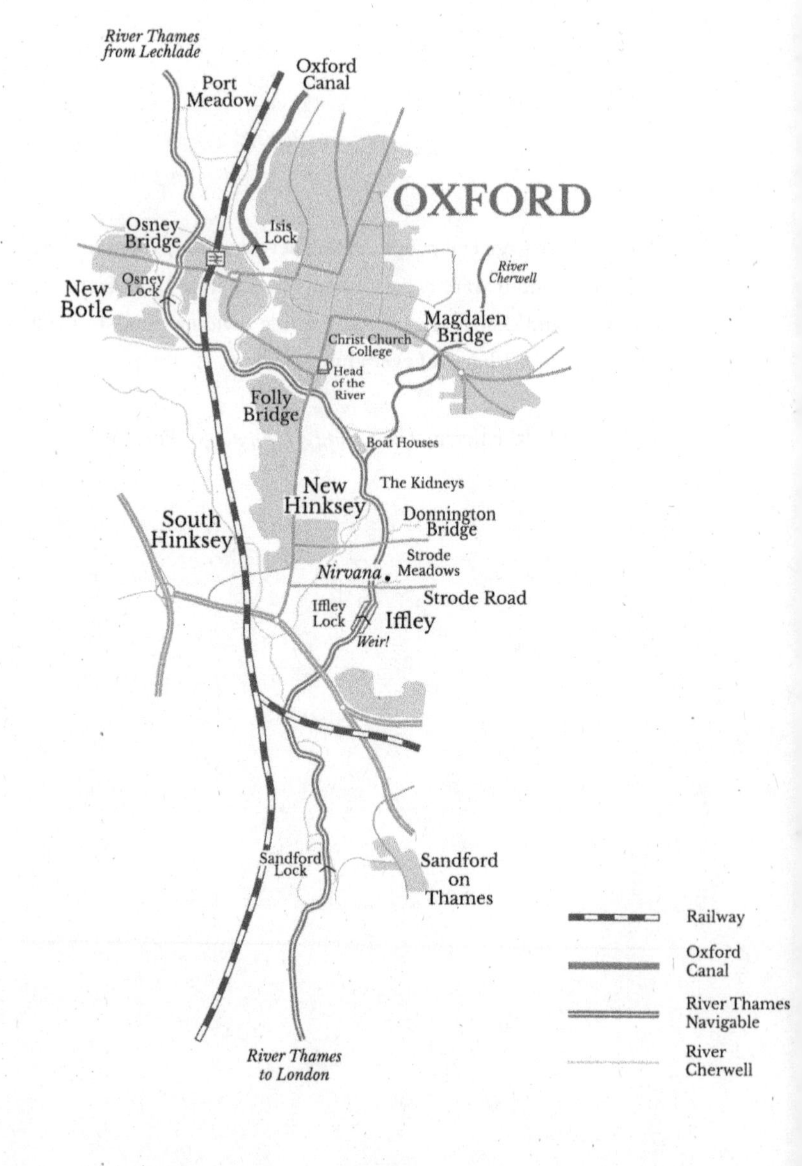
River Thames
from Lechlade
Port
Meadow
Oxford
Canal
OXFORD
Osney
Bridge
Isis
Lock
River
Cherwell
Osney
Lock
New
Botle
Magdalen
Bridge
Christ Church
College
Head
of the
River
Folly
Bridge
Boat Houses
The Kidneys
New
Hinksey
South
Hinksey
Donnington
Bridge
Strode
Meadows
Nirvana
Strode Road
Iffley
Lock
Iffley
Weir!
Sandford
Lock
Sandford
on
Thames
River Thames
to London
Railway
Oxford
Canal
River Thames
Navigable
River
Cherwell

A place where two gods meet to make love may be just as fatal to mortals as a place where the deities join to do battle. The weir at Iffley, where two rivers meet on the outskirts of Oxford, is such a place. Thamus – old Father Thames – flexes his still powerful physique and allows his long hair and beard to ebb and flow in the strong winter current. Isis, the Divine One, the queen of all gods and the origin of all life, swims to meet him, her long sheath dress clinging then billowing free as she moves gracefully towards her lover.

Often, in this place, the long limbs of the two river gods brush against each other with the gentlest of foreplay, slipping and joining gently as one. But at other times, in the embodiment of the seasonal renewal that is delivered by their namesake rivers, the lovemaking throws them together forcefully, thrashing fiercely against each other. Today is such a day. Giddy spiralling whorls on the surface of the water betray the frantic passions beneath. The shell-like shapes spin relentlessly, tighter and tighter, faster and faster, before they are pushed downstream into calmer water where they fade and vanish. This is the place where Thamus and Isis will eventually go to rest in the Spring and recover their energies in lazy post-coital bliss.

On this particular Saturday in January two men are standing on a wooden bridge between the Iffley bank and an island with a lock and the lock-keeper's cottage, staring down into the disturbed water. The bridge is narrow and stands a metre apart from another wooden construction, a weir gate with a tiled pitched roof covered by vivid green moss along its length. Barriers underneath the gate can be raised and lowered to control the flow of water.

The men, in their early twenties, were born two years apart but a casual onlooker might mistake them for twins. They are both tall and lean with close cropped beards, prominent cheekbones and jet-black hair tucked into woollen beanies. Both wear hiking-boots below waterproof trousers and thick fleeces zipped up to their chins to keep out the winter cold. One has his hand resting on the other's shoulder and their eyes are fixed on a line that stretches taut and enters the water ten metres in front of them.

'One more go,' says the older brother. For the fourth time in two minutes they both pull hard with their gloved hands. But the line fails to move even the slightest distance.

'I said we shouldn't risk it here,' says the younger brother. 'God knows what's under there.' He points to the wide expanse of dark and troubled water in front of them. 'And it cost a fortune.'

He is referring to an immensely powerful fist-sized magnet, currently stuck under the water before them. The pair began their magnet-fishing excursions a year ago, tossing their line into the Oxford Canal and retrieving a steady supply of lost windlasses, discarded bicycles, coins, scrap-metal, shopping trollies and, once, an entire mobility scooter. An unexpected end-of-year bonus has prompted them to invest almost a thousand pounds in the magnet marketed as 'The Beast'.

'I said we should have tried it somewhere quiet first,' he continues, spitting into the river in disgust. 'Cost a bloody fortune, that did.'

'So, you keep saying.'

'Well, what're we going to do then? Dry-suit and a tank?'

Both the young men are qualified scuba-divers and they keep their kit locked in the back of a carefully restored Land Rover, which is currently parked next to a pub in Iffley village.

The older brother shakes his head, staring at the whirlpools below. 'I don't like the look of this current.' He is thinking of a recent newspaper story about another pair of magnet fishermen, a father and his eighteen-year-old son. One had gone into the water near a steep bank and the other had followed – presumably on some kind of a rescue mission.

Police divers later found their bodies within touching distance of each other, still standing and swaying upright under the water with their feet buried in silt and weeds. The brothers have already registered the urgent warning signs sited around this particular lock and weir.

'What about the winch?' says the younger brother, relieved that he won't be expected to enter the turbulent river. His suggestion is greeted with a frustrated nod so he heads off to fetch the heavy piece of equipment from their vehicle.

Fifteen minutes later the winch is bolted to a sturdy wooden upright of the bridge and the line is coiled several times around its drum. The brothers both wrap their hands over the handle and pull back on it with all their strength. The handle slowly shifts towards them.

'It's coming!' says the older brother. 'Again.' Grunting with the effort, the drum slowly turns, and the wet line begins winding its way in. 'It's not stuck now,' he pants, 'but it's bloody heavy. Our old magnet would've come free by now.'

'Car engine block?'

'Who knows? Just turn the ... the handle.'

It takes five more minutes of exhausting inch-by-inch progress before the line is vertical below them.

'Lock it now.' The brake is flipped onto the cogs and the line is held taut. They both gratefully stretch their arms and shoulder muscles before peering down into the water. The powerful magnet can now be seen, just above the river's surface, and it seems to be clamped to a large round object covered by a blue canvas. The material stretches down around the disc until it can no longer be seen. Showers of rain have gusted along the river throughout the morning. A trickle of dog-walkers and joggers have hurried past the brothers on the bridge with their heads bent down, reluctant to linger in the wet and the cold to watch what they are doing. Now it begins to rain again, the drops spotting the surface of the river below them.

'Come on, one last effort.'

The magnet and the disc can now be seen through the gaps in the bridge's wooden balustrade. The canvas bag is pipe-shaped below the disc and appears hollow until it bulges into a shapeless mass which begins about a metre above the fast-flowing river.

'See if you can get the hook under it.' The younger brother flips the winch brake again and bends to pick up a wooden-handled boat hook from the floor. He leans out over the rail and tries to hook the curved metal point under the disc. They both pull and it comes closer towards them, but the hook tears a hole in the canvas and, as the bag begins to spin on the end of the line, there is a ripping noise. The weight of its load has created a jagged tear.

Then it happens. As the blue canvas load spins and the rip continues to lengthen, the head of a young woman suddenly lolls into the open air. Two open but sightless eyes stare up at the young men. Long, sodden black hair hangs down as her neck stretches taut with the weight of her head, as though it might snap at any second. There is a blue-black mark circling her throat in shocking contrast to the extreme whiteness of the rest of her skin.

'FUCK!' they shout in unison, leaping backwards as though it might save them from the dreadful sight. But it will haunt them for the rest of their lives. The bag, suspended under the disc, continues to rotate with the dead woman inside. Its lower end is buffeted by the water flowing through the weir gates. The woman's head, hanging backwards out of the tear in the canvas, spins slowly with it.

The police operation to recover the woman's body is complicated. The divers are worried that any further attempts to lift the bag from above will rip the canvas along its entire length and spill its contents into the broad expanse of river. But they too have taken one look at the dark and broiling water and are reluctant to enter it. Eventually, after much discussion, they loop another line around the middle of the bag and tie it tight. Then they take its other end to the bottom of the nearest riverside garden in the hope that pulling it horizontally through the water will put less stress on their load and keep it intact.

The garden belongs to a property called the Old Parsonage, a fifteenth-century clerical home that has been bought and restored by The Landmark Trust, a charity that leases it out to holidaymakers. Its current weekend tenants, three well-to-do middle-aged couples, have gathered by the remains of an ancient mulberry tree on the slope of the garden to watch the drama unfold. They have already pressed steaming mugs of tea into the hands of the two young magnet fishermen who are shivering with shock and cold. The bystanders can't help themselves from edging forward as the police divers slip into the water from the garden's edge and carefully lift the canvas bundle up onto some flagstones. Two plain clothes detectives are standing between the holidaymakers and the diving team, huddled in thick puffer jackets.

A long time ago, before Christians arrived with baptisms and ceremonies of hydromancy, ancient priests or adepts used this same spot for their rituals.

Some would throw pebbles into the sacred river water and count the number of circles that rippled across the surface, or interpret the significance of the colours of the water of the river. At other times, human skulls were thrown into the water as part of shamanic purification rites. Isis looked on from her watery depths with a smile as the Christians built St Mary's Church nearby in honour of their Virgin Mary. They said she was like her, another Mother of God who magically conceived her own son. Now, there is something unworldly and priestlike in the all-white appearance of the figures who are waiting at the bottom of The Old Parsonage's garden. When the river gives up its dead they bend over the body-shaped roll of canvas in their hooded suits as though in prayer.

One prises off the magnet and reaches inside to determine what it had been stuck to. He pulls out a heavy round metal disc and examines it briefly. It appears to be some kind of weightlifting equipment. He places it into a plastic evidence bag and then into a holdall before repeating the operation at the other end of the bag. Once again, he extracts a round metal weight of similar dimensions. Then the body, with river weeds still coiled around its makeshift shroud, is carefully rolled onto a large white plastic sheet. The sheet is sealed at both ends then transferred onto a stretcher and carried into the back of an anonymous black van that is waiting by the tall garden wall. Meanwhile, the river continues to flow by, as ancient as the world and much, much older than the flow of blood in human veins.

CHAPTER ONE

I pour myself another mug of coffee from the flask on the stern seat and adjust the tiller slightly to take *Jumping Jack Flash* into the centre of the river. There are no other boats on the water; those safely moored up are the sensible ones. It is a bitterly cold, grey day with low cloud cover and the threat of snow is in the air. The bleakness of the weather matches my mood. As I creep closer towards Oxford at walking pace, the extravagant promise of Matthew Arnold's 'city of dreaming spires' seems a hollow one. This has been a lonely journey from Bath, made worse by spending Christmas alone with my Border Terrier, Eddie, and a self-indulgent fifteen-year-old bottle of Dalwhinnie. Nina Wilde, the unrequited love-of-my-life, and the reason I'm heading for Oxford in the first place, has only joined me once on the trip – at Pangbourne. She has been busy wrapping up her life in Salisbury but soon she will be renting a flat in Oxford near her niece until she can find somewhere suitable to buy.

I had taken little comfort in Nina's Christmas present to me, which was the only gift I had to unwrap on the 25th of December. It was a beautifully printed copy of *The Wind in the Willows* and I had stared balefully at the images of Ratty and Mole messing about on the river, dismissed them as annoying propaganda and poured myself another drink for my festive breakfast. There is nothing joyful about cruising the Thames on your own at this time of year. Anyone who suggests otherwise has never done it – or has a book to sell.

Nina's niece, Anna, has just finished her first term as an undergraduate at the city's university and the two women spent Christmas together in a boutique hotel in Barcelona – a desertion that I felt only served to reinforce my position in the overall rankings of Nina's affection. Anna's mother, Marion, died of breast cancer and the young woman is estranged from her father, Nina's older brother, who left home for another woman during the immediate aftermath of his wife's diagnosis. I have gently suggested to Nina that Anna might not want her aunt breathing down her neck as she finds her feet at university. But Nina, who is still grieving for her army officer husband as well as her sister-in-law, describes Anna as the younger sister she never had and feels a keen sense of responsibility for her. And when Nina Wilde becomes determined on a course of action, it takes a better man than me to dissuade her.

So, I have trailed after Nina to Oxford and I am currently feeling pretty pathetic and cross with myself for doing so. It took much longer than I had anticipated to disentangle myself from my life in Bath. The boat's engine needed some maintenance work before I could be wholly confident of trusting it against the flow of the Thames in deep mid-winter. Then my landlord Robert, the wealthy businessman who had rented me my city centre mooring on the Kennet & Avon Canal, offered me generous compensation to delay my departure by a month so that I could keep an eye on his Georgian mansion while he decamped to Barbados with a young and very beautiful female companion.

I had still hoped to be snugly moored up in Oxford by Christmas, but my planned departure in mid-November slipped past in a miserable miasma of flu. My efforts to walk Eddie in a weakened state of health only made matters worse, and I eventually took to my bunk for a fortnight with a wracking cough, streaming cold, feverish nights and inadequate self-medication. Thankfully, an earnest young man from the Canal Ministry came calling with a bible and took pity on me. He left with my little dog and returned with a fresh supply of coal for the stove and a doctor who gave him a prescription to take to the nearest pharmacy. The saintly Jonathan called twice a day after that and I was grateful to him for walking Eddie and warming up the occasional tin of soup for me. However, he faded away as I slowly recovered my strength and he realised that I had no corresponding interest in the salvation of my soul.

I can see from my J.M. Pearson & Son Canal Companion that the river will swing very sharply to the right after Culham Lock and the Culham Cut before it then bends to the left on the final approach to Abingdon Marina. The book says Abingdon is reputedly the 'prettiest riverine town' on the Thames and I am looking forward to mooring up and finding a warm pub with some comfort food for lunch. My coffee has gone cold, so I toss the dregs over the side in disgust and drain the last few mouthfuls from the flask into the empty mug.

The river circles around on itself at this point, so that it takes five miles to travel between two railway bridges that are just two miles apart as the crow flies. It seems an apt metaphor for my meandering and slow-paced relationship with Nina – a one-way affair that's taking forever to arrive at any satisfactory destination. Perhaps this new start in Oxford will change things for the better? Or perhaps it will make things worse? Perhaps being surrounded by bright young things will accentuate the fifteen-year age gap between us? And yet we make a good team – our adventures in Bath with a small community of liveaboards eventually led to the imprisonment of two unscrupulous property developers, their violent henchman and a pair of corrupt councillors. I'm not sure if I'd have got involved without her urging. The newspaper and magazine sales of the story have topped up my small savings and I will be solvent for the next few months. However, I will need to find some work in Oxford as soon as I possibly can.

An excited yapping from the bow interrupts my gloomy thoughts. Something has set Eddie off. I peer along the 64-foot length of my floating home's roof, but the river ahead is still empty. Then I see them. Two women standing at the mouth of the marina, jumping up and down and waving their hands excitedly in the air. And in that brief moment, my mood lifts. The grim set of my mouth melts into a huge grin and I wave back furiously with one hand, keeping the other on the tiller.

I am still beaming like an idiot as I manoeuvre *Jumping Jack Flash* onto a short-term visitor mooring, throw a stern rope across to Nina and cut the engine. She neatly loops it through a large metal ring on the pontoon and brings it back onto the stern platform.

'Hello, you,' she says, going up on tiptoes to plant a kiss on my cheek and throwing her arms around the back of my neck. 'Surprised?'

'Yes, very!' I laugh and hug her back before taking the end of the rope and securing it onto a cleat.

'Good. Anna and I decided to join you for the last bit after I got your text last night. We've been waiting here for a couple of hours though, and we're bloody frozen.'

The tilted little ski-slope of her nose is pink with cold, but Nina's large dark eyes are sparkling with excitement and it looks like her Audrey Hepburn-style hair has been recently cut. She is wearing a blue and yellow sailing coat with black jeans, gloves, scarf and a large pair of walking boots.

'And this is Anna,' she adds as the younger woman walks along the pontoon from the bow, carrying Eddie against her chest. 'Come and meet the famous Jack Johnson, Anna. I can't believe you guys haven't met before now. But give me Eddie first. Hello, you lovely boy... have you missed me? Of course you have!'

Anna hands over the little dog who is wriggling frantically at the sight of Nina. Then she steps up onto the platform and holds out a hand to me.

'I've tied her up at that end but I'm not sure if I've done it right,' she says. 'Good to meet you, Jack.'

She is slightly taller than her aunt and I am surprised to see how fair-skinned and blonde she is in comparison. Her hair is long, wavy and attractively tousled. A pair of big blue eyes are framed by large tortoiseshell glasses above a set of very white and even teeth. She has a red duffel coat on over light blue jeans and trainers.

'I'm really pleased to meet you too,' I say, shaking her hand.

'Nina's told me a lot about you,' Anna says. 'You two seem to stir things up a bit wherever you go!' There is little trace of Nina's cut glass pronunciation in Anna's voice, which leads me to believe she didn't enjoy the same privileged home counties upbringing as her aunt.

Nina is laughing as Eddie's tongue flicks in and out like a lizard in a bid to connect with her face. 'Jack usually manages to get out of it, though.'

'With a bit of help.' I smile at Nina fondly. 'Come below and I'll get the kettle on.'

We all descend through the hatchway and down the short flight of steps flanked by two large cupboards. The boat's pair of single berths are immediately either side of the walkway and bisected with a swing door. I wave my hand to indicate to Anna where the loo is, immediately on the left, and then usher her quickly past my unmade double bed and into one of the easy chairs on the other side of the little kitchen galley. Nina follows with Eddie and collapses into the other larger chair while I fill the kettle and put it onto one of the gas rings.

Anna is looking around at the boat's interior with undisguised interest. 'It's cosy, isn't it? I love the idea of living on a boat.'

'Jack didn't have much choice to begin with,' says Nina.

'No,' I admit. 'It was all I could afford after my divorce.'

'It was all he could afford – and he didn't have the first clue how to operate it!' Nina says.

'True,' I say, spooning coffee into a cafetière. 'But luckily I met someone on the towpath who knew what they were doing ... and I've been trying to get rid of her ever since.'

'Yeah, sure,' Anna retorts, laughing. Nina joins in.

I don't imagine the two women have any secrets from each other so I have to accept the younger woman is probably fully appraised of my feelings for her aunt. It is a passion that is forlorn and unreturned to date, but I sincerely hope it will be one day – when she feels able to move on from the love and grief that she still feels for her dead soldier. Nevertheless, I feel a moment of hurt and annoyance at their laughter.

I distribute the mugs and pull out a chair for myself at the table. Eddie is on Nina's lap now, lying on his back, his front paws bent, his hairless tummy uppermost and his hind legs splayed wide. Nina has always been his favourite person. He had belonged to a young homeless man who had been deliberately drowned in a canal near Stratford-on-Avon, and Nina rescued the little dog and brought him to live with me. Anna shuffles forward on her knees and starts rubbing Eddie's tummy.

'And I've heard all about Eddie too,' she says. 'He's sort of Snowy to your Tintin, isn't he?'

Nina snorts with laughter. 'I think Jack's a bit older than Tintin.'

'True,' I say sadly. 'But we are both journalists ...'

'Resting journalists,' says Nina teasingly. 'Have you done anything about finding a job here?'

I give an exaggerated sigh and look at Anna. 'You see? She's only just come on board and she's nagging me already.'

'Someone has to.'

'Well, we can't all swan off to Barcelona on fancy Christmas holidays.'

Nina and Anna spend the next ten minutes describing their increasingly complicated manoeuvres to outwit the pickpockets who plague the Spanish coastal city. Then we lock up the boat and go in search of a pub lunch. Nina links an arm through mine as we trail behind Anna who has Eddie on a lead.

'She's lovely, isn't she?' Nina says proudly.

'Yes, she is. Just like her auntie.'

'She's done so incredibly well to get into Oxford. Her parents never had much money, and when my brother walked out after Marion was diagnosed, I worried Anna might go seriously off the rails. She took her mum's death very hard, but she's come through. I'm so proud of her.'

'She doesn't mind us descending on her?'

Nina scrunches up her retroussé nose to rebut my question. 'She knows I'm not going to be bothering her the whole time. She'll be in her college and I'll have my apartment. I'm looking for a job of some kind to keep me busy. She just knows that I'll be there for her if she needs me. But I've promised her I won't cramp her style.'

It is a promise I will come to remember all too clearly in the days ahead.

CHAPTER TWO

Finn Connolly spins the wheel of his matt black top-of-the-range Mercedes G-Wagon and turns swiftly off the main road. He cruises slowly into the centre of the sprawling housing estate and looks about him in disgust. He grew up somewhere very similar on the poorer fringes of Belfast, but now he finds it hard not to despise those who are too lazy or feckless to escape such a shithole. He believes everyone has it within them to make a success of their lives, no matter what their background has been. If he has overcome the poverty of his childhood, why can't they?

The large slab-sided four-wheel-drive vehicle is virtually brand new. He flares his nostrils to inhale the heady scent of leather mixing with his own expensive cologne. Better than drugs, he thinks to himself. Even better than sex. For him, it is the undiluted smell of money and he loves it. He takes satisfaction in the fact that the off-roader cost more to buy than a home on this estate.

A large crescent-shaped block of flats stretches out in front of him. Five storeys of discoloured grey concrete rise above a row of graffiti-sprayed garages at ground level. The peeling and patched doors of the flats can just be glimpsed beyond the walkways, which run from one side of the building to the other. He's prepared to bet that the architect who designed it in such brutalist style would never have deigned to actually live there. The entrances to stairwells and lifts are stationed at each end along with a jumble of plastic rubbish bins, many of them spilling their contents onto the ground. He knows from previous visits that the flats have small balconies at the rear and that residents don't usually choose to loiter on the walkways beyond their front doors. Today, however, he sees four figures staring down at him from the first floor. Their thin white faces below their hoodies betray undisguised interest in the arrival of Connolly and his expensive car.

He bumps it over the kerb and brings it to a stop in front of a garage door directly below the little group. He turns off the powerful engine with a final throaty blast of the accelerator. Then he rolls his head, laces his fingers together and presses his palms outwards until they give a small cracking noise.

Connolly weighs 12 stone exactly and stands 5 ft 10 inches tall in bare feet. Today, he is wearing a two-piece cashmere suit perfectly tailored to fit his muscled frame. He still smiles at the memory of the shock on the old man's face when he stripped to his pants to be measured in the fitting room of the shop in Pall Mall. Clearly, most of his clients did not have bodies that had been forged into the steel required for a successful career in professional mixed martial arts and boxing. Nor were they covered in blue, black and red tattoos, which begin just under Finn's closely clipped beard and stretch to his ankles.

It is just two years since he retired from the cage, narrowly defeated on points for the Ultimate Fighting Championship featherweight title. He still misses the adrenalin rush of the UFC, pitting his strength and wits against another fighter in a brutal head-to-head encounter. He misses the build-up to a big fight; the psychological warfare he deployed to unsettle his opponents long before either of them stripped to their bespoke silk shorts and began trying to maim each other with their bare feet and their thin padded four-ounce gloves.

But he believes it was a good time to stop. Finn is thirty-seven; he couldn't continue to rely on his cunning and experience to beat the relentless arrival of hungry new contenders younger, stronger and fitter than him. His lucrative sponsorship deals with a male-grooming brand and a watch company came to an end when he hung up his gloves. But he has been careful with his prize money and the income from his endorsements, and he still has almost two million pounds deposited with various banks, as well as an apartment near the Thames, wholly bought and paid for, and a nice new set of wheels. Finn bares his teeth in the driver's mirror and admires his gold incisor. Time to go to work.

He looks up as he closes the vehicle's door and activates the central locking mechanism with an audible blip. The four young faces look back down at him. He has no need to worry about the Merc. They know who he is and what he's capable of.

Connolly takes the piss-smelling concrete stairs two at a time and reaches the fourth-floor landing without needing to breathe hard. His daily exercise regime – two hours a day at home or in a nearby gym – keeps him in shape, as does his largely teetotal lifestyle and carefully controlled calorie intake.

The woman who lives in Flat 45 is expecting him and already opening the door before he needs to ring the bell.

'Alright now, Suzy? How's the new fridge then?'

'Ahh... it's bangin', Finn, it really is. And they took the crap old one away too.' The woman is in her mid-thirties and has made an effort with her make-up and hair for her visitor. Her Merseyside accent is as pronounced as Connolly's Northern Irish brogue once was. But he has trained himself over the years to soften it into a gentle lilt that can be alternately persuasive or menacing. 'D'you want a bevvy, Finn? I can get you ice-cubes now in no time!'

Connolly glances at the kitchen, where he suspects cockroaches scuttle away if a light comes on suddenly in the night. The woman's efforts to prepare for his visit haven't yet included washing the breakfast dishes. The flat smells of cigarettes, hairspray and bacon fat.

'No, you're alright, Suzy. I'm glad it arrived okay.'

He stands in front of the new silver-coloured American style fridge-freezer with its built-in ice dispenser and swings open the right-hand door. One entire shelf is already filled with a cheap brand of extra-strength lager.

'I expect you could do with a hand to stock it up.' He pulls a pig-skin wallet out of his jacket's inside pocket, fishes out three twenty-pound notes and folds them into Suzy's eagerly outstretched hand.

'Ah, thanks, Finn. You're boss, you are.'

'Have you had any thoughts about the carpet yet?' He can't help himself from grimacing as he looks through the kitchen door at the cheap nylon floor covering of the sitting room. He glances down at his handmade black Oxfords. 'It's about time you got rid of it.'

Suzy wraps a poorly painted set of fingernails around one of his biceps. 'I don't know where to start, Finn, I really don't ...'

'Okay, leave it with me. I'll send someone round to measure up and give you a quote for fitting something. They can bring some samples for you to choose from.'

Suzy squeals with pleasure and starts stroking Connolly's arm until he moves away. 'Thanks so much, chuck,' she says as she stuffs his cash into a cracked plastic purse. 'You're really good to us, you are.'

'So, is she ready then?'

'MIA!' Suzy shouts. 'Finn's here.'

A door in the corridor beyond opens immediately, as though someone has been waiting behind it for the signal. The girl who emerges is in her early teens. Suzy is wearing trainers, a pair of faded jeans, a sweatshirt and parka with a fur trimmed hood. Her face bears a strong resemblance to her mother's. There is the same sharp look about her, but without the tired eyes and the poor skin.

'Say hello properly then,' snaps her mother.

The girl wraps both hands around Finn and gives him an awkward hug. 'Hi, Finn.'

He shrugs himself free of her. 'Hi, Mia. Okay let's go. We'll be back when we're back,' he says to her mother over his shoulder as they make for the door.

'Alright, love, take care, have a nice day.' She has pulled the top off a can of beer from her new fridge before Connolly and the girl have even reached the ground floor.

Frustratingly for Mia, the boys are no longer there to witness the big Mercedes reverse fast and speed out of the estate with her sitting up front in the passenger seat. Thirty minutes later they are taking the slope of an exit slipway off the A40 and pulling into the car park of a drive-thru McDonalds. A young black girl dressed in similar fashion to Mia approaches the vehicle, opens one of the rear passenger doors and climbs onto the back seat.

'Hi, Grace,' says Connolly. 'Everything alright?'

'Yes, thanks, Finn,' she says, pulling the seatbelt across her. 'Hey, Mia.'

'Hi, Grace.'

'Right then,' says Connolly, looking at Mia. 'In the back with her.'

Mia pouts unhappily but does as she is told. Then Connolly opens the passenger glove compartment and pulls out two packs of cigarettes. He throws them casually over his shoulder where the girls claim one each.

'Not for now,' he growls, 'and never in the car.'

'Yes, Finn.'

'No, Finn.'

Connolly bends forward again and pulls out a packet of wet wipes. He turns and gives it to Grace. 'And wipe that muck off her face. I said no make-up.' Mia raises her face and unhappily submits as her friend rubs her eyes, lips and cheeks with the wet tissues. 'Take your rubbish with you,' he says, nodding at the crumpled wipes. The girls stuff them into their coat pockets.

Connolly punches a button on a touchscreen panel and the girls begin rocking their shoulders in time to the driving beat of the track. Connolly's fingers tap the steering wheel lightly as he accelerates back onto the dual carriageway and north towards Oxford.

CHAPTER THREE

Anna and Nina chatter excitedly, mostly to each other, as we tuck into three generous Sunday roasts at the Nag's Head. The listed riverside pub sits on its own island, with old stone bridges to either side of it, and must be a glorious spot to sit outside in the summer, but today we claim a table inside near a roaring wood-burner. Nina stays my hand as I reach for my empty glass, intending to head for the bar to refill it with one of their real ales.

'You've still got some boating to do, Jack, remember?'

This isn't like Nina, even though she has distinct head girl tendencies. Usually she takes a relaxed attitude to my alcohol intake, often matching me drink for drink herself. I imagine her sudden concern must be something to do with Anna. They have made their small glasses of white wine last all meal and clearly they are in no mood to linger.

'I've never travelled on a narrowboat before,' Anna says. 'I'm quite excited.'

'Hmm... it's the lack of excitement that I like,' I reply. 'Four miles an hour suits me just fine. And if there is any excitement, it usually means that something's gone wrong. Rivers still scare me a bit. Too unpredictable. Give me a nice dull canal any day.'

'Well, in Oxford you've got both,' says Nina. 'Just like Bath.'

I nod. I've been doing a bit of reading about the city and its history during my long, lonely evenings on the boat. Bath grew up around its hot spring but the reason for Oxford's existence was much more modest, apparently – a ford for oxen crossing the Thames.

'Where are you planning to moor?' asks Anna, stooping down to untangle Eddie's lead from his front legs.

'Good question. I don't think it's going to be easy without paying to stay at one of the marinas or boatyards. Oxford is a bit of a mooring hotspot, apparently, but I'm hoping that I can find somewhere where they'll turn a blind eye if I keep my head down and mind my own business.'

'Ha! That'll be a first,' says Nina. 'But it should be a lot less busy at this time of year.'

She can afford to be relaxed about the issue, I think to myself, cosily ensconced as she is in a warm hotel until she can find somewhere to buy. Nina's childhood involved pony-riding, an expensive boarding school and holidays on the Norfolk Broads where she became very proficient at boat handling. She now seems keen to demonstrate her skills to Anna, so I bustle about with the mooring ropes while she starts the engine and takes the tiller. Eddie is loitering at his beloved's feet and Anna is listening to Nina's explanation of some of the boat's parts – the gunwale, the windlass, the sterngear and the weedhatch.

'How heavy is it?'

'Eighteen tonnes. And *it* is a female in spite of the name and the picture on the side.' Anna has already admired the painting that decorates one side of *Jumping Jack Flash* – a grinning jester leaping into the air with his legs akimbo. 'High maintenance and very difficult to change direction.'

A short awkward silence follows my feeble joke and I see Nina raise her eyes skywards and shake her head. 'Why don't you take Eddie down to the bow, Jack?' she asks. 'He's getting in the way here. It's too crowded.'

I scoop Eddie up into my arms without saying anything and take him down the companionway and through the boat to the little open cockpit with its two bench seats in the bow where I sit and sulk. Anna seems lovely, but my long-anticipated reunion with Nina is not progressing in the way I had hoped. Her attention isn't so much divided as one-directional, although I hate myself for being jealous of her niece.

We motor on past the Capability Brown-designed grounds of Nuneham House, where Queen Victoria honeymooned with Albert in 1841, passing the estate's boathouse. I remember my guidebook mentioning that Charles Dodgson (aka Lewis Carroll) used to row Alice Liddell down to Nuneham occasionally. And I know there's another literary aspect to this stretch of river coming up because I spent some time researching it yesterday evening. It would be nice to share with Nina, but instead I stare balefully at the barren scrubland that has opened out on both banks. The march of electricity pylons over the terrain, carrying power into the city, does little to make it more attractive. The low grey cloud feels oppressive. My blues of the morning are returning with a vengeance.

'Hi there. Enjoying the view?' Anna's blonde mane pokes through the door. 'Mind if I join you?'

'Pretty bleak, isn't it?' I say, indicating that she is welcome to claim the little bench opposite me. Eddie jumps down from my lap and creeps through the door, clearly intent on making his way back to Nina. 'You're studying English, aren't you, Anna?'

'Yep. The workload is so insane. You should see the reading list they've given me for the holiday! I get a weekly one-to-one tutorial and I have to go to two or three lectures a day ... and then there are the essays. And everyone else seems so bloody clever.'

'You're enjoying it, though?' I ask, genuinely interested. The memories of my own time at a northern red-brick university are increasingly vague – the result of too many years having passed, and too many pints of Guinness in the Ducie Arms at the time.

'It's very heavy on the classics. I'm going to have to read the complete works of Shakespeare between my second and third year! I wish we could do some more modern stuff. But at the moment I just need to focus on getting through the exams at the end of this year. Then I won't have any more until my finals at the end of the third year.'

'So, you're telling me there's no time for partying?' I say sceptically.

Anna laughs and shrugs her shoulders.

'It was a bit manic at the start – it's tempting to go mad at first, I guess. You could easily party every night if you wanted to. But I was falling asleep in lectures, so I gave myself a good talking-to. I do feel slightly more grown-up than some of the others. Probably because I had to work solidly through my gap year to earn some money to be here. Anyway, now I ration myself to one party a week – preferably at weekends.'

'Very sensible. I'm sure your aunt would approve.'

'Ah yes, lovely Aunt Nina. She tells me you're in love with her.'

Her directness throws me. 'Er, yes. Did she? Sorry ... was that a statement or a question?'

'A statement, I guess. It's pretty obvious anyway.'

'Is it?' I use my middle and index fingers on both hands to paint quotation marks in the air. '"*I did love her in a way, but it was under the sign of doom.*"'

'Oh ... that's good. Who is that?'

'Iris Murdoch. *Henry and Cato.*'

'I've never read it.' Then she gives me a long searching look. 'Bloody hell, Jack – you really do have it bad, don't you?'

'"*The course of true love never did run smooth.*"'

She rolls her eyes. 'Cliché alert! But true enough in my limited experience.'

'Actually, we're coming up to Sandford, so this is a good place to talk about doomed love.'

Anna looks ahead towards the little settlement approaching on the bow. 'Why, what happened here?'

'The pool at Sandford-on-Thames is where J. M. Barrie's ward, the man who was the inspiration for Peter Pan, drowned in distinctly dubious circumstances.'

'Go on,' says Anna, intently scanning the riverbank.

'Michael Llewelyn Davies drowned about a month before his twenty-first birthday, along with another fellow undergraduate called Rupert Buxton. Davies was one of five brothers who were supposedly the 'Lost Boys' in Barrie's play.'

'So, what were the dubious circumstances?' Anna swings her legs off the bench to face me.

'The two of them were found in Sandford Lasher – that's a pool of water on a weir just upstream of the lock on the left bank,' I say, nodding ahead of us to indicate the place. 'The pool was known to have dangerous currents and it's about 20 to 30 feet deep in places. There were lots of warning signs even then, as well as a memorial to previous drowning victims.' Anna is listening intently. 'Davies – Barrie's ward – had a fear of water and wasn't a strong swimmer. I was reading about it last night. A witness told the coroner's inquest that he saw one man swimming to join the other, who was sitting on a stone on the weir. But the man in the water got into trouble and the other dived in to reach him. The witness said he saw their heads together, but they didn't seem to be struggling. When their bodies were recovered, they were clasped together.'

'A suicide pact?' says Anna quietly, her eyes round with horror.

I shrug. 'Who knows? The coroner concluded that Davies drowned accidentally, and Buxton had drowned trying to save him. But ...'

'Go on.'

'The *Oxford Magazine* published an obituary, which said they were "*intimate*" friends and that "*in their death they were not divided*". Two of Davies' brothers later said suicide was a possibility, and so did Barrie. And one of their contemporaries, a gay Tory politician called Robert Boothby, gave an interview in the seventies saying Davies and Buxton were in a relationship and that Buxton had a suicidal streak about him. He said he'd tried to warn Davies to stay away from Buxton because he had a "*feeling of doom*" about him.'

'How bloody sad.'

'Barrie became the guardian of Davies and his brothers after both of their parents died in 1910. Davies was ten at the time he was orphaned. The drownings happened in 1921 and Barrie wrote later that year that the death of his brilliantly clever young ward was, in a way, "*the end of him*".'

'And when did Barrie write *Peter Pan*?'

'1904. When Davies was just four. It's ironic, isn't it, Peter Pan was the Boy Who Would Not Grow Up and, of course, Davies never did either. The local paper called Sandford Lasher "the Pool of Ill Omen". And when the sculptor Sir George Frampton wanted a model for his statue of Peter Pan in Kensington Gardens, Barrie sent him a photograph of Davies dressed as Peter Pan when he was six years old. So Michael became immortalised as the statue.'

Anna gives an exaggerated shudder. 'I've always found the Peter Pan story a bit creepy.'

'I know what you mean,' I agree. 'I was taken to see it as a kid at Bristol Hippodrome one Christmas and Captain Hook scared the shit out of me. So did the crocodile.'

'And then there's Wendy's crush on Peter. All that stuff about the kiss ... and the suppressed sexuality,' Anna says. 'Ugh.'

Anna's mobile rings. She checks the screen, presses it and Nina's voice breaks into our conversation over the speaker. 'I thought you'd gone forward to fetch me a cup of tea?'

'Oops, sorry. I've been chatting to Jack about doomed lovers.' She grins naughtily at me and I grimace back at her. 'Sorry, I'll get onto it.'

After negotiating Sandford Lock and bypassing the dangerous weir, we motor on under a road bridge and approach Iffley Lock. This is where the Thames turns into the Isis for the duration of the river's presence in the city of Oxford. A large church and a handful of riverside properties appear on our right including one with an impressively sloping garden and a very ancient mulberry tree that has an elaborate arrangement of wooden scaffolding to hold its bare branches upright. By this stage I have taken the tiller and left the two women to sip tea inside the boat. An efficient but taciturn keeper helps us through the lock, which is sited on its own island, and we motor on for the final approach into the city. This stretch of river is occupied by the rowing clubs and, sure enough, the first boathouse appears on our left. It has a stone lintel under a partly timbered end gable which announces itself as the Isis Boathouse of 1815. There are empty water meadows behind it and a smart riverside path running along its frontage. It is quickly followed by a large white pub called the Isis Farmhouse and I see that a couple of narrowboats are moored up alongside the path. The first has a homely plume of smoke rising above a small chimney in its roof and I get a whiff of coal on the cold air. Well, if they're camping here, there's no reason why I can't too. I shift the rudder slightly, reduce the throttle and shout for Nina and Anna to come and help me tie up.

Nina looks around us as I finally cut the engine. A small road bridge spans the river about one hundred metres ahead of us. She folds her arms and pouts. 'Really? You're stopping here?' She looks across at the pub with its arched front door. 'Anything to do with having real ale on your doorstep?'

'This'll do for now. The canal isn't far from here but it's going to be a lot more crowded and difficult to find a mooring as I go closer to the city centre. I can suss out the area on foot first.' It is mid-afternoon and the sky is already starting to darken.

'Well, it's a nice walk up to my college,' says Anna equably. 'It's about twenty minutes along the riverbank. And I need to get back – I've got an essay to write and I'm dining-in tonight.'

'We'll walk with you then,' says Nina.

As we stroll along, I scrutinise the boats of my new neighbours. The first, the one with the smoking chimney, is about the same length as *Jumping Jack Flash* and looks immaculate. She is called *Raven* and the black paint of her superstructure is clean and glossy. Her ropes are neatly coiled and the rope fender protecting the point of her bow looks brand new. A small but neat-looking fibreglass dinghy is chained and padlocked upside down on the roof. Blinds have been drawn down at the windows, but I can hear the faint sound of what sounds like Bach coming from the interior.

The second boat is a much scruffier affair. Straggly plants are lined along the roof of *Madam Gipsy* and it is clearly a long time since the red and green hull was repainted. She is about 40 feet long and has portholes rather than windows. Tattered curtains behind the grubby glass make it impossible to see if anyone is onboard. I sense that both boats may have settled into this mooring for the winter and hope that I may be able to join them for a few expense-free months, at least until I can find a job.

The majestic walls, crenelated towers and gothic windows of Christ Church College make me want to laugh. It is a far cry from the concrete council flat in the Moss Side district of Manchester where I spent my university days. But then, it must be a bit of a culture shock for Anna too. She gives Nina a tight hug, then she gives me one too. 'It's really nice to meet you at last,' she says before adding, quietly in my ear, 'Hang on in there, lover-boy.' Then she grins and disappears through an impressive portal to the college grounds inside.

Nina is staying at a mid-range corporate hotel in the city centre and we begin to walk in its direction – although she is worried about Eddie being allowed inside.

'Well, it's too early to eat again,' I say. 'How about a drink?'

'Because it's never too early for a drink, is it, Jack?'

I choose to ignore her comment and use my phone's Good Pub Guide app to guide us to The Bear, just off the High Street, named after the pet bear of a previous landlord. It is snug, wood-panelled, fire-warmed and only about three hundred years old – although the app tells me there's been an inn on the site since 1242. I approve of its history, the range of beers on offer and the thousands of neck ties that adorn its walls and ceiling, donated by customers the barman tells me. Nina wants a chilled white wine so I forgo the ale and we finally settle in a cosy corner with a bottle of Chablis and a packet of peanuts between us.

'Cheers, Jack.'

'Cheers, Nina. Great to see you.'

'So, what did you really make of Anna?'

'She's lovely ... as you know only too well. And it sounds like she's coping okay with the workload – and being sensible about the carousing too.' Nina nods thoughtfully. 'What does she want to do?' I ask. 'When she finishes, I mean?'

Nina pulls a face. 'Didn't she tell you? She was probably worried that you'd think she'd be after a favour. She wants to be a journalist – God help her.'

I laugh and take a deep swallow of the wine. 'There are worse things in the world.'

'I don't know ... I've met a few horrors, remember?'

For one moment I think she is referring to me, and then I realise she's probably thinking of the famous newspaper columnist who attempted to force Nina into an exclusive interview after her disappearance in the wake of her husband's death in Afghanistan. It had prompted nationwide press coverage and the media had been relentless in their pursuit of her.

'I'll have you know that ours is a noble calling. It is our role in life to comfort the afflicted, and afflict the comfortable,' I say portentously, with one finger raised in the air.

'And sell papers.'

'And sell papers,' I admit, laughing.

But Nina looks at me seriously. 'I've got something to ask you, Jack.'

'Fire away,' I say, topping up both of our glasses.

'Well, I think I've found somewhere to buy. I might even be able to exchange contracts within a week or so. It doesn't make much sense to pay a deposit and sign a rental agreement for somewhere else in the meantime. And the hotel bill is mounting up. So I was wondering if I could reclaim my single berth on *Jumping Jack Flash*? Just until I can move into my new place?'

I notice how carefully she has worded this request. It most certainly isn't a declaration of intent, with its emphasis on the single-berth and the temporary nature of the arrangement. Nevertheless, I am delighted.

'Yes, of course. Eddie and I would be extremely pleased to have you. You're very welcome to stay.'

'Great. Thanks, Jack.' She leans across the table and brushes her lips against my cheek. 'I've paid for a couple more nights at the hotel but then I'll bring my things over. I've got a couple of huge suitcases, I'm afraid.'

'No problem. No problem at all. We'll stash them somewhere.'

Later, after a couple of whisky chasers, Eddie and I walk her to the hotel and we part on excellent terms. I pick up some fried chicken on the way back to the boat and drop bits for the dog as I go. It is very definitely dusk now and I am only a few metres away from *Madam Gipsy* when I see two teenage girls sitting on its roof, dangling their legs over the side and smoking. There are no lights on behind the grubby curtains and no sign of life onboard.

'Is this your boat?' I ask them.

One of the girls spits out a ball of pink chewing gum, which lands at my feet. 'What's it to you?' Her friend giggles and takes a draw of her cigarette.

'If it's not your boat, you shouldn't be sitting on it.'

'Piss off, grandad. We're not doing any harm.' She holds her cigarette between two fingers and flicks them so that it somersaults towards me, its glowing red tip spinning in the fading light. It lands close to Eddie, who jumps backwards with a little yap of fright.

'Okay,' I say, gritting my teeth. 'If it's not your boat, you won't mind me taking your photo and showing it to the owner, will you?' I begin to take my phone out of the back pocket of my trousers.

'Don't you dare!' says the other girl loudly. Now she too flicks the remains of her cigarette at me. 'Are you a paedo or something? We could scream and you'd be in a lot of trouble.'

But my threat seems to have registered with her friend who has put out a restraining hand. 'Come on, Grace. We're out of here.' They exchange looks and then quickly shuffle forward and jump down onto the path.

'Wanker,' says Grace, but they're already walking away quickly with an exaggerated roll of their shoulders, arms linked, heading towards the lights of the city without a backward glance.

CHAPTER FOUR

The big matt black Mercedes is idling in a lay-by on the main commuter road that passes through Cowley. The rush-hour exodus from the car factory and nearby business parks is dying away. Connolly taps his steering wheel impatiently, watching a bus-stop on the other side of the road. He has spent a pleasant day in an upmarket private health club, where he swam and did some weightlifting in the gym, then had a profitable business meeting over a light lunch. His plans for further diversification are on track and he's pleased with the figures that are being quoted. He drove to Summertown afterwards and kept an appointment at a Thai massage parlour. It took the girl nearly all of her wiry strength to push her heels into his tightly packed back muscles. Now he is impatient to get back to London. Where have the little bitches got to?

Two buses come and go, and he is about to send them a text when there is a knock on his side window. It's Mia, with Grace behind her. He checks all around the vehicle and then releases the central locking. The girls climb into the rear seat. They smell of some kind of fruity chewing gum and cigarettes. Connolly doesn't bother to turn around.

'How many?'

'About a hundred.'

'How many exactly?'

'Ninety-six, Finn.'

'Gimme.'

Mia hands him a cheap shiny plastic shoulder bag with a picture of Elsa from *Frozen* on the side. He puts it on the front passenger seat and eases out into the traffic. He has already been parked in this place for too long. Maybe next time he'll tell them to take a taxi? No, that would be even more suspicious.

When they have left the city behind he pulls into a motel car park just before the junction with the motorway. Then he counts the remaining plastic sachets in the bag, makes some marks in a small leather notebook and scoops up handfuls of loose ten- and twenty-pound notes. He counts and bundles them together with thick rubber bands before replacing them in the bag.

'Good girls,' he says. 'No trouble?'

'Nah ... piece of piss. Them students are supposed to be brainy, ain't they? Me and Grace are cleverer than them.'

The two girls have spent the day wandering around the city centre, meeting different people every hour who are desperate to supplement their student loans by selling the white powder on to their friends for a decent profit. Connolly never meets them and relies on a local go-between to make the appointments. The girls look young and the Disney bag is a deliberate ploy to make them appear even younger. He has also calculated that the police will hesitate to stop and talk to a young black girl. They don't want to appear racist, do they? The girls are street-smart so even if they do get picked up it would only be a temporary blip. They'd never shop him, would they? And when they're too old to distribute the drugs without attracting suspicion, he has other plans for them.

Connolly leans forward, opens the glove compartment and pulls out a quart of cheap vodka. He tosses it into Grace's lap.

'Thanks, Finn!' squeals Mia, grabbing the bottle before her friend can and unscrewing the metal cap.

'I'll give you something for your mum later,' he says, engaging drive on the automatic gearbox and turning up the volume of the car radio. 'Now we need to get you home. School day tomorrow.'

CHAPTER FIVE

I am usually awake before my phone alarm goes off, but this morning it summons me from a fathom down. I had tossed and turned restlessly, re-examining every hour of my reunion with Nina until I finally fell into unconsciousness about three o'clock. As usual, after I switch off the alarm I spend a few minutes scrolling through news websites and checking my social media feeds before Eddie loses patience and jumps up onto the bed to urge me to let him out.

The local BBC Oxford website catches my attention. The body of a young woman has been found in the water below Iffley Lock and police are still trying to identify her. The discovery was made two days ago by magnet fishermen. I'm surprised the lock-keeper didn't mention it when we came through yesterday.

I'm still feeling a bit frowsy so decide to brave the cold air and take Eddie for a jog back down the Thames Path towards Iffley Lock and back. As I run past the little island with the lock-keeper's cottage, I stop to stare at the weir. The water is running fast and the signs of violent disturbance below the surface suggest it would be a lethal spot to fall in. There are plenty of warning signs. Beyond Iffley the path becomes earth and recent rain makes it an unappealing prospect to continue.

Back on the boat, I quickly replace the calories I've just burnt with a bacon and fried egg sandwich and then jump in the shower. There is still plenty of water in the tank and the batteries are well-charged from my journey, so I won't need to worry about either for a few days. I am just towelling myself in the main saloon when my mobile rings.

'Deb, how are you?'

'Good thanks, Jack. Are you in Oxford yet?'

My ex-wife still keeps track of my movements via the occasional phone call or email and we have settled into a casual friendship that makes no particular demands on each other.

'Yep. Arrived yesterday. Nina and her niece Anna met me at Abingdon for the final stretch.'

Deb has met Nina once, briefly, and liked her.

'That's nice. No sign of her making an honest man of you yet?'

'And how is your love life?' I hit back swiftly. 'Still swiping right in eternal optimism, are you?'

She chuckles. 'So, paint me a picture. Where are you moored up and what are you up to?'

'Well, I've stopped on the Isis, just outside the city centre. There are a couple of other boats here so I'll see if I can chat to their owners later this morning. I need to find out if I can stay here or if I have to move on to the canal. And, at this precise moment, Deb, I am stark naked and drying myself off after a run with Eddie.'

'Too much information, Jack. And is Nina there too, enjoying the sight of your one-pack?'

'Nina is staying in a hotel. But she's found a flat to buy so she wants to camp with me on the boat until she can move in.'

'That'll be nice for you. But you sound a bit flat. Something wrong?'

I give an audible sigh. Deb knows me too well. 'Oh ... you know. Bloody winter. It seems to be going on for ever. I had flu and it was a tiring journey up from Bath on my own. And now I need to find a job.'

'Aha! Now that's something I can help with. That's why I'm ringing, in fact.'

'What?' I sit down at the table with the towel draped across my groin. Nosy gongoozlers peering through portholes from the bank are a constant headache for liveaboards like me. 'How d'you mean?'

'We've been doing a bit of a sales push in the Cotswolds.' Deb works for an outdoor furniture company. 'And I've been liaising with a glossy magazine over some advertorial.'

'Go on,' I say, my heart sinking.

'Well – it turns out they're based in Oxford and the guy I was talking to says they're really short-staffed. One of their reporters has just resigned and another has gone on maternity leave earlier than expected. Sounds like you should get in there quickly, Jack.'

We part on good terms after a bit more chat and I go online as soon as I am dressed. The prospect of working for a glossy local lifestyle magazine doesn't make my heart sing but an approach to the *Oxford Mail* has already been rebuffed and I do need to start earning again.

The website has the occasional piece of editorial but is largely dominated by property porn, expensive watches and jewellery, photographs of people grinning with drinks at a variety of social events, spa treatments, car ads and upmarket garden furniture. However, there is an email contact address and so I send a brief message and my CV to Ms Julia Goodfellow, Editor-in-Chief of *Cotswold Quality*. Then I head out to see if my new neighbours are up and receiving visitors.

I decide to try the nearest boat first and knock on the hatchway lid of *Raven*. The doors open and the lid slides inwards. A man's freshly shaven nut-brown face looks up at me. I estimate him to be in his late sixties or even early seventies. He has lively intelligent eyes and a friendly smile.

'Hello, there. What can I do for you?' The voice is clipped but amiable.

'I'm Jack Johnson. I moored up here yesterday and I wanted to find out how long I can stay, so I thought I'd knock and ask.'

'Ah ... delighted. Delighted. I'm Hugh Spencer, Hugh to my friends. Come in, come in. Coffee?' We shake hands slightly awkwardly, with him stretching up from below, and then I follow him immediately into a little galley where he ushers me to a stool. 'I haven't been out yet. What have you got?'

'64-footer with a cruiser stern. Four-berth. *Jumping Jack Flash*.'

'Splendid, splendid. Come far?'

'Up from Bath. It took just over a fortnight.'

The man is tall and broad-shouldered with a flat stomach and square jaw. He is as neat and trim as his boat's interior, dressed in a blue crew-neck pullover with a shirt and tie underneath and a pair of mustard yellow cords. He looks lean and fit for his years as he bustles about, turning the volume of Radio 3 down, grinding coffee beans and boiling a kettle.

I notice a framed set of medals are mounted beneath glass on a wall near the galley alongside some military-looking badges on wooden plaques.

'Navy?' I ask, nodding at them.

'Surgeon-Captain Hugh Spencer, OBE, at your service,' he says with a grin, splashing some milk into the coffee without asking and pushing a mug towards me. 'Formerly Officer Commanding Medical Squadron of the Commando Logistic Regiment, Royal Marines. What do you do for a living, Mr Johnson?'

'Please, call me Jack. I'm a journalist,' I say. 'An unemployed journalist, to be exact.'

'Ah. The Fourth Estate, eh? Jolly good. Jolly good. I met Max Hastings a few times – when he was single-handedly liberating the Falklands! And you can call me Hugh. What brings you to Oxford, Jack?'

'A woman, I suppose.'

His eyes twinkle. 'Capital. Tell all!'

Within minutes of meeting this energetic ex-Forces man with his rapid-fire questions, I am telling him about Nina. He is fascinated to discover that she is an army widow and asks for more details about her husband's death in Afghanistan.

'Sorry. Shouldn't be so damned nosy,' he says, changing the subject. 'D'you want a quick tour of the boat? She's about the same size as yours.'

The interior of *Raven* is as carefully maintained as its exterior and has been cleverly equipped with additional features of its owner's design. There is a small writing table tucked into one corner and another single medal hangs in pride of place above it. Hugh sees me studying it.

'Only one of its kind,' he says proudly. 'The *Orden de Mayo* – Argentinian for Order of May.'

'You fought in the Falklands?'

'I was Senior Medical Office of 3 Commando Brigade. I ran the field hospital at Ajax Bay.'

I whistle and look into his sharp grey eyes. 'And the Argentinians gave you a medal?'

'I got an MBE from the Brits and that one from the Argies. I was the only person to be decorated by both sides. I had to get special permission from Her Majesty to wear it.'

'Wow!'

'Yes, well ... I'll tell you all about it over a drink sometime.'

'I'll bring the drink. I'm a single malt man.'

'Excellent, excellent. Rum or Navy-strength gin for me usually, but I do like a drop of good whisky. Now then, you wanted to know about the mooring?'

'I do. I want to know if I'll be moved on from here very quickly.'

'Well, I've been here for three weeks so far. The boat next door has been here much longer – although it's empty most of the time. Chap from the Environment Agency called round once, but he wasn't too bothered. He said I'd have to move her when the university boat racing starts up again, but I'll be long gone by then. It's a very quiet time of the year and he was sympathetic about my situation.'

'Your situation?'

'Mrs Spencer is in the John Radcliffe. Serious heart problems.' He coughs, as though to cover his emotions.

'I'm sorry to hear that.'

'Yes. Well. We have a home in Gloucestershire, but *Raven* means I can be nearby. I can pop in and see her every day.'

'Yes, of course. Well ... if I can do anything ...?'

'It'll be good to have some company. Been a bit lonely but mustn't grumble. My wife's in very good hands and I should know. Now, you must forgive me, but I want to get a particular book from Blackwell's for her before I see her at lunchtime.'

The news about the mooring is good and as I disembark I text Nina to tell her I shall be staying put for the moment. Back on *Jumping Jack Flash* I fire up the laptop and check my emails. There is already a reply from Ms Goodfellow. She will see me at four this afternoon over tea at the Malmaison Hotel. That was quick. It has been an encouraging morning.

Nina arrives at the boat an hour before my appointment. Eddie behaves as though he hasn't seen her for a year rather than just twenty-four hours. She announces that she intends to inspect my appearance for the interview and make sure I leave on time. She will even walk part of the way to the hotel with me.

'Gosh, I wonder how I possibly reached the age of forty-six without you,' I say.

'Me too.'

I bring up the website for the Malmaison – I know it's a good twenty to thirty-minute walk. When I click on the little red marker balloon to establish its location, I am brought up short by its brief description as a 'sophisticated hotel in a former prison'. A former prison? I click through for more detail. *Housed in a former prison, the 95 rooms in our Oxford hotel are rather more spacious than your average jail cell and complete with luxurious beds, super-fast Wi-Fi and power drench showers...* No slopping out from a shared bucket in a corner then. It is as though the marketing copywriter was initially coy about admitting to the hotel's previous history but then got slightly carried away. *Be sure to stop by our neon-lit bar, where the only clink is the sound of glasses as you raise a toast.*

I groan. Is this the type of guff I'm going to have to write? I suspect so.

'Listen to this. "*This is without a doubt one of the most unique and thrilling hotels in Oxford city centre. So, who wants to escape? It would be a crime not to.*" Christ. What drivel.'

'Get over yourself, Jack,' Nina says brusquely. 'Copy like that will be exactly what's wanted at *Cotswold Quality* and you need the money. Now come on, you've got ten minutes to smarten yourself up. Mustn't be late.'

And so, like a condemned man, I set off to the prison/hotel while Nina splits off to meet up with Anna. We agree to catch up later so that she can hear how my interview with Ms Goodfellow has gone.

CHAPTER SIX

The woman in question is already settled in a large high-winged armchair in the hotel's bar. I recognise her immediately from her glamorous full-length photograph on the *CQ* website. She is wearing a large patterned green and white wraparound dress with a deep V-neckline. The upper part of her breasts, brown and slightly mottled, are on generous display and draped with a necklace of large blue beads that drop down into her lap. She is fighting the passage of time with rather too much make-up, and her slightly immobile forehead and upper lip suggest she is no stranger to the Botulinum toxin. The fuchsia-pink velvet-covered chair opposite her is empty and there is a bottle of prosecco and two glasses on the coffee table.

'Jack! Darling!' she gushes, remaining seated but holding out a heavily ringed and red-taloned hand for me to shake limply. She waves me into the empty seat. 'Pour yourself a glass of fizz. It's not the real thing but it'll do for this time of the afternoon.'

The heads of some other guests are already turning to identify the source of her loud sing-song voice. I do as I am told and try not to stare at her hair, which is immaculately coiffured but dyed the darkest shade of black that the hairdresser's art can produce.

'Now, darling, I know everything about you already, thanks to Mr Google. Oh, I say. Sweetie. Can you just ...?' She has broken off to try to attract the attention of a young waiter. 'Yes – you, darling. Can you find some nibbles for me and my friend here? Nothing much. Just a few little cakes, maybe some of those darling little coffee eclairs that you do? Thank you so much.' She watches the young man retreat with a stare that is indecently focused on his tight buttocks.

'Now then, yes ... where was I? Jack. So, you're not *just* a journalist, are you, darling? You're a real live author and you've had such an exciting time on your boat, haven't you? Being attacked by that Canal Pusher – what a horrid little man. And putting Russian property developers in prison. My goodness. You *are* famous. It's just all so exciting. And isn't it wonderful to live on a boat all the time? Footloose and fancy free. Just wandering around the country whenever the whim takes you. I am very jealous!'

I find it very difficult to imagine Ms Goodfellow coping with the cramped privations of a liveaboard life. In fact, it is difficult to imagine her on any kind of craft other than a cruise ship or a large Sunseeker gin-palace.

'Anyway, I'm sure you are just what we need at *Cotswold Quality*. And it's such good fun. The perks are just marvellous. My ex-husband used to tease me about it. A millionaire's lifestyle without the lolly, he used to say.' She shrieks with laughter, stoops down to retrieve a green leather handbag and fishes inside it. 'There you go, a free CQ pen and a memory stick, just to get you started.' The magazine's bright orange branded merchandise is tossed onto the table in front of me.

'Do you know what I had last month, darling? A free top of the range Range Rover for a whole month. Listen to me! A top of the range Range Rover – that's funny. I should have used that in my piece. And tomorrow I'm trying out a gorgeous new spa that's just opened at a lovely little hotel at Lower Slaughter. Ah ... here's that dishy young man with our cakes. Lovely, darling. Just pop them on the table there, would you, along with your phone number?' She screeches with laughter. 'Listen to me! I'm such a tease.' The waiter retreats and her hand hovers over the cakes before pouncing on a small éclair.

She takes a large bite out of it and I take advantage of her mouth being temporarily full of cream. 'So, what does the job pay?'

She dabs the corner of her mouth with a napkin and runs a tongue around the top and bottom of her lipstick. 'Two hundred pounds a feature, plus reasonable expenses. I'll give you a file to work through and I'll keep topping it up. You can start on these. Any order you like.' She empties her glass of prosecco and finishes her cake as I sift through the cardboard folder that she has given me. There are four A4-sized briefing sheets inside – each with a target number of words and a brief outline of picture requirements alongside the number and name of a photographer.

'I get first dibs on any freebies, darling. Privilege of rank and all that. But I'm sure you can churn this stuff out standing on your head. There's no shortage of it in an area like this. My goodness, the number of celebs and millionaires who live around here. It's just mind-blowing. There's gold in "them thar hills", and I'm not just talking about the famous honey-coloured Cotswold stone! And of course, CQ is their essential reading matter. My one rule is Town not Gown. Well, Town *and* Country, actually. But I don't want any boring stuff about the university or its dreary professors and their medical breakthroughs and so on. The only gowns I want to see in our magazine are Dior or Versace! Ha ha. I'm a scream, aren't I? Now, I'm just going to powder my nose. You stay there and have a look through the files.'

She totters off on a vertiginous pair of wedge-heeled shoes and I do as I'm told.

The first sheet in the folder indicates that an interview and 'action shots' are wanted with the youngest female eventer to win at the Badminton Horse Trials of the previous year. She should be interviewed and pictured at the large farm owned by her parents near Cirencester. Horses scare me so I move quickly on to the next sheet.

A photograph is attached of a plump and florid-faced man in a waistcoat and bow tie who, it appears, was the Oxford Chamber of

Commerce's Businessman of the Year. I like businessmen even less than horses, so I move on to the third page in the folder.

This suggests a visit to a ghastly-looking riverside mansion that has won a national prize for its interior design. The interior designer needs to be present as well as the homeowner in order to explain the 'concept' and where she got her 'inspiration'. Judging by the photographs attached to the sheet, her inspiration came from a quarry of Italian marble, a funfair's hall of mirrors and a tart's boudoir. I am beginning to understand why Julia has selflessly sacrificed these stories to my in-tray. There is a distinct shortage of perks associated with any of them. But at least the fourth story appears more interesting.

This sheet is attached to a formal head and shoulders shot of a policewoman in uniform. She has a round, cheerful-looking face with a suggestion of Anglo-Chinese heritage. She reminds me of a famous television actress whose name I can't remember. Detective Sergeant Jane Henry, aged 35, is being offered up by the Thames Valley Police force as a potential *Cotswold Quality* 'Citizen of the Month'. This appears to be a regular feature profiling civic-minded high achievers – unless they work for the university presumably? DS Henry has been conspicuously successful as part of the force's ongoing campaign to deal with county lines criminal activity on its patch. An accompanying press release from the force's communications department describes how she helped to expose one particular gang that had been ferrying young women into Oxford from Birmingham to sell drugs and themselves to a network of British-Asian men. The organisers of the criminal activity and many of their customers had received prison sentences as a result of her investigations.

The fifth sheet is another press release from the organisers of the Blenheim Palace Winter Balloon Lift-Off. Weather permitting, more than thirty hot-air balloons will take off over the ancient ducal home. Members of the press and media are being invited to bid for flights and the chance to take spectacular photographs of the estate from the air. I deduce that Julia can't have a head for heights as she has passed on this one.

'Right then, darling.' Lipstick reapplied, Julia has returned from powdering her nose. 'Everything alright? Work your way through those and I'll send you some more by email. I must love you and leave you, I'm afraid. I'm going to the opening of a gorgeous new Chinese restaurant in Jericho and they've said I can bring three friends along for dinner. Yum yum, dim sum! It'll be just too lovely having you to write for us, Jack.'

I stand to shake her hand and watch her sweep out of the bar. Then I sit back down, attach the orange memory stick to my keyring, pocket the pen and help myself to one of the remaining eclairs. I'm feeling quite cheerful and pleased with myself. I've only been in Oxford for one night and one day, but I already have a free mooring, a nice new neighbour and a writing job, and Nina is living in the same city as me. Then there is a discreet cough behind me. It is the young waiter.

'Would you like your bill now, sir?'

CHAPTER SEVEN

A text message from Nina has told me to meet her and Anna at a pub called the Head of the River on Folly Bridge – this suits me as it is probably the closest watering hole, aside from the Isis Farmhouse, to my new mooring. The name makes it sound pretty authentic, but it turns out to be part of a hotel owned by a big brewery chain and looks huge from the outside. I suspect it is trading heavily on its name and position to make a good profit out of a blend of overseas tourists, students and locals.

Today is the first day of Hilary Term and there is a young crowd filling its multi-levelled spaces tonight. I fight my way through the throng to find Nina and Anna and discover they are ensconced in a corner overlooking the river with a large, noisy crowd. My first impression is characterised by floppy fringes and braying laughter.

'Hey everyone, this is Nina's friend, Jack,' Anna calls out as I stand awkwardly on the edge of the group, feeling the full force of my advanced years. I look nervously at the table's jumble of glasses in case I am expected to buy everyone a drink. I have already shelled out a silly amount for the prosecco and cakes at Malmaison. Instead, a young man sitting on Nina's immediate left unfurls his considerable length and announces that it is his round before calling across the table to me.

'Hey, Jack, why don't you have my chair and I'll squeeze in somewhere?' His accent is American. He shuffles free of the group and grasps my hand firmly. 'I'm Caleb. Caleb Hopper. Call me Cal.

Nina and Anna have told me all about you. What are you drinking, my friend?' He looks older than the average undergraduate, maybe late twenties or early thirties. He boasts Hollywood star looks with an aquiline nose, chiselled cheekbones, clear piercing blue eyes and closely cropped blond hair. He also has an athlete's physique and stands taller than me. I estimate he is at least 6 feet and 3 or 4 inches.

I ask for a pint of bitter and he turns and counts the empty beer glasses. 'So, if I get six pints of real ale, three bottles of lager, a bottle of red and a bottle of white, that okay for everyone?' There is general assent and he heads for the bar.

'Do you want any help?' I ask after his repeating back, but he just waves a hand above his shoulder without looking backwards. I shrug and struggle past a line of knees to claim the empty seat next to Nina.

Both women turn to face me as I sit down. 'So? How did it go?' asks Anna eagerly. She has an open and generous smile and seems genuinely interested.

'Fine, thanks. I don't think there'll be much scope to win a Pulitzer, but I've been given a bunch of pieces to write. The pay is pathetic, but it'll do for now.'

Nina punches me lightly on the arm but rolls her eyes and addresses Anna. 'Listen to him! You think he'd be grateful. But no, Jack Johnson is already too good for ... what was it called? *Cotswold Quality*? Even before he's started.' Her words are slightly blurring into each other; it sounds as though I'm already several drinks behind, even allowing for the prosecco.

Anna clearly senses me starting to bristle and jumps in. 'Well, I think it's great news. Well done, Jack. We should celebrate.' She shares the depleted remains of a bottle of white between both of their glasses and raises hers. 'To Jack's new job!'

Nina raises hers as well and a few of the others automatically raise their glasses in salute. Caleb is back now and delivering the first drinks of his round.

He reaches across the table to hand me a pint. 'There you go, Jack. Enjoy.'

'Is he a tutor?' I ask Anna and Nina after he has turned for a return trip to the bar.

'No, Cal's doing a PhD and he's a rower. He's got a place in the Blue Boat for the boat race crew this year,' says Anna. 'He's got a room at Christ Church and a cottage somewhere in town. He's supposed to be loaded.'

Both of them are looking across the bar to where rich, athletic and handsome Caleb is tapping a plastic card against the bar's pay machine. The sleeves of his white shirt are folded back to display strong bronzed forearms and an expensive looking jumper is draped casually around his neck. Cashmere, no doubt. The phrase 'Over Paid, Over Sexed and Over Here' bubbles up into my brain.

Nina is laughing. 'You seem to be remarkably well informed about him, young lady!'

But Anna is far too self-assured and confident to blush at her aunt's clumsy attempt to tease her. 'Oh no. We're just mates. We met in Freshers' Week last term. Besides, I hear Cal's already taken ... he met someone recently but I haven't been introduced yet. Anyway, I don't go for his type.'

'And what is his type?' I ask.

'Oh, you know. Masters of the Universe. I prefer my blokes a bit more human. Flawed, sensitive and vulnerable – just like you, Jack – but a bit younger!'

I laugh along with Nina.

'But why would he have a room in halls *and* a house in town?' I ask, as the object of our curiosity turns to come back to the table with a bottle of wine in each hand.

'Because he can,' says Anna simply. 'It's the best of both worlds, isn't it? Sociable and convenient in college. Comfortable, quiet and private in his own house. He can take his pick.'

'Don't go getting ideas, young lady,' says Nina. 'I don't think Granny's savings or your student loans will run to that!' Anna lived with Nina's mother after her own mother died and she became estranged from her errant father. I have never met the old lady but I suspect she wasn't the easiest person for a teenage girl to live with.

Cal settles himself with a pint of lime and soda on the opposite side of the table just as someone behind the bar turns up the level of the music. Everyone raises their voices to be heard above it and it is no longer possible to have a conversation with anyone other than your nearest neighbour without shouting. This is not my favourite type of pub, or way to spend an evening, but Nina is obviously enjoying herself and seems wholly at ease with the young company around her. And, to be fair, I think to myself, as a thirty-one-year-old she should be.

I am now facing the type of social quandary that probably only keeps socially constipated English people awake at night. I want to leave. But I've already been bought a drink. But I arrived late, and it seems unfair to be forced to trade my single free pint for an enormous and expensive round of drinks. Nina spots me eyeing my empty glass and raises an eyebrow. I shrug. 'I've got a bit of a headache. I think I'll call it a night. I'll owe Cal a drink for another time.'

'Okay. I should get some news about the flat tomorrow. I'll call round and let you know what's happening.'

'You can come back to the boat for a nightcap now if you want.'

'I thought you had a headache?'

'I think I'm still tired from the trip – and this music doesn't help.'

'Thanks, Jack, but I'll stay on for a bit and walk Anna back.'

I look around the table. 'Won't they all be going back to her college with her?'

'Some are from her college and some are friends from her course.'

I lean closer to talk in her ear. 'What was that you said about giving her some space?'

Nina turns to look at me and narrows her eyes in annoyance. 'You've just arrived, Jack. Don't start judging me already.'

This seems particularly unfair. It is Nina who has been the most judgemental out of the two of us recently. I rub both eyes with the base of both thumbs. I do feel pretty exhausted. As I drop my hands, I can see Anna has sensed something in the atmosphere and turned towards us.

'I'm going to call it a night,' I shout to her across the front of Nina. 'I'll see you when I see you.' I give both women a peck on the cheek and stand to put on my coat and scarf. Cal is also on his feet by the time I have struggled to free myself from the table and given a little goodbye wave to everyone else. He's holding out a hand again.

'Great to meet you, Jack.'

'Thanks for the drink,' I mumble. 'Bit of a headache. I owe you one.'

'Yeah, sure. No problem. Nina tells me you're living on a boat. I'd love to see it sometime. I'm on the water a lot myself.'

'Look in at any time. It's just past Strode Road Bridge. Red and black with a jester painted on the side – *Jumping Jack Flash*.'

'Hey, I'll do that. I take a run down to Iffley early most mornings. We do our land training over at Iffley Road Sports Centre.'

'What do you call early?'

'Oh, you know, about seven a.m.'

I wince in mock pain. 'Well, if you do come calling, try to make it a bit later than that, will you?'

He laughs. 'Sure thing. Nice to meet you, Jack.'

Nice chap, I think to myself, even if he is American and a 'Master of the Universe'. The temperature drops almost as quickly as the noise levels as I leave the pub and let the door swing closed behind me. Thankfully, the boat is only a twenty-minute walk downriver and I am soon passing under the ugly concrete sweep of the Donnington Road bridge. There is enough moonlight to see the graffiti on the far bank. The Isis must be about 50 metres wide here, but I can make out that someone called Hussein has spent several hours spray-painting his name between a cartoon of a flying angel and a bicycle standing upright on a little green hill. The symbolism, if there is any, escapes me. I move on under the next smaller road bridge. Eddie barks furiously as soon as I step up onto the stern tiller platform and I am reminded of my neighbour's medals. I'm surprised that he keeps them on the boat rather than in the safety of his family home. Surely they must be valuable to him? Both emotionally and financially. And yet, without a dog, and moored near the centre of a city, there is always the risk of boats being targeted by burglars or vandals. I make a mental note to ask him about it whilst greeting Eddie and giving him a biscuit as a reward for performing his guard-dog duties.

I am too tired to light the solid fuel stove, so I pour myself a generous slug of J&B and burrow under the duvet and a pile of blankets. Before turning out the light, I send an email to the Thames Valley Police communications department requesting an interview with DS Jane Henry as soon as possible.

CHAPTER EIGHT

Although it is a very cold morning, at least there is a cloudless sky and a weak and watery sun can be glimpsed on my morning stroll with Eddie. In fact, I can see clear straight white contrails streaking across the bright blue air above me. I know aircraft don't leave these lines in the sky unless they are higher than 20,000 feet, so I assume they are on their way to Manchester or Scotland or somewhere more exotic rather than descending to land at Heathrow, Gatwick or Birmingham.

I give Eddie his breakfast and munch on a croissant as I turn on my laptop. I am delighted to see a crack-of-dawn email from the police confirming that DS Henry will be pleased to meet me during her lunch break. I am to meet her at one o'clock in the entrance foyer of the city's main police station. A quick Google tells me this is just across Folly Bridge on St Aldate's, opposite the main court building. I spend the morning doing a bit of online research and then Eddie and I head out for a spot of shopping. I'm waiting with the dog lead in one hand and a bulging grocery bag in the other when DS Jane Henry comes into the reception area, precisely on time.

She looks like her photograph but younger than her thirty-five years. She has jet black hair that is neatly cut, parted centrally and bobbed into two curls, which reach just to the end of her neck. I still can't remember the name of the television actress who she reminds me of, but I decide I must have fancied her a bit. She is dressed in smart-casual civilian clothes and immediately wins my approval by kneeling to make a fuss of Eddie.

'Hello, Eddie, what a lovely dog you are. There's a good boy.'

'How did you know his name?' I demand as she straightens up to look me squarely in the eyes. She is probably eight inches shorter than me, so about five feet four, and she has a neat trim figure which reminds me of Nina's.

'I'm a detective, aren't I?' she says, smiling.

'You read his name on his collar tag.'

'There's a school of thought that says it makes it easier for the baddies to steal your dog. Just put your phone number and postcode on it next time.'

'It's hard to put a postcode on him. I live on a boat and move around a bit.'

'Ah yes. I know that too.' She smiles. 'Just a mobile phone number then.'

'How do you know I live on a boat? Is it on my name tag?'

'Are you wearing one, Mr Johnson?' She stares up at my chest. 'A medallion with your name on? Bit seventies, isn't it?'

I have already decided that I like DS Henry, so that makes the next part easier. I lift up a carrier bag. 'I'm sorry you had to give up your lunch break. I've been to a deli. I thought we could do the interview on my boat.'

'On *Jumping Jack Flash*? Yes, lovely idea.'

'Okay, now you've got me seriously worried. How *do* you know I live on a boat called *Jumping Jack Flash*?'

We leave the busy reception area and turn left back towards the river.

'I told you, I'm a detective.'

'And ...?'

She takes Eddie's lead from me without asking. 'You can alternate hands with the shopping now.'

'And?' I persist.

'I checked you out as soon as the press office contacted me this morning. There are plenty of newspaper articles about you online, in case you didn't know. Well, of course you do, you wrote most of them. I also gave Detective Inspector Kerr, formerly of the Avon and Somerset Constabulary in Bath, a quick ring. She vouched for you. Actually, she's still quite grateful to you.'

'She should be,' I mutter.

'It ended well for her. She was promoted to a bigger job with the Met. So, what brings you to Oxford?'

'Wanderlust,' I say. With the emphasis on lust, I admit to myself ruefully.

We are soon settled around the little dining table in the boat's galley. I have transferred a range of intricate looking cold dishes into a motley collection of bowls and cut a crisp fresh baguette into slices. She accepts a small glass of red wine and so I pour two and wait for her to load her plate.

'This is a treat. It's usually a canteen sandwich in front of my computer.'

'How did you get into working on county lines?' I ask, beginning to load up my own plate.

'It's been a big thing for this force. Ever since the case review into the 2013 paedophile gang. D'you know about that?'

I shake my head. I haven't come across this in my morning's research.

She takes a sip of wine. 'It's all on record. Seven convictions, five life sentences. Rape, trafficking and organised prostitution. Operation Bullfinch picked them up in 2012 – but the judge gave the police and social workers a tongue-lashing for not acting sooner. There was a case review that said the victims, all young white British girls, should have been taken more seriously. The figures were horrendous. There were six girls involved in the case, but the review said more than 300 young people in Oxford might have suffered grooming and abuse or been at risk between 1999 and 2014.'

I open a notebook at the side of my plate. 'D'you mind if I take notes?'

'Can I see the article before you send it?'

'Just for fact-checking,' I concede.

'Okay. Just for accuracy. Anyway, most of the men arrested were of Pakistani heritage. It was a tinderbox issue – although the review said no one messed up due to what it called *racial sensitivities*.'

'So, it was cock-up rather than conspiracy?'

'Off the record?'

I nod briefly. 'We fucked up. Crap policing. There was one story about a beat officer who found a thirteen-year-old girl hiding in a car with an adult Asian man and condoms nearby. He just gave the man some "advice" and sent him on his way.' She shakes her head in disbelief.

'But that wasn't a county lines case?'

'Not really. Local men. Local kids. But the same underlying issues. Vulnerable children and teenagers being exploited by violent adults. Just a different business model. Then the gangs began bringing kids in from the big cities instead. They calculated it was safer to make them work for them in places where they had no previous connections.'

'What are they brought in to do?'

'Drug-dealing mainly. But they also act as couriers for stolen cash, stolen goods, illegal weapons. They act as runners between the dealers and the buyers. They're cunning too. Constantly changing their tactics to try to stay one step ahead of us. And the kids are getting younger and younger. Easier to pass under the radar.'

'How young?'

'Eleven or twelve in some cases. Young enough to be out on the streets but not too young to attract any concern or attention – unless it's a school day. And it's even more complicated if they are young, female and black. Some officers are frightened of being accused of unfair racial targeting, or even of inappropriate touching.'

'How are they recruited?'

'It usually starts with presents, then cash, then sex, then drugs. Sometimes the kids are with foster parents or in children's homes. But they start going missing for lengthy periods. There was a big bust in Birmingham recently. Same old story. Young teenage girls running drugs and even guns for a big Asian gang. There's a lucrative market for drugs anywhere that has a sizeable student population. And it makes sense to expand the business out of the big cities and into places where the county police forces are less well resourced. Lower risk. Higher profits. Here in Oxford, we're vulnerable to attack from both Birmingham and London. One recent study said there were 1,000 women or girls at risk of gang association in the capital.'

I go to top up her glass, but she holds a level palm over it to prevent me. 'No thanks, Mr Johnson, I'm back at work this afternoon.'

'Please call me Jack.'

'Okay. You're the skipper, I suppose. But only if you call me Jane.'

'It's a deal. Help yourself to some more food. I'll be eating it for dinner otherwise.' She helps herself to a few more spoonfuls of falafel and a samosa. 'So,' I go on, 'that brings us to your reason for being here.'

She smiles at me. 'You mean it's not just my natural charm in exchange for a decent glass of red and a delicious lunch?'

'I mean the Stronghold campaign, Jane.'

'You've got all the details in the press release. We had a week-long blitz. One hundred arrests, more than £65,000 recovered, plus 1,435 wraps of cocaine, crack cocaine and heroin, 17 weapons and 118 mobile phones. Pats on the back all around.'

'But what did you do specifically?'

'Look. I just did my job. But the press office and the high-ups want the warm glow of a successful operation to continue for as long as possible, so they send out a press release about a mixed-race woman detective because they think it'll play well. Sorry. It's cynical. But at least I've had a nice long lunch out of it.'

I shake my head. 'I don't buy that. What was your role as part of the Stronghold busts? If I don't get that, then there's no *Cotswold Quality* High Achiever profile and nobody wins. Your bosses won't be happy.'

'Okay. But I warn you, it's seriously boring. I run community liaison. I go out and talk to schools, taxi drivers, pub landlords, property landlords and hotel owners. I tell them what to look for, how to spot the signs of exploitation. I helped Stronghold to identify nineteen vulnerable people and one hundred addresses where "cuckooing" was suspected.'

'Cuckooing?'

'Yes, cuckooing. The OCGs target...'

'Wait a minute. OCGs?'

She sighs theatrically. 'Okay. OCGs are Organised Crime Groups. They entice vulnerable people into allowing their homes to be used for drug dealing. They give them free drugs, or they pay for their food or the household bills or buy them presents. These people can be lonely or isolated or they can be heavy drug users themselves. It's called cuckooing and when we identify them, it gives us a foot in the door to the whole operation. Well, actually it's usually more than a foot in the door. It's a big heavy metal battering ram with a bunch of armed officers behind it.'

'Okay. I get it. It sounds like a nasty business. And I thought policing in Oxford was all about driving around in a classic Mark II Jaguar, listening to opera and drinking real ale!'

She laughs but then suddenly turns serious. 'It's a nasty business. These people are evil. They exploit and hide behind the most vulnerable people in our society.'

'Well, it won't hurt to write about them, will it?'

She looks at her watch. 'Oh, look – I need to get back. There's already been a lot of banter in the station about that press release.'

'They're just jealous of the force's new poster girl.'

'Hah! Girl? I'm thirty-six next year and I'm still a DS. I was supposed to be on a graduate fast-track programme. But I don't want to have to leave Oxford to become a DI.'

'Do you have family here?' I ask disingenuously. I have already registered the absence of a wedding ring.

She shakes her head. 'No. Came here five years ago from Dorset after a quick marriage and a slow divorce. No kids, much to the disappointment of my Chinese mother. Married to the job. That was part of the problem really.'

'Me too, I suppose,' I say, closing my notebook.

She flicks it back open. 'Look, if you want to do something serious about county lines, rather than just a puff piece about me, you should talk to a few of the charities involved. Give me your pen.' She scribbles *Operation Shutdown* and *Gangsline* on an empty page and closes the notebook again.

'Thanks. I'd like to spend a day shadowing you – out on the road, if that's possible? It would give me a real insight into what you do.'

'You'll have to ask the powers-that-be,' she shrugs. 'It's okay by me. But if you do, we won't be eating a lunch like this.'

I escort DS Henry back to the hatchway, where she says goodbye to Eddie and shakes my hand.

'That was fun. Nice lunch. Nice dog. Nice boat. Nice meeting you, Jack,' she says. 'Don't forget to let me see your final draft.'

'I won't be writing anything until I've shadowed you,' I say.

She nods briefly and saunters away, waving to Hugh, who is pottering about on the stern of *Raven*. We exchange a wave too and then I duck down back inside. My mobile pings with an incoming text just as I am clearing away the remnants of lunch. It's from Nina.

Flat sale has fallen through.

No! What happened?

Gazumped.

Bollocks. I'm here if you need a shoulder to cry on.

Don't worry. Going to see Anna.

It's perfectly reasonable for her to seek solace with her beloved niece but it doesn't stop me feeling a tad jealous. Nevertheless, I return to my phone's screen and type.

Okay. Chin up. x

There is no reply.

CHAPTER NINE

I spend the afternoon reading, dozing and wondering if Nina will get around to crying on my shoulder as well as Anna's, but I don't hear a word from her. I give up waiting at four o'clock and spend a happy hour wandering around Blackwell's huge basement, where I pick up a few more books for my ever-growing to-be-read pile. At six, there is a confident knock on the hatchway door, which I assume to be Nina. But it turns out to be Surgeon-Captain Hugh Spencer OBE, standing there with a bottle of single malt and a roguish grin.

'Hello, Jack. Wondered if you were free for a tincture or two? Is this one alright? I picked it up on my way back from the hospital this afternoon.'

I register that it is a ten-year-old Talisker and scramble out of his way. 'Yes, of course, I'm all alone. Come on in. How was your wife today?'

'Not too good, I'm afraid. Still quite breathless and she's had a few complications since surgery. A leaky valve. But she's a fighter.'

I usher him into an armchair and fetch two whisky glasses and a jug of cold tap water. He efficiently dispenses with the dark blue foil and pours a generous measure into each of the glasses. We sniff appreciatively and then dilute the amber liquid with a little water.

'Slainte,' he says, raising his glass to clink mine.

'Good health,' I say. 'And a quick recovery.'

'Amen to that.'

I roll the liquid around my mouth to fully appreciate its fruity smoke and seaweed flavours. 'Robert Louis Stevenson said Talisker was one of his three king o'drinks.'

'Did he really? Well, well. It's a long time since I read *Treasure Island.*'

'I'm sure they'll have it at Blackwell's if you want to read it again. I was there this afternoon.'

'What did you get?'

I pull the unopened paper bag off a shelf and hand him one of the three books. It is one of Colin Dexter's Inspector Morse stories, *The Wench Is Dead*. 'You'll appreciate that one.'

'Ah yes. How appropriate. It's a while since I read this. Isn't Morse a patient, recovering in hospital?'

I nod. 'A stomach ulcer. And he solves a Victorian murder on the Oxford Canal without ever leaving his bed. I thought I'd re-read it as I'm here.'

'I confess, my main enjoyment from reading crime novels is to see how the authors cock-up all the medical bits!'

A sudden idea strikes me. 'Why don't you borrow it for your wife? She might be amused by the parallels. She's lying in the same Oxford hospital as the good inspector.' I wave at the bookshelf stretching along the length of the boat. 'I've got plenty to be going on with.'

The old man looks touched. 'That's very kind of you, Jack. I think she'd like that. I'll take it to her tomorrow, if I may?'

We clink glasses again to clinch the deal and I add some fuel to the stove. 'You were going to tell me about your Argentinian medal,' I prompt him.

'Ah, yes. Well, I think I told you that I was in charge of the field hospital at Ajax Bay. Pretty hairy situation, really. The only roofed buildings that were suitable belonged to an old refrigeration plant. And it happened to be next to an ammunition dump. That meant we couldn't paint a Red Cross on the building. Would have been contrary to the Geneva Convention, I'm afraid.'

The yellow glow of the wall lamps inside *Jumping Jack Flash* have given the veteran a sallow appearance, but his voice is strong and firm as he continues with his story.

'That meant we suffered air attacks and conditions were pretty bloody. It was dirty and dangerous work. We had two unexploded bombs to contend with and poor lighting that came and went all the time. But all in all, only three died out of the 580 British soldiers and marines who were wounded in action.' He takes a mouthful of whisky. 'And no one met their maker on my watch,' he adds proudly.

'Amazing,' I say. 'But I still don't understand why the Argentinians gave you a medal?'

'I went over there afterwards, to Argentina, for a visit in 1998. But before I arrived, I sent them a list of all the Argentinian casualties who we treated. I wanted to know what had become of them. As a result of that, the Argentinian Foreign Ministry learned for the first time about how we gave their lads battlefield medical care during the conflict. They held a reception for me in Buenos Aires and invited fifty of their chaps along, all soldiers and airmen who we'd treated. Bloody moving occasion, I don't mind telling you.'

Eddie is sitting in his strangely human upright position, leaning slightly on me with his back against the armchair, his rear legs splayed outwards and his front paws folded in front of him, watching the old man talk with his beady brown eyes.

'And so, they made me an *Oficial*, that's an officer in their lingo, in the Order of May. They give it to foreigners who ... how does it go? *Who distinguish themselves by service or personal achievement or have gained their nation's gratitude.*'

I give a low whistle. 'And you say you had to ask the Queen for permission to wear it?'

He nods and laughs. 'I had to ask her as it's a foreign decoration. She personally sanctioned that I should wear it "on all occasions *on behalf of the 300 British forces' medics who were involved in the war.*"'

'Hugh,' I say, leaning forward, 'is the medal safe on your boat? I don't know what it's worth financially, let alone emotionally, but well ... it must be priceless to you. Moorings here might not be so secure.'

He laughs and leans forward to pour two refills. 'I had a few replicas made. No one knows where my real medals are – except for Mrs Spencer, of course.'

I shake my head in admiration. 'You sly old dog!'

'Talking of sly old dogs,' he says, with a wink, 'I saw a very attractive lady leaving your boat this afternoon. Are you keeping a disreputable boat in the middle of the afternoon, Jack?'

I am just about to explain that my visitor was, in fact, a very respectable detective police sergeant when Eddie leaps off my chair, barking, and hurtles through the boat. There is someone at the hatchway and I can hear clattering and banging. I excuse myself and go to investigate.

It's Nina and she is grappling with two enormous wheeled suitcases. 'Oh, Jack. Thank goodness. Give me a hand with these bloody things, will you, please?'

I manage to edge them both sideways down the short flight of steps and put them side by side on one of the single berths. Nina follows and throws a shoulder bag onto the other unoccupied bed. She gives me a peck on the cheek. 'Thanks, Jack. You don't mind, do you? I can't stay in that hotel a minute longer. It was so depressing – especially after the flat fell through – and expensive. I'll find somewhere to rent as soon as I possibly can. Hopefully it'll just be for a few days. Hello, Eddie darling, are you pleased to see me?'

I help her out of her thick puffer jacket in the confined space of the bedroom and she shrugs herself free of a scarf, gloves and a tweedy flat cap.

'Come on through and meet my new neighbour,' I say. 'He's brought whisky!'

Hugh is already standing politely as we make our way through the boat. 'Surgeon-Captain Richard Spencer, Order of the British Empire and the Order of May,' I say. 'Hugh, this is my great friend Mrs Angelina Wilde.'

They shake hands and chat amiably while I fetch another glass and pull up an extra chair for myself. Nina has claimed my armchair and Eddie is already curled up on her lap. Not for the first time I reflect on how ungrateful the traitorous little dog is, lavishing his affections on Nina when it is me who feeds, walks and cares for him most of the time.

I am content to sit and listen while Hugh tells Nina why he is in Oxford and Nina does likewise. I wonder if he will return to the question that he asked me just before Nina's arrival, about Jane Henry, my lunchtime visitor. I suppose he must be slightly startled that another very attractive younger woman has come calling – one who is clearly very at home on board *Jumping Jack Flash* – but he tactfully avoids any further discussion about it. I prompt him to repeat the story about his amazing role in the Falklands, which he does succinctly and with modesty after Nina also urges him to do so. Then she tells him about how we first met on the towpath of the Stratford Canal and some of our subsequent adventures. This takes quite a while, but the old man is a good listener and slowly the level of whisky falls as the convivial evening progresses.

At one stage he asks Nina about her husband and Nina briefly describes how Captain Alan Wilde of the Parachute Regiment was killed during a firefight with the Taliban in Helmand province, and how he had been awarded a posthumous medal for trying to rescue two injured members of his platoon.

'How long had you been married?' asks Hugh gently.

'We got married six weeks before he left for his second tour of duty,' Nina tells him.

'I'm so sorry.' There is an awkward silence as Hugh realises that she doesn't want to say any more and so he deftly changes the subject. I know that Nina will only contemplate a life with me once she is on more easy terms with her grief for Alan. This exchange makes me realise, yet again, that this day is still a long way off.

At another point I slip away to empty the little fridge of the remaining nibbles from lunch and fill two plates of supper for my guests. 'Mmm, this is lovely, Jack,' says Nina. 'I'm impressed. You don't usually have such nice things on board. You must be very honoured, Hugh!'

Hugh raises a quizzical eyebrow above his amused grey eyes – but says nothing.

Eventually, with barely a couple of inches left in the bottle, Hugh gets to his feet rather suddenly. He is slightly unsteady, but he takes Nina's hand and kisses it with old-fashioned gallantry. 'And so to bed. This has been such a treat for an old warhorse. Thank you so much, both of you.'

I watch Hugh get back to *Raven* safely and then stand shivering on the riverbank path while Eddie cocks his leg one last time before bed.

Nina is still up when I return and filling two large tumblers with water.

'I'm really sorry the flat fell through,' I say, taking one of them.

She shrugs. 'As Anna said, "Shit happens". When did the young become so damned philosophical? I'll do another round of the estate agents tomorrow. But I'll prioritise looking for a rental now.' She gives a huge yawn. 'It's been a very long and trying day. I'm off to bed. I did like Hugh. He's lovely.'

'And I'm certain he liked you. Yet another male conquest, besotted by the beauty and charm of Mrs Wilde. Good night, Nina.'

She pokes out her little pink tongue. 'Good night, Jack. You won't help yourself to any more whisky, will you?'

Eddie trails behind her through the boat and beyond the swing door. I squint my eyes to examine the remnants in Hugh's bottle but, for once, I resist temptation, obey the head girl's orders and go to my own bed.

CHAPTER TEN

As usual, Nina is up and out and about long before I surface the following morning. I lie there, listening to her get dressed and then sliding back the hatchway to leave for a run with Eddie. Through the porthole by my double berth I can see a dusting of thick frost on the opposite bank. I hope she's wearing plenty of Lycra to stay warm this morning. Two Bewick swans fly down to land on the river while I'm watching. I never tire of seeing them spread their wings for balance just before their undercarriage touches the surface and they briefly water ski on their outstretched webbed feet. I find it amazing to think they have arrived here in mid-October to find a bit of warmth.

I'm still a bit fuzzy from the previous night's whisky, but the sight of the big white birds inspires me to get up and bustle about in a thick dressing gown, organising coffee and warming up the remaining croissants. Nina is flushed pink when she returns. She takes her breakfast quickly and standing up, before heading for the shower. I know she plans to leave early in order to have a full day of estate agent visits.

'Are you sure you don't want me to come with you?' I ask after she comes back into the main living area of the boat, dressed and towelling her short crop of hair.

'No, it's fine, thank you, Jack. It'll be much less complicated on my own. I don't want them to get the wrong impression.'

I assume that the 'wrong impression' would be that she is part of a couple looking for somewhere to live together and wonder why that should be a particular problem. But I know that it won't be worth trying to persuade her otherwise so shrug to indicate I don't agree but that it's up to her.

After Nina leaves, I send a text to DS Henry asking if there's any progress on my proposal to shadow her for a day. She replies almost immediately.

I'm happy but still waiting for permission from the high-ups. Thanks again for a lovely lunch.

The water that flows past *Jumping Jack Flash* originated at the source of the Thames, 360 feet above sea level, in a damp meadow called Trewsbury Mead on the edge of the small village of Kemble, near Cirencester in Gloucestershire. The water then meanders and falls for 229 miles from its source, gathering in size and strength as countless streams and other rivers flow into it. It becomes navigable for boats at Lechlade and flows on, getting wider and ever more powerful until it bisects and defines England's capital city before passing on through the Thames Barrier and ending in the grey expanse of the North Sea.

In London, that water also flows past Finn Connolly's 1,000 square foot riverview apartment. The 999-year lease on his home cost him just over £1 million and he takes enormous pleasure in the expensively restored light oak flooring and exposed brick walls of the converted warehouse. In the summer he transfers his exercise equipment onto a long outdoor balcony, but for now it is placed in front of a floor-to-ceiling window in the spare bedroom, along with an expensive set of loudspeakers connected to the playlist on his phone. One entire wall of the room is covered by a row of rectangular mirrors.

Once, the neighbour in the flat above was unwise enough to complain about the volume of Finn's music as he was working-out shortly after midnight. Connolly had won most of his UFC fights while remaining on his feet rather than wrestling on the floor of the cage. He'd become famous for deploying 'shock and awe' tactics, attempting to overwhelm his opponents within the first few seconds of the fight. His ferociously aggressive punches often resulted in quick knockout victories. However, he was also a brilliant wrestler and the much larger and younger city banker who lived above Connolly had failed to do any research into his new neighbour. He had pounded on Connolly's front door with his fists and started shouting and swearing as soon as it was opened. He had got only the briefest glimpse of the tattooed and virtually naked man who answered before he found himself being spun 180 degrees and forced onto his knees.

A flat hand snaked alongside the banker's neck from behind, then moved across his throat fast and locked onto the banker's bicep, so that the crook of the attacker's arm was pressing on his victim's windpipe. The attacker's other hand gripped the back of his victim's head so that the banker was now fixed in a human vice. Connolly knew that in this hold, the Rear Naked Choke, he could break the man's neck by simply twisting both his arms in opposite directions. Instead, he gripped, squeezed and pulled his neighbour's shoulders back so that the back of the man's head couldn't fly into his face. The arteries carrying blood to the man's brain were now being blocked and Connolly dropped him to the floor as soon as he passed out. After feeling for a pulse and placing the man in the recovery position, he returned to his flat, closed his front door and turned the volume on his sound system up further. His neighbour never complained again; the bruise around his neck lasted three weeks and he moved out after four.

Today Connolly is wearing a pair of silk fighting shorts and warming down by pedalling gently on an exercise bike, sipping a green coloured juice from a beaker with one hand. His smartphone is attached to the handlebars. He has spent the last thirty minutes talking to his solicitor about the completion of a contract to buy three new flats in Dublin, which he plans to rent out. But when he sees another incoming call he takes it, abruptly cutting off the lawyer.

'Hi there, Suzy. How's things?' he says, watching as two long white tourist boats cross in the middle of the river.

'Hey, Finn. I got your message about Mia and Grace and half-term,' says the hesitant voice on his phone's speaker.

'Yeah. Great. What d'you think then?'

'Well. I know it's hard for you, chuck, when they've got school.'

'Yeah, I'm missing out on a lot of potential business only going to Oxford at weekends.'

'You will look after them, won't you?'

Finn smiles to himself. Mia's welfare is the last thing on her mother's mind. He can picture Suzy in the chaotic kitchen of her skanky flat in Tower Hamlets. His riverside apartment is in the same East London borough, but it could be another world away.

'Course I will, Suzy. The girls will be together the whole time. Just running errands for me like usual. And you and Jo can have that well-deserved break in Tenerife. Christ, I'd love to get away for a whole week of winter sun myself.' He hears the woman giggle with excitement. 'And it'll be all inclusive, like I said. My treat.'

Connolly knows that both mothers understand the nature of their daughters' errands without him ever telling them. And at the moment, he calculates, the two friends won't be able to see further than a sun-lounger and a jug of sangria.

'Jo's really excited. She's had a tough time recently. She does need a holiday and I can't let her down,' says Suzy.

Her pathetic attempt at self-justification makes Connolly give a gold-toothed smile into the full-length mirror and shake his head.

'Yeah, well. Best to be out of the way when they fit the new carpet. You can get that done during half-term too.'

Mia's mum gives a little scream of excitement. 'Ooh yes, thanks Finn. That'd be great to come back to.'

'Okay, we've got plenty of time till February. I'll book it all online and send you the details,' says Connolly, stabbing the phone to hang up. He despises the woman and can only take her in small doses.

'Morning,' says a voice behind him.

Connolly glances in the mirror rather than twisting away from the view of the river.

'Good morning, my darling.' He can't remember her name for the moment.

A girl is leaning against the doorframe. She is wrapped in a short purple silk robe that he'd been given by an Arab fight promotor for one of his big stadium entrances in Abu Dhabi. Her hair is still bed-tousled, and without make-up she looks younger than she did in the nightclub the previous evening. She moves forward and slides between the exercise bike and the mirror. Her eyes are still half-closed, a result of the booze and the drugs of the night before, but they still scan Connolly's tattooed physique with unabashed fascination.

'Get yourself some breakfast,' he tells her, waving in the general direction of the kitchen, with its polished granite surfaces and state-of-the-art appliances. 'You're in my way,' he adds, indicating the view of himself in the mirror. The girl pouts and moodily slides round so that her back is now leaning against the window. Finn sighs theatrically and drains the last of his juice. 'And now you're blocking my view.'

She leans forward and tentatively traces her finger around the head and open beak of the eagle on Connolly's chest. He sniffs and flicks his head towards the door.

'Go on. I'll be through in a minute. I need a shower. There's some more merch in the bathroom. Help yourself. Be a good girl now and we'll have that break in Oxford together soon, just like I promised.'

CHAPTER ELEVEN

Eddie has already had a good run along the riverbank, so I leave him on guard and settle him into a basket by the door with a handful of gravy bones. Nina is off on her rounds of the city's estate agents and I'm feeling at a bit of a loose end so decide to stroll into town. Maybe DS Henry fancies a quick bite of lunch at a pub? It is still cold enough to steam my breath and there is no sign of Hugh as I stroll past *Raven*. However, this time there is a trail of smoke rising from the chimney of the smaller neighbouring boat, the scruffy-looking *Madam Gipsy*. I decide to be sociable and stop off to introduce myself. I bang a metal door knocker in the shape of an otter by the stern hatchway. A dog barks immediately and I can hear a man's voice telling it to shut up before mumbling something and moving through the boat towards me.

The face that appears from the gloom is thin with shrunken dark eyes, a beaky nose and overlong grey wispy hair framing a bare monk-like tonsure. His chin is also bristled with grey hair and he seems to have some kind of paint-spattered boiler suit on. I can hear the dog growling behind him, and he swats a hand backwards to push it away.

'Be quiet, Tod. Bloody dog. Aye?' he says, narrowing his eyes. I can't decide whether he does so out of suspicion or merely because he's dazzled by the light.

'Hi. I just thought I'd say hello. I'm moored up just the other side of *Raven*.'

The man sniffs and wipes his nose with a sleeve. Then he comes up the stairs and remains standing on them, half in and half out of the boat.

'Jack Johnson,' I say holding out a hand, which he takes after a slight pause.

'Aye, well, I'm John Turner. Pleased to meet you.' His accent is heavy Yorkshire, with those abrupt cadences that can often sound truculent – as though daring you to find fault with even the mildest statement. I doubt that I'm going to be invited in for a morning cuppa.

'I've got a dog onboard too. A Border Terrier called Eddie.'

'Aye well, Todd's a lurcher ... and a bit of a sod too. Don't do for strangers to trust him.' He's still standing on the stairs so he has to look up at me awkwardly. I back away from the waist-high doors to give him room to emerge and he hesitantly comes up onto the same level as me.

'I'm not sure how long I can moor here? Any ideas?'

'Week or so. Can't stay here for ever, y'know. It's not an official mooring.'

'No. I didn't think so. How long have you been here?

'Two years,' he says, jutting forward a chin as if to ask if I have a problem with that.

'Oh, right,' I laugh. 'What's your secret?'

'No secret. I work for council, don't I? Need to be nearby.'

'Ah, I see. What do you do, John?'

'I look after kidneys.'

I look blankly at him. He jerks a thumb backwards towards the big concrete road bridge.

'The Kidneys. Nature reserve over Donnington Bridge on the left. On the far bank.'

'Oh, I see. Nice. I'll come over with Eddie and have a look sometime.'

'Aye well, keep him on lead. Tod's only dog allowed off lead in Kidneys.'

'Yes. Of course.' There is an awkward silence. He is staring at me. I assume he wants me to make my excuses and leave. I'm happy to oblige.

'Well. I'd better get going. Nice to meet you, John. See you again maybe.'

'Aye, well sometimes I sleep on boat and sometimes I sleep in hut. Keeps bastards guessing.'

'Yes. Good idea,' I say, backing off his boat, although I haven't got the slightest idea who he means by the 'bastards'. Troublesome local kids, perhaps? I make a mental note to check out the nature reserve, possibly this afternoon, depending on how the day pans out.

I continue my walk along the riverbank path, under the two bridges and past the mouth of the Cherwell where it flows into the Isis. The line of university boathouses stretches along the other side on their own little island, just after the junction of the two rivers. I look across at them, admiring their 1950s styling with balconies above large ground floor doors. I can just about make out some people exercising on rowing machines behind some of the first-floor boathouse windows. A few of the big doors are open, revealing rowing eights on racks, and sculls and other boats. A couple of safety boats are zipping around on the water, so I suspect some mid-winter training is about to take place.

Suddenly, there's a shout from across the river.

'Jack! Jack! Over here!' I look across and see Nina with Anna and Cal, who are waving their arms from the balcony of a boathouse in the centre of the row of buildings. My mobile rings and the screen tells me it is Nina.

'I thought you were touring estate agents?' I say.

'Something's come up. Can you come across?'

'What is it?' I ask.

'Tell you when you get here, Jack.'

'Okay. But it'll take me about half an hour. I think I'll have to go up to Folly Bridge and come back on the other bank, through Christ Church Meadow.'

'Hold on a minute.' I look across to see Nina talking to the broad-chested figure of Cal who seems to be wearing some kind of vest or singlet and have a towel wrapped around his neck. Then Cal calls across to one of the safety boats and points to me. It looks like a beach pedalo for two, but it has an outboard engine at its stern. The couple on board wave back at him in acknowledgement and begin moving it across towards me. A young woman wearing several layers of woollen jumpers hops out and indicates that I should take her seat for the short crossing over to the boathouse.

'You know Cal?' says the remaining young man as he steers the stable little craft across the river.

'Not really,' I admit. 'I'm a friend of a friend.'

'Great. He's almost a cert to be in the Blue Boat.'

'Blue Boat?'

'The boat race crew. I roomed with him at training camp last week and his dedication is awesome – running during the night, staying in the gym longer than anyone else.'

'Are you in the crew too?'

'I was in the reserve boat. Isis. But I had a rib stress fracture on the last day. It's a real bugger. Anyway, I'm just helping out with some college coaching now.'

As we get to the bank, Nina walks across the grass in front of the club house.

'What's going on?'

'It's Cal. His girlfriend's gone missing and he's getting quite worried about her. He told Anna last night and she rang me this morning. I thought you might have some ideas about what to do. Have you got time for a coffee?'

We climb the stairs to the first floor of the Oriel College boathouse. Cal and Anna are sitting at a small round metal-topped table and a handful of other students, mostly dressed in sports gear, are scattered around the other tables. Anna fetches a coffee for me from a small kitchen area and Cal stands to shake my hand with his familiar no-nonsense grip but his brow is furrowed with concern.

'Jack, thanks for coming over. Nina thought you might be able to help us.'

'I'm sure there's a simple explanation. When did you last see your girlfriend?'

'The day before I went to training camp – so Tuesday the 6th. We both stayed in college for most of the holiday, but the rowing squad went to Caversham and I got back the Sunday before term started.'

'What's in Caversham?' I ask.

'The Redgrave Pinsent Rowing Lake. It's where the GB team trains, and our boat race crews are allowed to go there too. It's compulsory for the squad. We all stay at the Sheriff's Boathouse and we aren't allowed out. Usually the January camp is somewhere abroad but the coaches decided to stay close to home this year. It's intense. Phi and I swapped texts while I was away, but they stopped on the sixteenth – last Friday.'

'That's only a few days ago. Maybe she's lost her phone?'

'Yeah, but I spoke to her college again today. They thought she'd gone home for the rest of the holiday, but she wasn't back for the first day of term on Monday. That's not like Phi.'

'Phi? That's her name?'

'It's what I call her. Short for Ophelia. Ophelia McVeigh.'

'Have you spoken to her parents? Where does she live?'

'That's what's so strange. I don't have a number for her parents, but I got her tutor to call them and he rang me yesterday evening. They live in Edinburgh and say she hasn't gone home. She's just vanished. I'm worried about her.'

Anna puts a hand over his on the table. 'I'm sure she'll be okay, Cal. There's bound to be some kind of logical explanation.'

But there are three worried pairs of eyes looking at me and I sense they're expecting me to come up with something.

'May I see her last message?'

Cal hesitates and then goes to a nearby sports bag on the floor and pulls out his phone. He unlocks it with his thumb and scrolls through his messages.

'It's a little embarrassing, I guess. We only met in early December and we were really into each other. It was hard being apart for twelve whole days.'

I look at the phone. The last three texts are dated Friday 16th January.

Can't wait to see you on Sunday. Been training hard but still got lots of energy left for you! Xxx

Hi Cal! Xx Glad to hear it because I'm going to put you through your paces when you get home!

Outstanding! I'll get some fizz and we can stay in bed all day. Counting down the hours xxxx

I briefly scroll down his messages and there are similar exchanges on a daily basis for as far back as I can see.

'I got back from Caversham pretty early on Sunday morning and waited at my house for her all day. But she didn't turn up and she wasn't picking up. I figured it was strange when she didn't text me the day before, on the Saturday. I went to her college late on Sunday afternoon. Her room was locked but they let me have a quick look around. It looks like no one has seen her since Saturday the 10th and yet her last text to me was last Friday, like I said.'

'Which college?'

'St Hugh's. Over on the other side of town.'

'Have you tried the police?' I ask.

'Jack!' says Nina, looking worriedly at Cal. 'It's a bit early for that, isn't it?'

But Cal takes the question seriously and bites his lip. 'No. I haven't. D'you think I should? I don't know what to do next.'

'Did she have any other close friends?'

Cal shrugs helplessly. 'She never really mentioned anyone. It was her first term, like Anna – and me, I suppose. I think she was a bit lonely. She was on her own when she came over to the cathedral for an end-of-term carol service and we just hit it off.'

'Do you have any photos?'

'Sure,' he says, accessing his phone once again. He shows us all a selfie of the couple beaming towards the camera. It looks like they are in Christ Church Meadow. Ophelia is very attractive with long dark hair. They make an extremely handsome couple.

'She's lovely,' says Nina.

'Phi's very intelligent,' says Cal. 'I just don't understand where she's gone. I'm sorry to burden you guys with it, but Anna said you and Nina might be able to help.'

'Jack's a journalist,' says Nina, putting a hand on one of his bare forearms. 'He's good at getting to the bottom of things.'

'Anything. Anything you can do. I'd be so grateful.' His eyes have watered up and I feel genuine sympathy for the man. This particular 'Master of the Universe' does seem to have a sensitive and vulnerable side to him, after all.

'Let's think about this,' I say. 'Ophelia's last message to Cal was last Friday. So, she's been out of touch for five days. But she hasn't been seen at her college recently and she failed to meet Cal when he returned on Sunday.'

'She missed the start of term on Monday and she hasn't gone back home to Scotland,' adds Nina.

'Okay, I think maybe you're right, Nina. It is a bit early to go running to the police. I think my advice is to sit tight for the moment. Give it a couple more days.'

They all look at me doubtfully. 'You think?' says Cal dubiously.

'There must be something we can do,' adds Anna.

Nina looks at me crossly. 'Is that the best you can come up with, Jack?'

'You're the one who said it was too early to go to the police,' I remind her, but she is shaking her head in disbelief and Anna is looking at me pleadingly. 'And you didn't have any kind of argument?' I ask Cal.

'Jack!' says Nina. 'You saw her last messages to him.'

Cal just shakes his head.

'Ok ... perhaps ... perhaps we should go back to her college, St Hugh's, you say? We can ask around and try to find out if she said anything to anyone about her plans.'

'Great,' says Cal. 'It would just be great to be doing something. You don't mind coming with me?'

'No,' say Anna and Nina simultaneously.

'I'll just get a shower and we can drive over in my car,' he says.

It is barely ten minutes before he is back, dressed, smelling of shampoo and with a car key fob dangling in one hand. He waves goodbye to some of the other rowers and shows us to a small car park behind the row of boathouses where he blips open a silver-grey Jaguar SUV. The car looks brand new.

'Climb on in,' he says.

Nina claims the front passenger seat and I get into the rear with Anna. She leans over to me and whispers, 'Thanks for doing this, Jack.'

I shrug. I'm not too clear on precisely what I am supposed to be doing.

CHAPTER TWELVE

St Hugh's College is just north of the city centre, off the main road in the direction of Banbury. Cal has to do an entire circuit of its large perimeter before he finds an on-road parking space. I'm struck by how extensive it must be. The buildings look relatively modern in comparison to some of the other colleges I have walked past. The main entrance has a separate porter's lodge to one side of a set of brick pillared gates.

'Hi there again,' says Cal to a large bearded man behind a reception counter.

'Hello again, sir. Any luck yet?'

'No. I've brought some friends of mine. We thought we'd have another look in Phi's room, if that's okay?'

The porter inspects our little group and then swivels a visitors' book to face us. 'You'll all need to sign in, please. And I'll have to get someone to accompany you.'

We all do as we are told before the porter comes back with a younger man in the same kind of shirt, tie and flannels that he is wearing. 'This is Andrew. He'll show you up and bring you back out. And I'll need to tell Dr Romaine you're here. He asked to be kept informed.'

'Phi's pastoral tutor,' explains Cal.

We follow Andrew through the main door, zigzag along countless corridors that smell of furniture polish, and across an expanse of lawn into the Kenyon Building, a modern looking residential block. The young porter, who has been chatting amiably to Cal at the head of our little group, pulls out a key and opens the door of a room on the ground floor. The room smells musty and appears slightly soulless. There is a narrow single bed, a utilitarian desk, a chair by a window and a door that I assume leads into a small en suite bathroom. There are no pictures or posters on the walls but there is a photograph of Cal on the desk next to one of an elderly couple. Ophelia's parents, I assume.

The room is crowded with us all crammed inside and I decide to take charge. 'Look, we could do with a bit more space in here to look around. Andrew, would you mind staying by the door? And maybe you and Anna could sit on the bed?' I say to Nina. She looks about to protest but Anna just says, 'C'mon, Aunt!' and pulls her down alongside her.

Cal moves over to the desk and begins opening the drawers and rooting around inside them.

'Hey, hang on a minute,' says Andrew from the door. 'No one said anything about looking through her things.'

'Oh ... I'm sorry,' says Cal, pausing.

Anna gets up from the bed and moves the short distance to stand next to the young porter. She puts a hand on his arm and smiles sweetly. 'You don't mind, do you, Andrew? We're her friends and we just want to look for a note or anything that can explain where she's gone.' We are all looking at him and he looks back at each of us in turn, finally settling on Anna's big blue eyes.

'Well, I don't suppose it can do any harm,' he says uncomfortably.

I immediately open a wardrobe and find clothes hanging up and two suitcases at its base, one piled on top of the other. 'Do you know how many cases she had?'

'No idea,' says Cal.

There don't seem to be any signs of a purse or personal documents. Nor is there a phone charger or laptop. I pull the chair over and stand on it to look on top of the wardrobe. There is nothing there except a layer of dust.

I get down and move over to a small noticeboard by the door. It has a map of the city on it, alongside a timetable for lectures and tutorials and two fast food leaflets – a pizza delivery firm and a Chinese takeaway. I examine the map more closely, first looking to see exactly where St Hugh's is and then scanning our route back to the boathouses. But as my eyes follow the river towards my mooring, I notice a fresh pin hole has penetrated the paper. I look more closely and see that the pin had been located on a very small inlet on the far bank of the Isis, immediately after the small bridge by my mooring. The map indicates the bridge belongs to Strode Road; Strode Meadows is just above the pin hole. I scan the rest of the map and can see no sign of a hole anywhere else on it – it looks brand new and untouched otherwise.

'What is it, Jack?' Nina asks from the bed.

I shrug and shake my head. How could a mere pin prick be of any relevance?

'What about the rubbish bin?' asks Anna. 'Is there anything in there?'

I move over to the desk and pull a small grey metal bin out from under the aperture in the middle. Its only contents are a bright pink set of unused Post-it notes.

'How often are the rooms cleaned?' I ask Andrew, who is now leaning against the doorjamb and watching us.

'Every Friday, sir.'

'That's odd,' I say to the others. 'The texts stopped on Friday and the bin was emptied on Friday. So that means these Post-it notes must have been put in the bin since then, over the last few days.'

Cal gives me a puzzled look. 'Or Phi could have put the pad in the bin after the cleaners came. Like you say, she was still texting me last Friday.'

'Yes, but you said the last sighting of her in college was on Saturday the tenth?'

'That's what they're saying. Maybe she was in her room last Friday, but no one saw her?'

I can hear a voice behind Andrew in the corridor outside. 'Alright, Hargreaves. I'll take it from here. You can go back to the lodge. We'll talk about this later.'

I put the remaining pad of Post-it notes into my trouser pocket and watch as Andrew slips away to be replaced in the doorway by a man in his mid-forties. He's dressed in a blue three-piece suit with a collar and tie, his head is closely shaven, and he peers at all of us in turn through a pair of round wire-framed spectacles. He is easily as tall as Cal, but much thinner. He automatically bends his head as he enters the crowded little room.

'Good morning. I am Dr John Romaine,' he says stiffly. 'I'm Ophelia's tutor here at St Hugh's and I'm really not at all sure you should all be here, in her room, let alone searching through her property.'

Nina and Anna stand to introduce themselves and shake hands, followed by me, and then Cal.

'Ah yes, Mr Hopper. We spoke on the telephone, did we not?' The man has a precise, prissy way of speaking. 'Well, as you can see, Ophelia isn't in her room. Now, I suggest we adjourn to my study.'

We follow his ungainly frame back into the main building, up two wide flights of stairs and along a corridor into a book-lined room with a group of mismatched armchairs that circle a small round coffee table. A neat desk is sited under the only window.

'I use this room for tutorials and pastoral care meetings,' he says. 'Please take a seat and I shall put the kettle on. Tea? Coffee?'

We sit in a slightly awkward silence facing each other as he bustles about at a sideboard before finally distributing drinks in an assortment of different mugs. 'I have made a few more enquiries since our conversation, Mr Hopper.'

'Please, call me Cal.'

The tutor looks distinctly put out by this idea but then seems to come to terms with it. 'Yes, well,' he says, brushing an invisible speck of dust from one trouser leg. 'Thank you, er ... Cal. I last saw Miss McVeigh for a pastoral interview at the end of last term, before I went to France on a skiing trip.' That explains his unseasonal brown tan, I think to myself. Although he appears far too tall, skinny and awkward to be proficient on the ski slopes.

'And, as I told you, she was last seen in college on Saturday the tenth,' he adds, referring to a small leather-bound notepad on the arm of his chair. 'Most students were still away on holiday but, having spoken to our staff, that's the last time anyone can remember seeing her. We don't ask our students to sign in and out. Their identity cards are sufficient at the front reception. So, of course, I cannot be definitive about this. However, as you know I have now spoken to her parents and they are terribly concerned. She went home to Edinburgh for Christmas Day and Boxing Day, but they haven't seen her since then and their last conversation with her was by telephone on the weekend of ... let me just check, yes, that was also on Saturday the tenth.'

'How did you think she was getting on here?' I ask him.

'Well.' Doctor Romaine crosses one long leg over the other. 'She did seem rather agitated towards the end of last term. She was quite tearful when we last spoke, but I was unable to find out what was troubling her. In my experience it is usually boy trouble, money trouble or the workload. It can come as a tremendous shock in the first term to some of the students from less privileged backgrounds.'

'As far as I know, she didn't have any of those problems, sir,' says Cal firmly. 'And I would know.'

The tutor coughs at Cal's declaration. 'Yes, well, of course, I am sure you would. Nevertheless, Ophelia did seem rather distracted. I asked if she would rather talk to a female member of the college staff or our resident nurse, but she declined. I also spoke to her course tutor afterwards who said that she wasn't a spectacular student but that she seemed to be coping with the academic demands on her. And so, I feel I did all I could at the time. I am due to see her again this coming Friday and, obviously, we all hope that she will reappear by then and keep her appointment with me.'

It sounds to me like the good doctor is rehearsing a line of self-defence for some reason. I exchange a glance with Nina, who seems equally perplexed at the tutor's carefully chosen words.

'Mr and Mrs McVeigh are travelling down by train tomorrow,' the tutor went on. 'We have offered them a room in college. We have a number kept free that can be hired by members of the public. However, they said they would prefer to stay in a hotel in town. They're quite elderly, I believe. I will only be able to tell them what I have told you, I am afraid. I wonder if Miss McVeigh suddenly decided to take a last-minute holiday somewhere. Skiing, like me perhaps, or a winter break in the sun somewhere?'

'She would have told me,' says Cal adamantly. 'And her last text message to me on Friday was clear. She was looking forward to meeting me on the Sunday, when I got back from Caversham.'

I nod in agreement. 'That's what the text said.'

'Have you thought about reporting her missing to the police?' I ask.

The tutor looks horrified. 'Goodness me, no. Students often drop out for a few days or go on holiday without telling anyone, Mr … Mr Johnson, is it? No. I believe that must be a decision for her parents to take. The college authorities, of course, will co-operate in any way we can. I feel we have done all we can for now by informing Mr and Mrs McVeigh.'

CHAPTER THIRTEEN

'Look,' says Cal when we are back outside the St Hugh's entrance. 'It's nearly lunchtime. Why don't you guys come back to my house? I'll fix a bite to eat. I could do with the company.'

'Of course,' murmurs Nina sympathetically. 'And that would be lovely, wouldn't it, Jack?'

It's a short five-minute drive to Cal's rented home in Jericho and he talks for most of the journey. 'What did you make of Dr Romaine?' he asks. 'I'm not sure I cared for him suggesting that Phi was kind of distressed. She sounded just fine in her texts to me while I was away at camp.' He doesn't wait for an answer. 'But maybe something else was going on. I think she had a boyfriend in Scotland during high school. She told me they'd ended it painfully ... maybe he came back on the scene? What do you think? It's so strange that she'd just vanish like this. Here we are.'

Cal parks his car outside a pretty terraced cottage, which is separated from the pavement by a small stone wall. 'Welcome to Jericho. It's a pretty cool area. Someone told me it's called Jericho because it was outside the original city walls. Jericho means a remote place in the Bible. Phi used to tease me for bringing up the Bible all the time. But I guess it's natural when you've been brought up in the church. Did I tell you my pa is a preacher back home?'

He has barely drawn breath by the time he is opening the front door of the cottage and ushering us through a light wooden-floored sitting room and into the kitchen-diner beyond.

'Please take a seat. I'm sorry for rattling on. I'm really worried about Phi disappearing like this. Now I need some pasta for the carbs. I'll be back on the water at Wallingford to train this afternoon. Is pasta okay for everyone?'

Nina and Anna join him at a breakfast bar but he refuses their offers of help and sets to work chopping leeks, mushrooms and garlic, grating a fresh chunk of Parmesan and cutting some chives with some impressively fast knifework. I pull up a chair at the dining table nearby.

'Do you share this place with anyone, Cal?' I ask. It looks much more upmarket than the average student's accommodation and its location in a trendy bohemian quarter like Jericho must attract a premium rental fee.

'No, it's just me here. My folks give me a pretty generous allowance. They'll be coming over in April for the boat race and they wanted me to have the best possible chance of making the Blue Boat and finishing my PhD. For the moment, at least, I'm living on the bank of mom and dad. I have to confess, though; I haven't told them about Phi and me yet. They want *Doctor* Caleb Zachary Hopper to come home wearing a blue blazer and with a winner's medal around his neck – and nothing else will do. I think they'd view a girlfriend as an unwelcome distraction!'

'So, your father must make a good living as a preacher,' I say.

'Jack!' says Nina in an outraged voice.

But Cal just laughs, briefly showing his film star teeth. 'We're from the Bible Belt. Tennessee to be exact. Hence my name. Caleb was sent by Moses to find the land of Canaan. It means "faithful and wholehearted". My middle name is Hebrew originally, from the Bible too - Zachary means "the Lord has remembered."And Pa's a televangelist with his own cable channel. He's pretty successful at it and you could say he's inclined to be prodigal when it comes to his only son and heir.'

Nina is still glaring at me but I'm not exactly sure why. Cal certainly doesn't seem embarrassed talking about his wealth.

'So what is your PhD about?' I ask, attempting to divert onto safer ground.

Cal pulls a face at me as he loops a blue and white striped apron over his neck and ties it behind him in a neat bow.

'Major Sports Events and the Threat of Global Terrorism. I've been going at it for two years so I need to finish it this year. Oxford were keen on the topic, but, to be honest, I think they wanted me for my rowing ability rather than my doctorate. But hey ... I'm hoping to get a book out of it afterwards. And it won't hurt if I can promote it as a winner in the boat race!'

Nina and Anna join me at the table while Cal bustles about with a couple of pans on the hob. He breaks off to pour three glasses of chilled rosé and I wander into the sitting room with mine as the others chat. There is a well-polished revolving bookcase in one corner with a small collection of silver photograph frames on it. One has a picture of Cal flanked by an older couple in front of an impressive white clapperboard church. I assume these are his parents. There is a picture alongside it of the same older man, dressed in a cassock and surplus and standing in a pulpit. He has impressively chiselled features, like a mature Charlton Heston, and it looks like he is delivering a sermon into a microphone. There is a label on the pulpit which reads 'The 40-40 Ministry'.

Another picture shows Cal rowing. It must have been taken with a telephoto lens from the riverbank. It has caught him mid-stroke with a fierce look of determination on his face. He is wearing some kind of small camera on a headband around his forehead. A third photograph shows Cal again, but this time he seems to be in a hot-air balloon with the edge of a basket and a panoramic landscape behind him. He is reaching up with one hand to some kind of lever under the balloon. He is also giving the camera a thousand-yard stare and it is easy to see the resemblance to his father. There are no pictures of Ophelia, but then they haven't been seeing each other for very long.

'Lunch, Jack!' calls Nina.

'*Fusilli ai funghi e porri*,' he announces, placing a large pan in the centre of the table and spooning it onto four plates. 'Pasta with chestnut mushrooms, leeks and mascarpone. Phi loved it.'

'Yummy!' enthuses Anna.

'Delicious,' says Nina.

I am already forking a second mouthful when I realise Cal has bowed his head to say a silent grace. Anna, who must be used to this, has also paused before eating and I see Nina's cutlery is still on the table. Once again, she is giving me a reproachful look. I sigh inwardly and wait for Cal to finish praying and begin eating.

'So, what's it like being a Master of the Universe?' I ask, in an attempt to ease the atmosphere.

'Jack!' protests Nina, yet again. I really don't know what her problem is. She is treating the young American with kid gloves just because he hasn't heard from his girlfriend for a while. I decide to press on.

'No, I mean it, Cal,' I say, smiling. 'It's Anna's phrase.' Anna pouts at me for being so indiscreet. 'You must be the original Alpha male! Top-level rower. Studying for a PhD. You're writing a book and now we discover you're pretty handy in the kitchen. And what are you? Twenty-five? Twenty-six?'

Cal is laughing now. 'Twenty-eight, actually, and the average age for the boat race crews is twenty-three. That's why I have to train harder than the others. I'm an old man and this is my last chance.'

'...and that's not to mention the ballooning,' I add.

'Ballooning?' asks Nina.

'What can I say?' says Cal, holding out both hands and grinning. 'I like to do a bit of hot-air ballooning. I plan to take a few flights over the British countryside. It's too good an opportunity to miss.'

'You see. He's a bloody balloonist too,' I say to Nina and Anna. 'How the hell does an ordinary British bloke compete with all of these talents? And I haven't even got onto his looks yet!'

They are all laughing now. Cal spoons some more pasta onto everyone's plate and, of course, no one protests. It tastes as delicious as it looks.

'To Phi's safe return,' he says suddenly, looking around the table and raising his glass of water. We all repeat the toast and clink his glass. It is followed by an awkward silence. 'Speaking of which,' Cal goes on, looking directly at Nina, 'I was wondering if you might help me with Phi's parents tomorrow? I've arranged to meet them at the Randolph at ten o'clock. I've said I'll take them to see Dr Romaine and do anything else they want. I've spoken to my rowing coach and cleared the day.'

'Of course I will. I'd be happy to,' says Nina.

'Why, Nina?' I ask. But as soon as I utter the words, I register the green-eyed-monster lurking behind them. 'I mean ... rather than Anna?' I add lamely.

'Jack ...' Nina murmurs. But the protest is slightly half-hearted because I suspect that she too would like to hear the answer.

'I think they'd be reassured by Nina's presence,' says Cal simply. 'No offence,' he says to Anna. 'But Nina's a little older than you, so maybe she'd be a little more comforting for an elderly couple. But I don't think we should turn up "mob-handed", as you Brits call it.'

'No, I understand. It's fine,' says Anna. 'It's not as though I've ever met Ophelia ... Phi ... before.'

'Great,' says Cal. 'Thank you. Now, I'm afraid I need to get back to my training, folks. Did you know they reckon for every stroke we do on the day in the boat race, we've done about 600 in training during the run-up? Crazy! I only get the chance to work on my PhD in the evenings and I'm often too tired to keep my eyes open. They cut me some slack due to the rowing but now, with Phi disappearing like this ... well, I just can't seem to concentrate on anything else.'

We all turn down Cal's offer of a lift or a taxi, so he suggests we walk back along the towpath of the Oxford Canal, only five minutes away. The canal feels narrow and suburban after the broad majesty of the Thames and the Isis. There is no shortage of boats moored bow to stern, and a small fleet of hire narrowboats is waiting for the start of the season in the spring, but there is little sign of life. The towpath runs mainly along one side of the canal and at one place the plastic hoarding of a new housing development called Jericho Wharf drops straight down into the water on the far side. I predict another upmarket development marketing itself on the strength of its proximity to the towpath. And then, after a while, the new residents will begin to complain about the boaters' chimney smoke, noisy engines and allegedly anti-social habits. It's a pretty familiar dynamic for boat dwellers.

A stream runs parallel to the canal, but it is woody and overgrown and although there are some craft moored on it, they are largely rotting wrecks. We pass Isis Lock, which connects the canal to the river, and I am struck by a powerful poster that the Royal Life Saving Society has put up on the towpath. The top half shows a man in a t-shirt with his eyes half-closed and his head tilted backwards. The capital letter text says, 'ALCOHOL MAKES YOU MORE CONFIDENT. LESS CO-ORDINATED...' Underneath is a more shocking picture of the same man, but with a bare-torso and underwater. He is flailing his arms above his head as a stream of bubbles escape from his mouth. This time the poster says: ...WHICH YOU COULD DEAL WITH. UNLESS YOU ARE IN THE WATER. #DontDrinkandDrown.'

There can be few crueller ways to take another person's life or a more horrible way to die than a deliberate drowning.

The gloomy decay of the largely stagnant stream seems an appropriate backdrop to my mood, and perhaps the womens' too. Pull yourself together, Jack, I tell myself. However low you feel, how would you like to be an elderly couple travelling from Scotland and frantic with worry about the disappearance of your beloved, attractive and clever daughter? It is a bit baffling and I am full of sympathy for the young man who is struggling to make sense of it. If Nina can help find Ophelia, then who am I to begrudge it? Although it would be easier to accept if Cal wasn't quite so young, handsome and accomplished.

At the end of the canal we duck under a very low road bridge – a damp and sinister place, even in broad daylight – and continue to follow Castle Mill Stream to a main road that takes us back to Folly Bridge. We give Anna a quick hug and she goes on to Christ Church while we pause, leaning on a rail and looking down into the Isis.

'Penny for them,' says Nina, linking one arm through one of mine.

'Oh … nothing really. Just wracking my brains for any reason why Ophelia might have taken off.'

'Me too. I think perhaps her parents should go to the police after all.'

'You're probably right. You can suggest it to them tomorrow.'

'Do you think her tutor knew more than he was saying?'

'Possibly. He seemed a bit too keen to cover his arse.'

'Hmmm. I know what you mean.' She yawns. 'Sorry. I shouldn't have had that second glass of rosé. I'm hopeless if I drink at lunchtime. I need to cut back – and so do you.'

I ignore the repeated dig about my alcohol consumption. 'You do know you don't need to rent somewhere, don't you? You can save some money and stay on the boat.'

'Thanks, Jack,' Nina says, turning to look me squarely in the face. 'But I'll be more comfortable in my own space. And I can visit you and Eddie whenever I want to. Best of both worlds.'

'Just like Cal,' I say, again rather too quickly.

'What?'

'That's what Anna said about Cal having a room at college and his nice little cottage. The best of both worlds.'

'Oh, yes. I see. Well, I don't think poor Cal is feeling particularly lucky at the moment.'

'No. No, of course not,' I say, feeling genuinely chastened.

'You need to get back to Eddie,' Nina says, shutting down the conversation. 'I'll see you later.' She gives me a kiss on one cheek and strides off towards Cornmarket and the High Street while I wander slowly back to *Jumping Jack Flash*, alone with my thoughts.

CHAPTER FOURTEEN

I collect Eddie and slip him onto a lead to climb some steps to cross the Strode Road Bridge. Then I turn left and give him a run across Strode Meadows off his lead, before clipping him up again and joining a narrow residential road called Meadow Lane. I follow it past the rear of Salters Boatyard and cross Donnington Road, where I find the entrance to Kidneys Nature Reserve. The map on my phone shows kidney-shaped meadows that run alongside the Isis, criss-crossed with footpaths. A small sign at the entrance tells me to look out for water voles, small, spurred digger wasps, common toads, frogs and grass snakes. The reserve also allegedly contains greylag geese, mallards, dunnock, bullfinches, sparrows, song thrushes and the green woodpecker. The list doesn't sound hugely impressive to me, but it is a small patch of green bordering a river, so probably much appreciated by the locals regardless of the wildlife. The sign says dogs are welcome as long as owners clear up after them. It says nothing about keeping them on a lead, though, so in spite of the warning from my neighbour, I take a chance and let Eddie off.

My little dog scampers ahead of me, searching for squirrels on a path through some trees. As the path opens out into a patch of open land I can glimpse the river through the foliage on the far side, but we stay in the woods and I begin to circle around the edge of the nature reserve, which is bordered by a substantial spread of allotments. Eddie is darting happily in and out of the trees and bushes ahead of me, until he suddenly comes running back to my side with his ears flat and his tail clamped firmly between his legs. It doesn't take long to discover why, as a large lurcher comes galloping and barking from around the corner. I recognise the dog immediately: Tod from *Madam Gipsy*.

Tod stops a couple of metres in front of us and drops down onto his belly. But he continues to bark furiously, his long grey snout rising and falling to show a line of yellowing teeth. His owner now comes hurrying behind him, wearing a hard hat with a clear mask and carrying a petrol-powered brush-cutter. John Turner stops the engine and wriggles out of the harness holding the machine suspended from one shoulder. Eddie is cowering behind me as Tod is still barking.

'Hush thee row!' Turner shouts at his dog, who grumbles himself into a silence. 'Bloody dog.' He peers across at me. 'S'you, is it? From the boat?'

I bend to fix the lead onto Eddie's collar. 'Yes. Jack. Jack Johnson. I just thought I'd walk over and have a look at your Kidneys.' That doesn't sound quite right, but he doesn't show even a flicker of a smile. He takes off the hard hat. The top of his bald pate shines with sweat and his grey hair hangs lank and greasy around it.

'Warm work?'

'Aye. Just cutting back brambles. Bastards take over if you're not careful.' Tod is still eyeing us both suspiciously and chuntering to himself. I take the risk of moving closer to Turner and his dog.

'How big is the park?'

'Three hectares,' he says, rubbing his grey bristles. 'But there's couple more parks up there,' he says nodding in the direction of the city centre. There's River Greens, which takes you on up onto Cherwell, and there's Aston's Eyot a bit inland. Big patch for one man to look after.'

'And they give you a hut or something do they?'

Turner looks at me suspiciously. 'Aye. Need somewhere for me kit. And I keep guard now and then. It's just over there.' He nods over to my left, where I can just glimpse a concrete block outbuilding with a red tiled roof. 'No fencing, see? You wouldn't believe what some people get up to in here at night. Down and outs. Druggies. Doggers. It's disgusting it is – the mess they leave behind.'

I nod sympathetically. 'So, when you're not on your boat, you're staying here in the Kidneys?'

'Aye.'

Our conversation seemed to have come to its natural end and I was about to take my leave. But instead, Tod chooses this moment to spring forward unexpectedly and clamp Eddie by his neck to the floor. I still have the little dog on his lead and I'm immediately tangled up in the melee as both dogs snap and struggle for dominance. I'm definitely not going to risk putting a hand into the confusion of teeth and claws, so I aim a kick at Tod's head, which somehow connects. He is momentarily stunned, or just surprised; it's enough for Eddie to twist free and clamp his own strong little jaw onto one of the big lurcher's ears. Tod twists and shakes his large shaggy head to free himself from Eddie, who has all four feet off the floor and is hanging by Tod's ear. But Border Terriers were originally bred to run with hunts and go down tunnels to fetch the fox after it had gone to ground. If there is one thing Borders know how to do, it is to lock their jaws and hold on for dear life. Out of the corner of my eye, I now sense Turner entering the fray as Tod spins around in circles, trying to dislodge the smaller dog from his unrelenting bite. Eddie is almost flying horizontally, like some kind of circus acrobat, his hind legs splayed wide in the air. I have already let go of the lead and it too is flailing in circles.

'LIE STILL!' shouts Turner at the top of his voice and he darts in to give his dog a firm smack on the rump with the flat of one hand. To my amazement, Tod instantly drops to the ground and freezes. Eddie is still clamped on. I move in quickly, prise Eddie's jaw apart with considerable difficulty and carry the struggling little dog away from the lurcher.

'YOU BLOODY DOG!' Turner is bent over with both hands on his hips, shouting at his dog, who is darting looks between his master and us. Tod doesn't look very contrite, but thankfully he isn't moving from his splayed position on the ground either. Turner pulls a length of baling twine out of a pocket of his overalls and quickly ties it to his dog's collar. I'm not sure who is panting the heaviest, the dogs or us.

'Your dog started it,' I say defensively, as I examine Eddie for any wounds around his neck where Tod had initially pinned him to the ground. I can't see any sign of puncture marks or tell-tale trickles of blood. Tod, however, has a ripped and bloody ear.

Turner is red in the face from his exertions. 'Aye, and your dog finished it ... just about. Is it alright?'

'I think so.'

'Well,' he says as he bends to put his hands on both knees and take a breather. 'I don't know about you, but I could use a cuppa after that.' He yanks the piece of twine and nods at his nearby hut. I'm not sure about ushering the two dogs into a confined space but they are both securely on their leads now and befriending Tod's owner might be a way of securing a free long-term mooring. I follow Turner, carrying Eddie and maintaining a safe distance.

Turner unlocks a steel door with a key on a string around his neck and flicks a wall switch. Three neon strip lights blink several times before settling to spread their harsh light over a compact orange tractor, a jumble of smaller machinery and a kitchen unit. On the far wall, under a grubby window, is an equally grubby single bed with grey army blankets spread on top of it and some kind of kerosene heater standing where you might expect to see a bedside table.

'Tea,' says Turner, as he ties Tod's makeshift lead around a lever on the tractor. It's not a question 'I don't drink coffee.'

I agree that tea will be fine, and he fills a battered old plastic kettle and plugs it in. I wander across to the window. Tod is grumbling and growling at the idea of his small but worthy opponent sharing his space, so I keep him in my arms and move over to peer through the smeared panes at a wall of foliage.

'How's your dog?'

I put Eddie down on the floor and carry out a more thorough inspection, parting his coarse hair to look for wounds and moving his legs to see if he flinches. He is wagging his little tail and I swear his face is showing something between a smirk and a grin. 'He's okay, thanks.' I sip my tea. It is undrinkable. Turner hasn't asked if I take sugar and it tastes as though there could be three teaspoons in it.

'Are you sure?'

'I think so. I'm sorry I kicked your dog. But he could have killed Eddie.'

Turner nods and spreads his hands. 'Aye, well, I won't lie. If you make a complaint, I'll have to have Tod put down. He's done it before, see. He's an unpredictable bugger. There's been a few complaints and he's under caution, like. He killed a family's Chihuahua last year and they took us to court. Still can't bring myself to lock him up all day, though.'

The plea for mercy is why I have been invited back to the hut for tea. Tod is looking up at us with his chin resting on the floor of the hut. A few spots of blood from his ear have dripped onto the bare concrete. He looks as glum as his master. I get up to go. 'No. No, I won't be making a complaint. It was six of one, half a dozen of the other. No harm done – except to Tod's ear. You'll need to get that seen to.'

Turner is now smiling for the first time since I've met him. He moves across to shake my hand and ruffle the fur on Eddie's head. 'Tough little bugger, aren't you? That's grand. Thank you. Thank you very much.'

I tip the nearly full mug of tea into the filthy sink, make my excuses and leave. I am relieved to see that Eddie is moving okay and not showing any signs of being hurt in the fight. He runs ahead of me again and we stick to a main path, which circles the Kidneys and its neighbouring parks. For a while, the path runs along the river and then, at the mouth of the Cherwell, it swings right. I can just make out the end of the row of college boathouses on the other bank of the junction, where the rivers meet. Then I swing right again, along a large broad avenue of trees, and find myself back at the entrance on Meadow Lane.

The Kidneys don't have the opulence or elegant fixtures and fittings of Sidney Gardens, the eighteenth-century park close to my former city centre mooring in Bath, but they are still very pleasant and I'm lucky to have somewhere nearby where I can give Eddie a run. This time I cross Donnington Road Bridge and walk back along the far bank to *Jumping Jack Flash*. But before I get to Strode Road Bridge, I glimpse the mouth of a small inlet on the far bank. I can just see the protruding prow or stern of some kind of houseboat moored there. It has a slender flagpole; it's almost the height of the bridge. The area around it is quite densely wooded and, although most of the leaves have gone, it is still relatively well-hidden from the opposite riverbank's path. I must have already passed by several times. It piques my curiosity and I climb up to cross Strode Road Bridge and take a closer look.

Now, I can see much more. It's as broad as a Dutch barge with an elegant white superstructure stretching along its entire length. The hull, from what I can see, rises up slightly to a point. I am still not sure if I am looking at the bow or the stern. The flagpole could be sited at either end. It has a black hull, edged in a line of red paint. It looks like a barge or a houseboat of some kind that is designed to be pulled by another craft. I can see a row of four elegant wooden columns under a slightly curved roofline at the end closest to me. They form a porch and there are wood and glass doors under the canopy that lead into the boat.

A small dirt track slopes down to a gate in a tall chain-link fence that stretches from the mouth of the inlet and disappears into the trees – presumably circling the entire mooring. There is not the slightest sign of life on board, but it is an attractive and perhaps even historic craft in a very private setting. I can't imagine it is deserted for very long and I would love to find out a little more about this unusual boat. I wonder if Turner knows any more about it.

Back on my own boat, I pull out some chicken, vegetables and stock to prepare a coq-au-vin for two before checking my phone. There is a text from Nina.

Go ahead and eat. Back later.

I pack away the food, heat up a tinned steak and kidney pie instead and wash it down with half a bottle of red. I spend the rest of the evening with the other half-bottle for company while I read the latest Jo Nesbo thriller and doze. My boat doesn't have a television and it is the better for it. I hear Nina fumbling with the hatchway half an hour after I have walked Eddie and turned in. The little dog vanishes through the swing door to greet her. I hear her using the bathroom and see the line of light under her door go dark.

She probably thought I was already asleep, I tell myself. I guess she decided not to poke her head around the door and risk disturbing me.

CHAPTER FIFTEEN

Nina leaves the boat at nine the following morning after I've joined her for a morning run with Eddie. She is younger, fitter and faster than me, but she has the good grace to slow her pace to match mine. I glance across at her. 'Did you have a nice evening? I heard you come in. I was still awake.'

She keeps her head fixed firmly ahead and accelerates slightly. 'Not nice exactly. I called in at Cal's. He's in quite a state.'

I tell her about The Kidneys and Eddie's scrap with Tod as we jog upstream to Osney Lock and back, a distance of roughly two miles. She spends slightly longer than usual in the shower and dressing, while I wolf down a bacon sandwich. But the wait is worth it. Nina has dressed carefully and looks fabulous in a white collarless shirt, bunched at the wrists and belted at the waist, over black leggings tucked into knee-length leather boots.

'I hope it goes okay today,' I say as she puts on an elegant black raincoat and red leather gloves.

'It's not going to be much fun is it?' she says. Then she pointedly sniffs in my direction. 'Don't forget to shower.'

'What about your breakfast?'

'I'm meeting Cal first, before we meet Mr and Mrs McVeigh. I'll get something in the coffee shop.' And with that, she is off, pausing only to give Eddie a kiss as she goes.

She's right. It isn't going to be much fun dealing with Ophelia's worried parents. I should be pleased that I have been spared any part of it. But I'm not. Part of me is jealous of the time she will spend with Cal and the rest of me is curious about the next steps they will take to trace the missing girl. After my shower, which is tepid, I discover I have a missed call and a voice message waiting.

It is DS Jane Henry. 'Hi Jack. The ACC has approved you spending a day on shift with me. Subject to certain conditions. I'm a bit busy today but if you're free this evening, we could talk it through over dinner. Let me know. Bye.'

I am unexpectedly excited by this invitation and, if I am brutally honest with myself, see it as an opportunity to get even with Nina for her cosy evening with Cal. I send a text agreeing to the plan and she replies quickly with a text.

Porterhouse Grill. 7.30pm. Can you book a table?

I send a thumbs-up emoji in reply and open up the restaurant's website. The Porterhouse Grill is a restaurant with rooms. It makes a big thing of cooking all its dishes in a charcoal-fuelled Bertha Oven at temperatures reaching 350 degrees centigrade. The price list looks similarly over-heated for my bank balance. I am about to test the CQ editor's definition of 'reasonable expenses'. I send another text telling DS Henry that the table is booked and start cleaning and tidying the boat. I don't know how long Nina will be staying, but her standards are slightly higher than mine in this respect.

However, as I am stuffing my jacket onto a coat-hanger in one of the cupboards, I remember the pad of Post-it notes from Ophelia's room in its pocket. The little pink pad is probably half of its shop-bought size and I flick through it. The pages are all blank but then I notice the top one has the ghostly indentation of some writing on it – presumably caused by the pressure of the pen that was used on the previous top sheet. It's the oldest trick in the book but that doesn't mean it isn't worth trying.

I root around in a galley drawer for a pencil, sit down at the kitchen table and start to lightly shade the paper. But then I stop quickly. What if I cover the indentation and still can't make it out? The note could be ruined. I ponder this for a while and then fish out my mobile phone. A quick search on Google comes up with an alternative so I switch off the boat's wall lights and lay the pad flat on the table. I shine my powerful little torch across the paper. This picks up the shadows left by the pressure marks. Now I use the camera on my phone to capture the image which I enlarge to double its size. It is a single word in capital letters: NIRVANA.

I return to the Google search box. Unsurprisingly, the first page is full of references to the famous band. Wikipedia tells me it was formed in Aberdeen, Washington, USA, by lead singer and guitarist Kurt Cobain, bassist Krist Novoselic and drummer Dave Grohl. I click on Cobain's name, vaguely aware of there being some controversy about his death. I read that he was found dead at his home in Seattle, Washington in 1997, at the age of twenty-seven. He had died three days earlier and been found with a shotgun across his body, a visible head wound and a note nearby.

Is this some kind of indication that Ophelia had also been contemplating suicide? Is this why she had suddenly disappeared? I scroll through more pages of entries about the band until I get to another definition.

'*Nirvana – the cessation of individual existence, to which a Buddhist or Hindu aspires as the culmination of the meditative state; loosely, a blissful state.*' Perhaps Ophelia had been going to meditation classes? Or perhaps she needed to reference the term for an essay she had been working on? Or perhaps she was just a fan of an American rock band that, I now know, '*was the flagship band of Generation X*'. Or perhaps I am trying just a bit too hard to construct a reason for her to write a single word on a pad of Post-it notes? I put the pad back into my jacket's pocket and make myself a coffee.

I return to my cleaning and tidying and then run the engine for a couple of hours to recharge the boat's batteries. I still have plenty of water in the tank, thanks to my brief stopover at Abingdown Marina. There is a fine rain falling and hardly anyone is about on the riverbank apart from the occasional runner, dog-walker or cyclist. I am just preparing a sandwich lunch when my mobile rings. It's Nina.

'Jack?' Her voice sounds urgent and distressed.

'Hi, Nina. How's it going?'

'Oh, Jack. It's terrible. I'll have to be quick. I've got to get back to them.'

'Where are you? Are you still with Ophelia's parents?'

'Yes, yes.' She sounds impatient. 'But then we went to the police station – to report Phi missing ...'

'Right. So, what did they say?'

'Jack, just stop interrupting me, please. We went to the police station and a constable started filling in a missing person's report. He wrote down all her details and then her parents showed him a photograph. That's when he left us in the interview room. He said he'd be just a few minutes, but he was gone nearly an hour. He came back with two older men. Oh, Jack, it was horrid. One of them said they thought a body that was found in the Thames a few days ago might be Ophelia.'

I'm stunned. And then I remember the story on the BBC local news website.

'At Iffley?'

'Yes. How did you know that? Iffley Weir on Saturday. Cal and Phi's father had to go to the mortuary to do a formal identification. It's her, Jack. It's Phi. But when they told Mrs McVeigh she collapsed. We're at the hospital now with a couple of different officers. They think Ophelia was murdered. They took Cal back to the station, to help them. Why would they do that to him? He's inconsolable. I said I'd stay here with Mr and Mrs McVeigh for the moment.'

'What can I do to help? Do you want me to go to the station and wait for Cal? Or come to the hospital? Have you told Anna?'

'You're the first person I've called,' Nina says. 'Look, I've got to get back to Mr McVeigh. He's going to need some medication as well, I think. They're both in their seventies – Phi was adopted. Can you track down Anna and tell her what's happened? Tell her to stay in college and I'll call her later if there's more news. I must go.' The line abruptly goes dead.

Poor Ophelia. So, it wasn't suicide. It was murder. And it was natural that the police would want to question Cal first and foremost. For all their apparent sympathy, the detectives know that 80 per cent of murder victims knew their killer. The victim's boyfriend would be the first person they would need to eliminate from their enquiry. And Cal could shed light on what was going on in Ophelia's life and tell them who else might be in the frame. I remember him saying something about an ex-boyfriend in Scotland. Had the man reappeared in Oxford? Was he jealous and vengeful after they had split up?

I try Anna's phone, but it goes unanswered. She has probably switched it off for a tutorial or lecture. I leave a message asking her to call me and then clip Eddie onto a lead and make my way to Christ Church. The porter's lodge doesn't keep records of the students' comings and goings and there is still no answer from Anna's phone, so they direct me to the Faculty of English at St Cross Building in Manor Road. It's only a ten-minute walk away and although the rain is a fine drizzle, it manages to give me a good soaking. My phone rings just as I belatedly duck into a tourist shop to buy an umbrella.

'Hi Jack. What's up?' It's Anna. She has just emerged from a tutorial and can meet me within a few minutes so she names a coffee shop in the High Street.

Anna goes ashen when I tell her the news. Her eyes are huge and both her hands are pressed flat to her mouth in shock. 'No. Oh no. Poor Phi and poor Cal. And her poor, poor parents.'

We end up staying in the coffee shop for at least an hour, with Anna repeating the same sentiments and the same questions. How long do I think she might have been in the water? Why do I think the police believe it was murder? What kind of injuries do I think she might have had? Do I think she would have suffered much? Can the police tell if someone was dead before they went into the water? Do I think she was murdered there, or somewhere else? Would it have happened at night? How long will the police question Cal for? Won't they give him time to grieve first? Should we go to the hospital and see if Nina needs a hand? Or should we wait at the police station until they let Cal go home? On and on it goes, endlessly round and round, with me trying to answer her questions and buying repeat cups of coffee before, eventually, persuading her to eat something.

'Look,' I say, 'Nina said she'd call you later. She'll have her hands full with Mr and Mrs McVeigh and Cal, so it's probably best not to bother her. You can come back to the boat and wait for her if you want. I need to go back and change out of these wet clothes.'

'No.' Anna shakes her head. 'It's okay, Jack. Thanks. I'll go back to college and wait for Nina to call me there.'

'Okay. But if you change your mind just come down to *Jumping Jack Flash*.' I wrestle with my key ring which has the orange CQ memory stick attached alongside a small cork ball to make it float if I drop it in the water. 'Here's a spare key to the boat if I'm not there.'

She takes it, stands to give me a hug and makes her way sadly out of the door while I settle the bill.

I keep half an eye on BBC Oxford and the *Oxford Mail*'s website during the afternoon, but there is no breaking news to announce that the dead woman found at Iffley has now been identified. By six o'clock the sun is well over the yardarm and I am just cutting a slice of lemon and breaking some ice for a gin and tonic when my phone pings with an incoming text from Nina.

Phi's parents back at Randolph. Police family liaison officer is with them. I'm taking Cal home. May stay over. He's in bits. Talk later. x

She hasn't asked after Anna, so I text a brief reply.

Understood. Met up with Anna. She's waiting for a call from you. Take care. Sympathy to Cal x

I regret the message as soon as I press send. Sympathy to Cal? He has just found out that his girlfriend has been murdered! And I'm just sending my sympathy. What an idiot. But then, I can't imagine Nina saying, 'Oh, and by the way, Jack sends his sympathy.' So, no harm done – except possibly in Nina's eyes. But then, I reflect, I don't seem to have said or done much right according to her in recent days. My mobile pings again and I predict that it will be Nina again, with a caustic reply, but in fact it turns out to be DS Jane Henry.

Still on for 7.30?

Why not? It doesn't look as though I'm needed anywhere else and if Nina's staying at Cal's to give him a shoulder to cry on, she won't be coming back here this evening to cry on mine. I send Jane a thumbs-up emoji for the second time and head to the bathroom for a hot shower and a shave.

CHAPTER SIXTEEN

The detective is already seated and waiting for me by the time I get to the Porterhouse Grill. The dining area is painted blue-black and the lighting is low, but I can still see enough to appreciate the view. She is wearing a V-neck cobalt blue dress and her black hair has been pulled back into a short ponytail, a style which accentuates her high cheekbones. I go to offer her my hand, but she just laughs, stands up and kisses me lightly on the cheek. She smells great.

'Jack. You made it. You brush up well.'

'Thanks. As do you DS Henry!'

'If you don't call me Jane, I swear we won't split the bill.'

'Ah yes ... well, I'm hoping that this one is on the magazine.'

A waiter appears to ask politely if we want aperitifs. Jane opts for a vodka martini and I order a gin and tonic – my third of the evening so far after two on the boat. I am already feeling cheerfully mellow and hungry. The restaurant obviously treats its steaks very seriously. The menu boasts that they come direct from Smithfield Market and the beef is dry aged in-house for up to 42 days. Much of it is on display, great marbled slabs of red-blue meat hanging in chilled cabinets around the dining area.

'So, you're not a vegetarian, then?' I ask, nodding at the huge haunches of cow.

She laughs. 'This is my favourite restaurant in the whole of Oxford. I only live around the corner. I'd eat here every day if I could.'

We both order duck hearts as starters, two *cote de boeuf* mains with frites and a bottle of Haut Medoc.

'Have you been at the station today?' I ask. She nods. 'Did you hear anything about a murder enquiry into a woman who was found at Iffley? She was identified today, and it turns out she's the friend of a friend.'

'Yes, I heard a bit about it in the canteen. DCI Brian Philpott is in charge. He's a hard bastard – but he's experienced. Who's the friend of the friend?'

I explain briefly about Cal sharing the same college as Anna, who is the niece of my friend Nina. 'Cal and the girl's parents reported her missing this morning and then the body was quickly identified. All very horrible.'

'I assume the boyfriend has been questioned by Philpott?'

'I think so. Cal had to stay on at the station this afternoon. But he's been allowed back home now – he's with my friend Nina.'

Jane quickly picks up on the hint of something in my voice. 'I thought Anna was his friend at college and Nina the aunt?'

'Yes. That's right. But Nina lost her husband in Afghanistan. She's still mourning herself, and she's had some professional grief counselling. I expect she feels she can use her experience to help Cal at a time like this.'

'So, the dead girl is actually a friend of a niece of a friend. And Aunty Nina? Is she more than a friend to you, Jack?'

Her instinct and directness are an unsettling combination.

'Have you noticed this trademark on the cutlery? It's from France. It's called Laguiole. Look, you can see the bumble bee on it.'

'I asked you a question, Jack.'

I shake my head in disbelief. 'Once a detective ...'

'Well, is she?' presses Jane, her eyes sparkling mischievously in the candlelight.

'Okay, I surrender,' I say laughing and holding up both hands. 'I'd very much like Nina to be more than a friend but, well, as I say, she's still grieving for her dead husband and she hasn't really been able to move on.'

'How long has it been since he died?'

'Getting on for a couple of years.'

'How old is she?'

'Thirty. No, thirty-one now.'

'And you are ...?

'Forty-six. Have you ever thought about going into journalism?'

'And how old was Nina's soldier-boy husband?'

'About the same age as her. Where are you going with this?'

'Just marshalling the facts. And how old is Cal?'

'Twenty-eight.'

'Handsome?'

'Ridiculously so.'

'Rich?'

'Yes. Well, his father is. And yes, he's athletic, smart, American and an all-round nice guy. Oh, and he'll be in the boat race crew this spring and he's a hot-air balloonist. And he's a dream in the kitchen.'

'Wow! Can you give me his number when Nina has finished with him?'

'Not bloody likely,' I say refilling her wine glass. 'And Nina's not *with* him.'

Jane obviously hears something in my tone and turns more serious.

'So, this Cal,' she says. 'Could he be connected with the girlfriend's death?'

'No, I honestly don't think so. He seems to be an all-round good guy, as I said. And religious too. His father is some kind of television preacher with his own cable channel in the States. Cal was locked down 24/7 with the rest of the university rowing squad at a residential training camp in Caversham for over a week before she was found. And the girl was sending him texts up until the day before. I've seen them. They don't suggest there was anything wrong between them. Quite the opposite.'

Jane nods thoughtfully. 'And is Nina the reason you're moored up here in Oxford now? I remember you telling me it was wanderlust. Is the emphasis on lust , by any chance?'

'Sort of,' I confess. 'It's all a bit pathetic, really. Trailing around the country after her. What about you? Anyone on the radar?'

She takes her time chewing a piece of steak before answering. 'You just changed the subject but okay. No. As I told you before, I'm married to the job at the moment. My career should be moving faster than it is and I don't have time for complications.'

'Talking of which. The article for *Cotswold Quality*. Aren't we supposed to be discussing it over this dinner?'

She waves a hand airily. 'It's fine. All sorted. Permission granted. I'll take you to meet someone interesting. She was part of the London gang scene for a while.'

I make a mental note to fix a definite day and time for this to happen before the evening ends and I order another bottle of the same red for us to share.

'Did you say you joined Thames Valley from Dorset?'

'Yep. And I joined Dorset straight from uni on a graduate entry scheme. It's getting quite difficult to recruit detectives. So much of it is tedious computer work these days and even some of the uniforms aren't tempted. And, no doubt, I was good for their diversity stats.'

I shake my head. 'Don't talk yourself down. You're obviously great at your job. What did you study? Criminal psychology?'

She laughs. 'No. Classical Civilisations, would you believe? Astonishingly useful if you want to know the difference between a Doric, Ionic and Corinthian column.'

Our waiter reappears with a second bottle of wine, refills our large balloon glasses and talks us through the dessert menu. We opt to share a single cheese platter.

'Actually, if you're going to use a classical education anywhere, this city is the place to be,' she continues. 'Take the Isis where you're moored. What d'you know about the Goddess Isis?'

'Egyptian?' I guess. 'Connected to the Nile in some way? That's about it.'

She takes a big gulp of wine and grins naughtily. 'Yes. Okay. She's a lot more interesting than that, so pay attention. The ancient Egyptians believed the annual floods on the Nile were caused by her tears and that she was crying because of the death of her husband.'

'Okay,' I say slowly, wondering where this tale is leading and hoping it isn't circling back to Nina.

'Her husband was Osiris, a king of Egypt, but he had a nasty brother called Set who wanted the throne. So, Set has a beautiful wooden box made out of cedar, ivory and ebony and he tricks his brother into lying in it as a dinner party game. It's been made for his exact measurements and all the other guests don't quite fit. Then he slams the cover shut, seals it and throws it into the Nile. The coffin eventually floats out to sea and ends up in a city called Byblos, where a tree grows around it. Eventually the king of Byblos has the tree cut down and made into a pillar for his palace – with the coffin still inside it.'

'Don't you just hate a sloppy builder?'

'Isis visits the king and she finds the pillar and her husband's corpse.'

'Is this a true story?'

'Listen, Jack. It gets better. Set then steals his brother's corpse back and this time he means business. This time, Set hacks his brother's body into fourteen pieces in the hope that crocodiles will eat the flesh and he'll be gone forever.'

'Bloody hell! He doesn't mess about, does he? I'm so very glad that we've finished our bloody steaks.'

'Well, Isis is a stayer, though. She finds all of the remains of Osiris and joins them back together again. All except her husband's penis, which is missing because it has already been eaten by a crab.'

'What? You've got to be kidding me? His penis has been eaten by a crab?'

'Straight up. But Isis is resourceful. She makes a new todger for him out of gold and wax and this finally makes the body whole again. And this means that she can have posthumous sex with her old man and, as a result, she magically conceives their only son Horus, who turns out to be the sun god.'

'Of course he does. And what happens to Osiris and his golden balls?'

'Well he's a god now, obviously, and he descends into the Underworld and becomes its lord. Although he does still pop back up to visit his wife and son occasionally.'

'Probably to pay his child maintenance ...'

'But Isis goes a bit mad, cuts off her beautiful black hair and tears her robes to pieces. The End.'

I clap my hands in admiration and Jane half rises from the table to take a bow.

'To Isis and beautiful, clever and loyal women everywhere,' I say raising my glass to hers.

She smiles. 'To Isis,' she says, raising her own in reply.

There is a moment while we look at each other. I am suddenly reminded of Waugh's famous line from *Brideshead Revisited* when Charles Ryder 'caught a thin bat's squeak of sexuality, inaudible to all but me.' That was in Oxford too.

'What are you smiling about?'

'I'm enjoying myself.'

'Me too.'

She asks me about my dealings with the police in Bath over our wine and cheese, and I ask her about county lines over coffee.

'You called the OCGs evil,' I remind her. 'You sounded angry at the time. Is it okay for the police to be angry?'

'Yes,' she says immediately. 'Controlled anger is a good motivator. But we can never allow that anger to cloud our judgement or prompt us to cut corners.'

'Even if the evil people get away with it?'

'Yes. It's a slippery slope. We need to follow the rule of law scrupulously otherwise the guilty go free anyway. The courts will see to that. We can't ever allow our anger at social injustices or heinous crimes tempt us to take shortcuts. It always comes back to haunt us when we do. And anyway, don't journalists have to play by the rules too?'

'It's a fair question. Up to a point, I guess. But our industry still largely regulates itself.'

She rolls her eyes. 'Even after the phone-tapping scandal?'

'The courts are still holding the press to account for that. And the *News of the World* went out of business.'

'And a lot of lives have been ruined. Police enquiries disrupted.'

'Okay. I'm just saying the press can be a force for good too, just like the police.'

'As long as we both work within the rules.'

Jane has the final word on this exchange and I take care of the bill by stopping at the reception desk on my way back from the gents and break the news to her as I sit back down.

'Jack! I said we'd go Dutch.'

'Don't worry. I'm sure I can claim it on expenses.'

'But what if you can't?'

'Then I certainly won't regret having had such a lovely evening.'

'Well, at least let me give you a nightcap. You can walk me home.'

The temperature outside is freezing in contrast to the intimate warmth of the restaurant and Jane immediately links an arm through mine. She gives an exaggerated shiver. 'It's only two streets away but let's hurry.'

Her flat is half of the ground floor of a large Victorian house that has been turned into apartments. It has high ceilings and an original fireplace framed by images of poppies on tiles. The tiles are flanked by floor to ceiling bookshelves that are spilling over with erudition. The grate has already been stacked with newspaper, kindling and logs. I am instructed to set fire to it while Jane switches on a couple of lamps, turns off the main ceiling light and fetches an unopened bottle of Johnnie Walker Black Label from the kitchen.

'Can you open it while I get some glasses? Would you like ice?'

I wince. 'Just water, please.'

We clink glasses and sink back into the depths of the squashy sofa. The fire is crackling and already beginning to blaze and throw flickering shadows around the large and comfortable room. I recognise the Jacques Loussier Trio playing Bach softly in the background.

'That was a hell of a story about Isis,' I say, and she chuckles softly.

'As one of my tutors used to say, the Gods can be mad bastards.'

'A golden penis,' I say, shaking my head and taking a huge swallow of the smoky blended whisky.

'A 22-carat hard-on!'

Now we are both laughing.

'This is a lovely apartment. It feels so big after the boat.'

'I'm sure the boat's really cosy,' she says, topping up my fast-depleted glass.

'Yes. But after a while it begins to feel very small. It's only 6 ft 10 inches wide – a floating corridor really.' I feel a pang of disloyalty to *Jumping Jack Flash* even as I say this. It's is a short step for me to register an even greater pang of disloyalty to Nina at this precise moment. But why should I feel disloyal to her? I have just shared a wonderful meal with a beautiful, clever and independent woman who is pursuing her own career and doing her bit to make the world better. Where is the harm in that? And where is Nina tonight? With Cal. In Cal's lovely rented home. Cal, Master of the Universe, getting lashings of sympathy and understanding from Nina. And what if one thing leads to another? What if he reaches out to her for more than words? What if he seeks physical comfort in the depths of his grief? Would she deny him? They are virtually the same age. And look at him, for God's sake. What woman wouldn't?

I sense Jane looking up at me. 'Slow down, Jack. It's too good not to taste it, isn't it?'

I've been drinking my whisky on autopilot, unthinkingly taking rapid sips which have matched my rush of unwelcome thoughts. She's right. I haven't appreciated it at all. But the spicy aftertaste is still there at the back of my mouth. A small brass antique carriage clock on the mantlepiece chimes softly, twelve times, marking the end of the day and the beginning of the next.

'The iron tongue of midnight hath told twelve; Lovers, to bed; 'tis almost fairy time,' she says softly.

There is a brief silence. Our eyes lock onto each other and she makes the slightest, infinitesimal move closer to me. I do the same. Then our mouths fuse together.

It takes at least five seconds for me to realise where I am the following morning. The ceiling that usually presses down on me a few feet above my bed now seems to stretch upwards to infinity and it is decorated with a small chandelier hanging in the centre of a circle of plaster flowers. The watery grey morning light is filtered by vast hessian curtains drawn across a huge bay window instead of streaming through a little porthole. The familiar odour of diesel, damp and dog has been replaced by the remains of a scented candle and a woman's perfume. That woman is pressed, warm, naked and asleep, along the length of my equally bare body. I check my watch. It is only seven a.m. and my brain is foggy, but I am not too hungover to forget that Eddie has been alone on the boat all night. He will be desperate to cock his leg. Perhaps even as desperate as me.

The call of nature prevents me from pulling the duvet higher and simply sliding back down into temptation. As noiselessly as I can, I slip sideways out of the bed and onto all fours on the carpet. Then, crouching, I pad to the en suite bathroom, scooping up discarded bits of clothing on the way. I run a trickle of water into my mouth for a good minute, splash it over my face and run my fingers through my hair. Dressed, except for my shoes, I head for the sitting room where the remains of a log are still smoking slightly in the grate and two-thirds of a bottle of whisky reproaches me from the coffee table.

I am writing a short note in the kitchen when Jane appears in the doorway, wrapped in a white towelling robe. Her hair is attractively tousled. She gives a huge yawn and folds her arms in front of her.

'Morning, Jack.' She smiles. 'You're busted.'

I move over towards her and kiss her on the lips. She kisses me back forcefully. Stale whisky breath. 'Good morning. I've got to dash. Eddie's been on the boat all night. I need to let him out.'

She nods sleepily and yawns. 'I think I'll go back to bed.'

'Wait,' I say, holding one of her arms. 'Jane. It was great. I had a wonderful evening. A wonderful night.'

She moves to the sink, fills a glass with water and gulps it down before turning back to me. She yawns again. 'Me too. But it was what it was. No strings attached and none expected. Uncomplicated. You run off now. Back to Eddie – and Nina if she's still there. Mum's the word. I watch her shuffle back towards her bathroom before quickly slipping on my shoes and coat and heading for the door.

I try jogging back to the boat, but rapidly abandon the attempt. I suspect there is still too much alcohol in my blood to allow me to drive legally and my head is telling me not to try running either. As I walk, I try to marshal my thoughts about spending the night with Jane. It's curious. I feel a degree of shame and guilt – both towards Nina, who I recognise that I am in love with, but also towards Jane for … for what? What happened just seemed to happen naturally. I didn't set out to seduce her. Okay, I accept there was an element of flirting involved. But on both sides. All that stuff about Isis and her husband's golden penis? And her parting words suggested that she was relaxed about our night together. Two ships that humped in the night? Could it be that simple and uncomplicated?

My jumble of thoughts is brought to an abrupt stop when I see a light shining through the porthole of my bedroom on *Jumping Jack Flash*. Someone is onboard. It must be Nina. She must have come back last night after all. Suddenly I remember her text message said that she might stay over at Cal's place. 'Might', not 'would'. Oh bollocks. A pain stabs between my eyes and my stomach heaves but it's nothing to do with my hangover.

There is a small bark from Eddie as I tentatively unlock the hatchway cover and slide it back so that I can open the two little doors beneath. Now my mind is racing. I am fully awake and increasingly sober. But there's no going back. I descend the steps.

'Jack? Is that you?'

The voice is coming from Nina's bed but, although it is similar, it doesn't belong to Nina. It's Anna. She is sitting up now, cuddling Eddie and peering at me curiously.

'Anna? What are you doing here?'

'Nina rang me. Quite late. She said she was staying over at Cal's to keep him company.' Anna looks slightly tearful. 'I said that was good of her. But then, afterwards, I kept wondering why she should be there. Cal's my friend, not hers. Oh Jack, I'm sorry. That sounds really petty and horrible now in the cold light of day. Phi's dead, for god's sake.

Cal must be in a terrible state. But last night Nina told me to give him some space and I wanted to talk to someone about it. Someone who knows both of them. So I came down to the boat like you said I could, but there was no one on board except Eddie. I let myself in with the key you gave me, and I gave him a little walk and waited for you to come back. I thought you must be out at a pub or a club. But then you didn't come back, so I gave up and went to sleep in Nina's bed. I hope that was okay?'

'Yes, of course it was fine, Anna,' I mumble. 'Thanks for looking after Eddie.'

Anna scrunches her nose and frowns in a look of genuine puzzlement. 'Anyway, where have you been all night?'

CHAPTER SEVENTEEN

Before I can answer, Anna's face assumes a sudden look of realisation. 'Jack! Have you been there as well?' She looks like she's going to cry and I hurry to reassure her.

'No, Anna, I promise you I haven't been with Nina and Cal. I had too much to drink with a friend and I crashed out at their place.'

Fortunately, she does not cross-examine me further. We retreat to the galley, where I grind some coffee beans and make a large cafetière to go with some life-saving bacon sandwiches and two aspirin tablets.

'I feel such an idiot,' says Anna, legs tucked under herself on my little sofa and wrapped in a dressing gown of Nina's. It's more of an oversized armchair really, a so-called 'loveseat' that I had bought in hope and with Nina in mind. Eddie is intimately curled into the crook of Anna's neck but watching me with his big brown eyes. He is most definitely a lady's man. 'I'm sorry, Jack. You know how close I am to Nina. But when we spoke last night, she just sounded so cold and distant. It was weird and upsetting. I know that I don't *really* know Cal that well. We only met last term and I didn't know Phi. But I do know him better than Nina. Surely it should be me comforting him rather than her?'

I don't know how to answer this. She is rattling on in her innocent way without recognising that Nina's readiness to comfort Cal is a dagger to my heart too. 'Look,' I say. 'Why don't we both go to his place now? We can pick up a breakfast for them and find out if we can be useful.'

Anna looks like a doubtful little girl. 'D'you think it would be alright?'

'Of course,' I say more bullishly than I feel. 'In fact, it would be odd not to, don't you think? Come on. Get dressed. I'll see if my next-door neighbour will have Eddie.'

Hugh is already up and about, immaculately dressed and halfway through the Times cryptic crossword and a pot of Earl Grey. I avoid telling him all about Ophelia for the moment but he's delighted to have Eddie for the morning and says he'll walk him downriver and back before lunch. I belatedly ask after his wife.

'On the mend, on the mend. She's loving *The Wench Is Dead,* by the way. Canals and crime – wonderful combination! She sends her thanks. I think she'll be out in a week. Then I'll get her back home in style. Might even splash out on a driver and a limo. You'll keep an eye on *Raven* for me whilst I'm gone, won't you?'

I know that Hugh usually keeps his boat in a marina at Upton upon Severn, which would mean a return trip via the Oxford Canal, onto the Grand Union and then down the Worcester & Birmingham to Worcester itself where he would need to join the River Severn. 'Perhaps I could give you a hand to get her home?' I say. He's shaking my hand enthusiastically before I can properly consider what I have said.

'Wonderful. Wonderful. It would be capital to have your company, Jack. Thank you so much. That's a great relief.'

Anna and I take the waterside walk to Jericho alongside the Isis, Castle Mill Stream and the canal. We are both quiet with our own thoughts for most of the way. I sense that she is nervous about arriving unannounced on Cal's doorstep after the conversation with Nina the previous evening.

I know the feeling. My own thoughts are wavering all over the place. One minute I am thinking of Cal and the dead girl. Then I am thinking of Nina. And then I am remembering what I can of my night with Jane.

What an idiot. We stop off at a trendy coffee shop to collect a bag of warm pastries and four large cardboard cups of Americano.

Nina answers the door. It is just after nine a.m. She is bare legged and bare footed below a large white linen shirt that must belong to Cal. Her eyes are dark with tiredness. 'Anna! Jack! Cal –' she says turning to shout back into the house – 'Anna and Jack are here with breakfast and coffee.' She turns back to look at us, closes her eyes briefly and shakes her head. 'He isn't in very good shape,' she whispers, giving us each a brief hug.

Cal is slumped at the breakfast bar in a sports singlet and a pair of shorts when we enter the kitchen. 'Hey, guys,' he says in a voice that is heavy with defeat. Anna moves straight towards him and receives a long hug while I wait awkwardly on the periphery. Eventually, he breaks free and grasps my hand in his iron grip. 'Jack,' he says.

'I'm very sorry, Cal,' I reply.

He pats my shoulder with his free hand and then breaks free.

'Look, fresh croissants and pains au chocolat,' says Nina, putting the bag into his hands. But Cal just transfers it onto the breakfast bar without looking at it.

'Thanks. Thanks a lot. Hey, look. I'll just get dressed okay?'

Nina watches him pad miserably towards his bedroom and I watch Nina. 'What exactly happened yesterday?'

She picks up one of the takeaway coffees, curls her feet under herself in exactly the same manner as her niece, and glances at the corridor where Cal has retreated. She lowers her voice. 'Well, we took Phi's parents to see Dr Romaine. He repeated what he said to us although obviously he was a bit more tactful and sympathetic with Mr and Mrs McVeigh. They're a sweet couple but pretty elderly and frail. They adopted Phi quite late in life and obviously thought the world of her. There was no doubt that they wanted to report her missing to the police. They were already a little puzzled and worried because she usually called them every weekend, but she had missed two calls. She was home for Christmas, but only for a couple of days, and she had also told them that she had met a boy and seemed very happy about it. Phi told them she had been doing some kind of part-time job, as a secretary, to top up her student loan.'

'So, you went to the police station,' I prompt her, eager to hear as much as I can without causing Cal additional pain.

'Yes. And the officer who was taking down Phi's details took one look at the photograph and connected it with the dead body at Iffley. But, of course, we didn't know anything about that until a senior officer came back into the room – DCI Philpott. He could have broken the news more gently, to be honest. Mrs McVeigh collapsed almost straight away, and I volunteered to go to the hospital with her and Mr McVeigh. Cal stayed to talk to Philpott. Phi's mother was treated for shock and we were given a lift back to their hotel by a hospital volunteer. By then, a police family liaison officer had joined us and so I went to the station to wait for Cal.'

Cal re-enters the room at this point. He is still barefoot but dressed in chinos, a check shirt and a chunky fisherman's jumper. 'Yeah. They kept me waiting around for ages and then questioned me for a couple of hours while they searched this place. It was pretty damn upsetting,' he says. 'I'd only just found out about Phi being murdered and seen her mom faint clean away. They wanted to know when I'd last seen her, when I'd last heard from her, whether we'd had a row of any kind.' Cal slumps into a chair. He has brought a pair of socks with him from the bedroom but is just wringing them between his hands. 'Did I know if she had fallen out with anyone else? What was the name of her ex-boyfriend in Scotland? On and on it went.' His voice wavers and he looks up at all of us, his eyes glistening with tears. 'I wanted to help them, I really did. But it's just .... oh my lord. Who would do this to my sweet, lovely, clever Phi?' He buries his face in his hands and his shoulders heave as he begins to sob.

Nina unfolds herself and is by kneeling on the floor by his side almost instantly. 'It's okay, Cal, it's okay. Let it all out. Don't bottle it up.'

Cal uses a forearm to wipe his eyes and looks at all of us again. 'I'd like to see the place where they found her. Would that be okay? Would you all come with me?'

'Of course,' says Anna quickly.

'Are you certain?' says Nina quietly, putting a hand on his. 'It's not too soon?'

He nods and swallows hard. 'I'm sure it will help,' he says simply.

'I'll just get some clothes on,' Nina says. 'Are you okay to drive or shall I order a taxi?'

'Or we can walk,' I suggest. 'It'll take about 40 minutes from here.'

'I'll drive,' says Cal decisively. He looks directly into Nina's eyes. 'Thank you.'

The interior of Cal's Jaguar is silent during the journey to Iffley. Cal drives into the village, navigates his way around a complicated one-way system and past a big church before parking near a pedestrian footpath that cuts down through some houses to the river. Nina has her arm through his on one side and Anna the other. I trail along behind them to a small wooden bridge where the weir races underneath. We pause halfway along the bridge and look down at the dark swirling water with its eddies and counter-eddies.

'It must have been here,' says Cal. 'The police said some magnet fishermen found her. Magnet fishermen,' he says wonderingly. 'I never knew that such a thing existed.'

'What did the magnet fasten on to?' I ask.

Cal just shrugs his shoulders. 'I have no idea. They didn't say.' We stand quietly. I had never met Cal's girlfriend, but it was impossible not to be moved by the moment. He looks around at each of us in turn. 'Would you mind if we held hands while I say a prayer?'

Nina and Anna, who are already holding one of his arms each, slip them down to grasp his hands. I shuffle across. I'm feeling slightly embarrassed, as usual, when I am in the presence of any declaration of strong religious faith. I take hold of Nina's other hand. She gives it a little squeeze, which I find ridiculously reassuring.

'Dear Lord,' says Cal suddenly, in a strong, firm voice and looking upwards. 'Almighty God, who has given us grace at this time to make our common supplications unto thee with one accord, we don't know why you have taken Phi, our beloved Ophelia McVeigh, to be with you before her allotted three score years and ten on this earth. And we don't know exactly what happened to her before she was found in this place. But we pray that we may come to understand and ... and even to forgive the person who did this to her. For they know not what they do. And please do what you can to comfort her parents, and all those who loved her, in their suffering at this time. Thank you for the comfort of my friends here today, for Nina, Anna and Jack, and we all of us beseech you that Ophelia is granted your eternal mercy and love. From all the deceits of the world, the flesh and the devil, Good Lord, deliver us from evil. Amen.'

Only the sound of the rushing water and the far-off traffic breaks the silence that follows. Anna gives a little sniffle. We have all been affected by the passion and fluency of his prayer. There is little doubt that he is a preacher's son. As an atheist, I am also impressed by his declaration of forgiveness for Phi's killer. I know that such a sentiment would be well beyond me. Cal lowers his head and smiles quietly to us on either side of him. 'Maybe each of you would like to say a few short words? It doesn't have to be a prayer. Anything at all.'

Anna shoots a panicked look at me which I am more than happy to return. But Nina begins talking quietly.

'I can't pray as eloquently as you, Cal. And I am very sorry that I never met Phi before her death. She was obviously a lovely young woman. But I hope you won't mind if I just say the Lord's Prayer.' She does so, quietly and with a depth of feeling that almost moves me to tears. 'Our Father, Who art in heaven, Hallowed be thy name ...' We all say Amen and then Cal smiles sadly at me and Anna.

'I won't say a prayer,' says Anna, 'but I will recite some words about another young woman who was called Ophelia, in the hope that the poetry brings you some comfort.'

There is a willow grows aslant a brook,
That shows his hoar leaves in the glassy stream;
There with fantastic garlands did she come,
Of crow-flowers, nettles, daisies, and long purples
That liberal shepherds give a grosser name,
But our cold maids do dead men's fingers call them:
There, on the pendant boughs her coronet weeds
Clambering to hang, an envious sliver broke,
When down her weedy trophies, and herself,
Fell in the weeping brook.

She breaks off with a little sob. I wonder if Anna was picturing the painting of 'Ophelia' by Millais when she decided to recite from *Hamlet*. But, in truth, there couldn't be a greater contrast between the picture's summer floral colours and natural tranquillity, and the bleak wintry stretch of water flowing fast and bleak in front of us. And there is a world of difference, I think, between the accidental drowning of Shakespeare's poor unbalanced maiden and the murder of this twenty-first century Oxford student. But who am I to quibble? Cal has already murmured his thanks to Anna and now he is looking at me. My mind is racing nowhere fast. What can I possibly say? I am just about to plead to be excused when a mobile phone starts ringing. Cal fishes it out from a back pocket and puts it to his ear.

'Hi. Oh, hi.' He pauses quite a long time to listen to the caller. 'Yeah, okay. I can do that. What time?' He pauses again and holds a finger in the air to ask for our patience. 'Okay. No problem. I'll need to go home and change ... You will? That's great. You've got the address. Okay. Bye.' He hangs up and turns to us. 'That was the police. They'd like me to do a press conference. They want to ask for the public's help. Phi's parents aren't up to it, but they'd like me to read a statement from them. I need to go and help them with it. The police are going to give me a lift from home. I need to change. Put on a suit and tie, I guess.' He gives a long juddering sigh. 'What a nightmare.'

'I'll come with you,' says Nina, squaring her jaw and shooting a look of stubborn determination at me. It is a look with which I am very familiar. 'Mr and Mrs McVeigh know me now, I can help. It's only ten minutes back to the boat along the riverbank from here, Jack. Why don't you walk back there with Anna?'

'What time is the press conference?' I ask.

'Two pm. At the central police station.'

'Okay, we'll see you there. Good luck. Come on, Anna.'

CHAPTER EIGHTEEN

A conference room at the police station is already nearly full by the time we arrive. I flash my out-of-date NUJ card to gain entry and Anna explains that she's a friend of Cal's. A table has been set up at the front of the room with a Thames Valley police logo hanging from it. A few microphones and recording devices are also in place and pointing at two chairs, which are waiting to be occupied.

A door opens and a short, stocky man with a red face, white hair and a black moustache appears first. A double-breasted suit fails to hide a prominent beer belly and a triple chin prevents his collar from being buttoned behind his tie. Behind him is Cal. He is also in a dark business suit, but this one is well-tailored and fails to hide a physique of a very different kind. The two men sit side by side. Nina has followed Cal into the room, but she slips around the side of the table to take a seat in the first row. Then a woman police officer in uniform bustles in and puts two printed cardboard name plates in front of the two men. The first says DCI Brian Philpott and the second says Mr Caleb Hopper.

Cal nods at me and Anna without smiling while Philpott calmly surveys the gathering of press and media people. There are about a dozen in total. Two television cameras have also been set up at the back of the room and I note that one of them has the police force's logo on it. It seems that the police are making their own recording of the press conference. It makes me wonder if this is some kind of deliberately staged test for Cal.

'Good afternoon, ladies and gentlemen,' says Philpott. There is a slight sneer in his Glaswegian accent as he says this, as though he doesn't believe there will be many ladies and gentlemen present amongst the assembled journalists. 'Thank you very much for coming.' This too sounds less than sincere. 'I will make a brief statement followed by Mr Hopper here and there will be a limited opportunity for you to ask some questions.'

'As you will know from our press release, the body of a young woman was found in the Thames by some magnet fishermen last Saturday January 17th at Iffley, just below the lock. It was recovered by a team of police divers. The dead woman has been subsequently identified as Miss Ophelia McVeigh who is …' He corrects himself and frowns. 'Who *was* a first-year student at St Hugh's College and studying for a Computer Science degree. We have reason to believe that Miss McVeigh was deliberately killed before her body entered the water.'

The policeman looks down at his notes and then looks back up, directly at the news camera. 'We would now like to appeal to the public for any information they can give us, particularly about Miss McVeigh's movements in the days before her death. Miss McVeigh was last seen at her halls of residence on Saturday January 10th, a whole week before her body was found. However, she continued to send daily text messages to her boyfriend, Mr Hopper here, until the following Friday, January 16th, when they stopped abruptly. Mr Hopper was away at a residential training course for the Oxford rowing squad throughout the period in question and did not return home until Sunday January 18th – the day after the body was found. Mr Hopper and Miss McVeigh's parents became concerned for her whereabouts and the body was subsequently identified after they reported her missing at this police station yesterday morning. Photographs of Miss McVeigh will be made available to you and we are asking for anyone who knows anything about her whereabouts during the week before her body was found to contact us immediately. Mr Hopper will now make a brief statement.'

Cal's head has been turned sideways throughout the policeman's statement, and now he turns to face us. There is a slight tremor of the paper he is holding in front of him but when he speaks, his voice is calm and under control. His absurd good looks and smart suit give him the air of a television newsreader about to begin a bulletin. But this bulletin is a much more personal and painful affair.

'Good afternoon, ladies and gentlemen.' I see a few of the journalists registering his American accent with surprise. 'Ophelia's parents, Mr and Mrs McVeigh, have asked me to convey their deep shock and overwhelming grief at the death of their daughter Ophelia. They loved her very much and they were very proud when she was offered a place to study at Oxford University. They ask that anyone with any information about Ophelia's death should come forward to help the police and they also ask that their privacy is respected in the difficult days ahead.'

Philpott glowers around the room meaningfully at this request and nods his head threateningly. He clearly regards the press as a necessary evil and would rather have nothing to do with them. 'Thank you, Mr Hopper. Right. Any questions? Please say who you represent first.'

Several hands go into the air and Philpott nods at a woman in the front row. 'BBC Oxford. Can you tell us how Miss McVeigh was murdered, Chief Inspector?'

'A post-mortem examination has determined strangulation as the cause of death.'

'And did the post-mortem say how long the body had been in the water?' asks the same woman.

'We know that she sent her last text to Mr Hopper on Friday January 16th, the day before the body was found on Saturday 17th – so we believe the answer to your question is barely 24 hours. Next.'

'The *Oxford Mail*. Do you have any reason to believe there was a sexual motive for her murder?'

The man has phrased the question carefully, but we all know he is asking if Ophelia was raped before she was murdered. Cal is looking down at the table, the fingers of both hands interlaced in front of him.

'There was no evidence of a sexual assault on Miss McVeigh, but we are obviously keeping an open mind on the motive for her murder. Next.'

'Cotswold News Agency. May I ask Mr Hopper how long he had known Miss McVeigh and what he is doing in Oxford, apart from being a member of the Oxford University Boat Club? And how old he is?'

Cal raises his head to look at the crumpled middle-aged reporter. 'I'm twenty-eight. I'm here doing my final year of a PhD at Christ Church. And I met Ophelia towards the end of last term.'

'And how do you feel about her murder?'

It's a crass question but I suspect the police have deliberately put Cal into this position. It won't hurt their investigation to see how he behaves under extreme pressure like this.

'How do I feel about it?' says Cal. His voice is still calm and controlled but there is also a steely edge to it. 'How do you think I feel sir? I am sick with grief, just like her parents. She was a wonderful girl. Beautiful, clever and with her whole life before her.' He glances at Philpott alongside him. 'I'd also like to ask that anyone with any information about her death comes forward and talks to the police. Whoever did this should be put away for a very long time.'

There is a moment of silence which the agency man eventually decides to break. 'Can you tell us what she said in her last text messages to you, Mr Hopper?'

Cal suddenly looks angry. 'What? No. Can I hell!'

He looks at Philpott who in turn looks at the reporter. I expect him to reprimand the man, but I'm mistaken. He takes out a handkerchief and blows his nose noisily before telling the room, 'Mr Hooper has shared all of his text messages from Miss McVeigh with us and they are the kind of loving messages you might expect between a young woman and her boyfriend. That's as far as we are prepared to go.'

Cal is still shaking his head in a gesture of disbelief. The agency man will be filing copy for most of the national press. The tabloids in particular will be hungry for any additional juicy details. He decides to have one last go. 'Can I just ask then ... was Miss McVeigh's body dressed or undressed when it was found in the water?'

Cal rears back with his head and gives the man a blazing stare. The muscles of his square jaw are clenched furiously together, and his mouth is a grim thin line.

But again, Philpott smoothly intervenes. 'The body was fully dressed and found in a blue canvas bag. Two round weights, like those from a bench press or exercise bench, had been put in both ends of the bag. The magnets of the fishermen had fixed onto one of these weights.'

The reporter is scribbling furiously onto a notepad. 'How heavy were they?'

Philpott shakes his head. 'We'll be keeping some details to ourselves for the moment. But if anyone in the Oxford area has noticed that any weights have gone missing in recent days, we'd be interested to hear from them.'

Cal is looking at the policeman in surprise. It seems that this is the first time he has been given this detail.

'So, any more questions? No? Right then ...' The policeman pulls his handkerchief out again and rubs his nose vigorously with it. I think he must be coming down with a cold.

'Sorry, sorry, just one more question if I may?' It is the agency man again. Philpott now looks exasperated and Cal looks as though he's going to explode. But the man presses on. 'Is there any suggestion that Miss McVeigh was having a relationship with any other men recently? And can I ask Mr Hopper, had she been dating any other members of the university boat crew?'

Cal is now on his feet and pointing at the reporter. 'Ophelia ... Phi ... didn't deserve to be killed and she certainly didn't deserve to have creeps like you asking questions like that about her. She was lovely ... and loyal ... and ...' His eyes are wet now, his words interrupted by deep intakes of breath. Suddenly he sits back down and puts his head in his hands and sobs. This is the money shot and every journalist in the room lifts their cameras or phones and rattle off several pictures. A professional reflex makes me reach for mine, but I manage to control it.

'Right, that's it,' says Philpott emphatically. He still has his soiled handkerchief in his hand and for one moment I wonder if he is going to offer it to Cal. 'This press conference is now over. Photographs of Miss McVeigh can be collected at the door or emailed to you digitally.'

Nina has rushed around the table to put an arm around Cal and I notice a few of the remaining journalists also taking pictures of this touching scene. I would be doing the same in their shoes. No doubt, they will all be trying to identify Cal's attractive friend, the woman with the short hair who is trying to comfort him. She isn't thinking straight. She risks stirring up renewed press interest in herself, the young war widow who walked out of her home and prompted a nationwide search. Philpott ushers Cal and Nina through a door behind them and the crowd begins to disperse.

'Gosh,' says Anna, looking at me with wide eyes. 'What do you make of that?'

But before I can answer, the door has re-opened and Nina is making straight for us. The agency man is already trying to intercept her. 'Excuse me, love? Can you tell me what your name is? How do you know Cal?'

She gives him a furious look. 'Piss off, you reptile.' He backs away grinning, both hands held up in the air placatingly. She turns back to us. 'Cal and the Chief Inspector are just having a quick chat. He's very upset ... upset and angry. I'll hang around and go back with him in the police car. I'll catch you both later.' Then she is gone, back through the door and ignoring another attempted question from the same reporter.

'Well. Here we are again,' I say to Anna. 'Come on, let's go.'

We make our way out of the room, pausing to collect a photograph of Phi on the way. It is a head and shoulders shot of her, caught in mid-laugh with her head thrown back and her dark hair flying. She looks vivacious and beautiful, full of laughter and fun and without an apparent care in the world.

As we are leaving the station, we come face to face with Jane coming up one of the two shallow ramps that flank the main public entrance. She has three box files pressed to her chest. She stops and smiles at me. 'Hello again, Jack. Here for the press conference?'

I can sense Anna looking curiously between us both. 'Anna, this is Detective Sergeant Jane Henry who I am profiling for a CQ article. Jane, this is Anna, the niece of my friend Nina.'

'Ah yes, your good friend Nina,' says Jane, still smiling. She struggles to free a hand from her burden and Anna shakes it. 'Nice to meet you, Anna. How did the press conference go?'

Anna interrupts before I can answer. 'Nice to meet you too. Sorry, but I need to get back for a tutorial. I'll see you later, Jack, maybe?'

'Attractive girl,' says Jane after Anna has joined the passing throng of pedestrians. Her eyes are twinkling with mischief. 'Does she resemble her aunt?'

But we are interrupted by the agency reporter who has just come out of the station. 'Hi. Hi there. Excuse me, but I saw you talking to the woman who was comforting Mr Hopper at the end there. Can you tell me who she is?'

'No. But, as one journo to another, I can tell you there isn't a story there.' I turn back to Jane. 'Coffee?'

'Sorry.' She indicates her files. 'No time. Busy, busy, busy. Catch you later.'

I am left alone, standing on the steps while the hopeful agency reporter lights a cigarette and loiters nearby. There is only one thing to do.

Two minutes later I am settled in the nearest pub, the Old Tom, with a pint of bitter in front of me and some 'Thai-style tapas' on order. Events have been moving very fast and I feel the need to do some quiet reflection on my own. Through the street window, I see the agency reporter striding past purposefully. I duck my head and he doesn't see me. He's probably on his way to file some copy. It will be interesting to see how the nationals pitch the story. I am two thirds of the way through my pint and halfway through a spicy prawn salad when my mobile vibrates with an incoming text. It is Nina.

> Just got back to Cal's place. He's gone for a lie down. Don't tell any press where he lives. Phi's parents are going back to Scotland. Talk later.

CHAPTER NINETEEN

'One. Two. Three. Four. Five. Six. Seven. Eight. Nine. Ten.'

'Faster this time,' says Connolly. The girls, one on each side of him, do as they are told and count from one to ten slightly quicker as he raises and lowers the weight-training bar above his chest.

'Oof. That'll do.'

Mia and Grace step forward and help him guide the bar and weights back onto their supporting metal struts. He lies there for a moment, his broad bare chest heaving with the effort of his half-hour workout. Sweat beads and glistens on his brow and biceps. The girls giggle. They are still in awe of Connolly's body, which is naked save for a pair of his silk fighting shorts. His taut pecs taper to a washboard abdomen which then widens into strong, muscular thighs, a stark contrast to the flabby white upper halves of their mothers' occasional boyfriends. They are also fascinated by Connolly's tattoos and the reasons for each one – a special victory in the cage or, more recently, a good business deal. He has previously allowed Mia to trace a finger along the letters of his name which is stretched across his six-pack, slowly spelling out each letter as she did so – CONNOLLY. She continued to trace out I LOVE U and blushed pink when he laughed in understanding.

The girls have come straight from school to clean his flat, as they do every Friday. They are still dressed in an approximation of their uniforms, but their white shirts are now hanging outside their short non-regulation length skirts and their ties have been stuffed in their shoulder bags.

Today, they have sneaked several mouthfuls of vodka from a bottle in the fridge and replaced the missing alcohol with two inches of tap water before Connolly returned home. He knows when they do this because he can smell the alcohol on their breath, and it amuses him to keep a cheap brand chilling precisely for this purpose. At some stage he will make it clear that he knows they have been stealing from him – and he will scare them silly about it.

He has already inspected every inch of the riverside apartment before changing and working out. He wipes his finger along shelves to make sure they have been dusted properly, looks into the bleached toilets, sinks and shower tray, stands on a chair to see that the top of the fridge has been wiped and looks at himself in all the mirrors to make sure they are sparkling and without a single smear. They know that if he finds any fault, he will stand over them until it is put right and some of their pay might even be docked. This is all part of his programme of training for them. It isn't about keeping the flat clean – although that's an added bonus. It is about instilling an unquestioning obedience of him and a clear understanding of his carrot and stick approach. With these two, he has rarely had to use the stick – just the flat of his hand once or twice which left their ears ringing.

No, this pair were much greedier and eagerly responsive to his treats of alcohol, cigarettes and money. He hasn't given them any drugs yet. He may wait another year for that. And in the meantime, both of their mothers set them the right kind of example – whinnying with pleasure at his regular present-giving and turning a blind eye to the errands he asks of their daughters.

He unfolds himself upright on the padded bench and swings both legs to one side. 'I'm having a shower. Going to Oxford tonight. Watch the TV for a bit if you want.'

'Thanks, Finn,' says Grace, racing Mia across the room to grab the remote.

Connolly pads barefoot to his rainforest shower. It's already programmed to go through a cycle of different sized droplets and different temperatures until it finishes with a pounding tempest that pummels him with ice cold water. Different coloured lights have come on with each change of the programme – finally ending with a flashing green and blue display, which the manufacturers describe as 'Northern Lights'. He loves his shower – it's large enough to have hosted two guests plus himself in the past and he would cheerfully kill anyone who tried to take it away from him.

As he soaps himself with an expensive cedarwood shower gel, Connolly thinks about his business plan. He has been watching YouTube lectures about economics on his free evenings. He wants to make sure that he approaches his strategy for wealth-growth in the most professional and business-minded way. It's all about demand and supply. He has worked out that he is active in a market characterised by 'inelastic demand'. This means that once he has his customer base established, he can vary the price without much impact on the level of goods being demanded. That is to say, his customers are addicts of one kind or another and need his merchandise to an extent that they stop worrying about the price after a short while. It's all about knowing when to increase the price for a particular customer, he tells himself. And then there's the supply side of the equation. That's the trickier bit. He needs to maintain and grow an effective pipeline to market for his goods – both the drugs and the girls and, on rare occasions, the boys. He can't afford to take his eye off the ball there.

Finally, there is his choice of markets. Oxford is working out well for him. There's a lot of money, a lot of wealthy students and the cops are a lot more sleepy, or under-resourced, than they are in London. His business plan includes a list of small cities that he might expand into at the right time, and he intends to start carrying out some research trips in the near future. Cambridge, Salisbury and Worcester will be next to receive his consideration. His ambition is to triple his turnover and double his profits over the next twelve months. But he also knows that a good businessman also carries out careful risk assessments. He intends to stay at arm's length from both his suppliers and his customers – using go-betweens to fetch the merchandise and take it to market. That's the tactic for the drugs part of the business anyway.

For the girls, he has decided to be more hands-on and run an upmarket 'boutique' operation. He has no appetite to rely on the East Europeans or Asians for their women. Illegal immigration brings additional risks that he isn't keen on, and he wants to avoid getting dragged into doing any kind of business with established gangs. He believes this is the way to stay under the radar and avoid unnecessary aggro. He can handle himself, but he also doesn't want the expense or trouble of having to hire more muscle. He won't have any problem finding, grooming and delivering his own girls. Okay. It'll take longer and mean smaller profits – but he's in this for the long haul. Well, at least until he delivers on his business plan anyway. Five years, he has promised himself. Five years and a strategy that will take his original fight money and grow it five-fold to more than ten million pounds. That's when he will cash in, invest in more rental properties and go back to live in a mansion in Ireland. Maybe he'll set up a gym. He has it all worked out and will remain ruthlessly clear-eyed about delivering his objectives. And if anyone gets in his way, he will wipe them out.

Connolly raises his head to the big round showerhead directly above him and gives a loud wolf howl of triumph. He wraps a towel around his waist and pads into his bedroom. Mia and Grace, who are sitting on his black leather and chrome sofa, temporarily abandon the early evening news to watch every step of his progress. He bangs the door shut and dresses for work in black jeans with a black cotton shirt and a hoody.

When he comes back into his lounge, a police press conference is being screened on the gigantic flat television mounted on the wall.

There is a Thames Valley Police badge on the front of a table where two men are seated. An older one and a clean-cut younger one who looks like some kind of actor.

'Alexa. TV louder,' he says, and the volume of the television rises several notches.

But just as this happens, the action swings away from the conference to a reporter standing in front of the entrance to the police station.

'A spokesperson for St Hugh's College said Miss McVeigh was a bright and charming student who will be much missed.' A picture appears on screen. The girl's head is tipped backwards, and she is laughing. 'Her murder has shocked the small academic community who knew her here in Oxford and anyone with any information is asked to contact the police.' The picture dissolves back to the reporter. 'This is Shamira Bayer for BBC News, Oxford.'

'Alexa. TV off,' says Connolly. He straddles a cow hide and chrome Le Corbusier lounger to put on some black socks and a pair of dark blue trainers. 'You see,' he says, nodding at the blank television screen and smiling at the two schoolgirls. 'Nasty things can happen to girls when they don't do what Finn Connolly tells them. Now fuck off home.'

CHAPTER TWENTY

I switch off the early evening BBC News and lean back in my chair. Eddie takes the opportunity to leap up onto my lap and get comfortable. The first half of the regional news programme is being presented from Oxford, but there is a handover back to a different presenter in Southampton halfway through. The more localised service means that Ophelia's murder gets a lot of prominence in the headline sequence and it is the lead story in the programme.

Several clips from the press conference are included along with pictures of the water below Iffley Lock, an expression of sorrow from Dr Romaine at St Hugh's and the photograph issued by police of the dead girl. DCI Philpott is featured twice, talking about the cause of death as strangulation and then describing the bag that the body was found in with its weights. A sentence of Cal's from the statement by Mr and Mrs McVeigh is included, but the report takes time to linger on the moment of drama when Cal stood up and then slumped back down into his seat. Fortunately, it does not linger on his distress. Nevertheless, he comes across as genuine, grief-stricken and anxious to find his girlfriend's killer. I imagine the same report, or a version of it, will have also been transmitted in London and even perhaps on the national news. Television transmitter coverage can be a poor match for local boundaries. But I know that news broadcasters liaise closely and swap reports between regional news programmes when it makes sense for their audiences. As well as playing in London, the story will be on several local radio stations and, no doubt, it will be in all the national newspapers tomorrow. I wonder if all this coverage will net a vital scrap of information. That'll be what the police are hoping for. You can see why they invest in their media departments with their mixed staff of serving officers and ex-journalists. To help catch criminals *and* to portray the force in its best light. Hence the press release from the Thames Valley force about DS Jane Henry.

Jane Henry? What am I to do about her? As the day has gone on, I have felt increasingly remorseful about the previous night. I am a bloody fool and I know that I have risked my long-term happiness with Nina. I have tried blaming the drink, my annoyance at Nina's apparent indifference, her closeness to Cal and even Jane for being such good company. But in the end, I know I have only myself to blame. It is small comfort that Jane seems to be so casual about the entire episode. It must not happen again I tell myself firmly. I just need to finish the magazine profile of her and make a quiet and tactical retreat. I check my watch. It is 7.15 p.m. and dark outside. Nina hasn't been in touch at all since her text saying that she had gone back to Cal's house and ordering me not to tell the press where he lived. As if I would! It rankles that she has felt the need to give me this instruction. And it rankles that she hasn't been in touch since. I decide to grasp the nettle and telephone her, which I do after pouring myself another glass of red wine.

'Hello, Jack.'

'Hi Nina. How's it going? How's Cal?'

'Hold on a minute.' I hear her saying she'll take my call in another room and wait for a few moments of silence. 'Hi. That's better.' Her voice now has a slight echo and I imagine she has gone into the tiled downstairs bathroom. 'He isn't very good, I'm afraid. The press conference was a real ordeal for him. He insisted on watching the news tonight too.'

'Yes, I saw it.'

'He's furious with himself for losing his temper with that reporter and showing his emotions. He really wanted to remain calm and in control of himself.'

'I thought he came across okay.'

'It's not about how he came across for him, Jack.' She sounds impatient with me. 'It's about how he's feeling inside ... it's how he's coping with Phi's death and the news that she was murdered. You can't imagine what it must be like.'

'No. No, of course I can't.'

'I think I can be of real help to him because of what I've been through myself. Because of what I'm still going through over Alan. I'm going to stay with him for a few days. All of his family and his closest friends are in the States. I don't want to leave him on his own. I couldn't live with myself if he harmed himself in any way. I spoke to his rowing coach earlier and he's given Cal a week off training. Cal says he can't face it anyway. I think that resuming his normal routine would be good for him, but he's worried about the press hassling him now they know he's in the boat race squad. And he doesn't want the rest of the crew to be hassled either. He's also worried about his parents finding out about all this. He thinks they'd be on the next flight over to support him and he doesn't want them involved. It's heart-breaking to see him worrying about all of this, Jack ...'

I am dimly aware of Nina rabbiting on about Cal but realise I haven't taken much of it in since she said she was going to move in with him for a few days.

'Jack? Jack! Are you listening?'

'What yes, yes. Umm ... that all makes sense,' I say lamely.

'What makes sense? I asked you a question. I said could we come over first thing in the morning and pick up a few of my things? I've got your spare key, so you don't have to wait in if you don't want to.'

'I'm not doing anything now. I could wheel one of your suitcases over to you if you like?'

'No. No, don't do that. He's too fragile to cope with visitors now. And I know exactly what I want. It's Saturday tomorrow. I'll be there about ten o'clock. I'll bring Cal if I can.' She drops her voice to a stage whisper. 'I don't want to leave him on his own and the fresh air will do him good.'

'Okay, Nina,' I say. I can hear the stiffness in my voice. 'I'll wait in to see you in the morning.'

'Great. Night, Jack.'

'Good night.'

Now I have nothing to do but sit and brood. I don't want to be unsympathetic, but Nina's unrelenting focus on every aspect of Cal's well-being seems slightly excessive to me. Does she really need to be with him for every second of the day? Does she really need to move in with him, for god's sake? She only met him for the first time this week. Or am I just jealous? And if I am, how can I justify that emotion after my night with Jane?

I angrily snatch up Eddie's lead and try to settle my swirling thoughts with a walk along the riverside path to Folly Bridge and back. But as I pass the entrance to the little spur of water after Strode Road Bridge, some music drifts across the river towards me. I look across and can see lights through the foliage. They are shining out from the large white houseboat with its ornate columns and flagpole. Soft music and laughter are also coming from the boat. It seems that some kind of party is taking place. I shrug and walk on but just as I reach the point opposite the line of college boathouses, I see Hugh marching vigorously towards me with a carrier bag in one hand.

'Evening, Hugh.'

'Jack, old boy. Well met. Well met,' he says, transferring his bag to the other hand and shaking mine with the one that is now free. 'Just about to rustle up some food. Fancy joining me?'

'I'm not sure I'll be very good company to be honest.'

'Nonsense. Nonsense. Bit of the Black Dog, eh? Soon shake you out of that. Trust a medical man. Got just the cure,' he says grinning and shaking his bag at me. 'Come on.'

I obediently fall into step alongside him while he rattles away. He is in good spirits because his wife's recovery is still going well. We make our way onto *Raven*, where he pokes the stove into life and turns up his heating. Two armchairs are slanted towards each other on the other side of the galley and he pushes me into one, pours me a glass of Argentinian Malbec and puts a bowl of water on the floor for Eddie.

'Now then,' he says, peering at the plastic and cardboard packaging of some supermarket ready-meals. 'One Chinese meal coming up. Absolutely masses. Plenty for two. Won't be long.' He gets his small oven going and sits down next to me while he waits for it to reach the temperature on the instructions. 'Cheers, old boy. Or as they taught me in Argentina, *Sálud y amor y tiempo para disfrutario* – health and love and time to enjoy them!'

'Health and love and time to enjoy them – especially love,' I reply.

'You haven't got any problems there, have you, Jack? You seem to have an endless supply of fine young fillies beating a path to your boat!'

I just shake my head. 'I don't think I want to go there tonight, Hugh, if you don't mind?'

He leaps up to load the oven with his meal containers. 'Not to worry, mum's the word. What else have you been up to then?'

I sit back and run through the developments of the last three days as sweet-and-sour aromas begin to fill the boat's interior.

'Good god!' says Hugh as I finish. He has been a very good listener, not interrupting once, just sipping his wine and looking at me with his lively intelligent eyes. 'I missed the evening news tonight. She was found at Iffley Weir, you say?'

'Just below it, yes.'

'Chance in a million that she was found by those magnet fishermen, I'd say. The river runs fast, wide and deep there. Hardly any chance of anything being found if it was properly weighted down. Whoever the murderer was, they knew what they were doing.'

'I know. And yet the body was found only twenty-four hours after her last text message. It was a chance in a million.'

Hugh ushers me to his table where we greedily tuck into the contents of five different piping hot cartons. The two of us are sitting side by side on a banquette, facing the river through a large rectangular window. The moon is quite bright tonight and gives the water a glossy sheen, making it look deceptively still. Hugh catches me staring at it as I chew a sweet and sour pork ball.

'There are worse places to be for dinner, eh, Jack?'

I nod. I am miserably aware that I am not the best company this evening.

Eventually he puts his knife and fork down. 'I did enjoy that. Although I'm looking forward to some proper home cooking again when Mrs Spencer is fully fit. She's a fine cook, as you'll find out if you help me bring *Raven* home.'

He clearly hasn't forgotten my offer. 'I'll look forward to it,' I say.

'Capital. Capital. Now then. Some more red or a drop of the hard stuff?'

'I'll stick to the red, if you don't mind.' I am ruefully remembering Jane's whisky from yesterday evening.

He stands and heads for a galley cupboard. Outside, I see a small boat mid-river, moving slowly against the current from right to left. It's an odd sight at this time of night, ten minutes past ten. There are three figures with their backs to the little boat's bow, heavily wrapped in coats, scarves and lifejackets. I peer closer. They all seem to be middle-aged men, carrying excess weight and bald or thinning on top to judge by the moonlight on their scalps. Another man is in the stern, dressed in a dark hoody and steering the boat with a small outboard motor that I can hear now. The boat is about ten metres from *Raven* and as it passes the helmsman turns to look through our window. He seems to be much younger than his passengers and his stare is cool and appraising before he turns back to look ahead.

'Good grief,' I say suddenly.

Hugh looks up from his tussle with a corkscrew. 'What is it?'

'Quick, Hugh. Binoculars.'

Like any good ex-Navy man, Hugh has a pair readily to hand. He clamps the bottle between his knees and uses his free hand to toss them to me. I quickly move across to the riverside window and train them on the transom of the retreating little boat. There is a single word elegantly painted in black and gold on it. As I thought. It clearly says: NIRVANA.

I watch as the boat begins to veer across to the other bank so that, by the time it reaches the road bridge, it is almost as far over to the starboard side of the river as it can be. Could it be heading for the party on the houseboat? And if so, where could it have come from? And why?

NIRVANA. The same name that had been scribbled on the missing top sheet of the Post-it notes that I found in the bin at Ophelia's room. Coincidence? Possibly. And yet there was also that little hole left by a missing drawing pin in the map on her wall. And that pin prick could easily have been indicating the little inlet where the houseboat is moored.

CHAPTER TWENTY-ONE

I explain to Hugh why I am suddenly interested in any connection between what may be happening on the other bank and the murdered young woman. As I am talking, I catch myself examining the older man's eyes. They are crinkled with age but still seem to generate an infinite calmness about life. They are the confident eyes of a surgeon who has seen many dreadful things in his life but remained sure of himself and his skills and in command of any situation that fate throws his way. I am jealous of such calm self-assurance and wish I felt more sure about my own lifestyle and relationships.

'Why don't we have a wander over the bridge and see what's going on?' he says. 'I'm sure Eddie could do with a pee.'

Having crossed the bridge, we pause and lean on the rail to look down across the fence towards the little inlet. There are still one or two cars moving in both directions behind us, but the faint sounds of laughter and music drift across from the houseboat on the still night air. The mooring is still too far away to make out what is going on. Hugh pulls his binoculars out of his waxed jacket and puts them to his eyes.

'Ah ha!'

'What is it?'

He passes me the binoculars. 'See for yourself.'

The raised black hull comes into focus. Above it, under the little porch created by the white pillars, the lights are on behind the glass panels of the door and its adjacent windows. But any view inside is prevented by drawn curtains. Then I see what Hugh is getting at. Painted neatly, on both sides of the prow, is the boat's name.

'Nirvana!'

'Nirvana,' confirms Hugh.

The little tender we saw must belong to the houseboat and share its name. Sure enough, I can just glimpse it now, tied to the starboard side of the bigger boat. I can also see a gangplank with a handrail that spans the water between the boat and the bank on the boat's starboard side.

We make our way back across the bridge and stroll upstream until we are opposite the inlet. The music, laughter and hum of conversation is slightly louder now, but not raucous. However, we are still unable to see into the boat's interior and Hugh is starting to shiver. 'She's a lovely looking vessel,' says Hugh as we walk back to our respective boats. 'I suspect she was one of the college barges.'

'What were those?'

'An old boy told me about them. They originally came from the livery companies in the City who had them on the Thames. The college boat clubs adopted them as club houses and floating changing rooms. People also stood on their roofs to watch the racing during Eights Week apparently – they were sort of floating grandstands. Some of them were built by Salters here on the Isis. But between the 1930s and the 1950s they were gradually replaced by the row of brick boathouses on the island. It was a lot easier to store and maintain boats on the ground floor and have a top floor for club facilities and a viewing balcony. And you didn't have to keep refloating the barges when they sprung a leak and settled on the bottom of the river.'

'Gosh. There can't be many of them left.'

'Not at all. This old chap was a student here in the fifties. He could remember being invited to a rowing club party on one. Apparently, the invitation stipulated that no one was allowed to wear any clothes other than a hat!' We chuckle at the story and say goodnight.

Eddie and I repeat our walk on the following morning. I can't see anything going on from Strode Road Bridge and *Nirvana* seems to be silent and empty. We go on across Strode Meadows to the Kidneys. The ground is cloaked in a hoar frost and the absence of any other footprints on its virgin surface suggests we are the first to visit that morning. There is no sign of John Turner and his work shed is chained and padlocked. Eddie has a happy half hour, which includes 'Border-terrorising' a couple of pheasants, as we make our way around the nature reserve and back.

As I begin to cross the Donnington Road bridge, the smell of hot fried food wafts enticingly across the road. There is a rowing boathouse on the other pavement with a huge plastic banner saying OPEN on it. The City Boathouse, home of the City of Oxford Rowing Club, allows members of the public to walk into its first floor, on the same level as the bridge, and get fed. I smuggle Eddie under a table in a bright wood-floored area that leads onto an outdoor patio and order a 'Rower's Breakfast' after seeing the menu's injunction to 'Remember Food Is Fuel'. I suspect this is aimed at people who have already burned a few hundred calories rowing on the river rather than just a couple of dozen on a dog walk, but I decide to go with the flow. The mountainous Full English that arrives gives me plenty of time to have a think as Eddie and I make our way through it.

The pin prick on the wall map and the Post-it note at St Hugh's must mean that *Nirvana* had some kind of connection with Ophelia. And if the historic barge is being used for occasional parties, could it be connected to her death in some way? I realise, even as I think this, that it is quite a leap. Ophelia could have had any number of reasons to be connected with the boat – all of them innocent. But then, what about Nirvana's little tender? It seemed to be ferrying passengers to the party on board the larger boat. It is a strangely furtive way to arrive. Why didn't they just arrive by car and walk through the gate in the chain-link fencing? There seems to be nothing more I can do at the moment, but I am intrigued, and I make a decision.

Back at the boat, I start up the engine of *Jumping Jack Flash*, untie my mooring ropes and slip the gear lever into the forward position. Hugh pokes his head out of his hatch to see what's going on. As I pull out and draw level with him, I call across. 'Just going to move upriver for a bit.' He waves. He understands what I am doing.

I steer the boat to a new mooring just before the Strode Road Bridge and tie up again. This now gives me a diagonal view across the river and straight into the mouth of the inlet, but I think I am still far enough away not to attract attention. I'm surprised that I still haven't been visited by someone from the Environment Agency – although, my boat's registration number may have been recorded without my knowledge and I may already be under supervision. Moving my boat a mere hundred metres or so won't be enough to satisfy the requirements of my cruising licence. But then again, the riverbank is hardly crowded and maybe they will turn a blind eye for the moment. They seem to have done that for *Raven* and *Madam Gipsy* and the handful of other boats scattered along the bank all the way to Folly Bridge.

I am still uncomfortably full of my self-indulgent breakfast, but I can manage a coffee with Hugh when he comes calling shortly afterwards. He has brought his binoculars and spends a few minutes with them trained on the adjacent barge.

'No. Nothing happening over there. Nice looking craft, though. Now I can see her properly I'm even more certain that she's an old college barge. Presumably they just towed her into position. I'd love to see what she's like inside.'

We chat for a while and then he heads off for visiting hours at the hospital. I open up my laptop and trawl though some of the press conference coverage on the newspapers' websites. The tabloids boast a range of headlines including 'Oxford Student Strangled to Death',

'Boat Race Star Sobs After Lover's Murder', 'Student Strangler At Large in Oxford' and 'Student Strangled and Body Dumped in River'. The stories are all fairly similar, describing Ophelia variously as brilliant, beautiful and besotted. One story describes Cal as looking like 'an all-American hero, with chiselled features and the physique you would expect of a world-class rower'. Most are sympathetic to him, although one snidely refers to his time at the training camp as 'an alibi'. None refer to his wealthy televangelist father, although I suspect it is only a matter of time before this detail emerges. The poor sod. Cal won't enjoy reading this morning's coverage in the British press.

I send a text to Nina letting her know that I've moved the boat a short distance. A message arrives on my phone a few minutes later. However, it isn't from Nina. It's from Jane.

Free for lunch today? I've got someone you should meet.

I know I need to crack on with writing the story or I risk underwhelming my new employer. And I need the money and my expenses to be approved. But do I really want to reacquaint myself with Jane so soon after what happened between us? Nevertheless, I find my fingers rapping out a rapid reply.

Where and when?

12 noon. Your boat?

OK. Thanks. On a new mooring closer to the bridge.

Another text arrives. I imagine it to be Jane again with more information, but this time it is Nina replying to my earlier message.

> We'll find you. Running late though. Cal had a bad night.
> Will call round for my stuff early afternoon.

Jane arrives at ten minutes past twelve. I let her take the lead on what kind of greeting she wants to extend, and we settle for a professional handshake. This may be because she is accompanied by another woman who she introduces as Imani. I assess her to be in her mid-twenties, but she has the tired eyes of a much older woman who has crammed a lot of experience into her life – and not all of it pleasant. Her hair falls to her shoulders in tight beaded braids that click softly when she moves her head. She is swaddled in a quilted coat that reaches to her ankles. She peers around at the interior of the boat while I put a pot of tea in front of them.

'So, you're a journalist, yeah?' she demands.

'That's right. I'm sure that Jane … er, DS Henry has told you that I'm writing a profile of her and her county lines work for *Cotswold Quality* magazine.' I flick open a notebook.

'Yeah, cool. I call her Jane. You can call her Jane too, if you like. She won't mind.'

Jane laughs delightedly and I shoot her a warning look. 'So how do you know, Jane?'

'We met at the food bank. She was givin' and I was gettin'.'

'You work at a food bank?' I ask Jane.

'Weekends. Sometimes.'

'I gotta job, though,' says Imani quickly. 'Cleaning at the Mini factory. Just don't pay enough. Kids – they always wantin' something. Maybe we should live on a boat like this! You pay much for it?'

'Er … no. Not really. Not compared to a flat or a house.'

'Tell him how you came to Oxford,' prompts Jane.

Imani rolls her eyes. 'I was just fifteen. Been hangin' round with a gang in London since I was ten. That was when I saw me cousin stabbed in the head. Man, that was bad. Newham was bad, you know.'

Jane and I fall silent as Imani talks on. I can tell she has told this story many times before and there are moments when she seems to be talking to herself rather than to Jane or me. She describes how an older man made her reliant on drugs and, after sleeping with her several times himself, installed her in a bedroom in a large house on the outskirts of the city. She was locked in for long periods, monitored closely by the man's friends and forced to entertain older male visitors – sometimes more than one at a time. This continued for two entire years until there was a police raid on the house.

'We found ten girls there,' says Jane. 'None of them was older than nineteen. They'd all come from London. All been in gangs.'

'Kids got no chance there. Stabbin's are worse than ever,' says Imani angrily. 'No way I'm taking my kids back there.'

Imani's story makes me sick to my stomach. How can anyone sink to such depths of depravity that they imprison teenage girls and sell them for sex to their friends? And how could the girls become so vulnerable in the first place? Absent or indifferent parents must be a big part of the problem. Parents with their own drug habits, caught in a vicious cycle of addiction and carrying out the crimes to pay for it. But even then, it must take particularly malevolent individuals to seek out the young and vulnerable, groom them and use them in this way. I remember Eddie's owner, a young man called Sam, who was homeless and penniless having been thrown out of his home, only to end up drowned in a West Midlands canal. And I remember Tammy, a teenage girl in Bath who betrayed her father and her friends in return for cash from a violent hitman. And even beautiful Anna – with her dead mother and deadbeat father – could have been at risk from this. What twist of fate prevented any of them from ending up as the victims of these vile people? I feel an ice-cold fury growing inside me.

'How many children do you have?' I ask.

'Two,' she says. 'Two boys. Four and six. Their dad's gone. Good riddance, I say. We're better off without him. We're okay,' she adds defiantly. She looks across at Jane. 'That okay, Jane? Can I go now? Things to do. You know?'

Jane exchanges a questioning look with me.

'Yes, of course,' I tell her. 'I'm really grateful. It's been great to meet you ... and to hear your story. Would you mind if I put your photograph in the article?'

Imani likes this idea. She pulls two huge hooped earrings from her bag and puts them in before striking several poses on her own, and then with Jane on the riverbank, before giving her a hug, bumping my fist and swinging away, back towards the city.

'Useful?' asks Jane, as she settles back in the loveseat with Eddie.

'Yes, absolutely. It's given me a real insight into what you do and why you do it. I understand why you should be angry. Christ, it makes me feel sick ... and furious. These people are ruining young lives in such a callous and deliberate way.' I pause, tempering my emotions. 'But I should be able to crack on with the piece now, thank you. And I'll send it over to you before I submit it, like we agreed.'

Jane nods thoughtfully, smiles and cocks her head on one side. I recognise it as some kind of unstated question.

'Umm ... I should have said thank you properly,' I say awkwardly. 'For the other night. I enjoyed our evening very much.'

'Me too.'

'But, look ...'

'Aha! I suspected there might be a "but" coming.'

'Well,' I say awkwardly.

'Like I said, it's not a problem. I'm not looking for complications – let alone confetti and a carrycot. We had some fun. It was mutual. End of. Just do me a favour and stay schtum. I get pestered a lot at the station and I have no desire to get pestered even more. Better to stay aloof and mysterious. In fact, I'm thinking about encouraging them to think I'm gay. Or maybe not. You have no idea how twentieth century the so-called banter is in a police canteen. Did you ever see *Life on Mars*? They reckoned it was a drama, but I call it a fly-on-the-wall documentary!'

'Hi there!'

Nina has come through the swing door at the stern followed by Cal. The tall American is being forced to stoop his head slightly. Nina advances on us with a look of curiosity at my visitor. I stand but Jane remains seated.

'Nina, this is Detective Sergeant Jane Henry. I'm doing a profile about her for *Cotswold Quality*.' The two women shake hands with Nina reaching down and Jane reaching up. 'Jane, this is my good friend Nina, Nina Wilde. And this is her friend Cal. Cal Hopper. She's just come to fetch a few things as she's staying with Cal for a few days.'

Jane raises an eyebrow at me and I sense Nina stiffen as she registers this.

Cal bends to shake Jane's hand too. I can't help noticing that he is no longer radiating a picture of bronzed good health. His features are as enviable as ever, but there is a clammy pallor to his face and his eyes are rimmed red with dark bags under them.

'I hope you don't mind me stealing Nina away for a short while, Jack,' he says sheepishly to me. 'She's being such a great comfort and I'm not sure what I'd do without her at the moment.'

'Sure,' I say. The three of us are still standing. 'No problem.'

Nina gives a brittle little laugh. 'You don't need to ask his permission, Cal. I'm not Jack's property or anything!'

'No, no sorry,' he mumbles.

I am desperate to bring an end to this awkwardness. 'Well, you know where your stuff is,' I say, with a laugh that rings hollow. 'Leave whatever you don't want to take.'

But Nina is looking down at Jane appraisingly rather than across at me. *Beam me up, Scotty*, I think to myself.

'So, what prompts this profile for the magazine?' she asks.

'Oh ... I'll let Jack explain,' says Jane coolly.

If only Nina would sit down. It would all feel so much easier. But then, I don't want Nina to sit down. I want her to get off the boat as quickly as possible before something irreversible is said. 'Jane has been a key player in busting some of the county lines criminal activity in Oxford. She works with the community to identify where it might be happening.'

'County lines?' asks Cal. 'What's that?'

Jane peers up at him. 'It's mainly drugs and prostitution – sometimes underage – being run by organised criminal gangs out of London and other big cities like Birmingham and Manchester. They set up operations in smaller cities and towns in the surrounding counties – hence "county lines".' Jane suddenly stands up and looks Cal square in the face. 'Look, Cal, as a policewoman, I know what's happening – what's happened.' Cal looks momentarily stunned. 'I know about you and Ophelia, the dead girl. And I want to say how sorry I am for you.'

'Uh yeah, sure, thanks, thanks a lot. That's nice of you.'

'I'm sure DCI Philpott will catch the person responsible. He's very experienced.'

'Yeah. Yeah, thanks.'

I think Jane has handled the moment well, but the look on Nina's face suggests that she is less than impressed. She gives a theatrical sigh and looks pointedly at her watch.

'Well, we need to get on. I'll just take both my suitcases, okay? They're virtually all still packed anyway. And I don't know how long Cal will need me.' She leans in to give me a peck on the cheek and we watch them turn and make their way back down the boat.

I slump into a chair and put a hand over my eyes while Jane chuckles quietly to herself. I part my fingers to sneak a look at her and she is smiling back at me.

'It's Saturday. I'm on a day off, I've just done you a favour – and I'm not talking about Imani,' Jane says, grinning. 'So, I'd quite like a drink and, to be honest, Jack, you look as though you could do with one too.'

I wait until Nina and Cal have walked past on the riverbank, each pulling a roll-along suitcase, before collecting a cold bottle of Pino Grigio from the fridge and pouring two very large glassfuls.

'They make a nice-looking couple, don't you think?' says Jane.

'Just don't,' I warn her.

'I had an interesting time reading your cuttings again yesterday evening. Sounds like you and Nina have quite some history together.'

'I told you, we're just good friends.'

'And you also told me you'd like to be more than that. I have a pretty good memory – even when considerable drink has been taken. But I'm talking about your encounters with the criminal fraternity – first the famous Canal Pusher of the Midlands, and then the Russian Mafia in Bath. Great stuff! Jack and Nina, the crime fighting duo on a canal boat!'

I laugh in spite of myself. 'And Eddie the dog.'

'And Eddie the dog,' she repeats. Hearing his name, Eddie springs back into her lap and a small amount of wine is spilt. 'But poor Jack,' she adds as I go to fetch some kitchen towel. 'You follow Nina all the way to Oxford and suddenly she's moving in with a vulnerable six-foot-plus American hunk who is just two years younger than her.'

I scrunch the kitchen towel into a ball and throw it at her head. Eddie gives a little bark of excitement. It reminds me that Nina barely acknowledged the little dog's presence when she came on board the boat. And if she behaved jealously with Jane, it was prompted by Cal rather than me. She is clearly infatuated. But I realise that falling into bed with Jane wasn't much of an answer either.

'So why did you move the boat up to here?' she asks. I hope this signals that she has finished teasing me.

I explain about our visit to Ophelia's room at St Hugh's, the pad of Post-it notes and the pin hole left in the map. Then I tell her about the previous evening's party on the boat and the men who were being ferried to it.

'So, you've moved closer to see what's going on?' she asks, helping herself to some more wine, which more than replaces the drop spilt by Eddie.

'That's the plan,' I say. 'Of course, it could be something and nothing. But it seems odd, don't you think?'

'I think the girl's murder changes everything,' she says firmly. 'You may have found evidence in her room that's relevant to a murder rather than just a missing person's case. You need to tell Philpott what you've got. Or I do. Remember what I said about doing things by the book?'

I'm not really concentrating on Jane's instructions, though. Right now I can think of little other than Nina leaving with Cal and moving into his home with both of her suitcases. She seems to have an obsession with helping him. It cannot be healthy given her own fragile and grief-stricken personal history.

'Penny for them?' says Jane.

I sigh. 'Have you got any plans for this afternoon? I feel the need to get out of Oxford for a few hours, stretch my legs and breath some country air.'

Jane grins. 'Great idea. Have you ever been to Bagley Wood?'

CHAPTER TWENTY-TWO

Jane drives Eddie and me out of town in her little Japanese car. She says we are heading towards the Cumnor Hills on the west of the city. We park at somewhere called Kennington Playing Fields and enter the wood via a footbridge that crosses a main road. The road is busy and there are electricity pylons marching across the landscape.

'I had somewhere more bucolic in mind,' I tell her.

'Stop being a grouch,' she orders, taking Eddie's lead and charging ahead.

A metal gate into the wood has a sign indicating that it is owned by St John's College and says entry is by permit only. It's a reminder of the extraordinary wealth built up by the Oxford colleges over hundreds and hundreds of years. They have assets stretching far beyond their connoisseur wine cellars. I have read that Anna and Cal's college alone has reserves totalling £500 million.

'St John's has owned this place since the dissolution of the monasteries. Before that, it was owned by Abingdon Abbey,' says Jane.

'Well, they don't seem to want to share it,' I say indicating the sign, but Jane insouciantly walks past it. 'Okay, officer. I'll risk it if you will.'

'There's nothing to risk. There used to be a system of permits controlling access, but anyone can come in now, as long as we stay on the paths and keep Eddie on a lead.'

I hate having to walk Eddie on a lead in a place like this, but I concede that he does have a tendency to get lost in unfamiliar woodland. So far, he has always come back, but it's too cold to have to stand around for an hour while he does so in his own sweet time.

'I come out here quite often,' says Jane. 'Seen a few deer and there are wonderful drifts of bluebells and wild garlic in the spring.'

We follow well-maintained paths and rides through the ancient wood which is a mixture of mature Leyland cypress, oak, hazel, larch and Scots pine. There isn't another person to be seen.

'A lot of Oxford poets used to come out this way for inspiration,' says Jane as we walk past a carefully stacked pile of wood. 'Oscar Wilde wrote a poem calling this area "The Garden of Eros" – it was where he escaped from what he called "the tiny waxen town". I don't think he was that keen on Oxford. Am I talking too much?'

'Not at all. It's nice to have such an erudite guide. Although I'm still recovering from your story about Isis!'

She laughs. 'Wilde talked about "summer hours spent in some cool grassy field, far from the cricket field and noisy eight, at Bagley".'

'Yes, I don't imagine he had much time for the hearty sporting types.'

She laughs. 'On the contrary, I think he would love to have spent time with the "hearties" – just not with their sports! Talking of which, I thought Cal looked pretty broken. All joking aside, it's probably a good thing he has Nina to look after him.'

'For him, yes. But I'm not so sure it will be very good for her.' I explain how Nina ran away from her family and friends after her husband's death and how the depth of her grief has made it very hard for her to move on with her life in any way. 'I hoped that the move to Oxford, and her closeness to Anna, would all be part of her gradual recovery – if you can call it that. But I'm worried this Cal thing could unbalance her again. It seems to be all-consuming for her. An obsession, if you like. She's just suddenly turned her back on Anna, on Eddie ... '

'And on you?' says Jane quietly.

'Yes, on me too. Although I wonder if that was ever going to go anywhere anyway.'

My hands are thrust deep into my coat pockets for warmth. She transfers Eddie to her other hand and links her free arm through mine. It's a nice gesture of support but I worry it might be more than that. How much weight should I give Jane's declarations of independence?

'Cheer up. That's why we've come out here remember? Now, what other literary anecdotes can I bore you with?'

'Has it ever occurred to you that you are ridiculously over-educated to be a police detective? Are there many intellectuals like you in the Thames Valley force? Is it the lingering impact of Inspector Morse? He liked opera, didn't he, and crosswords?'

'Ah … as Auden said, *to the man-in-the-street, who, I'm sorry to say is a keen observer of life, the word intellectual, suggests straight away, a man who's untrue to his wife*!'

'If that's the case, almost the whole population of Oxford must be cheating on each other.'

'No, Jack,' she says quietly. 'Firstly, and contrary to its image, there are an awful lot of people in Oxford who aren't privileged intellectuals. It's a manufacturing city too. And secondly, it's only cheating if it means something.' There is a lengthy pause while I digest this, then she uses her arm to push me into a 180-degree turn. 'Come on, let's get back to the boat. You can cook me a nice dinner. We can stop at a farm shop on the way back for ingredients.'

Jumping Jack Flash can be the cosiest of boltholes on a cold wet evening in January. The golden glow from its wall-lights is reflected in the varnished wood interior and the solid fuel stove is giving out a good heat in the corner. Eddie is curled up on a small beanbag, sleeping off his walk, twitching occasionally and giving a little whimper as he dreams. A small but high-quality portable speaker is linked to my phone's playlist and Nigel Kennedy is playing Vivaldi's *Four Seasons* to accompany my labours at the gas ring. Appropriately enough, it is the first movement of the final Winter concerto. Jane is settled crossways in the loveseat with her legs draped over the armrest and completing my half-finished crossword. I continue stirring the paella, add a pinch more saffron and another glug of fish stock and a glass of white wine. One for the pot, one for me. I can think of worse ways to spend a winter evening.

The rice is just absorbing the last of the liquid when my eyes catch some movement on the opposite bank. A vehicle has pulled up on the track near to the chain link gate. It's a nondescript estate car and I watch through my binoculars as a portly man in a flat cap opens the gate, and then the car boot, and carries a cardboard box up the gangplank and into the boat. He repeats this four times and then drives away after padlocking the gate behind him.

I take a large bowl of paella to Jane and sit opposite her to eat my own. The smell of food has woken Eddie and I slip him a prawn, which vanishes in seconds. 'I think there could be another party on *Nirvana* tonight,' I tell Jane. 'Some supplies were just delivered.'

She shrugs. 'No law against it. This is very good, Jack. Top marks. Thank you.'

I position myself at the table where I can look across at *Nirvana* and Jane eventually joins me to wrestle with the last remaining crossword clues. It is eight o'clock and I am just opening a second bottle of wine when I see car headlights through the arch of the bridge. I can make out two large 4x4s next to the chain-link fence. The headlights show a man unlocking the gate while the car doors open and three passengers from each of the cars gather behind him. 'Look,' I say to Jane urgently. 'New arrivals.' I train my binoculars across the water again. 'They're all women, seven of them.' Although it is dark, and they are all wrapped up, I can tell this from their high heel shoes and the way they are tiptoeing in small steps across the grass to the boat.

They all file behind the man, up the gangplank and into the houseboat where lights come on. The blinds and curtains are already drawn. Then the man comes back down the gangplank, locks the gate behind him and drives away, followed by the second vehicle.

After half an hour, I persuade Jane to join me and Eddie for a walk. We go over the bridge and look down and then we go back along the riverbank path until we are opposite the houseboat. Again, there is the faint sound of laughter and music but nothing to see so we make our way back to the welcoming warmth of *Jumping Jack Flash*.

'If it's a re-run of last night, the smaller boat will be bringing the other guests,' I say.

I train my binoculars across the river again but can see no sign of the tender. It must have already left to pick up its passengers. Jane yawns. I sense that she is less interested in the coming and going of my neighbours than I am. But she has shown no sign of wanting to make a move and she has been drinking steadily throughout the evening. I'm beginning to wonder whether she has plans to stay the night and try to resolve my conflicted feelings about the prospect. In the meantime, I slow my pace of alcohol intake and keep vigil at the window where I am trying to look downstream as far as I can.

At ten o'clock my patience is rewarded. I see a small white bow wave first as the tender emerges into view, in the centre of the river. 'Jane. Quick. Come here.'

She has been washing and wiping a few things in the galley and now she kneels next to me at the port hole by my bed. 'Turn the lights out,' I whisper to her urgently.

'I thought you'd never ask,' she giggles. Seconds later, we are pressed together side-by-side in darkness. The lack of light makes a small improvement to my night vision. The tender comes on towards us, twenty metres, ten metres, and now it is opposite us and beginning to move across under the bridge and towards the inlet where it motors up alongside *Nirvana.* It looked like the same man at the stern, dressed in the same hoodie and I have a feeling he is one of the men who delivered the women to the boat earlier. The three passengers climb a short ladder on the boat's side and enter the boat followed by the helmsman.

I put the binoculars down and look at Jane. 'Bloody hell! I know one of those men. It's Ophelia's tutor from St Hugh's. The tall thin one with the shaven head. It's Dr John Romaine. What the hell is going on?'

But Jane is staring back at me with a look of shock that more than matches my own. 'I know one of them too,' she whispers. 'And he's an assistant chief constable in our force.'

CHAPTER TWENTY-THREE

Jane is now as intrigued as I am. We agree to take half hour shifts at the window, and we are just changing over at one a.m. when we hear the outboard cough into life across the river. It's too dark to attempt a photograph but we watch the three passengers – Dr Romaine, the senior police officer and another man – being ferried back past us, downstream. Half an hour later, the two 4x4s are back to collect the group of women. Jane has my binoculars.

'Damn, I couldn't make out the registration numbers,' she says, throwing them down onto my duvet and flopping backwards with her head on a pillow.

We have been batting the same questions back and forth between us since we saw the small boat arrive, but to little effect. Are we watching a private party take place or some kind of illegal prostitution? If it is prostitution, could there be a county lines angle? How old are the women? Or are they underage girls? What is the policeman's involvement? Could it be possible that he is acting as an undercover agent? But why would a man of his senior rank be doing that? And what is the connection between the evidence I found in Ophelia's room and what is going on across the river? How is her tutor involved? Could he be in some way connected with her death?

'We've got plenty of questions but no answers,' I say quietly into the darkness as I lie on my back next to Jane, looking up at the wood-panelled ceiling.

'We need to focus on what to do next,' she says. 'I'm going to play it by the book and talk to Philpott. The murder investigation is the most important thing for the moment. And I'll tell him about the policeman and Dr Romaine. It'll be his call how to handle that.'

'Makes sense,' I say. There is another lengthy pause. I am still buzzing with what we have seen but sense the warmth of Jane's body alongside me.

'I'll crash here if you don't mind? It's too late to go home now and I'm knackered.' She gives an exaggerated yawn and rolls against my side with one hand on my chest. She begins to stroke it gently downwards, then across my stomach. I have a rush of feelings: guilt, resentment, self-justification and finally resignation and excitement.

'Of course, you're very welcome to stay. I hoped you would.'

'Did you, Jack? That's alright then, isn't it?'

The visibility through the porthole above my berth is just a matter of inches when I pull back its little curtain the following morning. A thick swirling grey and white wall of fog is blanketing the view. Jane is already up and boiling a kettle for coffee. She is brusque and businesslike and doesn't say anything about our second night together and so neither do I. However, she does say she is keen to get home, change and see the Detective Chief Inspector as soon as she can. She declines anything to eat and is gone by 7.30 a.m. I desperately need a shower but decide to walk Eddie first and clear my head. The fog hangs dense in the bitterly cold air as I cross the Donnington Road Bridge with Eddie. I look over the parapet but can't see the river. It feels as though I am up in a balloon, hanging in the misty clouds. The café is invisible too, but my sense of smell is compensating for my blindness as the scent of freshly fried pork products wafts into my nostrils. Eddie and I manage to walk on past the temptation and grope our way around a circuit of the Kidneys. I am worried that Turner and his dog Tod may be hidden in the dense riverside mist and suddenly ambush us. Eddie and I have no appetite for a return match.

We walk back along Meadow Lane until its junction with Strode Road. I take a small detour before the bridge and go down the track to the bank and the gate in the chain link fencing that leads to *Nirvana*. The fog makes it impossible to see if there is any sign of life in the little inlet and I certainly can't hear anything, but there are three black bin bags on the floor that Eddie is sniffing around. Each one has been tied with a knot and they have been left to one side of the gates alongside a large cardboard box full of empty bottles.

Without thinking, I pick up one of the bags. It's not heavy, just an awkward shape. The fog provides a convenient cloak as I take it back across the bridge and throw it into the well of my boat's bow. Then I find an old bedsheet, which I spread across the floor. Nina has left some yellow rubber gloves under the sink and I use these and some wooden chopsticks to start sifting through the rubbish. Luckily it's fresh and doesn't smell too bad. There is a vast quantity of wet wipes and tissues smeared with lipstick and mascara as well as the remains of some party food, half-eaten cocktail sausages, cardboard plates, the foils of four empty condom packets, the condoms themselves (used and wrapped in toilet paper), cotton buds and used cotton wool. An occasional dark shape passes on the riverbank, a dog-walker or jogger, but I can't make out their details and so I assume they can't see mine either. I bundle it all back into the black plastic bag, retie it and return it to the gate. Then I come back with another one of the remaining two bags. This one has much of the same detritus plus empty crisp packets and a generous quantity of chicken bones. It too is quickly repacked and returned to the gate.

The final bag is more of the same, but my probing rubber-clad fingers finally come across a creased and grubby business card. It reads: *Garden of Eden. High Quality Companionship for Discerning Professional People*. It includes an address in town and a website address. It takes me another fifteen minutes to repack the bag and take it back to join the others. Then I take a photograph of the business card and Google the website's homepage.

'Garden of Eden can help you to meet the partner of your dreams. We really get to know you – so that you can get to know the person who will be your perfect match. We offer a highly professional and personalised service to successful and discerning people who can't afford to waste their time. We have years of experience and nothing is too much trouble for our clients. Contact us now for a free tailormade no-strings consultation. You won't regret it.'

The copy is surrounded by photographs of good-looking older couples staring into each other's eyes over candlelit dinners, walking hand-in-hand by the river, laughing on park benches and sharing the front seats of expensive-looking sports cars. I send my photograph of the business card and a link to the website to Jane and my phone rings about a minute later.

'Really, Jack? Going through rubbish bags?'

'Professional hazard, isn't it? Both for the press and the police.'

'Seriously, Jack – it's not on. This could be evidence and we have to gather evidence properly. You should have left it to us.'

'Yeah – and it would've been in the back of a bin lorry before you lot got around to it,' I say. I think my efforts of the morning deserve a bit more gratitude. It hasn't been a pleasant task.

'Look. Philpott has said he can see me in an hour, after the morning briefing to his team. I'll tell him what you've found.'

'Okay. Let me know what he says.'

A text arrives on my phone 90 minutes later.

Brace yourself. We're coming to see you.

However, it isn't Jane and the DCI who are knocking at the door ten minutes later. It's Hugh.

'Hello there, old chap, bit of a pea-souper, eh? Got time for a coffee?'

Once he has a mug in his hand, I tell him about the sightings of the previous night. He raises an eyebrow when he discovers that Jane has shared my night-time vigil but lets it pass without comment. Then I show him the card and the website. 'So now she's coming back with the man in charge of the murder investigation.'

'Well, well, well. Of course, there could be a perfectly innocent explanation. But it's certainly intriguing. I'm sure the police will get to the bottom of it.'

'Maybe,' I say. But then any further conversation becomes difficult because the bells of Christ Church cathedral start to ring, and it sounds like there are a lot of them. They continue for ten entire minutes. Hugh leaves during the middle of the call to prayer and, as they come to an end, there is a vigorous banging at the hatchway. Philpott is standing on the stern platform, a hand on each hip and his chest puffed out in the classic Mussolini pose. Jane is standing awkwardly to his side. Philpott ignores my outstretched hand. He is wearing the same double-breasted suit from the press conference. I'm not surprised. A fresh murder enquiry isn't going to pause just because it's Sunday and he fancies a round of golf. He jabs a short stubby finger at me.

'You and I need a serious talk, *Mr* Johnson.' He stresses the *Mr* to indicate that any hint of politeness isn't deliberate.

'You'd better come in then.'

Jane is hovering behind him with an anxious look on her face. Philpott's nostrils look red and sore and his voice is nasal.

'Tea? Coffee?'

'You have seriously pissed me off, *Mr* Johnson,' he growls.

'Good morning to you too,' I say, retreating onto a chair by the dining table. Philpott remains standing. He seems satisfied that he can look down at me now.

'DS Henry has given me a full briefing about your so-called discoveries. I've a good mind to throw the book at you for interfering with a police investigation.' Unfortunately, the power of this threat is diminished by the sneeze that follows it. It sends him scrabbling in his pockets for a handkerchief.

'You'd be entitled to do that,' I say, more calmly than I feel, 'but only if I had done anything to obstruct or hinder you. But actually, I think I've helped you.'

'Helped me!' he explodes. He steps forward, puts both palms on the table and brings his head down close to mine. His breath smells of throat lozenges. 'You stupid bastard. You've tampered with evidence.' He sniffs. 'You took evidence out of the dead girl's room. And now you've been going through bin-bags.'

'No one knew she was dead when we went to her room. She was just missing at that stage. And I went through the bin-bags in case they were taken away before you could get around to it.'

'And he did tell us ... tell me about them as soon as he could,' adds Jane tentatively.

Philpott wheels on her. 'You stay silent, Henry,' he snaps at her. 'You stay quiet and stick to babysitting little scrubbers from Birmingham. D'ye hear me?'

Philpott has been on my boat for less than a minute, but I've already decided that I really don't like him or his winter cold very much. He swings back to look at me. 'I know all about you, Johnson. I know all about your history. Trampling all over police investigations in order to get a book or a cheap story out of it. Well, I'm warning you, you stay off my turf. D'ye hear me? I don't want any fucking celebrity amateur detectives getting in my way. Is that understood?' Once again, he sneezes, but this time he just wipes his nose with the back of a hand.

'Where's this Post-it note?' he snaps.

I retrieve it from my jacket pocket and Jane gets me to slip it into an evidence bag. 'It's interesting, though, isn't it?' I ask, examining my fingernails. 'The girl's tutor and a very senior police officer visiting women on a boat for a party? A boat which Ophelia McVeigh knew about for some reason. I'd be interested to learn what you're going to do about that.'

Jane has closed her eyes and is shaking her head from side to side behind the stocky little man, who clenches a fist and brings it banging down onto the table. Eddie gives a little bark but stays firmly behind my feet.

'Last warning, Johnson. It's no business of yours what I do with this information. And if you come anywhere near my investigation again, you'll find yourself spending some time in our cells. Is that clear? Well? Is that clear?'

'Perfectly.' I push a half empty box of tissues across the table at him. 'Please, help yourself. You need to be careful this fog doesn't settle on your lungs. It's always worse on the river.'

'Gahhhh ...' He throws his hands in the air with frustration and stomps back along the length of the boat. Jane frowns at me and hurries after him. I follow them both and stick my head above the hatchway to watch the leaden air swallow them up. However, I'm interested to hear Philpott tell Jane to 'Show me this bloody boat' as they go. She'll have trouble showing him anything until the fog clears – and that's unlikely to happen for hours in these freezing temperatures.

Jane phones me about half an hour later. 'Ouch. My ears are still burning. I don't think that did my so-called fast track career much good.'

'The man's an idiot.'

'He isn't. He just doesn't want you involved, Jack. He was already on to the dating agency. It turns out the dead girl's bank account shows regular payments from them during the first part of December. He's already spoken to the woman who runs Garden of Eden. One of his team told me. They obviously thought she might be working as an escort for them and met the wrong kind of client. But the owner was adamant that Ophelia only worked there as a temp in the office and it seems to have all checked out. And that's as much as I could find out. I think he's interested in the *Nirvana* connection though – and especially Romaine, Ophelia's tutor. They're trying to find out who owns it. I expect they'll try to get a search warrant. But there's not much evidence to justify one at the moment.'

'Apart from a business card connecting the boat to a dating agency which employed a murdered girl?' I ask sceptically. 'And a university tutor who knew Ophelia well and who goes to parties on board in the middle of the night? I think that should be enough for most magistrates.'

'Yes, well, he's only just found out about all that, hasn't he? And it was a business card you stole from a bin bag.'

'Can you actually steal anything from a bin bag? Hasn't it already been thrown away?'

'That's not the point is it? If it is evidence of some kind, you could have contaminated it.'

'Well,' I say stubbornly. 'Philpott wouldn't have any connection between *Nirvana* and Ophelia if it wasn't for me.'

'The Post-it note? More dubiously acquired evidence. Forensics would have picked that up in the end.'

'Would they? Would they have noticed the pin hole? Could the wastepaper bin have been emptied before they eventually got there?'

'We have to do things properly, Jack. You know that. It could end up making the difference between a successful conviction and an acquittal.'

'If I was Philpott –'

But Jane cuts me off abruptly. 'But you're not. So, behave. Philpott knows what he's doing, and he's seriously pissed off with you.'

'Really? I'd never have guessed. Well the feeling is mutual. I feel sorry for his germs, having to live with him.'

She sighs. 'I've got to dash.' She has rung off before I can answer.

CHAPTER TWENTY-FOUR

My next unexpected visitor of the morning is Anna. Her big blue eyes aren't sparkling as much as they usually do, although her cheeks are pink and flushed from the cold.

'Hey this is a nice surprise,' I say as she gives me a hug. 'I didn't expect to see you this morning.'

She looks glum as she slumps into the loveseat without taking off her coat. 'Yeah, I'm sorry I didn't call – I got a text from Nina this morning and … well, I just need to talk to someone. I hope you don't mind?'

'Don't be daft.' Eddie doesn't wait for an invitation but jumps onto her lap to nuzzle her neck. 'What was the text about?'

'What? Oh, some of the staff and students at St Hugh's are saying prayers for Phi in the college chapel after lunch today. Cal wants to go along.'

'Are you going to go?' I ask, handing her a mug of coffee.

'Yes. I think so. But that's not what I wanted to talk about.'

'Go on then. I'm a good listener.'

'How do you feel about Nina moving in with Cal?'

Gutted is my immediate reaction but I realise it won't do in the circumstances. 'Oh … you know. Nina clearly thinks she can help him. She's gone through a lot of grief therapy herself in the last year and I expect she'll be trying to help Cal with what she's learnt now.'

'But that's just it,' says Anna with urgency, leaning forward. 'She's not a therapist. She might know the right words to say but what's going to be the impact on her?'

'I know what you mean. I'm worried about that too.'

'I spoke to one of my tutors who trains volunteers for Samaritans – not mentioning names, just, you know, sounding his opinion out. He said that, in the abstract, he'd be very concerned if a badly grieving person was actually trying to counsel someone else. Especially in the unique circumstances where a loved one has been murdered.'

'I know,' I say. 'It could all have a regressive impact on Nina. But I'm not sure how we can tackle that.'

'Someone needs to talk to her,' says Anna firmly. 'It can't be healthy for her and Cal to be shut up on their own in his house.'

'I think I agree with you,' I say warily. 'But are you sure we aren't over-reacting because, well, frankly because we're jealous that they seem to have latched onto each other?'

Anna sips her coffee with both hands wrapped around the mug. Her evident misery doesn't prevent her from giving my question serious consideration. 'Not really,' she says finally. 'That might be true for you, Jack. But I'm not in love with Cal or anything. He was just a friend I bumped into occasionally in college. It's Nina I'm really worried about.'

'Me too.'

'Right then,' says Anna decisively. 'Let's see if one of us can get a chance to talk to her properly about this – alone. Without Cal. Shall I see you at the St Hugh's prayer service?'

I shrug. 'Well, I'm not particularly religious. But I haven't got anything else on.' And it would be nice to see Nina, I think to myself.

'We can walk over together if you like?'

We agree to meet up in town before Anna gives Eddie a parting cuddle and makes her way off the boat where she too is quickly swallowed up by the fog.

I spend the next couple of hours writing my article about Jane for the magazine. I still haven't shadowed her for a day, but I can't afford to spend any more time on it. I read it back. It's okay. It won't win any prizes, but at least it's more than a public relations puff for the police. It describes the wider issue of the constant battle with organised crime groups and Imani's personal testimony is a very powerful extra ingredient. I attach it to an email and send it to Jane, and then separately to Julia Goodfellow along with a recommendation for taking some photographs. There is something uncharacteristically lifeless about the head and shoulders shot of Jane in her uniform that has been provided by the force with the press release. It's as though the police photographer is too used to taking pictures of crime scenes and dead people.

Eddie mopes when he realises that he won't be coming out with me, but I don't imagine he'll be very welcome at a prayer service. I meet Anna at Folly Bridge and we walk slowly across town. The fog is much more dispersed on the busier streets where bright shopfronts leak rectangles of light from their large plate glass windows. I brief Anna as fully as I can about the strange goings-on at the inlet opposite *Jumping Jack Flash* and my morning visit from DCI Philpott. She listens attentively, but I can tell from her half-hearted questions that she is distracted and still worrying about Nina and Cal.

The St Hugh's college chapel is up a flight of stairs in the main building. It's a tall vaulted room painted in various shades of pink and green with an altar covered in a white cloth in front of a large arched window. A large pink and white organ, which looks like a slice of wedding cake, is burbling away gently on one side of the dark wooden pews, and I'm surprised to see that a sizeable congregation has already gathered. There is a moment's silence and then a small choir rises to its feet and begins to sing something mournful in Latin. As they are singing, Cal and Nina walk down the centre of the chapel, between the pews to a space that has been kept for them on the front row. Anna and I have squeezed in at the back and for one moment, I feel giddy as I watch the pair of them walk slowly past us, arm in arm. I experience some kind of perverse premonition that they are on their way to take their marriage vows. But their faces, white and serious, give the lie to this unwelcome image.

As the singing ceases, a chaplain appears in a splendid red and gold robe. He thanks everyone for coming on this Sunday to remember Ophelia and to extend their Christian love to her closest friends. He particularly welcomes Cal at this difficult time and says Ophelia's parents are in his thoughts too. My attention begins to wander as he urges us to our knees and begins to intone prayers in a slow singsong voice. I hear the door of the chapel squeak slightly and look across the aisle. It is the tall and stooping figure of Dr John Romaine. He pushes his wire-framed glasses back up onto the bridge of his nose and sidles apologetically into the rear pew. He pulls a kneeling cushion towards him and drops onto both knees. One hand covers his eyes and forehead, but I can still see his lips moving silently in a private prayer.

We are invited to stand and sing a hymn that is too modern for me to recognise. Then we sit and are asked to quietly summon our memories of Ophelia while the choir sing some more psalms in Latin. After about a minute, I see Romaine rise from his pew in a crouch, mouth an apology to the person next to him and creep towards the door.

'Back in a minute,' I whisper to Anna, and follow a few steps behind him.

'Dr Romaine. Can I have a quick word?' He is standing in the centre of the wide carpeted corridor outside the chapel and peers back at me with a puzzled look. The penny drops.

'Ah yes ... it's er, Mr Johnson, isn't it? Have I remembered your name correctly? You were with Miss McVeigh's American boyfriend.'

I close the distance between us. 'Yes, that's right. I came to see you with Cal, when Ophelia was still missing. Before we knew that she had been murdered.'

His thin beaky face blanches and worry frowns crease the front of his closely shaven head. 'Terrible business. Quite terrible. Of course, I have spoken to the police, but I could only tell them what I told you and her parents. Now, if you will excuse me, I must get back to my family for what remains of the weekend. I just felt that I ought to show my face, you know,' he says nodding at the chapel door and beginning to move away down the corridor.

I fall into step alongside him. 'I have a feeling the police will want to talk to you again quite soon.'

He stops and looks across at me. We are both roughly the same height. 'Why should they want to talk to me again?'

'Well. I think they'll be wondering why you're being ferried to a party on a houseboat with a lot of women – or girls – on it in the middle of night.' He looks at me in astonishment as he assimilates what I have said. 'Particularly when you were tutor to a murdered girl who seems to have had some connection with the same houseboat,' I press on.

Romaine looks as though he is going to vomit. His eyes are wide with sudden panic and his prominent Adam's apple is bobbing furiously as he tries to swallow. 'What? What do you mean? I don't know what you're talking about. The police haven't said anything to me about Ophelia and any houseboat. Now, please, leave me alone.'

He sets off fast now. He has chosen flight over fight and he's making for the stairs, his elbows flapping as he almost, but not quite, breaks into a run. I'm seriously tempted to rugby tackle him but continue to snap at his heels instead. 'I saw you, Romaine. I saw you being taken onto *Nirvana* last night and I saw you coming off it. So, come on. What d'you know about the Garden of Eden dating agency?'

This last question clearly strikes home as he darts another look of horror at me from over his shoulder. 'Damn you! Leave me alone. I told you, I've already spoken to the police.' As he says this, he pushes open a door off the corridor and slams it behind him. I hear a key turn in the lock. The door is unmarked apart from a number.

I amble back to the chapel. The academic couldn't have appeared more guilty and I wonder why the police haven't yet hauled him in for questioning. It's been a few hours since Philpott was told of our sighting during the night. Could the presence of another senior police officer in the boat be making them drag their heels? But it's a murder enquiry, for god's sake. Surely they'll be rigorously following up on what Jane and I have told them?

I can hear another subdued hymn from behind the chapel doors and slip back into my seat alongside Anna, who shoots me a curious look. The chaplain gives a final blessing and then moves forward to give Cal a hug. I watch the fiercely protective passion on Nina's face as this happens and, in that instant, I sense the absolute truth that the pair of them are now in some kind of relationship. The sudden realisation winds me and I sit back down, blowing hard as though someone has punched me hard in the solar plexus.

'Jack? Are you okay?' Anna has bent over and put a hand on my arm.

I look up and stare across the length of the chapel at Cal. He has broken free of the chaplain and his good looks are momentarily framed by the whiteness of the arched window behind him. Nina has now moved in to replace the chaplain and she is holding Cal tight. But he is easily a foot taller than her and his eyes look across the top of her short crop of hair. They fasten onto mine and we look at each other for what seems an eternity. Then he gently prises himself free from Nina and strides up the aisle towards me. His eyes are watering and red-rimmed and he appears deeply moved. I stand and automatically stretch out a hand, but he ignores it, steps inside my reach and puts both his hands around my shoulders.

'Hey, Jack. Thanks for coming, my friend. Thanks to you and to Anna for coming. Why don't you both come back to mine for a drink?'

I look questioningly at Nina who puts a hand on my arm. 'Yes. That would be nice. You've been a bit of a stranger recently, Jack.' I wonder, for a millisecond, if I detect a hint of guilt in her eyes as she says this. She must realise it is her who has been the stranger. But then the moment passes and I decide it is a look of pity rather than guilt.

CHAPTER TWENTY-FIVE

The fog is starting to spread itself more thinly now and the four of us walk the short distance to Cal's home in Jericho, where we sit around his coffee table. He pours a large glass of iced water with a slice of lemon for himself and Nina, but thankfully takes a bottle of Cloudy Bay from the fridge for me and Anna.

As Cal builds some kindling into a pyramid for a fire, I look around and register the small but significant signs that Nina has made herself at home. There is the book she was reading, split open and face down across the arm of an easy chair. I recognise the green silk scarf that her husband Alan gave her shortly before he went to Afghanistan and her carelessly discarded running shoes by the fireplace. Our walk has been largely silent – each of us lost in our own thoughts – and this is still the prevalent mood as we sit and sip our drinks.

Cal slumps back on the sofa next to Nina once the newspaper twists are flaring and the wood is crackling in the grate. 'Thanks again to you all for coming to the service. I felt very emotional when I saw how many had turned up.'

'It was lovely,' murmurs Nina.

'And once again, Jack. Thank you for loaning me Nina here in my time of need.'

I think we all register the word 'loaning' with its clear implication that at some time, she might be handed back. Did he mean to deliberately imply this? The look on Nina's face is unfathomable.

I cough. 'Yes, well, as Nina said previously. She's not mine to loan. She's very much her own woman.'

'Yes, Cal. You make me sound like a library book.' Then she leans across to Cal and whispers something discreetly in his ear. He looks slightly abashed and takes a drink of water to cover the moment. Then he suddenly puts both hands on his knees and straightens his long back. 'Well, life goes on, I guess!'

Anna seems to gulp in surprise at the suddenness of this comment. She looks from Cal to me and back again. However, Nina covers one of his hands with hers and gives him a look of profound encouragement.

'Nina's been talking me through the different stages of the grief process.'

Nina sips her water and looks at me. 'Denial, anger, bargaining, depression and finally acceptance.'

'She's persuaded me to make a real effort to get back in the saddle.' Nina is happy to hand out advice which she has struggled to take on board for herself, I think sourly as Cal goes on. 'So tomorrow I'm going to start working on my PhD again. I'll stay off training for another few days but I'm going to fly the balloon first thing tomorrow. Nina thinks it'll be a good thing, to kind of rise above all the misery and get my head up above the clouds. See the bigger perspective.'

Nina beams at us all. 'It's a good idea, don't you think?'

'The weather forecast is really good. Unusual high pressure for this time of year, decent visibility and stable light winds of less than five miles an hour,' Cal says. 'If we go at the crack of dawn it should be fine.'

'We?' I ask. 'Are we invited?'

'Why not?' Cal seems to be transformed by his enthusiasm. 'I'm booked in for an event at Blenheim and I could really do with a practice flight before then. The conditions are exceptional, and you'll be completely safe. I've flown a lot in the States and it's my own balloon. I had it shipped over. I know how it behaves. We could have an early morning picnic over the Oxfordshire countryside.' He pronounces the word in four syllables, Ox-ford-shy-er.

'That sounds amazing,' says Anna.

Nina is grinning too. 'You see. Just what the doctor ordered. You sound much more cheerful already. Jack? Are you up for it?'

I check to make sure she is serious about the invitation. 'Sure,' I say, surprised. 'Actually, I've been asked to do a feature about the Blenheim Palace balloon event for the magazine, so it'll be good practice for me too. I might learn enough from Cal to sound as though I know what I'm talking about.'

'Wow. This is great!' says Cal. 'I've got two pals from the boat who can be our land crew. They can follow us in my car and pick us up when we land. I can't get more than five in my car, though, so another set of wheels would be handy. We can fit one more person in for the flight – and an extra pair of hands would help us with unpacking the balloon before the launch and handling the rig on the ground. Any ideas? I guess I can ask someone else from the boat.'

'Maybe Jack's new friend would like to come?' says Nina. I give her a questioning look. 'The policewoman, Jack ... what's her name. Jane, is it?'

Nina is smiling but her black eyes are watching me coolly. Anna too has turned to look at me closely. I don't know what to feel. Is Nina being deliberately provocative? She has only met Jane briefly, on board the boat, and the police officer was only introduced as someone I was writing about. Why would she suddenly invite Jane on the flight? Perhaps she has sensed something? Or perhaps she has learned something from someone – maybe Anna mentioned my early morning appearance after a night with a 'friend'? Her suggestion has come out of the blue and seems designed to stir things up. Okay, I think to myself, two can play at that game. 'Yes, sure. If it's okay with Cal, I'll ask Jane ... DS Henry.'

'Fine by me,' says Cal smiling broadly. 'This is all part of my therapy and I'm completely in Nina's hands for that.'

'I'll just give her a call then.'

'Rendezvous at 6.45 a.m sharp!' calls Cal as I leave the room to make the call. I head towards the rear of the house and end up in a small utility room with an old-fashioned drying rack attached to the ceiling by a pulley system. The proximity of his and her underwear on the rack strengthens my resolve to give as good as I get.

'Jane. It's Jack. Hi. Look, it turns out Cal is a hot air balloonist. Conditions are ideal tomorrow apparently and he's asked if you'd like an early morning flight with us. Him, you, me, Anna and Nina. It's a crack of dawn start – you'll need to pick me up at six-thirty – but we should be back down in plenty of time for you to go to work. Breakfast in the sky – interested? ... Great! Wrap up warm, it's going to be freezing up there ... Okay, yes ... I'll text you the rendezvous point. See you tomorrow.'

'She's up for it,' I say, re-entering the room.

'Excellent!' Cal replies enthusiastically.

'Oh good,' says Nina, with no detectable sign of sarcasm.

I am finding the atmosphere exhausting, however, and my late night will now be compounded by a very early start tomorrow morning. So, I drain my second glass of wine and stand up. 'I think I need to get back to Eddie. Thanks for the drink, Cal.'

'Oh, do bring him tomorrow,' urges Nina. 'I have been missing him.' Him, not me.

'He can't fly with us, obviously,' warns Cal, 'but he can travel in the cars with the support team and have a good run round at the launch field. Get Jane to meet us in the railroad station car park at Islip. We'll be leaving at 6.30 a.m. – so we'll see you fifteen minutes later?'

We shake hands. 'This is good of you, Cal.' I look across at Anna. 'Do you want me to walk you back?'

'Why don't you stay here with us for the night?' Nina says quickly to Anna. 'Then you'll be here for the early start. You can go in the spare room.'

'Sure,' says Cal. 'You can borrow one of my shirts to sleep in. That's what Nina does.'

Anna readily agrees and looks happy as she pours herself another glass of wine and settles back comfortably. I wonder if she will have an opportunity to warn her aunt about the potential consequences of her untrained grief counselling. The front door closes behind me and, as I begin to walk back through the streets of Jericho, I wonder to myself exactly how many spare rooms there are in Cal's house.

CHAPTER TWENTY-SIX

There is just an hour of daylight left as I make my way back to *Jumping Jack Flash*. Instead of following the route of the canal, I cut into the city centre this time and begin to head back along the straight run of wide streets that will eventually lead to Folly Bridge. I pass between the sides of the Ashmolean Museum and St John's College and dart across the street in front of the mid-road island which is shared by the Martyrs Memorial and St Mary Magdalen Church. It is Sunday afternoon and the car traffic is unusually light. As I begin to cross the next road junction, I glance to my left along the aptly named Broad Street and see a familiar figure. It's not hard to recognise the tall thin frame of a man with distinctive straggly grey hair framing his bald spot.

John Turner has just emerged from the large arch at the centre of Balliol College. He is trundling a metal wheelbarrow in front of him which makes a prosaic contrast with the honeycombed stone and gothic grandeur of the building he is leaving. The frontage of the college with its tall central tower flanked by pointed gable roofs makes a haughty statement to passers-by. I detour and close the distance between us until he registers me calling his name and looks up. His dark deep-set eyes squint in recognition as he lowers the barrow's handles and straightens up. As I get closer, I can see that the scratched and dented scoop contains an assortment of gardening tools.

'Hi there, John, I thought it was you.'

'Now then, Mr Johnson. How's that little dog of yours?'

'Fine thanks. No sign of Tod today? You're off your beaten track.'

He wipes his large bent nose with the sleeve of his donkey coat. 'Aye, I do a bit of extra work in college gardens at weekends. Just on my way back to *Gipsy*.'

'That's quite a trek with a barrow. Would you like a hand?'

'Nay. I can manage. But I'm happy to have your company if you're going back to your boat.'

I fall into step alongside him and we turn back onto the main drag of Cornmarket Street with its shops and shopping centres. The wheelbarrow is an incongruous sight and there are tuts and heavy sighs as the pedestrians coming in the opposite direction are forced to become a human bow wave on either side of Turner.

As we go, the Yorkshireman surprises me by abandoning his usual taciturn manner and waxes lyrical about the university's gardens. 'It's amazing,' he enthuses. 'People walk past these colleges with their stone walls and they've got no idea what's inside. Lovely gardens they are, private Fellow's gardens, quadrangles with their lawns and flower beds, orchards, lakes, meadows, even deer parks!' He pauses to straighten the handle of a rake. 'You look at early maps of the city,' he continues. 'Full of green spaces – even cornfields – right here in city centre. And a lot of it is still here,' he says proudly. 'And I help keep it nice and tidy like, for a bit of extra brass.'

I hadn't really considered this aspect of Oxford before, but now I realise Turner must be part of a small maintenance army employed by the colleges. 'What's your favourite college garden?'

He stops and puts the barrow down to give this question serious consideration and before he has the chance to protest, I nip in, pick it up and begin wheeling it in the same direction. He quickly catches me up. 'Aye, well that's a very good question, Mr Johnson. The wisteria in the cloister at Magdalen is a bit special and there's a nice herbaceous border, rudbeckias and climbing roses. But I reckon me favourite spot is the orchard at Worcester, next to Provost's Lodgings. Lovely varieties and they make their own apple and pear juice! I do a bit of mowing and pruning in there when they need me.'

Turner resumes control of his barrow at Folly Bridge after declining the offer of a quick pint at the Head of the River. 'Nay thanks, full of students gassing away – and their beer's full of bloody gas too.'

There is an occasional jogger or dog walker on the riverside path, but we have it largely to ourselves. 'Do you know the houseboat, *Nirvana*? It's on the inlet near our mooring, on the opposite bank.' We are passing the row of college boathouses across the river, so I add, 'I think it was previously a college boat.'

'Aye,' he nods. 'Fancied that spot meself when it came up for auction. Would save me moving *Gipsy* every time the bloody racing is on. But it went for silly money.'

'D'you know who bought it?' I ask quickly.

'Not a clue. It's hardly ever used. Expect they'll wait for a bit and then build a bloody fancy house there. But it'll need to be on stilts!' He laughs bitterly.

We part at Donnington Bridge, where he heads off to secure his tools in the shed at the Kidneys and I walk on under Strode Bridge towards *Jumping Jack Flash*. Sure enough, there is no sign of life on *Nirvana* as I pass by.

CHAPTER TWENTY-SEVEN

Thwack. Thwack. Thwack.

Connolly's gloved fists are remorselessly pounding the punchbag hanging in front of him. It is a state-of-the-art Mixed Martial Arts bag, leather and stuffed with padding around a hollow core that has been filled with water. He has been doing this for a solid hour now. Occasionally he alternates with a vicious roundhouse kick, lifting his knee while pivoting on his supporting foot and swinging around in a rapid semi-circle. But he always makes sure it is his shin rather than his foot which bludgeons the bag. It gives much greater potential for causing damage without hurting himself. Sometimes he aims for his long-suffering opponent's inner thigh, sometimes his outer thigh and occasionally he stretches higher for the ribcage and even the head. Sweat is dripping down his bare torso and he is breathing hard.

His work ethic and levels of aggression are well known to the other members of the private health club near his flat in Wapping. The well-paid young city workers who go there also know about his UFC career. As a result, they find themselves gravitating to his spot in the gym where they stand quietly to watch him work out. They watch his cords of muscle and sinew tighten and relax as he goes through his routines. But there is nothing routine about his exercise on this particular Sunday evening.

Today Connolly is a spitting, snarling ball of tightly compressed energy and he has been working himself in to a frenzy. Thwack. Thwack. Thwack. If the punchbag was a person, it would have died of blunt force trauma long before now. He stops to take a few deep swallows of water, his head tipped right back. Then he glowers at the small circle of on-lookers around him. 'Piss off.' They disperse quickly. Sometimes he has been known to answer questions or explain the finer points of a muay ti technique, but this evening he is in a dangerous mood. He resumes pounding the bag without mercy.

His ugly temper is the result of a text and a phone call that he received from Oxford earlier that same evening. The text informed him that police officers had been sniffing around the boat and asking local people if they knew who owned it. Then Marcie had phoned. She had been visited by the police about the dead girl and questioned about her work for the agency. They had been prepared for that. He knew Marcie wouldn't give them anything to work with. But how did they make any kind of connection between the girl and *Nirvana*? Thwack. And what if the police were now bugging Marcie's phone? Could they do that? He was livid at her for ringing him on his mobile. Thwack. He would need to throw his phone in the Thames on the way home and activate one of the new ones that he had waiting in a drawer at his flat. Thwack. And he will need to return to Oxford tomorrow and have a proper face-to-face conversation with her. But what if they were watching her house or office? No, the Thames Valley plod wouldn't be that clever ... would they?

He steps back from the bag and imagines it is his business partner. Bang. Bang. His shin cracks into it, twice in rapid succession. He could bloody well throttle her. Two young men, newly arrived at the gym, have wandered over to watch Connolly's second bout of exercise but he is oblivious to their presence and now he is muttering to himself as he attacks the bag. The first group of spectators has dispersed to various pieces of equipment, but they are all continuing to watch Connolly warily. Some consider whether they ought to warn the newcomers but decide it's safer to mind their own business.

Connolly wipes the sweat out of his eyes with a tattooed forearm and steps back from the bag, his chest heaving and his mouth gulping in air. He will not allow his personal wealth creation plan to be derailed. Full stop.

He takes a few steps backwards and then suddenly he accelerates forward into a flying kick so that his body is horizontal in the air and both his bare feet smash into the bag at head height. He would never have used the taekwondo move in a real tournament, but his ability to deliver it reassures him about his mental preparation and athletic condition. It is a kick that took him several months to perfect and it is considered to be one of the most difficult and advanced techniques to perform in martial arts. The two young men watching him are open-mouthed and one of them swears in admiration.

Connolly puts both hands on his waist and struts towards them until his face is barely inches from the one who swore. The young man flinches but stays rooted to the spot. The entire gym falls silent as the running and rowing machines come to a stop.

'SHIIIITTT!' he screams at the top of his voice into the other's face. The man staggers backwards, loses his balance and falls onto his backside on the floor where he sits, legs spread-eagled and looking up at Connolly with a look of naked fear on his face.

Connolly stoops to take up his bottle, fills his mouth and then directs a stream of water onto the head of the young man in front of him. He stands there, his legs braced apart, and his arms slightly bent forward in challenge. He is willing the young man to launch himself at him. The second onlooker yanks his friend to his feet and pulls him away. Connolly's eyes sweep the gym and he laughs. 'Posh twats!' Then he turns and saunters to the changing room, in the kind of cock-of-the-walk strut that he used for entering the fighting arena. He imagines that he can hear the roar of the crowd and his ear-splitting entrance anthem and, for one second, he admits to himself how much he misses it.

He showers and changes quickly, hurls his phone into the Thames on the way home and pours himself a small vodka and tonic before sitting down to think some more. He mentally ticks off The Principles of War Applied to Business. He has read and memorised large parts of the book by Peter Drucker who studied the military leadership principles of Carl Von Clausewitz, a Prussian who fought in the Russian Army against Napoleon in the early nineteenth century. He sips the chilled drink and decides he will focus on the principles of security, surprise and simplicity. He cannot afford to permit his opponents to acquire an unexpected advantage. So, he will decisively shift the balance of combat and momentum by striking the enemy in a totally unexpected way. It will be a simple and uncomplicated act. He has resolved what he needs to do. *Mens sana in corpore sano*. The motto is tattooed on one of his biceps. A healthy mind in a healthy body. His work in the gym has addressed his bodily needs and helped him to clear his mind and get his thoughts in order. He has decided what his next move will be. He drains his glass and goes to look for his car keys.

CHAPTER TWENTY-EIGHT

It's early evening. There are still lingering wisps of fog clinging wraithlike to the surface of the river. I feel exhausted after our early morning observations of the goings-on at *Nirvana*, DCI Philpott's visit and the chapel service, not to mention the emotional strain of the tension between me and Nina and my mixed feelings about the nights shared with Jane. I crash out onto the bed and sleep for a couple of hours before waking at 7.30 p.m. The prospect of an early morning start for the balloon trip sends me briefly to the galley for some fish fingers and beans and then back to bed after a brief stroll with Eddie. However, I find it difficult to fall asleep again as my thoughts swirl around and about the same people – Jane, Nina, Anna, Cal and poor dead Ophelia. I also feel some regret about tackling Romaine during the chapel service. I had acted purely on instinct – and the man had looked genuinely terrified. But I had seen him being ferried onto *Nirvana* at night. That wasn't the action of a wholly innocent man. Nor was his reaction to my questions. Nevertheless, I am uneasy about the encounter.

My thoughts are interrupted by laughter and loud music on the water and I sit up to peer through my porthole. A large tourist boat of some kind is sliding past, heading down river. All of the windows are lit and there is obviously some kind of party taking place on board. It's an unusual sight for a Sunday night in January, but the long cruiser slides past before I can properly take it in. Eventually, the slight rocking of my berth helps me to fall into a light slumber and at some stage I sense Eddie circling to make a nest in my duvet and finally collapsing at my feet.

Suddenly, we are both jolted awake as the interior of the boat is filled with light and noise and there is a discernible jolt as something collides with the side of *Jumping Jack Flash*. I scramble to look at my watch. Ten o'clock. There is another boat immediately alongside mine and its lights are shining directly through the porthole above my berth. Dance music is playing loudly. I look out at a large rectangular window on the other craft that has appeared opposite. It is brightly lit but steamed up. As I watch, several hands begin to clear the steam from the inside. And, as the moisture is wiped away by outstretched palms and napkins, I begin to realise the people connected to the hands are all stark naked. They are waving at me and grinning and talking excitedly to each other. A cluster of men and women with red faces, pink flesh and bare brown nipples point back at me excitedly through the window. There are more people clustered behind them who seem to be in a similar state of undress. What the fuck is going on? Who are these nude people who have clamped themselves to my boat in the middle of the night? Eddie is barking madly at the sight and I know how he feels.

I scramble to pull a dressing gown over my own nakedness and make for the stern hatchway as quickly as I can. It's locked but eventually I pull the cover back and yank the doors inwards. By the time I make it onto the stern platform, the boat, which is much longer, higher and wider than mine, is pulling back out into the middle of the river and heading towards the city. All of its moist windows are ablaze with light and a confusion of bare human flesh can be seen through all of them. The sound of the chatter and the music slowly fades away as the boat moves off into the darkness. This is surreal, like some weird kind of dream.

Then there is a cough from the bow of *Jumping Jack Flash* and I realise there is a naked man standing on the boat's roof, about 55 feet away from me. One of his hands is holding the handles of a shoulder bag and the other is clamping a white linen napkin in front of his groin.

'Hi Jack!' says Will. 'I bet you weren't expecting me!'

It is William Simpson, my oldest and closest friend, who has been letting me down regularly since our days together at boarding school. He begins to make his way gingerly along the roof.

'Bloody hell, I'm freezing my balls off.'

'Well, I suppose that's not surprising. It's January and, just in case you haven't noticed, you haven't got any clothes on,' I say. 'Hello, Will. What are you doing here?'

His choirboy face breaks into laughter. His strong-shouldered build, flat belly and lustrous curls never seem to age and help ensure that he stays in regular employment as an occasional film, television actor and womaniser. 'It's a long story... but a very, very good one,' he says. 'Let me in first. I need a drink – the stronger the better.' Having reached the hatchway, he hurls the napkin into the river, climbs down and precedes me into the boat where Eddie hurls himself up and into Will's arms. 'Hey little buddy, great to see you too,' he says as the dog tries to wash my friend's face with his tongue.

I fetch him my second-best dressing gown and he huddles close to the solid fuel stove, which I feed before opening up its vents to get it roaring again. Then I pour two large whiskies and we sit opposite each other on the armchairs.

'Cheers, matey,' he says, emptying the glass and holding it out for a refill. 'Christ, I needed that. How are you?'

'Never mind how I am. It's gone ten on a Sunday night in Oxford and you have arrived without notice and bollock naked on the roof of my boat. What the hell is going on, Will?'

'Okay,' he sighs theatrically. 'I suppose I owe you an explanation.' He grins, showing his perfectly photogenic teeth.

'I presume there's a woman involved?' I say, sipping my drink. Will is the same age as me and has never married, but he never has any shortage of female admirers and seems to develop problematic short-term relationships at almost every theatre or venue where he performs.

'Yes,' he says, 'Well ... sort of. But not in the way you mean.'

'Go on then.'

'Okay, so a while back, just before we met up in Bath, I changed my agent. I'd been unhappy with the old one for a while. He wasn't getting me any film work and that's the stuff that really pays.'

'Maybe you're just getting too old?'

'Piss off, Jack, you're the one that's showing your age. Anyway, this new agent is a woman and one thing sort of led to another.'

'So predictable.' I shake my head sadly at him.

'Well, everything ticks along fine until her husband, who's a banker, a right banker, finds out. He's loaded and gives her an ultimatum – so yours truly gets evicted from the marital bed.'

'And suddenly you don't have an agent?'

'No. That's the weird bit. She still wanted to represent me. But I had a better offer from a much bigger agency who'd heard the gossip and so I jumped onto their books. Well, she was mighty pissed off and we had a bit of a barney over a restaurant lunch. Drinks were thrown – at me – and someone told *Private Eye*. They ran a paragraph about it. *Ugandan Relations* were mentioned and, of course, she was very embarrassed and the hubby was a bit cross.' Will shrugs. 'I thought that was the end of it.'

'You had your big new agency looking after you?'

'Exactly. Then I got a phone call from her last week. She was begging me to do one last job for her. It had come in just before I jumped ship and it was a favour for a friend. And it was going to pay extremely well for just one night's work.'

'On a boat in Oxford?'

'Exactly. The Oxford League of Naturalists wanted an actor to read excerpts from literature about fauna and flora during their winter dinner cruise on the Thames. I wouldn't even have to learn any lines. Money for old rope. Or so I thought.'

The penny drops. 'Only they weren't naturalists, they were naturists!'

Will shakes his head at me in wonderment. 'The bitch stitched me up. I bet she's leaking the story to *Private Eye* even as we sit here. I had no idea. I got on the boat and everything seemed normal. The head guy showed me where I'd be performing – a little stage right in the middle of the boat. Then, straight after we set off, they all started taking their kit off. Every single one of them. Even the skipper and the crew. Of course, I had to do the same. I'm no stranger to nudity in the theatre, Jack, but Christ, even I didn't know where to look. They were all served a fish and chip supper with mushy peas and then the DJ invited me to go centre stage. I start to read them the stuff I'd prepared, and it all kicks off. There's booing and slow handclapping and they're throwing half-eaten bread rolls at me. They've all been drinking for a solid couple of hours. And I'm standing starkers in the middle of the boat reading something about a woman training a bloody goshawk. It turns out I'd been booked to read a selection of great romantic scenes from literature – smut in other words.'

I am roaring with laughter. And my friend is grinning. He knows he has an anecdote for the ages. No doubt it will be polished and embellished over time, but I have been the first person for him to rehearse it on.

'So then I look out of the window and bugger me, it's *Jumping Jack Flash*. I'd recognise that picture of your jester anywhere. And I suddenly remember that you'd been planning to come to Oxford after Bath. I race to the skipper with my bag and promise him £50 if he'll drop me off. He's killing himself with laughter, but he moves over close enough for me to step onto your roof ... and you know the rest.' Now we are both laughing, tears streaming down our faces. 'I have never been so happy to see your ugly mug in my life. More drink needed please.'

I top him up, but he notices when I don't do the same to my glass and raises a questioning eyebrow.

'I'm due out at the crack of dawn tomorrow,' I explain. 'I have an appointment with Nina and a hot-air balloon at six-thirty a.m.'

He sits forwards eagerly with one eyebrow arched. 'Ah... the lovely Mrs Angelina Wilde. How is she?'

It's a simple enough three-word question but I spend the next hour answering it. I tell my old friend about everything that has happened since I arrived in Oxford while he slowly demolishes the remainder of my whisky. He only tries to interrupt when I confess to him about my trysts with Jane, but I shush him and continue.

Finally, I sit back and close my eyes briefly. 'And so it's all a bit of a mess really. There's a murderer on the loose. Nina is living with Captain America. I've slept with a Detective Sergeant, twice, and I think there's some kind of floating brothel on an historic barge across the river. *Plus ça change*.'

Now it is Will's turn to shake his head in utter disbelief. Then he breaks into a grin. 'Hey, at least there's another book in it!' I narrow my eyes at him. 'Okay,' he says holding up his hands placatingly. 'Just a joke. I'm starving. Got anything to eat?'

I put my remaining fish fingers under the grill, and he eats them greedily with four slices of bread. How the hell does he maintain his washboard stomach? However, the makeshift supper doesn't prevent him from continuing to cross examine me between mouthfuls.

'So. Nina and Cal? Are they an item?'

'I honestly don't know. Maybe not physically yet – but mentally, yes, I think so. She seems pretty smitten by him.'

'And it's killing you?' asks Will seriously.

'You know how I feel about her.'

'Okay. So that's the reason you slept with Jane.' It's a statement rather than a question but I refuse to accept Will as a credible agony uncle or relationship counsellor.

'Let's just leave it, Will. I need to turn in.'

'Hey. I'm out of here early too. Maybe not quite as early as you. I've got to be at the Old Vic for an audition by nine-thirty. But all I'm saying is that you and Nina were made for each other. Remember our trip to Bradford on Avon? She told me that if she could ever love anyone again, it was you. Don't lose faith, my friend. Don't fret about Jane. But don't tell Nina about her either. It'll all work out okay. I promise.'

CHAPTER TWENTY-NINE

Jane's little car pulls up at one end of the bridge just before six-thirty a.m. The morning is cold and frosty, but the sky is largely clear of any cloud or mist and there is only the gentlest of breezes as promised. We are both wrapped up in several layers of clothing and I am wearing a pair of tight-fitting jogging bottoms under a pair of thick cord trousers. It's still too early for the morning rush-hour traffic to be queueing to enter the city, but we are heading in the other direction anyway and make rapid progress.

I yawn and try to rub some life into my eyes. 'God, it's early.' At least I slept deeply after my late evening with Will, but my batteries are still far from fully charged.

Jane seems to be a little more alert than me. 'I've never been up in a balloon before. It'll be interesting.'

'Nor me. I'm supposed to be writing a piece about the Blenheim Winter Balloon Lift-Off, so it'll give me an idea of what to expect. Were you okay with my piece about you?'

'Yes thanks. It was fine. I'm pleased you moved the focus away from me and onto the larger OCG issue.'

'Okay. Well, let's wait and see what the editor thinks.'

We lapse into a comfortable silence and Jane leans forward to put the radio on. It's BBC Radio Oxford and we are just in time to hear the news jingle that tees up the short half-hourly news summary.

'Good morning. A prominent Oxford academic, Dr John Romaine, has been found dead at St Hugh's College. Dr Romaine, a married

father of four who was an expert in medieval history, is believed to have fallen from the roof of a tower at the college in St Margaret's Road yesterday evening. Police are continuing their inquiries into what happened. In other news ...'

'What the –?' Jane signals and immediately pulls over. A horn blares in outrage as another car whips past us from behind.

I am stunned. Did Romaine commit suicide? I spoke to him just after two o'clock. Did the police interview him afterwards? If they did, and they released him, killing himself sounds like a pretty convincing admission of guilt.

'Suicide?' I ask Jane.

'Wait a minute.' She is texting someone. 'I'm just asking my friend who works for Philpott. I hope he's up by now.' A ping indicates that a reply has come through very quickly. 'Phew. They already know about it. Of course they do. Oh, wait a sec.' She reads on. 'They had arranged to speak to him again later this morning, at 10.30 a.m.' She puts her phone down and pulls back out into the traffic.

'But that's crazy!' I say. 'Why the hell didn't they see him yesterday? It was early morning when you told Philpott about Romaine being on *Nirvana*.'

'He obviously didn't think it was as significant as you did,' says Jane. She is very matter of fact about it.

'I wonder if Romaine left a note?'

Jane turns to look at me. 'Jack, it's none of your business, remember? You've been warned off – and so have I.'

I am about to reply but break off when I see we are already pulling into the car park outside a small railway station. Cal's Jaguar is waiting with the engine running and vapour is coming from the twin exhausts. It has a trailer behind it on which is strapped a balloon basket and a big glass fibre box. His hand waves out of the driver's window and he immediately sets off, with us following closely behind.

The take-off site is a grassy field on a farm a few miles away where there are no crops growing and no livestock grazing. Nina, Anna and Cal pile out of the car along with two other tall and powerfully built young men. Cal introduces them as Ben and Simon and looks around with satisfaction. 'Great. It's a great spot and the weather is just fine. But it'll be cold up there. I hope you've got some layers on! I've already spoken to the farmer. Come on, let's get this thing unloaded.' The sky is lightening but it's still half an hour until sunrise so Cal leaves his engine running and his full-beam headlights on to help with the operation.

Eddie charges happily in and out of the hedge around the edge of the field after giving Nina an enthusiastic greeting. Cal strides confidently around issuing instructions and stepping in himself to help with the unloading of the basket. He climbs easily into it, pulls a lever to check the propane-powered burners are firing reliably and then we all tip it onto its side. Next, the enormous green balloon fabric is pulled out onto the ground. He positions us around the envelope to spread it flat in a sequence of co-ordinated movements. It's all made much easier thanks to the muscle power of Cal and his two rowing friends. When it is flat, Cal directs a large fan into it, filling it with cold air. The size of the huge sack becomes ever more impressive as it inflates. Next he directs a steady flame from two gas-fired burner nozzles into the open mouth of the balloon, heating up the cold air inside. Slowly, it starts to move into a vertical position, tipping the basket upright at the same time. A rope is anchoring it to Cal's tow bar for the moment. The entire process has taken less than half an hour. Cal looks supremely confident, but it seems a strange thing to rely on just hot air and fabric to prevent you plummeting thousands of feet back to earth. I try to give Anna a confident smile, but she is looking a little pale and nervous too.

'Okay,' says Cal. 'Jane, give your car keys to Simon and he can follow Ben who will be tracking us. Eddie can go in the back of my car. We'll stay in touch by walkie-talkie. Climb in, everyone.'

He helps the three women take up their positions in the basket and I manage to scramble in, clumsily but unaided. Cal, Jane and I have all got a quarter of the basket each and Nina and Anna are sharing their compartment.

'How high will we be going?' asks Anna.

'Oh, around a couple of thousand feet,' says Cal. 'You'll love it. The amazing thing is how quiet it is when I'm not using the burners. I've seen some wonderful wildlife at home because they're not scared off by a balloon. And, of course, we're much closer to the ground than we would be in a plane. You'll get some great views and it's very peaceful.'

'And how far will we travel, do you think?' I ask.

Cal shrugs. 'That kind of depends on the wind speed. But the main factor is finding a good landing spot. We'll need somewhere like this. No crops. No livestock. And with a gate near a road so the cars can easily get to us. And if the farmer is pointing a gun up at us, it's probably not a good idea to land either.' Anna looks shocked and Cal laughs. 'That's a joke, Anna. They're usually fine about it. Especially if you give them a little financial token of gratitude.'

Cal signals to his ground crew to untie us. They coil the rope neatly and stow it in our pilot's segmented quarter of the crowded basket. He pulls on a lever to send long blasts of more hot air up into the canopy above us. Then, almost without realising it, we are off the ground and rising gently into the early morning daylight.

'Oh my gosh!' says Nina. Jane grins at me and gives me a thumbs up. Anna's knuckles are white as she grips the top of the basket on both sides.

The whoosh of the burners eventually becomes shorter and less prolonged and the English countryside drifts past below us; fields, hedgerows, copses and woods, houses and their gardens and the occasional pond or swimming pool. We are all transfixed. Even Anna is peering gingerly over the side now. Everyone is wrapped up well in gloves, scarves and hats and it isn't as cold as I had first feared.

'Look, there,' says Cal pointing. We can all see a russet-coloured fox trotting happily along the edge of a field. It has the corpse of a rabbit hanging limply in its mouth. 'You wouldn't see that from a plane or a helicopter,' adds Cal happily. But the sudden sight of death reminds me with a jolt of the morning's radio news bulletin. We have been so preoccupied with the business of the balloon launch that I have barely given it a second thought. But, of course, Cal deserves to know about it. Perhaps they already do?

'Did you hear the news this morning?' Cal shakes his head and Nina looks mildly annoyed, as though I am going to spoil the balloon ride with inconsequential stuff about some new virus outbreak or a ministerial resignation. Jane gives me a warning look, but I decide to press ahead. 'It's Ophelia's tutor. The one we met. Dr Romaine. He was found dead at St Hugh's yesterday evening. It appears that he fell from the college roof. That's all they're saying for the moment.'

'Woah! You're kidding me!' says Cal. Nina and Anna are both shaking their heads in disbelief. 'Do you think it was an accident?'

'Unlikely. Why would a college lecturer be on the roof of the college tower? Suicide, I would have thought. It'll be interesting to hear whether he left a note.'

'Do you think ...?' begins Nina. We are all thinking the same thing, but no one wants to say it.

'Do I think he killed Ophelia and then himself in a fit of remorse?' I immediately realise this sounds unnecessarily blunt. 'I'm sorry, Cal. Was that what you wanted to ask Nina?'

Nina has reached across the basket to put a hand on Cal's arm. 'Surely, if that was the case, he'd leave some kind of note. Some kind of confession?' she says.

'Maybe. Maybe not. Maybe he just thought the police were closing in on him and he took the easy way out.'

'But why would he think the police might be closing in on him?' asks Cal, staring at me in total bemusement.

I sense that we may be starting to descend. 'Don't forget you're supposed to be flying this thing.' I give a false little laugh to try to indicate that I'm not serious, but he immediately checks the horizon and gives a long blast on the burner. When he finishes, he turns to me again.

'Why would the police be closing in on him?' he repeats.

'Because we saw him going to a late-night party on a houseboat full of girls that's moored opposite *Jumping Jack Flash*.'

'What?' says Nina. 'When did this happen? Why haven't you told us about this before now, Jack? And who is "we"?'

'Jane and I saw it on Saturday night. We were staking it out after I saw the same thing on Friday night with Hugh Spencer. A bunch of women were dropped off at the houseboat opposite. Then Romaine and two other men were delivered via the river, in a smaller boat. There was some kind of party. Jane told DCI Philpott all about it. And I'm telling you now because I haven't really seen anything of you. It didn't seem like a good time to mention it yesterday after the service.'

Nina looks at me angrily but says nothing.

'But how does that have anything to do with Phi?' asks Cal. He looks utterly bemused.

'I found something in Ophelia's room which seemed to suggest she knew the name and the location of the houseboat. Then I found something from the boat that connected it to a dating agency in town called Garden of Eden. Apparently Ophelia did some work for this agency in December. The police found this out from her bank statements.'

'Jack!' protests Jane. 'That's confidential information.'

But I am getting into my stride now. No one else seems to be joining up the dots here, or they are doing so very slowly. And I confess to feeling angry at Nina's reaction so far. 'So that potentially connects Ophelia and her tutor at St Hugh's with some dubious parties on a houseboat and a so-called dating agency.'

Cal yanks on the burner for a minute or so and it is impossible for any conversation to be heard. But when he finishes, he turns to me angrily. 'So, what exactly are you suggesting, Jack?'

'I don't know any more than you. But I can make some guesses. Maybe Ophelia and her tutor were having some kind of affair?'

'No,' he says vehemently. 'That's not even remotely possible.'

'Okay,' I say. 'Unlikely, I agree. In which case perhaps he propositioned her, she rejected him, and it all turned nasty. Or perhaps the dating agency is actually an escort agency. If it's organising parties and bringing middle-aged men to meet women in the dead of night by river, it doesn't exactly sound respectable, does it? We know Ophelia was working for Garden of Eden and she knew the houseboat was called *Nirvana* and where it was moored. So maybe she met him as one of their escorts?'

'NO!' Cal is shouting now. 'You take that back immediately.' He is poking his forefinger at me. 'Phi wasn't some kind of hooker! She did some shifts for them as a secretary because she needed the money and that was all.'

Nina looks furious, and Anna is looking aghast at me. Jane just shakes her head. I've overstepped, and I know it.

'Look, I'm sorry, Cal. I'm just thinking out loud,' I say, apologetically. 'We don't know what the truth of Ophelia's murder is yet. But Romaine probably killed himself last night and there must have been a very good reason.'

Cal still looks upset and angry with me. 'There's no way Phi would have had anything to do with parties on that barge.'

'Apologise, Jack,' demands Nina.

I ignore her. 'Maybe not. But her tutor, the dear departed doctor, did – even though he denied it to me yesterday.'

'What d'you mean?' demands Jane immediately. 'When did you see Romaine yesterday?'

I look at her levelly and take a deep breath. 'I saw him come into the college chapel during the prayer service for Ophelia.' Cal is shaking his head in disbelief. 'It's true,' I say, and Anna gives a slight nod of her head to confirm what I'm saying. 'But he left quite quickly afterwards, and I followed him. I challenged him about his night-time parties on the river. But he just denied it and ran away.'

Now Jane is staring at me in horror. 'What? You are fucking kidding me, Jack! You'd been warned to stay away from this murder investigation and instead you blunder up to one of the key suspects and tip him off. And now he's dead! Brilliant. Utterly bloody marvellous. Philpott is going to eat you alive.'

'I thought the police would have already spoken to him,' I say defensively. 'They'd had all morning. I had no idea they would wait until after the weekend.'

'No,' snaps Jane. 'But that's what happened, isn't it? So you had already told him what it was all about.'

'In which case,' says Nina quietly, twisting the knife, 'if he killed himself, you're the one to blame.' This had been my immediate thought when I heard the radio news bulletin but it hurts a lot to hear Nina say it out loud.

'Nice going, Jack,' says Cal.

'It was a spur of the moment thing,' I admit quietly. 'I saw him leaving the chapel and so I just set off after him.'

'And you told him what *exactly*?' demands Jane. 'That he'd been spotted going onto *Nirvana*?'

'And that there was some connection between *Nirvana* and Ophelia,' I continue. 'And that the police would be speaking to him again.'

'Oh, that's just brilliant.'

'There could be underage girls on that boat,' I shoot back angrily. 'I thought it was your job to protect them.'

I can see a bright red flush spread up Jane's neck. 'You stupid careless bastard,' she snaps at me.

'Wait a minute,' says Nina. 'How did you find some kind of connection between Ophelia and this houseboat?'

'The boat's name was written on a Post-it note in her room, the indentations were on the top sheet of the Post-its that I found in her bin when we went there. And there was also a pin-hole on her map showing the location of the boat.' I should stop now but I am still feeling the need to justify myself. 'And then I found the business card for Garden of Eden in the boat's rubbish bags after the Saturday night party.'

'The one you watched with Jane,' says Nina, looking at us both in turn.

'You went through their trash?' says Cal in amazement.

It is now dawning on me that this is one balloon debate I am destined to lose. Only Anna has spared me so far, watching every twist and turn in the conversation with a look of amazement on her face.

Now she decides to wade in. 'Well, it sounds to me like Jack's the only one who has been doing much about anything. The police should be grateful to him,' she declares, looking pointedly at Jane from under her woollen bobble hat.

'Yeah, well,' says Jane back at her, 'I'm going to have to tell a Detective Chief Inspector with a bad cold and an even worse opinion of Jack that he spoke to Romaine yesterday, before he could interview him this morning. And before his suspect committed suicide, apparently. And believe me, that's going to get ugly and career limiting for yours truly.'

'Career limiting?' asks Anna in disbelief. 'Is that all you care about?'

'Anna ...' says Nina warningly.

'Just get me down and out of this basket, will you?' Jane snaps at Cal. 'I need to make some calls.'

Cal nods back at her without saying anything. There is silence apart from the wind, the creak of the basket and the faint sound of faraway traffic on the ground. Nobody seems to trust themselves to speak – especially me. As we descend, I spot another fox but decide to keep the sighting to myself. This one is skinny and skulking across the middle of a field. He is looking over his shoulder warily, as though a pack of red-coated huntsmen, horses and hounds is about to burst onto the scene and spoil his day. I sort of know how he is feeling.

Cal begins to liaise with Ben and Simon over the walkie-talkie and manages to find a landing spot which meets his criteria. We are all warned to hang on tight in case the basket tips over but it settles comfortably onto its base with the slightest of bumps. The support vehicles arrive just as we are beginning to push the remaining air out of the balloon's vents as it lies sideways on the ground. The ground crew are ebullient that they have managed to track us across country and reach us so quickly. They cheerfully ask if we have enjoyed our flight and exchange curious looks at the lack of enthusiasm in our answers. Eddie is released again to have a run around for a while until the balloon and all of its kit is packed away onto the trailer. Jane is already in her car, speaking on the phone. Cal squashes my hand without any friendliness in his eyes but Anna gives me a hug. I whisper thanks in her ear. I am surprised when Nina falls into step with me after I approach her with Eddie on his lead to say goodbye.

'Well, that turned out to be quite some experience.'

'Oh, Jack,' she replies resignedly. 'You always act with the best of motives, but ...'

'Bull in a china shop?'

'Something like that.'

Jane is beeping her horn impatiently. I stop to look at Nina. 'I shouldn't have come. To Oxford, I mean.'

'What? Why not?'

'Because ... because I'm out of sorts, to be honest. I'm doing things and saying things that I shouldn't. I'm not myself. And that's because I'm missing you,' I tell her. 'Missing your company. It would have been easier if I'd stayed in Bath. You wouldn't be so near, and yet still so far off.'

'Jack,' she says sympathetically. Jane is beeping the horn again. 'Come on.'

Nina takes my arm and walks me to the car. She even opens the passenger door for me.

'See you soon,' she says, lifting Eddie up and putting him onto my lap.

'Really?' I say in exasperation. 'When?'

'When we're both ready,' she replies, closing the door firmly.

Jane gives me a look that manages to convey disbelief and disdain in equal measures. 'Fasten your seatbelt, lover. You're going to need it.'

CHAPTER THIRTY

'They want you to give a statement about your conversation with Dr Romaine yesterday,' she says to me tersely.

'I'll need to drop Eddie off first.'

'Good. I don't want to be around when you come into the station. I'll drop you off at the boat.'

A tense silence continues for several miles as we make our way back into the city. The traffic is much heavier now. 'Look, Jane –' I begin but she cuts me off.

'I am so bloody angry with you,' she snaps without looking at me. 'That man could still be alive.'

'What? Says who? Are you really saying he wouldn't have topped himself if I hadn't spoken to him before the police? And that's if he did actually kill himself. We don't know that for certain yet. And if he did, he did it for his own reasons. And on the face of it, that was either the result of a bad conscience, or to avoid the consequences.' Even as I am saying this, I acknowledge to myself that she may be right. And yet it was Jane herself who made me aware of the full horror of young women being exploited for sex. Surely I was right to challenge Romaine if that's what he was mixed up in?

Jane clenches her mouth shut and just shakes her head. We complete the rest of the drive without saying anything to each other. Finally, she pulls in just before Strode Road Bridge, takes a deep breath and turns to look at me. 'I know the police can be hard bastards and we have to do some unpleasant things occasionally. But we still have to follow the rules. Unlike you. You think you can just do anything you like, don't you? Phone tampering, evidence tampering ... we discussed this.'

'I'm not involved in this for a story,' I protest.

'Yes, you are, Jack,' she says quickly. 'You're always in it for the story, aren't you? Even if you have to make it happen for yourself. It comes first, second and third for you, doesn't it? I haven't known you long, but I can see that now. You must have a splinter of ice in your heart and no thought for anyone but yourself in your head. And I really don't think I want anything to do with that. They're expecting you at the station. Now get out.'

This is clearly my cue to leave. I hold Eddie in my arms on the pavement and watch her drive across the bridge until her car is out of sight. I realise that something, however fleeting, has well and truly ended. 'It's just me and you again, matey,' I say, burrowing my nose into the coarse wiry hair on his neck. 'Just you and me and a lingering whiff of badger poo.'

I think carefully about what I am going to say during my short walk up to Folly Bridge and on to the police station. Philpott is a thug and I anticipate he's already cracking his knuckles in anticipation of our conversation. I'll just keep it factual, I think to myself. I'll report exactly what I said to Romaine and what he said to me and I'll say nothing more. I'll follow the old British Secret Service rule: never complain, never apologise, never explain. I'll just stick to the facts and Philpott can rant as much as he likes.

But when I arrive at the station, I am told that DCI Philpott has taken the day off to nurse his cold. A detective sergeant on his team ushers me into a small interview room and I complete a very straightforward statement about my conversation with Romaine outside the chapel. The verbal fireworks I had expected are non-existent. In fact, the DS seems quite bored and uninterested in my account, folding her arms and yawning. All the signs suggest this particular murder investigation is winding down. I decide to try my luck.

'So,' I say, looking up from the paperwork. 'Did Romaine leave a note admitting the murder?'

She smiles at me. 'Nice try, Mr Johnson. All I can tell you is the official press line. We are no longer looking for anyone else in connection with the murder of Ophelia McVeigh.'

There must have been a note! Romaine must have confessed and then killed himself by jumping off the four-storey tower at St Hugh's. I am surprisingly relieved. I may have tipped him off that the police were closing in, but I didn't push an innocent man over the edge.

The DS shakes my hand in a perfunctory manner and I am ushered outside. Right, I think, rubbing my hands together. Coffee time.

The walk back to the boat with my hot drink gives me a bit more thinking time. Do I feel bad about frightening Romaine? No. Not really. Not if he was guilty of Ophelia's murder. He hadn't escaped justice. He'd just escaped a lifetime of rotting in a prison cell. He delivered his own death penalty. But something else is bothering me. The police may be scaling down their investigation and its senior officer may be sitting at home in his slippers and sipping cold-cure drinks, but is that the end of it? What about the parties and the dating agency? Surely, there is still something very suspicious going on there? Shouldn't the police be looking into that in much more depth?

By the time I have reached *Jumping Jack Flash* I have made a decision. I walk on a little way farther and call in on Hugh. We spend half an hour refining my plan before I return to my boat and open up my laptop. An email is waiting for me from Julia Goodfellow.

Hi Jack. Many thanks for your piece. It's a peach, darling. We'll just use one of the shots you took of the lovely DS Henry and Imani. We won't sell any advertising to go with this so let's not shell out on a

snapper unless we really need to. I may need to cut it back a bit too – unless you want to do it yourself? Just lose a couple of hundred words, please, love. What's next? Keep them coming.
x

My heart sinks but I grit my teeth and send a brief reply that agrees to cut my own copy and suggests the Blenheim Winter Balloon Lift Off as my next story. My morning flight may have been a bit of a disaster, but it still counts as research.

After a solo lunch, I decide to have a doze to recover from the very early start. Eddie curls up with me and we are soon both sound asleep. But I'm awoken by Eddie barking. There is a knocking on the glass of the porthole above my bed. It can't be. That's the river side. Perhaps it is swans banging on the boat with their beaks? There it is again. I sit up bleary-eyed and see Nina's face filling the round glass window with a grin. This is ridiculous. Even I know that she can't really walk on water. She must be standing up in a boat.

I scramble outside onto the stern platform and there are Nina and Cal, holding onto the side of *Jumping Jack Flash* and each standing on a white paddleboard.

'Good afternoon, Jack!' calls Nina. 'Did we wake you up?' Like Cal, she is wearing a black wetsuit and a baseball cap. Both of them have rested their paddles horizontally on the gunwale, the narrow walkway that stretches along both sides of the boat, and they are holding on with both hands. 'We've paddled down from the boathouse.'

'Hi, Jack,' says Cal, waving one hand. 'Sorry to disturb you. Nina says you were asleep.'

I rub my eyes and yawn. This is a big surprise. I would have thought that I was still persona non grata after this morning's balloon trip. 'Coffee?'

'Great,' says Nina, and she begins to work her way along the boat, hand over hand followed by Mr All-America. They haul their boards onto the stern and lean them against the rail with their paddles. The tight-fitting rubber wetsuits show off both of their lean, fit physiques to maximum effect and the fact that they are matching makes them appear even more like the perfect couple. They exude good health and seem excited by their joint venture onto the river. It all makes me feel even older than usual.

'I didn't know you could handle one of those things,' I say to Nina as she takes a mug of coffee from me.

'Alan and I hired them almost every day on holiday in Greece,' she says smugly. 'If anything, it's easier on the river than in the sea. Fewer waves. Lot colder than Calynthos in the summer though.'

'She's very good,' adds Cal. 'I was secretly hoping she might get a ducking and need me to save her.' They both laugh while I force a smile. 'I shouldn't really be doing this while I'm training. But I'm not training at the moment and Nina talked me into it.'

I watch Cal sipping his coffee. They are sitting side by side on the banquette and it feels strange. The tight contours of their wetsuits almost give the impression that they are sitting there in the nude. Adam and Eve in the Garden of Eden before the snake and the apple got involved?

'Say, Jack, I almost forgot why we called in.' Cal puts down his cup. 'The police have been in touch. And they've also called Phi's parents in Scotland this morning. They're pretty sure that Romaine killed her. The murder enquiry is closing down. It seems he did leave a note after all.' This explains Cal and Nina's sudden cheerfulness and the unexpected visit. Cal seems to read my thoughts. 'I know Phi's still gone, and I'll never get over that.' He looks at Nina, who looks back sympathetically. 'But at least they got the bastard. And he won't be doing that to any other girls. He was supposed to be her pastoral tutor, looking out for her welfare,' he adds with a disbelieving shake of his head.

'Did they tell you what the note said?'

'Not the exact words,' says Nina.

'No,' agrees Cal. 'But the family liaison officer gave us the gist of it. He said he'd betrayed his wife and let down his colleagues, felt guilty beyond words, couldn't face his family and couldn't live with his conscience. Said it was the only way to stop the nightmare from continuing.'

'So, he didn't explicitly say he'd killed Ophelia?' I press. I am secretly anxious to determine my own level of culpability for his death.

Cal shrugs his powerful shoulders. 'As good as. The police seem satisfied. Maybe they've got some other evidence that we don't know about. His DNA on Phi's body or something?'

'Well, there will need to be a coroner's inquest – for both Romaine and Ophelia. I'm sure more information will come out then.'

Nina nods. 'But at least Cal can start rebuilding his life now, without this uncertainty hanging over him.'

'Jack, I'm kinda sorry I lost it with you in the balloon this morning.' Cal gives me a conciliatory smile. 'I didn't like the theories you were coming up with about Phi – but you were my guest, and I apologise.'

'And I shouldn't have said what I did,' I say. 'I was just theorising. I'm sorry too.'

Cal laughs. 'There's an American phrase, "All hat and no cattle" – let's just smoke a peace pipe and move on. The bad guy may not be in jail, but at least we know who he is. Or was.'

They stay for a further half an hour and we chat about Cal's boat race ambitions. 'It's coming up fast. Just a couple of months. I need to get back on the water A-sap. That's partly why we've come down to the river. I've been to see the coach – I start training again tomorrow. I need to reassure him that my head's in the right place after all of this. And that my body is still in good shape.'

'It's fine. You'll be fine,' says Nina reassuringly.

They stand to leave, and I begin to follow Cal through the boat. But I feel Nina's hand on my arm from behind.

'Jack, can I have a quick word?'

'Sure.'

'Cal, you go on and get the boards in the water. I won't be a moment.' She waits until he has gone through the swing door beyond the little shower room, then turns to me seriously. 'What are you planning?'

'What do you mean?' I say, playing for time.

'I know you. I know that look. You're like a dog with a bone and there's something you're not saying. What's going on?'

I'm not about to share my plans with Nina if it means she immediately tells Cal. I don't want Cal running to the police.

'Like a dog with a bone? I used to know someone else like that.'

'I haven't changed,' she says, jutting out her elfin little chin. 'Unlike some people.'

'What the hell does that mean?'

'You just seem … I don't know. Cavalier. Careless. Damn the consequences. I'm not sure what's going on. I think you're drinking too much. And then there's you and Jane … '

'Me and Jane?' I splutter disbelievingly. 'What about you and Cal? Jane hasn't moved in with me!'

'Oh Jack,' she says, frowning. 'That's beneath you. You see, that's what I'm talking about.'

'There is no me and Jane,' I say quietly. 'I would have thought that was obvious from our chat in the balloon this morning. I don't know why you invited her on the balloon trip. You were playing games and that was beneath you.' She shakes her head but doesn't say anything. 'Okay, I admit it,' I continue in a rush. 'I'm jealous of Cal and your relationship with him. And so is Anna in a different way. We both are.' There, I've said it. 'Of course, I feel sorry for him but, well … oh bloody hell.'

'Nina!' Cal is calling from the stern.

Nina shakes her head crossly. 'Keep Anna out of this. We're fine.

I don't know what you're up to, Jack. But whatever it is, try to think it through properly first. We'll be in touch.' It is telling, I think to myself, that she uses the first-person plural rather than the first-person singular.

And with that, she swings around, and all I can do is admire her figure as she pads back through the boat, away from me.

CHAPTER THIRTY-ONE

It is midnight when I hear and feel a little bump against the stern of *Jumping Jack Flash*. Eddie gives a short bark. We have been sitting in the dark as I don't want the boat's lights shining out across the water. I am dressed in a black sweatshirt, black jeans, black trainers, black gloves and a black beanie hat. Hugh is similarly dressed as he waits in his little dinghy on the water. However, the experienced Royal Marine has also streaked his face and neck with something black. I climb down into the little open boat as he holds it steady. Without saying anything, he brandishes a little tin of black shoe polish at me, indicates that I should lean forward and quickly adds streaks of polish to my face.

Silently, he pushes us off and begins to row directly across the river. There is a strong current running, but Hugh is a confident oarsman and we are quickly across to the other bank. I look up at the night sky. There is a bit of cloud cover and hardly any moonlight, so these are probably the best conditions we could hope for. Hugh makes a few powerful strokes with his starboard oar and we swing around to point upstream and towards the road bridge. We move steadily towards the little inlet where *Nirvana* is moored. There is barely a sound from Hugh's rowing as the paddles dip in and out of the water cleanly and without any tell-tale splashing. He still hasn't uttered a word and I take my cue from the old warrior.

He pauses just before the mouth of the little inlet and holds the boat steady in the current. We both scan the area intensely but there is no sign of life; no lights, no music or voices. Hugh nods at me and begins to edge forward again until we are up against the riverside hull of the barge. I take the painter and tie it around a stanchion of the larger boat with a quick-release knot. Hugh pulls the dinghy up close and I stand up, grip the stanchion with both hands and lift one knee up and onto the deck of the other boat. I use this as a lever to hoist my whole body up, as though I am climbing out of the deep end of a swimming pool, and remain on all fours. It is still all quiet. Crouching low, I edge around the full circumference of the boat.

There is an impressive carved crest above the doors at the end nearest Strode Meadows. Under it is a brass plate with 'St Michael's College' etched onto it. The crest is red and black and topped with a clergyman's mitre. It has the legend *Honi soit qui mal y pense* painted around its edge in gold lettering – Evil be to him that evil thinks. Is this a warning to me? Are my suspicions unfounded and am I about to come a cropper? Unsurprisingly, the doors are firmly locked. The land side of the boat is identical to the water side with eight latticed oval windows interrupted by a cluster of three small rectangular windows and one large latticed rectangular window.

When I get to the end with the flagpole, I go under the little pillared porchway and try its door handles with my gloved hands. It too is firmly locked. I continue back to the spot where Hugh is moored. He is looking up at me with his darkened face. I signal to him with a thumbs-down and begin moving back along the boat, giving a little push on each of the windows in turn. I do the same all the way around and return to the third from the end on the river side of the mooring. Unlike the others, this one seems to rattle slightly under the pressure of my hand. I have brought my small pencil torch and risk turning it on. I shine it around the edge of the glass. It's hard to figure out whether these big oval windows even open at all. They have been lovingly made and subdivided into eight smaller panes of glass. A semi-classical decorative pillar is carved on both sides, dividing each window from its neighbour. This is clearly a boat that has been built for status and comfort, rather than to go anywhere. Its occupants would have wanted to be able to open the windows occasionally – particularly if they wanted to watch their pals racing on the river. There must be a big hinge on the inside of the windows to allow them to pivot open and some kind of retaining mechanism opposite the hinge to prevent them falling the whole way. The narrow beam of my torch indicates a hook and eye latch on the inner right-hand side of the rattling window. There is definitely a bit more give in this one.

I see the bare branches of a willow tree hanging down over the boat's stern. I swiftly creep over and snap off a piece, then back at the window I poke the twig through the narrow gap by the latch. I have to hold the torch in my mouth and wiggle with both hands before the stick catches the hook and pushes it up, out of its little circular eye.

Now the whole window tilts forward a few inches from the bottom and creates a couple of inches of space at the top. My torchlight shows some kind of metal retaining clip that juts out from the wall above the window. Presumably the clip can be released so that the whole window can fold back into the gap below and leave the frame open to the air. But if I am able to free the clip, will the window go crashing back onto itself, causing the glass to smash and making a lot of noise? Is it time to retire, regroup and rethink? I'm about to return to Hugh when I have an idea.

I undo my leather belt, pull it free from my waist then push the end through the top of the window and around the piece of metal that sticks up into the restraining arm. I loop the end through the belt's buckle to create a small lasso, which I pull tight. I hold the belt firmly about a foot from the loop and reach in with my other hand to push the restraining mechanism upwards and release the window. It immediately slips back a few inches and now I need both hands to grip my belt and take the weight. Slowly, I begin to feed the belt through the space and the heavy mass of glass and woodwork slips backwards until it has dropped by about forty-five degrees. What now? I have created a problem for myself because if the window slips further, past the ninety degrees point, I doubt that I'll be able to prevent it crashing down into a vertical position.

I contemplate calling Hugh to help. But will the old boy be able to haul himself up onto the deck from the dinghy? My belt is straining with the weight of the window and I can feel my arms beginning to tire. Brilliant, Jack. Think, damn you! But as my arms begin to shake, I realise there are only two options. I either use all of my remaining strength to pull the window closed again or take the gamble of letting it fall.

Sod it. There's clearly no one on board. I just hope there isn't anyone in the immediate vicinity who is alerted to call the police.

I feed more of the belt through my gloved hands and the window tilts back further and further. As I get to the belt's end, I use the remaining leather to wind it once around one of my hands to establish a really strong grip. I wedge both my feet hard into the point where the deck meets the wooden wall below the window and brace myself as much as I can. The window drops through the horizontal and its weight immediately takes over, yanking me forwards with tremendous force so that the belt shoots out of my hands and there is a definite bang. However, it is quieter than I feared and no glass shatters. The wooden frame has taken the brunt of the blow. The small latticework of panes must be very solidly built.

My heart is pounding as I wait for any reaction to the noise. God knows what Hugh must be thinking. The inlet is completely silent again and the open gap now looms in front of me. It is easily large enough and low enough for me to hook one leg over the bottom sill and climb inside. But, instead of standing on the boat's deck on the other side, I find I am kneeling at the pillow end of a double bed. The window didn't fall completely into a vertical position because it was stopped by the bed and although it must have banged into the headboard slightly, the pillows helped to cushion its fall.

I re-thread the belt around my waist and lift the window closed behind me so that nothing looks abnormal from the outside. The first thing I notice is the smell. The usual odour of onboard dampness is mixed with the lingering scent of perfume, hairspray, cigarettes and strong spirits. There is no doubt that this is the aftermath of the Friday and Saturday night parties that we saw taking place. I use the torch to look around me. I've entered the boat roughly in its centre and I'm standing in a small bedroom with little room for anything other than the bed, which has been stripped down to its bare mattress, and a wardrobe to my left.

The cabin door swings outwards into a passageway opposite another of the oval windows on the land side of the barge. I turn right, towards the flagpole end, which I now assume to be the bow. I try the handle of two more doors leading into similar cabins. One of them has a cheap hand-painted sign fixed to it that reads: 'If the boat is rocking, don't come knocking!'

After the third cabin, the passageway opens out into a large saloon furnished with comfortable sofas and armchairs, curtains, lamps, paintings and rugs. A bar stands in one corner with optics above it. A pair of French doors leads outside.

I turn around and set off to explore the stern of the boat. I pass the cabins again and find a fourth immediately before a large and well-equipped galley that occupies the last bit of the boat's interior before more French doors lead out onto the stern deck. So, the living quarters comprise a galley at the stern, four double cabins off a passageway and then the large saloon in the bow. It's strange – from the outside, the boat seems bigger. I prowl along its length again, opening doors and taking longer to inspect each space with the thin beam of my powerful torch. I check my watch. It is now twenty minutes since I climbed on board and I have promised Hugh I will be no longer than half an hour. It is going to take me another five minutes to close and latch the window behind me, so I have five minutes left to explore. I walk the length of the passageway for a third time and that's when it strikes me.

From the outside, I remember registering that the line of oval windows was interrupted two-thirds along by three small rectangular windows. They had been grouped together in the shape of a L. And yet, from the inside, I haven't seen these three windows at all. All I have seen is the succession of oval windows and one large rectangular window in the galley. Sure enough, the length of passageway between the third cabin, where I entered the boat, and its neighbour seems unusually long compared to the space between the others. I go into the third cabin again and inspect its wall. The wardrobe! I open it and look at its rear wooden panelling. It looks perfectly normal but when I put my hand on it and push, there is a small click and it moves slightly towards me. It is some kind of magnetic catch of the kind you get on smart kitchen cupboards owned by people who don't want to use conventional handles. It proves quite easy to curl my fingers around the side of the panel and it pivots towards me. I climb through into the space beyond where the three rectangular windows in the shape of a L are immediately on my left.

The space is roughly the same size as the other cabins, but this one has an office chair in front of a substantial wooden worksurface. It has a large and very modern computer and wireless keypad sitting on it. Above this, on a long length of shelf at head-height, is a row of small video monitors. I count seven in all, each with a little metal switch. I click one downwards and an image immediately fills the screen. It shows the approach to the gangway of the boat. It also seems to be artificially bright considering the darkness of the night outside. I go along the row, flicking the switches of all the other screens. The interior of the galley, each of the cabins and the saloon appear in quick succession; all of them appear as bright as day, albeit in black and white. The seventh shows the main gate in the chain link fence. The monitors must be capturing the output of night-vision cameras. And the cameras must be very carefully hidden. I have seen no trace of them during my inspection of the boat so far.

My mind is racing. The conclusion seems obvious. *Nirvana* is acting as some kind of floating honeytrap, recording video pictures of the professional men of Oxford as they entertain themselves as the paying guests of Garden of Eden. They may think they have been discreetly delivered by boat in the dead of night, but whoever has been organising these parties must have other ideas as far as discretion is concerned. Blackmail? Almost certainly.

And that's when my blood goes cold. I am staring at the screens, rapidly trying to absorb what I have discovered, when I see the main gate swinging open. The dark figure of a man is coming towards the gangplank.

CHAPTER THIRTY-TWO

Think fast, Jack. Do I stay where I am or try to flee?

The little viewing room feels like a trap with just one entrance and nowhere to hide. I decide I need to get out of it as quickly as possible. I flick off all the monitors and move back through the wardrobe into the adjoining cabin. Now where? If the man is coming on board, he'll probably use the main entrance at the bow. Or will he? He could just as easily enter through the stern and come directly into the galley instead. It's a fifty-fifty call and I gamble by turning left and rushing along the passageway to the stern. I've already checked and I know there is no key in the locks of the rear or front doors, so there is no way I can make a quick exit through them. I'd resigned myself to leaving the boat in the same way that I had come in, through the oval window, but this is impossible now. My eyes scan the galley frantically. I need to hide – and fast. I can hear a metallic noise at the bow. It is a key turning in a lock.

I yank open the louvre door of a cupboard to one side of the French doors. It's shallow and houses an ironing board. I lean the board against the wall, climb into the empty space and pull the door closed. The cupboard is only about a foot taller than the ironing board and about a foot shorter than me so I am forced to flex my knees as far as I can and bend my head sideways. It's far from comfortable and my fingers are hooked around the inside of a slat of the door to prevent it swinging open again. I try to get my breathing back under control. Who the hell is wandering around *Nirvana* past midnight on a Tuesday? Apart from me, that is. And why? It must be the owner. And if it is, they have more right to be here than I do – whatever time of day or night it might be.

Then I remember Hugh. What will he do? Will he have realised that someone else has come on board? And if he has, will he wait? Or will he slip away and return to *Raven* in his dinghy? Our carefully prepared plan is unravelling fast.

I push an eye up to the narrow gap between two slats. A torch is moving about at the far end of the passageway, in the saloon. So, the newcomer isn't anxious to switch on the boat's interior lights either? Interesting. The torch begins to move closer towards me, ever closer and finally into the galley. I can't see the figure behind the bright light until the torch is placed on a work surface, pointing up at the ceiling, and the fridge door opens. The light from the fridge's interior and the light being spilled from the torch now show the man's face. He has a flat boxer's nose, sharp cheekbones and a strong jaw. The torchlight catches something shiny in one side of the man's mouth, which I realise must be a gold tooth. He isn't as tall as me, but he looks strong and he moves with a lithe assurance. I am sure that I have seen this man somewhere before, but I can't think where.

Something is pressing painfully into my back. My knees and neck are starting to protest at the uncomfortable position they have been forced to adopt. How much longer can I do this without needing to adjust my stance and risk making a noise? What about the ironing board! Will the man notice it is out in the open? Even worse, will he try to tidy it away? My heart is hammering against my ribcage and my knees are shrieking in painful protest.

I hear a drawer pulled open. There is a rattle of cutlery. Could he be reaching for a knife? I begin to brace myself to rush him if the door to my hiding place is opened. But then I hear soft footsteps retreating back along the corridor. I shift position slightly and put my eye back to the tiny gap between the slats. There is no sign of the man or his torch, but I can hear doors being opened in succession. Then I hear a slight grunt and the sound of metal striking metal. The smell reaches me before the man reappears in the galley. I can't see him, but I am almost certain I know what he is carrying. Petrol. I can hear it slopping out of some kind of container and the smell of it tells me that some is already flowing across the deck of the historic barge. It starts puddling at my feet inside the little cupboard. The fumes are threatening to become overpowering. Overpowering and terrifying. One spark and this old wooden boat will be a raging inferno with me trapped inside.

I have to get out. I imagine the long passageway stretching away in front of me. It would be madness to try to run down its entire length. I open the cupboard, prepared to take my chances with the man rather than suffer the fumes any more. But just as I emerge into the galley, I hear glass smash and the whoosh of an explosion at the far end of the boat. Almost immediately, I can feel heat prickling my skin and the passageway has become as light as day. The saloon is alight. I only have seconds to save myself.

I snatch up the ironing board, pivot and, holding it horizontal, rush towards the stern French doors. My impromptu battering ram forces them to bow outwards, but they hold firm. I see two bolts at floor level, yank them open and try the handle again. It's locked. There's intense heat at my back now. I rush forward again with the ironing board for a second time aiming it directly at the lock with all of the strength I can muster. This time the doors spring backwards and I hurl myself through them. Instinctively I turn right instead of left, vault up onto the boat's handrail with one foot and leap out and across the short ditch of water between the boat and the land. I make the bank with barely inches to spare, falling the height of the boat's hull, rolling forward with the momentum and landing on my back. Behind me, bright orange and yellow is filling the windows along the entire length of the boat and flames are leaping out of the doors at the bow. They climb upwards, licking hungrily around the flagpole and stretching up into the night sky.

I turn onto all fours and take in huge gulps of air. Hugh! What has happened to Hugh? But one look at the blazing boat convinces me it would be very unwise to try to reach its other side. If there are gas cannisters on board, which is likely, *Nirvana*'s a floating time bomb and liable to go up at any second. I pray that Hugh has made himself scarce and begin to stagger clear of the mooring. That's when my right ankle hits something hard in the long grass and I am brought down. It's a lump of sharp metal, possibly an old anchor that's been carelessly discarded. The pain is excruciating. I am still less than ten metres from the gang plank, and I can see flames starting to lick through the roof of the boat. I try to rise up, onto my feet, but my ankle gives way under me. I'll have to crawl.

'Now then, lad, what have you been up to, eh?'

I look up. The thin face of John Turner looks back down at me. 'I think you'd better come with me.'

He pulls me upright and I throw an arm around his neck as he half drags, half carries me back towards the gate in the chain link fencing, which is now wide open. Beyond it, on the track, there is a big black 4x4 vehicle, its lights on and its engine running. As I stare ahead, clinging to Turner's thin shoulder and hopping alongside him, the vehicle roars away at speed. But even before it has completely disappeared, there is an enormous explosion from behind us. The night sky is suddenly as bright as day and we feel the shockwave buffet our backs. We turn to see the bare winter branches of the trees hanging low over the boat are also on fire.

'Where to then, lad?' asks Turner.

'The *Raven*. As fast as we can,' I gasp. We are halfway across the bridge when the sound of the first sirens reaches us. I grit my teeth. 'Faster!' I urge him and he picks up his pace while I am dragged along at his side.

As we descend to the riverbank, I feel another shoulder prise up and under my spare arm to share my weight with Turner. 'You got out, then? Well done, old chap.'

'Hugh! Thank god you're alright.'

'Quiet now. Let's all get down below and fast.' Turner and Hugh virtually frogmarch me along the path before I collapse gratefully down the steps into *Raven*'s dimly lit interior. I am manoeuvred onto a banquette where Hugh takes charge. 'Put your foot up. I'll look at it in a minute. Wipe that stuff off your face in case anyone comes calling.' He gives me a hot, damp tea towel. Turner is sitting quietly opposite us in the dark, watching our every move with his hands patiently folded in his lap.

The sirens are now very loud as emergency vehicles begin to gather on the far side of the bridge. 'When did you bail out?' I ask Hugh.

'I heard the chap go on board but stayed in case you managed to get out. But when I smelt the petrol, I guessed what he was up to. I'm afraid I had no choice, Jack. I had to leave then, or I'd have gone up with *Nirvana*. I tried to stay on the river in case you had to swim for it. I was bloody relieved when I saw John bringing you back across the bridge, I don't mind telling you.'

I notice the use of the first name. 'John? You know each other?'

'Aye, lad. Captain Spencer and I know each other. We've been neighbours on river for a few weeks now. I was waiting and watching from the Meadows just in case I was needed. Didn't take long to cut through the fence.'

'I briefed John about our reconnaissance mission this afternoon, Jack. Always helpful to have a contingency plan and trusted reinforcements on hand – just in case.' Hugh inspects my face and rubs a few remaining smears of boot polish off. 'Now, let's have a look at that ankle, shall we?' He prods and manhandles my leg before announcing that nothing seems to be broken. Then he ties a pack of frozen peas around it and bustles off to pour three generous measures from a bottle of J&B.

Even here, on *Raven*'s mooring, it is possible to feel the heat, smell the smoke and see the remaining glow of the fire for a couple of hours.

The generators from the fire engines continue to disturb the peace until the early morning. It's clear it will be useless trying to sleep so we sit up while I bring them both up to speed on the apparent suicide of Dr Romaine, the end of the police's murder investigation and what I discovered on board *Nirvana*.

'Ah well,' says Hugh matter-of-factly. 'No battle plan survives first contact with the enemy. You were lucky to get out alive.'

'I'm certain that I've seen our friendly neighbourhood arsonist before,' I tell them. 'But I'm damned if I can think when or where.'

'Describe him,' orders Hugh briskly.

'Short. Powerful looking. Broad shoulders. High cheekbones. Boxer's nose – not broken but kind of squashed flat. He had a gold tooth. But he had a dark hoodie on, so I didn't see his hair.'

'Well,' says Hugh, sipping his drink and looking at me with those clever grey eyes of his. 'It sounds to me rather like the helmsman we saw on Friday night. The one who delivered the guests to the party in the little tender.'

Of course. That was it. We only had a fleeting glimpse of him when he turned his head towards us. But it had to be the same man.

Eventually, we doze in our seats and I am only dimly aware of Hugh making his way to bed as a grey dawn begins to seep through his boat's windows. It seems just minutes later that Hugh is shaking me gently awake with a mug of tea. It is seven o'clock and I see that John Turner has gone, presumably back to his boat or his shack in the Kidneys.

'Come on, Jack. Shake a leg. I think it's a little suspicious for us to show no interest in the aftermath of a fire and an explosion on the opposite bank. We need to have a wander over there. Why don't we pick Eddie up on the way?' I tentatively stand on my ankle. The surgeon-captain was right. Although it still feels sore, it takes my weight. I feel as though I may have a slight limp for a day or so.

Hugh is also right about the neighbours. A gaggle of curious onlookers are standing on the bridge, looking down at the charred and smouldering wreckage and sniffing the smoke that still pollutes the cold early morning air. Almost the entire barge has been razed to the waterline; just a few blackened ribs are left poking above the surface. As we stand there, looking down, a steady rain begins to fall. I see two black umbrellas go up and begin making their way through the gate. They stop and one umbrella tilts backwards, so that the face of the man underneath it springs into view. He is looking upwards, directly at me. It is the short squat figure of Detective Chief Inspector Brian Philpott and he is beckoning me to join him with an insistently wagging finger.

CHAPTER THIRTY-THREE

I ask Hugh to take Eddie back to his boat and I make my way down to meet Philpott. 'Good morning, Chief Inspector. How's the cold?'

Philpott narrows his eyes at me and ignores the question. '*Mr* Johnson. What a surprise, I don't think. You wouldn't happen to have any information about this, would you?'

'I heard the sirens in the night and saw the fire, obviously. Came over first thing to see what had happened.'

'Really? You must have realised it was *Nirvana* burning – the same boat that you were so interested in. Yet you restrained yourself and stayed in bed until now, did you?'

I smile sweetly at him. 'You ordered me to stay away from your enquiry. In fact, I understand the investigation into Ophelia's death has been closed now?'

'That's none of your business,' he says truculently.

'It was arson, I take it?'

'And how would you know? This is none of your business either.'

'Interesting, though, isn't it?'

'Enlighten me,' he says, buttoning up the front of his raincoat over his paunch.

'Well, *Nirvana* was somehow connected with Ophelia. And Dr Romaine was a night-time visitor to the barge. And there also seems to be a connection between *Nirvana* and a dating agency in town. The same agency where Ophelia worked. Then the academic kills himself ...'

'After a conversation with you, Mr Johnson. I haven't forgotten that. It'll be interesting to see what the coroner makes of that.'

'After a *brief* conversation with me and *before* you'd bothered to re-interview him. The coroner might also be interested in why you didn't respond to our information faster than you did.' Philpott flushes angrily. 'And now *Nirvana*, which might have unlocked some more secrets after a proper search by the police, is no more. Too late again, Chief Inspector?'

'Now look here,' he says angrily. 'We were going to search her today. We've got rules to follow and I can't get a search warrant unless I can prove we're not going to get permission from the owner. We've just spent 48 bloody hours trying to find the bloody owner.'

This is interesting. 'And did you? All boats on inland waterways have a unique registration number.'

'She's registered alright,' he snaps. 'But to a false name and address in Manchester. We also have to convince a magistrate that a crime was probably committed on that boat in order to get a search warrant. But you and DS Henry witnessing a party on board doesn't mean any crime has been committed, does it, Johnson? We do things by the book. And remind me, why am I telling you all this? I don't have to explain anything to you.'

I notice that I am no longer 'Mr' Johnson. I'm also getting steadily soaked through, although Philpott is probably the last person in the world who would offer to share his umbrella with me.

I shake my head sadly at him. 'I haven't forgotten the other person on that boat being ferried to the party on Saturday night. DS Henry recognised him. One of your force's very senior officers, wasn't he? And sharing a boat with a man you now believe to be a murderer? That could be pretty embarrassing if it gets out. Especially if there are rumours that you were slow to interview Dr Romaine. And now you've been too slow to search the boat where your murderer attended suspicious parties. Someone leaning on you to drag your heels, are they, Chief Inspector?'

Philpott turns an unhealthy shade of puce. He advances on me so that I have to duck back or risk a poke in the eye with a spoke of his umbrella. He pokes me in the chest instead. 'I thought so. I said it, didn't I? You're just another dirty muck-raking hack who's after a story and you don't care who gets in the way.'

It's hard for me to take my eyes off the small white bit of spittle in one corner of his mouth. He pokes me again.

'Final warning, Johnson. Stay away from me. Stay away from DS Henry. And, ideally, stay away from Oxford. In fact, why don't you just point that boat of yours in the opposite direction and get lost? You're not wanted here.'

I shrug and step back from him. But before I turn to leave, I pull out my mobile phone and take a picture of the boat – just because I know how much it will piss him off. Then I grit my teeth and try to disguise my limp with the appearance of a jaunty saunter back to *Raven*. It's childish, I know, but riling Philpott has already brightened up my morning and goaded him into giving me some useful information.

The policeman is probably right, though. If he'd been trying to get a search warrant for the boat for the past 48 hours, that would have been before Romaine killed himself. So Philpott had been following up our report of odd goings on at *Nirvana* and any connection they might have had with Ophelia's murder. And to be fair, unlike me, he would have had to jump through various legal hoops to obtain a search warrant and get on board the boat – like establishing who the owner is. But the fact is, I now know something that the police don't know about *Nirvana*. I doubt that the police will find any remaining evidence of the secret filming system that was on board. The fire, the water and the explosion of the gas tanks will have seen to that. They won't be looking for it, anyway. Why would they, unless I told them what I'd found?

But that would mean admitting to a spot of breaking and entering. I would also love to identify the man who burned the boat to the water. I can describe him. But how can I let the police know all this without admitting to a crime myself? Having seen Philpott's fury at me, I am certain he would love nothing more than to have me arrested.

I am desperate to have a shower and a shave and get into some dry clean clothes. But first I need to collect Eddie and I end up sharing a debrief with Hugh over a warming coffee. It's amazing that Philpott didn't smell the petrol and smoke on me. But we were standing near the remains of the boat and that would have disguised my individual aroma - and maybe he's still suffering from his cold.

'Well, obviously,' says Hugh, 'I'm not too keen on you advertising my involvement in last night to the police. Although,' he adds with a grin, 'it was the most tremendous fun!'

'Any sign of Turner?'

'No. He'll probably be in the Kidneys with his dog. He's a rum chap, but solid.'

'He won't go to the police?'

'No, no, no,' says Hugh confidently. 'I'm sure he won't. John and I get on quite well and he told me that he owed you a favour for not reporting his dog. He also has a bit of a grudge about whoever owned *Nirvana*. He wanted to buy her for himself to live on, or at least to put his boat on the same mooring. But she was sold in situ for a lot more than he could afford and the new owners didn't want neighbours. Perhaps he'll get his wish now. What do you think the police will do?'

'I honestly don't know. I'm not even sure that Philpott would have gone through with the search of *Nirvana* in the end. He was finding it difficult to get a warrant and now he thinks his murder investigation is all cut and dried. Obviously, he turned out this morning when he heard the boat had been torched. But, if he doesn't know about the secret recording equipment, then I'm not sure that he'll investigate it any further. Especially if one of his bosses is at risk of being seriously embarrassed.'

'And you?'

'Ah. That's different. I'm going to try to find out a bit more about Garden of Eden.'

'The dating agency? I thought you already had enough women trouble,' he says with a laugh that freezes when he sees my look.

'There's something very wrong about all this. There are people in this city selling young women for sex with powerful men and I aim to get to the bottom of it – whether it's linked to Ophelia's murder or not. But first, I badly need a shower and a change and some more sleep. Thanks for all your help, Hugh. D'you want a hand to stow the dinghy?'

'No. Not yet. I'll leave it tied up on the water for now. We don't want your policeman seeing us putting it back on the roof, putting two-and-two together and making four, do we?'

CHAPTER THIRTY-FOUR

Connolly pours himself another glass of high-protein smoothie from the jug in front of him and stares thoughtfully across at the Thames from the granite island in his kitchen. As he lifts it to his mouth, he catches the faint whiff of petrol that remains on his hands despite the extensive soaping he gave to his whole body when he got home. Now, wrapped in a thick blue towelling dressing gown, he is taking stock.

He knows that there is no longer anything that can connect him with *Nirvana*. The barge had been snapped up via a discreet solicitor and a brokerage. Its registration papers were a cul de sac leading nowhere. And there would be nothing left of her now. No fingerprints. No sign of the recording studio. Nothing. It was a shame to lose her. Not that he cared much about her 90-year history. She just happened to be the right size and in the right place and she'd worked out well for the last eighteen months. But he couldn't risk a police search after he'd been told that they'd been sniffing about. No, it was a good swift decision efficiently executed according with the principles of war applied to business. Now he must consider how to replace her.

He has already seen that a large three-storey house near Folly Bridge is for sale. The building, Grandpont House, is built on three stone arches over a small tributary of the Isis. Connolly wonders if he would be able to ferry his guests straight into one of the tunnels and up into the house. It would be a longer journey if he kept the same rendezvous point. And maybe it's too close to the city centre to be completely safe from prying eyes?

On the other hand, it's a handsome and historic-looking building with big and impressive windows. He could easily recreate the ambience of a discreet upmarket private members' club. It would have more bedrooms than the barge so there could be a bigger turnover. He could even introduce an element of illicit gambling and other sinful temptations. He wonders if there is a cellar that could be made to look like a dungeon. Some clients might get off on that and the blackmail potential would be even greater. The idea excites him even as he realises it probably carries too much risk. Marcie Lopez is a risk too but she could be useful. She can pretend she's looking for larger office premises for Garden of Eden. Maybe she can even buy it with his money and run it for him? That might give him the layer of insulation he would need? It would also add to his growing property portfolio. He knows that the house is set back from the road. Nice and private behind a big wall. So, perhaps he wouldn't even need to use the river to deliver clients – not unless someone particularly wanted that as an option. Most guests could simply drive through some high gates and park out of sight. It might work. Garden of Eden would be great cover for something like that.

Then he could continue to focus on his part of the supply chain. Marcie would continue to source their guests and he would continue to bring some of the younger boys and girls in from London and help out on party nights. Just to make sure things didn't get out of hand. Right now, though, half-term is approaching fast and he will need to find a suitable short-term replacement for *Nirvana*. An Airbnb perhaps? That might do as a temporary fix and Marcie could make the arrangements. It needs to be somewhere quiet in the country. Maybe even Marcie's place? He'll suggest it to her.

His mobile rings and the display screen shows him it is the woman he is thinking about. She knows now that she must use a cheap throwaway phone to ring him. He has the same kind of device to communicate with her.

'Hi. I was just thinking about you and half-term. Seven days of solid business.'

'The boat,' she says abruptly. 'Hath it gone?' Marcie has Spanish parents and you can still detect her heritage in the pronunciation of some English words.

'Yep. She was well ablaze when I left. She was covered in petrol and I'd had some extra gas bottles delivered. She went up like a bomb. Potter sent some pics this morning. There's nothing left.' Connolly has been paying a barman who works and lives at the boathouse café on Donnington Bridge to report on anything he sees or hears. He had already tipped Connolly off about the police asking questions about the boat.

'Good. Just in time.'

Connolly senses something in her worried tone. 'What's happened?'

'It's Romaine, Finn. He's topped himself.'

'Shit. How d'you know?'

'I've only just picked it up in the paper. It happened on Sunday. But it's strange.'

'Why?'

'Well, it seems the police think he killed Ophelia. It turns out he was her university teacher. I'm worried. What if –'

'Shut up, will you?' he snaps. 'I'm thinking.' Connolly remembers the tall, thin man from Saturday night. He'd been as nervous as hell. It was only his second time on *Nirvana*. 'Had you given him his bill?'

'Yes. As agreed. I sent him the video on Sunday morning on Snapchat and called him an hour later. He'd viewed the movie alright, just the once before it vanished. There'll be no trace of it left on his phone.'

'And the bill?'

'I told him. Ten thousand pounds. To be paid within a month.'

'How did he take it?'

'He was a quiet one. No swearing. No raging. Just quiet. Stunned. The paper says he had four *descendencia*, four kids.'

'How did he do it?'

'Jumped off the tower at his college. Later the same day.'

'Shit. Did he leave a note?'

'I don't know. That's what's so odd. There's just a police statement that says they're no longer looking for anyone else in connection with the girl's death.'

'Ask Simon Carter. He'll know what's going on.'

'*Mierda*! Do you think that's wise?'

'Just do it. There's no way the police can connect Romaine with us. But Carter will be shitting himself. He was in the boat with Romaine on Saturday.'

'What if he refuses to help us?'

'Just remind him what we've got on him. And it hasn't cost him a penny yet. I knew he'd come in useful one day. He can start paying us back now.'

'Alright. And Finn ...'

'What?'

'Maybe we should put a hold on things? Just until we know it's all okay?'

'The police would have been knocking on your door by now if Romaine had said anything. I think we're in the clear. And if they think Romaine killed the girl that's even better, isn't it? Speak to Carter and ring me back.'

He hangs up, spreads both his hands wide and flat on the kitchen island's top and tilts his head back. The new couple living in the flat above are having a lie-in, but they can hear Connolly's loud bellow of anger and frustration come loud and clear through their floorboards. They know better than to complain about it.

CHAPTER THIRTY-FIVE

I text Anna to see if she is free to meet me. She says she's working on an essay at the Weston Library and agrees to let me buy her lunch in its café. I potter about on the boat for the rest of the morning before heading out to the corner of Broad Street and Parks Road. The café is in the large open atrium of the library's entrance, and Anna is sitting at a table inside when I get there.

'Nice place to work,' I say, looking around as we queue at the counter.

'It's part of the Bodleian,' she says. 'Well, strictly speaking it's part of the New Bodleian. They built an extension to the Old Bodleian for extra storage during the war. Most of it is underground. Then they rebuilt it again as the Weston in 2015. They do quite good exhibitions here now. You should have a look at the current one,' she says with a smile. 'It's called "Sappho to Suffrage: women who dared". It's marking the centenary of Votes for Women.'

'Women should be running the world, as far as I'm concerned,' I say. 'Talking of "women who dared", I have a proposition to put to you.'

'Well, you can pay for a poor student's lunch first,' she says. I do as I am told, and we return to a table with our Brie-filled baguettes and fizzy water. 'So, what's the proposition, Jack? I hope it's not an indecent one.'

'First off, thanks for sticking up for me in the balloon.'

She rolls her eyes. 'Well honestly. All that righteous indignation. You weren't to know Romaine would respond like that. Like I said, at least you were trying to do something.'

'I thought Cal was going to throw me out at one point.'

She giggles. 'And I thought Jane was going to put you in handcuffs.' She raises an eyebrow and it makes me wonder if she suspects something.

'There's something else, though. The boat I was talking about. The one Romaine went to for the party. *Nirvana*. Someone set fire to it last night and it blew up. There's nothing left of it.'

'Bloody hell. Really?'

'There's more. I was on board her when it happened. I broke in to have a look around.'

'Jack! You're kidding me.'

'No. The police may be trying to shut everything down now that they think they've got their killer. But I don't think they know the half of it.'

'Why? What do you mean?'

'There were three cabins inside. Three bedrooms. And then also hidden on the boat was a small video recording studio. I think they were ferrying their guests in to meet young women and then secretly filming them.'

Anna's eyes are wide with surprise. 'Why? Porn?'

I shake my head. 'I doubt it. Not with balding middle-aged men – who'd pay to watch that? No, it was probably a prostitution racket with a nice little line in blackmail on the side.'

'And you still think Phi might have been caught up in it?'

'It's possible. Maybe she discovered something when she was working at Garden of Eden. Maybe she threatened to expose Romaine and he silenced her. Or maybe she threatened to expose the whole business and they shut her up, permanently. There was a guy on the boat last night who set it alight. He looked more than capable of handling himself.'

'Did he see you?'

'No, I was hiding in a cupboard and I managed to get off the boat just after he left – although things got a bit warm for a while. I saw him, though, and I'd recognise him again.'

'Why don't you tell the police? Get them to do a photo-fit or an artist's impression?'

I laugh at this. 'Not a chance. I've been warned off, remember? The guy running the show would just love to bang me up for interfering with a police investigation. Technically, I've already tampered with evidence and tipped off a suspect that the police were on to him. No, I can't go down that road. Not yet anyway.'

Anna sips her coffee thoughtfully. 'Okay. So, what's your proposition? I take it you're buying me this expensive lunch for a reason?'

'It's the dating agency where Ophelia worked. Garden of Eden. Their business card was also in the rubbish from *Nirvana*.' I show her the photograph of the card on my phone. 'I'd like to suss them out a bit more. Well, actually, I wondered if you would like to suss them out a bit more for me?'

'Me! How?'

'Say that you're interested in going onto their books. Get an interview with them. Then we can get a handle on who's running the business and whether it feels legit or not. We might be able to find out if Ophelia really was just a part-time secretary there, as they told the police, or whether she was involved in something else.'

'But why don't you just sign on as a client?'

I shake my head. 'No. I think we need to approach it from the other direction. They'll be much less suspicious of you.'

'It could be dangerous,' Anna says, thinking out loud. 'One girl has already died.'

'You don't need to actually go on any dates. Just apply to the agency and go and see them. Find out how they work and who is in charge. Then you can quietly melt away.'

Anna's lips part into a grin that reminds me of her aunt. 'Okay. I'll give it a go. It's actually quite exciting, isn't it!'

'Atta girl. But, there's one more thing.' She looks at me quizzically. 'Not a word about this to Nina.'

'Because?'

'Because firstly, she might tell Cal – who might tell the police. And because secondly, she'd kill me for involving you.'

We spend the next half an hour huddled over Anna's laptop in the café. There is an online application form which she completes and then she uploads a glamorous photograph of herself in a bikini on a foreign beach. Having pressed send, she agrees to keep me fully in touch and returns to her work while I go back to the boat and give Eddie a nice long walk along the banks of the Cherwell. There are no punts or rowing boats on the water today; the hire businesses close in mid-October and don't reopen until mid-March. But we both enjoy our afternoon stroll along the bank of the lovely river. I am just admiring the stone arches of Magdalen Bridge when my mobile rings. It's Anna.

'Jack, they've come back to me already! They're asking if I can go in at four o'clock today for an interview. It's the same address as the one on the business card.'

'That was quick. Mind you, I'm not surprised after they saw that picture of you on the beach.'

Anna giggles. 'I'll shoot back to college and glam up a bit.'

'Listen, Anna, I'll wait outside when you go in. Just in case. I'll be there at ten to four and we can talk after you come out.'

It is actually twenty to four when I arrive at the tiny lane off Beaumont Street called Friars Entry. I discover a separate front door and a discreet sign that says nothing other than Garden of Eden. It seems to lead to a first-floor office rather than the biblical paradise, so I take Eddie across the road and we set up camp in the window of a pub opposite called The White Rabbit. At least, it calls itself a pub. It's actually decorated like a 1980s disco and also thinks it's a pizzeria. I text Anna to say I'm in position, order a pint and sit there munching a mozzarella and pepperoni calzone until she swings into view. I dart out to the pub's front door and give her a discreet nod. She is wearing high heels, a tight-fitting trouser suit under a belted raincoat and her mane of blonde hair cascades alluringly around her shoulders. I watch as she presses a button, talks into an intercom by the door, pushes it open and walks in.

It takes two more pints and a slice of apple pie before I see Anna come back out of the door. She sets off through a series of confusing little lanes around the Gloucester Green market space before emerging onto George Street where she makes for a pub called the Wig & Pen. Once I'm satisfied that she hasn't been followed, I join her at the bar. 'Glass of dry white wine, please,' she tells the barman. 'He's paying.' I collect her wine and a whisky chaser for me, and we perch on stools at a high little table in a corner.

'Cheers. You look fabulous, by the way.'

She grins. 'Thanks. I wasn't quite sure what to wear for a little spot of espionage.'

'Tell me they didn't snatch your hand off looking like that? You were in there ages.'

'They did seem quite keen to put me on their books,' she says, still smiling. 'The woman who met me was called Marcie Lopez. Middle-aged, short, straight black hair, Spanish probably. But she spoke good English.'

'Go on.'

'Well, she gave me an interview. Asked about boyfriends. Asked what my parents did. Wanted to know what I was studying, hobbies and so on. She said she had lots of nice, wealthy and generous older men on her books who wanted young, attractive, intelligent women to accompany them to dinners, functions, dances, the theatre and so on. Sometimes, she said, it was for business hospitality. She said she concentrated on university students because she knew we needed the money and we could mix confidently in the company of the kind of professional men she had as clients. She said she also had some dishy male students on her books who were popular escorts for her female clients.'

'Did it all seem above board?'

'I asked her what would happen if any of her clients tried to misbehave with me.'

'Well done. What did she say to that?'

'She said her business was all legit and above board but that if any of her boys or girls wanted to make any personal deals with the clients – for "added levels of intimacy", as she called it – then she wouldn't object but she wanted to know about it! She wasn't exactly saying it was off-limits.'

'What were the offices like?'

'Plush. And we had a glass of fizz each. There doesn't seem to be any shortage of money. And the fees for a four-hour lunch or evening engagement were pretty eyewatering. I can see why she's got a lot of students on her books.'

'So, it's more of an escort agency than a dating agency?'

Anna nods. 'It definitely sounded like it to me. Although you're right. That card makes them sound like a dating agency. Maybe it's one story for the clients and another for the escorts? She said they'd arrange for some professional studio photographs of me if I wanted to take things further.'

'Were there many staff there?'

'Just Marcie and a secretary. A young woman.'

'No muscle? No security guy hanging around? No-one with a gold tooth?'

'Not that I could see. I'm not sure where all this gets you, Jack? Should I have asked if she knew Phi?'

'No, I don't think so. We know she told the police that Ophelia worked for her as a temporary secretary. She'd have smelled a rat if you suddenly brought up her name. No, let's just leave it there for now. Don't go back and don't get in touch with her. Leave it with me now.'

'Are you sure?' she says, smiling naughtily. 'I might develop a taste for older men if it pays what she says she's paying.'

'I mean it, Anna,' I say seriously. 'We don't know what she might be mixed up in. Keep your distance now. Promise?'

Anna nods. 'Okay, cross my heart and hope to die.'

I frown at her. 'We don't want anyone else to die. And remember. Not a word to Nina. Please.'

CHAPTER THIRTY-SIX

I wake dry-eyed with lack of sleep and dry-mouthed after an evening with Hugh. I'd delivered a sixteen-year-old Lagavulin to *Raven* as a heartfelt thank you for his help on the previous night and he insisted that we share some of it immediately. His wife is still recovering well, and he anticipates taking her back to Gloucestershire within a matter of days, so he was in good spirits. We relived our raid on *Nirvana* like a couple of veterans and I brought him up to speed on Garden of Eden. It was a very pleasant evening and I am even more full of admiration for the old boy.

I decide to start the chilly but dry morning by walking Eddie across Strode Meadows and around the Kidneys. But first I take the opportunity to peer through the chain link fence at the mouth of the little inlet under Strode Road Bridge. The emptiness is striking and very sad. *Nirvana* had been a lovely looking barge with so much history. Now, presumably, she is just an insurance claim being made by a person or persons unknown. Or maybe not. That would mean asking the police for a crime case number and I suspect the owner of *Nirvana* is very reluctant to reveal their identity to the Thames Valley force.

I hear a noise behind me as I stare through the wire and find John Turner a few metres behind me. I'm amused to see Tod skulking behind him, eyeing Eddie with considerable wariness. Eddie too seems to think it's best to stay close to me – so I'd say a canine ceasefire has been declared.

'Now then. Mending okay?'

'Hi there, John. Yes thanks, and thanks again for your help the other night.'

'It was nowt. Shame about the boat, though. She were a beauty.'

'And you have no idea who owned her?'

He shakes his head. 'Like I said, she's been there a while. She went for a tidy sum. Captain Hugh reckons she had a bit of history to her.'

'How often did they have the parties on board?'

'Oh. Pretty well every weekend, I reckon. Well, Fridays and Saturdays, anyhow. More often during the school holidays.'

Why would that be I wonder, unless it was easier for underage girls to be procured more easily? 'Have the police spoken to you about the fire?'

He rubs the grey bristle on his chin and gives me a sly look. 'No. They might have called round while I've been at work. But I've got nowt to tell them, have I? Sound asleep, I was. Tires you out, working all day in the open air.'

The lack of police curiosity about the arson seems crazy to me. But then I was on-board to witness what happened, and I know about the recording studio. Perhaps they think it was an accident and even if they don't, there isn't an owner jumping up and down at them for some action to be taken. And yet they know what Jane and I saw – and who we saw.

'Thanks, John. I don't know what's been going on over there but I'm determined to find out.'

'Aye, well, you know what they say? It's not the size of the dog in the fight that matters, it's the size of the fight in the dog. Looks like you and Eddie there have got something in common.'

After finishing a circuit of the nature reserve, Eddie and I call in to the clubhouse café on the bridge to share a round of sausage sandwiches. The guy behind the counter is probably four stone heavier than he should be, with a shaved head and a red spade-shaped beard. He reminds of Holbein's painting of Henry the Eighth – not a healthy look. He stoops to pat Eddie after depositing the sandwiches and a mug of coffee at my table.

'Shame about the barge,' I say, nodding downriver. 'Quite a blaze.'

'Did you see it then?' he asks, straightening up with a grunt at the effort involved. 'The explosion woke me up – I live here in the boathouse.'

'Yes. I live on board the narrowboat that's moored opposite. I haven't been there long.'

'Welcome to the Isis,' he says.

'Thanks. I'm Jack Johnson,' I hold out my hand.

He seems a bit startled but gives me his in return. 'Um Potter, Stephen Potter ... '

'Any idea who owned her?'

He stops shaking my hand but retains it in his. 'Why d'you want to know?'

I shake my head as casually as I can. 'Just curious. She was a lovely looking barge.'

He releases my hand, puts both of his into his pockets and shrugs. 'No idea. Doesn't matter now, does it? Bloody kids, I expect. I hope the police catch them.'

'Is that what they think?'

He shrugs again. 'Who else? Little bastards. What d'you do for a living then?'

I take a bite of my sandwich to give myself time to think. So far, Stephen Potter has answered most of my questions with a question of his own. I'm beginning to suspect he knows more than he wants to suggest. 'I'm a journalist.'

'You working, then? Looking for a story about *Nirvana*?'

It's interesting that he knows the name of the barge. Even though it was moored nearby, it was hidden away on its little inlet and it was quite difficult to see its name unless you were looking for it. I shake my head. 'No. I've only just arrived in Oxford. Just curious because my boat was almost opposite the fire.'

'Yeah? Well, I expect they'll be moving you along soon. They're not that keen on boats permanently cluttering up the river and that's not a proper mooring. The university gives them hell about it. Gets in the way of the racing. See you around.' He heads off back to the kitchen.

I check my phone to see a text. It must have arrived during our walk.

Lunch today? Ashmolean Rooftop? 1pm. Julia x

Back at the boat, Eddie and I while away a few hours before I leave him to keep the appointment with my editor. The restaurant she's chosen has bleached blonde furniture and trendy light fittings that look like oversized puffer fish. A large and well-stocked shiny metal bar stretches away at one end of the room. The place is buzzing, considering the time of year, and I imagine it must get rammed at the height of the tourist season. Julia hasn't arrived yet so I claim our table opposite a huge panoramic window that offers a view of the city centre skyline. The jumble of spires, cupolas, gables and turrets remind me of the Oxford rooftops that are clambered over by Lyra and Roger in the first book of Philip Pullman's *His Dark Material* trilogy. The memory prompts me to make a mental note to re-read the books. This in turn sets me musing on the daemons in the books – spirit animals which accompany each character and demonstrate the kind of person they are. I have always seen myself as having a Border Terrier daemon, mirroring my tenacity and tendency to ignore orders. And Nina? I think of her as having an otter: sleek, lithe and elegant, good on the water but relentlessly determined when she needs to be. How about Jane? A Siamese cat, I think. Very seductive and clever, but self-centred and aloof. Even as I smile to myself, I realise how unfair this is to Jane. I am mentally searching the animal kingdom for an alternative when Julia arrives, followed by a young waitress carrying two gin and tonics. She puts a wet kiss on my cheek and dismisses the girl.

'Lovely to see you, darling. I've got a quiet day today so thought we might have a little editorial conference.'

'Fine by me,' I say looking around. 'Popular place.'

She sighs theatrically. 'Oh, it's too popular. Did you know, we had seven million visitors to Oxford last year? That's nearly 20,000 a day. Apparently Oxford is the eighth most visited city in the UK for people who stay over. It just seems to be an all-year-round thing now. You can't bloody move for those godawful trails of tourists, blocking the pavement and standing around in groups while the guides drone on and on.'

'It must bring a lot of money into the place,' I say.

She flaps a hand in frustration. 'Yes, of course. But it just gets so boring for the rest of us after a while. The coaches clogging up the streets and the language-school kids barging into you. They have no sense of personal space.'

She orders a niçoise salad and a steak, and I do the same. Then she makes a last-minute decision to order a bowl of chips and a bottle of Sauvignon, 'For both of us to share.'

'Interesting piece on the pretty detective sergeant,' she says, smiling roguishly. 'Did you get on well with her?'

'Er ... yes. She was nice.'

'Sorry you had to cut it back a bit. All that county lines stuff wasn't really the point of the piece, was it?'

'It was interesting, though.'

'Yes, well. We got there in the end, didn't we? You see, I can't let CQ get too serious. Too cerebral.' I privately doubt that there's much chance of that happening. 'This place is split down the middle between gown and town, Jack darling. Always has been and always will be. Oh, thank you, sweetie.' She has paused to admire the floppy fringed young barman who has delivered the wine and poured us both a generous glassful. 'There was a riot once between the students and the townsfolk over the quality of some wine in a pub.' There doesn't seem to be anything wrong with her own wine, I think, watching her glug it with evident satisfaction. 'It lasted for three days, some students were killed, and some colleges were ransacked. That was in thirteen-hundred-and-something and it's not that much better now! Anyway, CQ is on the side of the town – well those with money in the town – and of course the monied countryside around here too. The famous Chipping Norton set and so on.'

'Yes. I think you can tell that from the adverts,' I say.

'Exactly, Jack! And the editorial has to complement the adverts. We know our readership and they're highly aspirational.'

'Materialistic.'

'Exactly! You've got it. They don't want to read about issues.' She draws the word out in contempt, so that it sounds like 'ishoooos'. There is a moment of peace while the food arrives, and I top up her glass for her. 'Forget the university. Our lifeblood is the business community here. There are 4,700 businesses in this city and they all love seeing themselves knocking back the plonk at dinner dances and networking at business and charity events. They all want to read about themselves and their new product launches. And they all want nice new ideas on how to spend their money on life's little luxuries. We're here to give them what they want – for a price, of course.'

'I understand,' I say, finding solace in my wine glass. I can't think of anything more soul-destroying than all of this, but it's my only hope for an income at the moment.

'Of course you do, Jack darling,' she says, shovelling about two thirds of the bowl of chips onto her plate and slathering them with mayonnaise. 'That's why I'm so looking forward to your piece about the hot air balloons at Blenheim. Ballooning and polo. They're tailormade sports for us. Lovely pictures and lots of lovely advertising off the back of them. Oh yes, the luxury retail trade love a bit of ballooning or polo. When is it? The day after tomorrow?'

'Yes. Umm ... I've done a bit of research. That is to say, I've been up in a friend's balloon. How d'you want me to play it? What angle do you want?'

'Oh, you don't need to go up with them again. Just hook up with our snapper and scoot around on the ground before take-off and get as many names into it as you can. Try to look out for the sponsors, the people with money, and the blue-bloods – anyone with a title, darling. And get lots of pics of people drinking bubbly before they all take off.' My heart sinks. 'Oh ... and do me a favour. A friend of mine in the Chamber of Commerce is sponsoring a balloon. It looks like Paddington Bear apparently. He owns the local Mercedes dealership. Make sure you get a nice little interview with him before it takes off. Here's his card. I need to scratch his back, if you know what I mean. He gave me a lovely big discount on a new car recently.' She draws breath to greedily inspect the dessert menu. I'm wary that she might pull the same trick as last time and leave me with the bill. Only this one will be considerably larger.

'Umm ... is this on the magazine?'

'No, sweetheart. It's on the Ashmolean. I do a monthly restaurant column. Four or five places at a time. And they all pay for the privilege.'

'Can you get much copy out of two steaks with salads and a bowl of chips?'

She laughs delightedly. 'Don't be silly, darling. That's why you're here. Just send me a couple of hundred words, will you? Now I fancy a chocolate brownie. How about you?'

I pull out a notebook while we wait for our desserts and scribble a few thoughts about the décor, service and food. Then a thought occurs to me. 'Julia, have you heard of a dating agency in Oxford? It's called Garden of Eden.'

'Oh yes,' she says immediately. 'Everyone knows Marcie Lopez. She's very active in the Rotary Club and she shows up at most of the social events on the Oxford business scene. We often picture her – she's a great networker. Why d'you ask? Are you using her to find the new love of your life?' She shrieks with laughter and an equally noisy group of American businessmen on a neighbouring table pause to look over at her.

'Is she a friend of yours?'

'I wouldn't go so far as that far, but ...' Julia leans forward towards me and drops her voice to a whisper. 'But I have used her a few times to provide me with a lovely young chap to be my escort. It was just after my divorce, when I had to go to a few dinners and things. I gave her a "Cotswold Movers and Shakers" profile in return. She's Spanish but you can hardly tell. She's always very well turned out. I think her business must be doing pretty well. So come on, Jack darling. Spill the beans. Why are you interested in her?'

'Oh,' I say vaguely, 'a friend of a friend is thinking about going onto her books. I just wanted to make sure it was all legit and above board.'

'Oh yes. I'm sure it is. At least, my young man from Garden of Eden was a perfect gentleman.' She pauses. 'A perfectly well-behaved gentleman – it was *such* a pity!' She cackles with laughter again. 'And I have a friend who used Marcie to organise a dinner at her house for a bunch of single ladies. Well ... I didn't know where to look! It was served by "Butlers in the Buff" – all these lovely fit young male students were just wearing aprons and nothing else! It was hilarious. Every time they turned around you could see their bare bums. She said they were all university rowers or rugby players. But it was all harmless fun. Now then, I can't sit here all afternoon gossiping. I must dash. Lovely lunch, darling. Just a couple of hundred words about lunch by the end of play tomorrow. Nothing too nasty. Enjoy Blenheim. Toodle-oo.'

CHAPTER THIRTY-SEVEN

Nina is stretched out in the saloon on *Jumping Jack Flash* with Eddie. He is sitting upright in the crook of her arm and looking insufferably smug.

'Hi Jack,' she says brightly. 'Cal's training on the Thames at Wallingford, so I thought I'd pop down and see you both. How are you?'

I yawn. 'A bit knackered, actually. I had a heavy evening with Hugh and I've just had a slightly liquid lunch with the CQ woman.'

'Who? Jane Henry?' she asks sweetly. 'Haven't you finished her article yet?'

I scowl at her. 'No, Julia Goodfellow. The magazine's editor.'

'Oh. Anywhere nice?'

'The Ashmolean Rooftop. And now I have to write a 200-word restaurant review for the privilege. My Meal in a Museum with an Antique.'

She giggles. I realise I am slightly discomfited by her sudden appearance and good mood. 'Don't look so grumpy about it. There are worse things in life.'

'I know,' I sigh. 'Drink?' I open the fridge door where half a bottle of white wine is waiting.

'No thanks. I'm not drinking at the moment. Cal isn't either because he's in training. And it sounds like you've had enough for the day too.'

I sigh and put the kettle on. 'I've got to start making arrangements to cover the Winter Balloon Lift Off on the day after tomorrow. I'll need to organise transport out to Blenheim and start sussing out which Hooray Henries are taking part.'

'Well, Cal isn't a Hooray Henry, but I think he's still planning on a flight,' she says. 'Although maybe you two should avoid sharing a basket at 2,000 feet for a while.'

I nod ruefully. 'I think I'll have to stay on the ground this time anyway. It sounds like she wants a glorified social diary piece. Anyway, how is he now? He seemed a lot more cheerful when you called in on the paddle boards.'

'He does seem a lot better now the police have identified Phi's killer. Although, I think he's still trying to put a brave face on it all. And I know precisely what that's like. He still hasn't told his father about Phi's death. I'm not even sure he had told him he was seeing someone. I think that might be worrying him. He respects his father hugely and doesn't want to let him down.'

'At least he's back in training.' I decide that's enough discussion about Superman. 'And what about you? What are your plans now? You were going to start looking for another apartment when all this kicked off.'

'That's still the plan,' she says. 'But there's no rush. Cal says I'm welcome to stay for as long as I want. It's a very comfortable house and I think he still needs me for the moment.'

I look hard into her large black eyes to see if she is deliberately plunging a metaphorical stiletto into the organ which pumps blood around my body. 'You're always welcome to move back onto the boat,' I say. She has opened her mouth to reply when there is a knock on the hatchway. 'Cal?' I ask, somewhat bitterly.

Nina ignores my tone. 'No. I don't think so. He was going to be a few hours.'

I make my way to the stern. A thin man is standing by the tiller under a black umbrella. He has a scraggy little beard that fails to hide cheeks pockmarked with acne scars. I hadn't noticed previously, but sleet is starting to coat the boat's roof and the riverbank with a layer of white crystals.

'My card,' he says, showing me a plastic rectangle on a lanyard round his neck. I hold it for examination, forcing him to bend towards me at an awkward angle. He has a prominent Adam's apple. The pass reads: Allan Wood. Leisure Enforcement Officer, Environment Agency. 'Can I have a word?'

'Sure. Come on in.' I introduce Nina to Mr Wood, and she gives a little smirk at his job title.

'Does that mean you enforce people to take their leisure for a living?' she asks brightly. 'That must be nice. Ordering people to have a lie-in!'

'Or to go to the cinema?' I add.

'Or the pub?' says Nina laughing.

Our visitor purses his lips. 'I enforce the rules so that everyone can enjoy their leisure time on the river,' he says without a trace of humour. 'In this instance, I am calling to warn you to leave this mooring or face a penalty fine.' He looks at us both. 'Who is the owner of this boat?'

'Uh, that's me. Jack Johnson.'

He nods. 'Well, here's a notice to move on within 24 hours or face the consequences. There are no official moorings here.' He hands me a slip of paper.

'Look, wait a minute,' I say. 'It's hardly rush-hour round here at the moment, is it? It's mid-January and it's snowing. There's plenty of space for any other boats that want to moor up along here.' I stop short of pointing out that Hugh and John have been moored on this stretch of river much longer than me. I don't want to cause trouble for them too.

'Not everyone agrees with you, Mr Johnson. I'm just doing my job.'

'What? What does that mean?' asks Nina. 'Has someone complained about Jack's boat being here?'

Wood shakes his head. 'I'm not at liberty to go into details. Suffice to say we are acting in response to certain representations of concern and the regulations are very clear – as you'll see from that note when you read it.'

'Oh, come on,' I explode. 'If someone has complained about me mooring here in January, when there's plenty of space, I have a right to know who it is.'

But the man just clamps his mouth shut and shakes his head. 'No, you don't. I'm sorry, Mr Johnson. You need to move on, and it needs to be a *meaningful distance*. Good day to you.'

I don't bother to show him off the boat and slump into a chair. 'Bugger it. I thought they'd turn a blind eye.'

'It sounds like someone's shopped you.'

'I know. And I think I know who.' Nina raises one of her highly arched eyebrows in enquiry. 'Detective Chief Inspector Brian Philpott. He ordered me to get out of Oxford when I saw him after the boat fire. He's got the clout to put the right word into the right ear.' But I also remember the waiter at the boathouse cafe this morning warning me that my time on the mooring might be limited. Could it have been him rather than the policeman? But why would he do that?

Nina is looking at me curiously. 'What boat fire?'

'*Nirvana*. The houseboat that was moored across the river. She was burnt to a cinder the night before last. Her gas bottles went up and there's virtually nothing left of her. And, conveniently, it seemed to happen just before the police were due to go on board and have a look around. They'd been trying to get a search warrant ever since we saw Romaine being ferried to the onboard party. After Jane told them about it.'

Nina tugs an ear thoughtfully and gives me a level look. 'And this fire, you had nothing to do with it?'

I am very tempted to share every detail of my narrow escape and describe what I saw on board the barge. I have already told Anna. Nina and I have gone through a lot together and it seems the most natural thing in the world to draw her in to helping me solve the puzzle. But I still suspect she would tell Cal and Cal would tell the police and I would quickly have DCI Philpott knocking on my door with a set of handcuffs. And after all, it's Nina who has effectively walked out on me. If she wants some space, she can have it. So, I swallow hard and prepare to tell less than the whole truth to the woman I love.

'No, Nina. Surprisingly enough I didn't set the boat on fire because I'm not an arsonist – and anyway, I thought she was a rather lovely. She was an old floating clubhouse for St Michael's College – before they built the row of brick boathouses on the island. It's a crying shame.'

Her eyes are still narrowed suspiciously. 'So why did Philpott tell you to get out of Dodge?'

I shrug helplessly. 'Call it a personality clash. He knows I don't think much of his half-arsed murder investigation.'

'And?'

'And I asked him if the sighting of a senior police officer in the party boat was prompting him to drag his feet.'

'Oh Jack!'

'What?'

'The murder enquiry is finished. Why can't you just accept that? Unless ...'

'Unless?'

'Unless this is all about trying to prove yourself to me,' she says quietly. 'You know you don't need to do that. In fact, I'd rather you just stopped whatever it is that you're doing and call it a day. Something tragic happened between Phi and her tutor. Whatever it was may come out in time and it may not. But you're just going to cause more unnecessary pain and hurt if you go blundering around.'

'You mean to Cal?' I demand.

'Yes. Don't you think he's gone through enough? And Phi's parents? Maybe she *was* working as some kind of escort? Who knows and who cares now? Will it help anyone to drag her name through the mud?'

I shake my head. 'But don't you see, Nina, there could be other girls out there. Being exploited. Putting themselves in danger. Aren't you interested in helping them if we can? What if Phi was just the tip of the iceberg? You should hear Jane talk about the organised crime groups and their county lines activities around here. They're evil bastards and they need to be taken on.'

'Ah yes, the blessed Detective Sergeant Henry,' says Nina. 'You seem to have been very impressed with what she's had to say.'

I feel like a man who has run out onto an iced pond and feels it cracking and splintering beneath his feet. 'She's a proven expert in her field,' I say sullenly.

'And it was very clear from our balloon flight what she thinks about you running around trying to do the police's job,' snaps Nina. 'So listen to her if you're not going to listen to me. Don't you think you've caused enough damage already?'

I try to protest at the injustice of this, but she has the bit between her teeth now.

'You should never have spoken to Romaine before the police and you know it, Jack. If you hadn't, he might not have killed himself and the police might have discovered everything that happened between him and Phi. Now we'll never know. That may be pretty hard for you to stomach but it's the brutal truth. I'm amazed Cal didn't throw you out of that balloon. You've got to live with yourself but don't try to justify it by mounting your charger and chasing more windmills. Just stop it!'

Nina's eyes are brimming with passion. I am stunned by her tirade and still groping for the words to answer it when she angrily wipes her face with a sweep of a forearm and stands up. 'So, no, Jack. I won't be coming back to stay on board *Jumping Jack Flash* with you. Not until you bloody well sort yourself out!'

CHAPTER THIRTY-EIGHT

I am fuming to myself, both about Nina and the notice to quit my mooring, and so I decide to go in search of Hugh as a calming influence. He readily accepts an invitation to the Isis Farmhouse and so we wander across the riverbank to the large white building and settle down in its cosy interior with two pints of the local real ale. He can't do much about Nina, but he does have a short-term solution to my mooring problem.

'Look at this,' he says, opening his smartphone and showing me a website labelled Thames Visitor Moorings. It's showing that the official Environment Agency status of the river has moved from 'Normal' to 'Yellow Boards Increasing.' Apparently, this means the river is rising and flowing faster. There has been a fair bit of rain recently and this makes sense. 'When the Thames is on this level of flood alert, we're supposed to find a safe mooring and stay put,' says Hugh. 'Stay put means don't move. You can show this to your official visitor and tell him to bugger off for now!'

'But what if it gets even worse?' I ask with genuine concern. I am way out of my normal comfort zone of relatively tranquil canal waters.

'Ah well, if it increases to "Red Boards" then we probably ought to find somewhere a bit quieter. Like the canal or a marina, perhaps? The Thames does occasionally flood over the riverbank and onto the path here, and if the river comes up an exceptional amount we could even risk the boats floating over the bank and being left high and dry when the floodwater recedes. I was going to move *Raven* somewhere safer anyway, rather than leave her here when I take Mrs Spencer back to Gloucester.'

Hugh seems quite blasé about the whole thing, but I am already worrying about my ability to move *Jumping Jack Flash* to safety through fast-flowing water in order to avoid the 'Red Boards' situation. I have no desire to see my precious boat swept out and across the nearby water meadows. Unlike Hugh, my boat is also my only home.

'Don't worry,' he says, sensing my anxiety, 'I'll keep a close eye on things for now and we can double up and move the boats if we need to. Mooring is a huge issue in this city and a lot of boats are here without official consent. It seems as though you've rubbed someone up the wrong way.'

I say my thanks, finish my pint and return to *Jumping Jack Flash* as Hugh heads off to the hospital. Nina has given me a lot to think about. But the more I mull over her words, the more indignant I become. After all that we have been through together! She was quite careless about announcing that she going to continue sharing Cal's house with him. She showed no appreciation of how difficult I might find that decision. And then, to accuse me of causing Romaine's death! Did she really think that? It was a low blow on a sensitive bruise. No, it was all about her precious Cal and the fact that Romaine could have explained how Phi died and given the American some peace of mind. Although no doubt they would both call it 'closure'. She was seeing absolutely everything from his perspective now. And then, to warn me off any more investigations. Outrageous. What if there were more girls in Phi's situation? What if an organised crime group was behind her death rather than Romaine? Why is no one else interested in exploring this possibility?

I have worked myself up into a toxic blend of self-pity and indignation that can only be resolved by doing something. The sleet has eased up a bit and the light is fading when I snatch up a quilted jacket, a flat cap, scarf and gloves and head back out to the city. I am soon ensconced in the window of the White Rabbit again, with a pint and a pizza, watching the door of the Garden of Eden offices opposite. At five o'clock precisely, the door opens and two women emerge. The younger one bustles away while the older woman, who I assume to be Marcie, carefully locks up behind her.

I fall into step behind the woman, munching on a last triangle of pizza as I follow her. A brown leather briefcase hangs on a strap from her right shoulder and she is wearing a distinctive orange scarf over black hair. This makes it easy to spot her in the throng of late afternoon shoppers and tourists, so I hang back at a safe distance. Eventually, she turns off a main street and enters a multi-storey car park. I follow her up two flights of stairs to a level where I watch her through a small glass window in the door. She moves quickly to a large new-looking maroon BMW saloon and I hear the beep of her key as she opens its doors.

I immediately turn, race back down to street level and run across the road to a line of taxis I had spotted a moment ago. Thankfully, there is no queue of people waiting and I jump into the back of the first one, some kind of Skoda SUV.

'Right then, chief, where to?' says the driver, punching his machine to indicate the start of a passenger journey.

'There's a big maroon BMW about to come out of that car park. I want you to follow that car.'

The man turns to look at me. I see from his taxi licence that he is called Karl Rose. 'You've got to be kidding?'

I reach for my wallet. 'Don't worry. I've got plenty of cash on me. Just follow the car when it comes out.'

He grins at me. 'D'you know, I've been a taxi driver for twenty years and no one has ever asked me to do that!' He looks very happy about it and shakes his head in disbelief. 'Honestly, I've been waiting a lifetime for this to happen!' He starts the engine and looks eagerly across the street until Marcie's car appears at the ticket barrier.

'There it is. Try not to make it too obvious.'

'Leave it to me, chief,' he says excitedly. We are soon snarled up in traffic as it inches its way out of the city. The taxi has slotted into a position two cars back from our quarry. 'What's this all about then? You a private detective?'

'What? No. I'm a journalist.'

'Oh right. So, what's this all about then? What's she done?'

'Sorry. Need-to-know basis. It's er ... connected with the National Lottery.'

'Understood, chief. No problem. Big winner, is she?'

'Massive.'

'Roger Moore said it once, in a Bond film.'

'What?'

'Follow that car! That's what he said. And Inspector Clouseau did too. What was his name? That guy in the Pink Panther films?'

'Peter Sellers.'

'That's him. Peter Sellers. He said it too. And there was another one. Arghh ... what was it?'

'Okay. I'm sorry. It's a cliché. But I just needed you to do it.'

'Not a problem, chief. What else would you say? Follow that car. Been waiting twenty years for them three little words. I tell you, it's made my day. Made my year! That's all I'm saying. Wait till I tell my mates down the pub.'

We are speeding up now as the traffic escapes the endless roundabouts and traffic lights of the city and the road opens up into the surrounding countryside. Karl Rose is concentrating hard on the task in hand. Having waited a lifetime for this, he clearly doesn't want to blow it. Luckily, his car is black and won't be too noticeable. He's probably half a mile behind the big BMW when it starts signalling right and turns into a much smaller country lane. We follow the same route. We're barrelling along between high hedges when we shoot past a large high wooden gate which is in the process of sliding shut. I just get a glimpse of maroon through the remaining foot-wide gap. 'Pull in here,' I order.

The taxi skids to a halt on the slick surface of the lane and Karl turns around with a panicked face. 'What? What d'you mean? We don't want to lose her!'

'She's turned off into that house back there. The gate was closing just as we went past.'

'Thank Christ for that. I wouldn't want cock it up for you, would I?'

'You did great, Karl. Would you mind waiting while I go and knock on the door? See if I can get an interview?'

'Sure thing, chief. In fact, why don't we say the trip's ended and I'll start a new one when you're back? Take as long as you like. I've got my paper.'

'That's very good of you, Karl. Just drive on a bit and find somewhere to pull in and wait, would you?'

He drives forward until he can swing into a space in front of a gate into a farm field. 'Right then. Shall we synchronise watches? That's what they do in the films, isn't it?'

'What? Yes. Okay. It's 5.25 p.m.'

'Right you are, chief. No rush. See you when I see you. Good luck. Most fun I've had on the job in years.'

CHAPTER THIRTY-NINE

I climb out of the car and walk back down the lane. We have driven further past the automatic gate than I thought, and it takes me five minutes to get back to it. It's impossible to see over the top and there is an equally high and impenetrable yew hedge stretching away to either side. I retrace my steps to the start of the hedge where it joins a wooden fence as tall as me. It stands at a right angle to the lane. The fence looks new and well-maintained. I follow the fence until it turns again, presumably to form the rear perimeter of the property. However, this area is more wooded. A number of trees have been pollarded along the line of the boundary, presumably to prevent them shedding leaves onto the garden. One in particular has a stout branch at knee height and it gives me the chance to climb up. I cautiously poke my head over the top of the fence.

In front of me is a neat lawn that slopes slightly upwards to a long stone-built terrace with well-clipped topiary in pots and a large all-weather seating area under rain covers. Beyond the terrace is an enormous wall of glass that leads on to the kind of kitchen that is showcased in *Cotswold Quality*. It is brightly lit by a miniature galaxy of downlighters in the ceiling. Marcie has taken off her orange headscarf, but she is still in her outdoor coat and talking on a mobile phone whilst fumbling in her briefcase.

Then she juggles the phone with a cigarette and a lighter and steps towards the glass wall. I shrink my head lower but continue to watch.

She slides back a large glass panel and steps out on to the terrace, where she takes a lungful of tobacco and blows the smoke out into the cold night air. Her voice carries easily to the back of the lawn. 'Yes … yes … I know, Finn. But I wouldn't want to go over five hundred with my share. We'd need to spend quite a bit on it. But it's big. It's Grade 2 listed. Loads of history. It could work … Yes, there's direct access off the river, just like you thought. I think you need to come up and have a look for yourself. Okay. *Adios mi amigo*.'

I watch Marcie finish her cigarette and return to the kitchen after closing the glass door against the chill of the evening. She opens a tall red fridge and pours herself a large glass of white wine. Now she shrugs off her coat, opens her laptop at a long wooden dining table and sits down in front of it, still taking occasional sips of her wine. She has her back to me, and I can see the white glow of the screen over her shoulder. After a couple of minutes, she stands, stretches and leaves the room. While I am watching, an upstairs light goes on – presumably a bathroom or a bedroom.

The laptop is still open, and its screen is still awake. I check the upstairs window. A blind has been pulled down, but the light is still on behind it. A blind would suggest it's a bathroom – she might be in there for a little while. I'm quickly up and over the top of the fence, running in a crouch across the lawn and up the steps of the terrace. I'm now standing at the threshold of the glass panel. Did she lock it? Will there be an alarm? Is she just changing and about to return any second? I notice that the glass of wine has gone upstairs with her. That's a good sign. But what if she's just a wholly innocent Oxford businesswoman having a drink and a shower at the end of a tiring day? What am I doing here? On her property? I can almost hear the chorus of Jane, Nina and Cal shrieking in my ear and asking exactly the same question – especially Jane.

But the laptop is too tempting. I slide the glass panel a short distance. It isn't locked and no alarm sounds so now I slide it wide enough for me to enter, close it behind me and cross the kitchen. Some music has been switched on upstairs and I think I can hear the faint sound of gushing taps. Is a bath being filled? I haven't done a single sensible thing since I arrived in Oxford and I'm not going to start now. I've also had a bit to drink which is making me a bit gung-ho. I sit down at the table in front of the laptop. My heart is pounding. If she returns now, she'll scream blue murder and call the police. Or attack me? What if she owns a gun? I could get six years for burglary. I shake my head to clear my mind and focus on the immediate issue.

I push the spacebar on the keyboard to prevent the laptop from timing itself out and stare at rows of neatly arranged folders in the documents file. They are all labelled GE, presumably standing for Garden of Eden, and each one has a different set of initials. I try opening one. It seems to be some kind of timesheet for an employee. I am about to open another when I hear a phone ringing upstairs and Marcie begin talking. How much longer have I got? She could come back down at any moment and I am already miles across the line and on the wrong side of the law. Then I remember my keyring – or more specifically the bright orange CQ memory stick that Julia gave me at our first meeting. I push it into the laptop and save the entire contents of the documents file to it. It's taking a while to download. I can still hear Marcie talking upstairs and calculate it's safe to wait while I can hear her voice. Come on, damn you, faster. Faster.

Suddenly, I can no longer hear Marcie's voice. There is definitely the sound of footsteps descending the stairs, getting louder and coming closer. I am tempted to snatch the memory stick out of the device, but I know it would leave a message alerting Marcie to its forcible and improper removal. It's also pulsing with a little light, which tells me that it hasn't finished its task. There's no time to make the door to the garden and so I drop onto all fours under the table and pray she won't return to it or her laptop.

At the far end of the kitchen, I see a pair of Birkenstocks below bare shins and the bottom of a towelling dressing gown. They slap across the tiled floor, disappear behind the central island and emerge by the glass door. I can see all of the back of her now, her jet-black hair contrasting with the white of her robe. She drops a catch before turning and moving to a row of light switches on a side wall. The room goes dim rather than dark and I watch intently as Marcie's ugly sandals slap noisily back out of the kitchen. I hear them reclimb the stairs.

I wait another couple of minutes for the memory stick to do its job and then eject it properly and return it to my pocket. Now what? If I leave through the glass panel, I won't be able to lock it from the outside. She may realise that someone has been here. I peer along the hall towards the front door. It's on some kind of latch. But the stairs lead up, off the hall, and Marcie is in a bath somewhere at the top of them. Would she hear me opening and closing the front door? Her music is still playing – classical flamenco guitar. It's not loud. For the first time in my life, I wish that someone was a heavy metal fan.

There may be other doors I can leave by, but I don't want to start exploring the entire floorplan of the house. No, there's nothing for it. I creep forward along the hall, thankful that it has a thick carpet. A control panel for some kind of alarm system is next to the door. I pray that she only activates it when she leaves the house. There is no way of knowing. The Yale lock twists sideways, and I pull the door back, just wide enough for me to slide through. There is no piercing shriek of an alarm. However, I know the lock will make a noise when it shoots home as I pull the door shut behind me. Will it be loud enough to carry upstairs? If it does, I calculate I will have seconds to get out of the garden unnoticed. Should I try to scale the automatic front gate or make my way around the house and escape the same way that I came in?

I turn and ease the door into its closed position. I do this incredibly slowly, a fraction of a millimetre at a time. I can feel the Yale lock beginning to spring back but maintain control of the door, closing it in fractions of movement until there is a little click and it is home. I don't believe the sound would have been audible in the upstairs of the house and above the music. Maybe she even had her head underwater with a bit of luck? I weigh up the wooden gate at the end of the drive but decide it's a bit taller than the rear fence and there could be unknown dangers in trying to climb it, perhaps some broken glass stuck to its top edge or someone passing on the lane at the moment I climb over. I make my way along the side of the property and across the lawn where I sprint the final few metres, leaping up to rest my stomach on the top of the rear fence. It scrapes and bites into me painfully, but I scramble to get one foot out to my side and over the top of the fence. I manage to pull myself over sideways and fall into a large clump of nettles. I lie there for a moment despite the stinging to my hands and face, flat on my back and with my chest heaving. I really am too old for this.

Eventually I make my way back to the lane and jog over to Karl and his waiting taxi. 'Well?' he says eagerly. 'How did it go?'

'Nah ... false alarm,' I reply, slightly breathlessly. 'It wasn't the right woman. Looked like her, though. Back to Strode Road Bridge please, Karl. You've earned your tip.'

CHAPTER FORTY

Eddie is pleased to see me and even happier after I have fed him, walked him and he is settled down on the banquette next to me. I open my laptop. First, I check the status of the river. The Live River Conditions page from the Environment Agency tells me it is still 'Yellow Boards Rising' on this stretch of the water. It could go in either direction, either worsening to 'Red Boards' or becoming 'Yellow Boards Decreasing' and then reverting back to 'Normal'. I check the weather forecast. There is no more rainfall due until midday tomorrow, but there's a strengthening wind for the Oxfordshire area, rising to ten miles an hour. This sounds too much for hot-air ballooning and so I search up the Blenheim website. Yes, sure enough, the Winter Lift Off scheduled for the following morning has been postponed 'due to adverse weather conditions.' I send a quick email to Julia to let her know and ask her to cancel the photographer.

Next, I insert the memory stick and open the documents folder. One file is labelled GE/OM and sure enough, the attached content all seems to relate to Ophelia McVeigh. It includes an initial job application, which stresses her typing, administrative and computer skills and there is a brief aide memoire about her initial interview. The job offer and job description are included. It looks like a list of typical administrative and secretarial duties. There is a timesheet, which shows that she did ten part-time shifts during December and the early part of January. The spreadsheet also shows a sequence of modest payments for the work.

There is absolutely nothing to suggest that she was working as a highly-paid escort. This makes me regret my words to Cal in the balloon. He was right to be outraged about my speculations. Finally, there is a brief, slightly terse email from Ophelia tendering her resignation with immediate effect. It is dated Friday January 9th. But there is nothing particularly odd or suspicious about it other than the brief length of employment and the lack of a reason for leaving.

I scan the other folders quickly. They are in alphabetical order and I stop at one labelled GE/JR. John Romaine? Sure enough, the first file is a client registration document, which includes a head and shoulders picture of the thin bespectacled academic. In the comments section, someone has typed: Married. Four children. Doctorate in Medieval History. Tutor at St.Hugh's. The second folder, GE/JR (2) is a spreadsheet of dates and payments which begins two months ago. I count two initial payments of £500. The third is for £750 and the fourth has suddenly increased to £2,000.

I click on a third folder GE/JR (3). It takes slightly longer to open and then I see why. It is full of black and white photographs. The first one shows the long and entirely naked skinny white frame of Dr Romaine lying on his back on a double bed. The picture has been taken from directly above and I am almost certain it must be in one of the cabins on board *Nirvana*. In fact, I see that Nirvana is typed in small lettering below the photograph alongside an automatic time and date stamp. Romaine has his eyes closed and the absence of his glasses makes his face look young and vulnerable – which is ironic because on either side of him is a totally naked girl, also asleep by the look of it. But these girls look much younger and even more vulnerable – in their mid-teens, perhaps? If they're over the age of consent then it must be barely so. I scroll down to look at more photographs in a sequence below this one. It shows the same trio, and in these pictures, they are most definitely not asleep.

This has to explain why Romaine killed himself, doesn't it? He was obviously being blackmailed. The sums of money he was paying out had suddenly risen sharply. How could a mid-level academic possibly afford to keep them going? Of course, this doesn't necessarily mean that he didn't kill Ophelia. The man obviously liked younger women. He could still have tried it on with his student and something might have happened which led to her death. But equally, his so-called suicide note could have just been referring to his nocturnal gymnastics with underage girls on *Nirvana*. I wish I knew the exact wording of the note. My mind is racing as I sip my coffee. When I told him that the police wanted to speak to him about his partying on board *Nirvana*, he must have assumed that his secret life was about to blow wide open. And that would explain why he threw himself off the tower at his college. Had the police jumped to the wrong conclusion about his involvement in Ophelia's murder because they didn't know about the blackmail?

The question now is what to do with this information? Of course, I should take it to Philpott and let him question Marcie a lot more closely about her business relationship with the dead man. But would he be able to use these files as evidence? Technically speaking, they've been obtained by a house burglar. I honestly don't know the answer to this, although I can predict the initial reaction of the aggressive little policeman. He's unlikely to be recommending me for a *Cotswold Quality* Good Citizen award. Perhaps I can find a way of getting this stuff to the police anonymously? After all, Romaine could just be the tip of the iceberg. No doubt he was just one of many who had been tempted by the outwardly respectable Garden of Eden before being trapped in a sordid underage sex scene that finally lead to blackmail and extortion?

The other rows of files are still lined up in front of me. I open a few at random. GE/OB. GE/ST. GE/SG. Naked middle-aged and older men fill the screen of my laptop alongside different girls, some slightly older and some, to my utter disgust, younger than the ones in the Romaine pictures. I continue along the row of folders feeling like a grubby voyeur. Christ. Some of the night vision photographs also show men with boys. University students, perhaps? A couple of much younger boys begin to appear in some pictures. The file for one of these identifies the client as a senior clergyman, aged 55, who lives in London with his wife and two daughters; another is a Tory Member of Parliament from the Home Counties. Most of the pictures are location and time stamped.

It would presumably be easy for Marcie to get some of the undergraduate escorts on her books to go a lot farther for the right kind of money. But some of these kids are definitely too young to be at university. How are they being supplied? It must be some kind of county lines operation, I think to myself. Of course! Jane. She's the expert. I need to show her all of this. She'll know what to do with it. Or will she? She might go running off to her superiors, just as she did last time. She certainly wouldn't approve of how I obtained them. I suddenly remember that somewhere in these files there are likely to be incriminating photographs of a very senior police officer. Another guy paying out handsomely to keep his respectable career and his marriage intact whilst enjoying a spot of paedophilia. I realise Jane has never told me his name. I feel sick to my stomach and there is a rancid taste in my mouth which the coffee isn't helping to dispel.

I'm opening folders on the final row when I see that the last folder is labelled CZH. I pause, as something stirs in my memory. CZH. I drain my coffee cup and pour myself a whisky. Surely, it can't be? But the initials are so unusual, I know that it must be him. CZH – Caleb Zachary Hopper. Somewhere in the far distance I can hear a clock tower chiming midnight. I am scared of what I am about to discover, but I know that I need to continue. I roll a mouthful of whisky around and swallow before pressing my mouse to open the file. Eddie gives a little whimper in his sleep.

Cal's registration form includes some studio photographs of himself in a dinner suit. It seems clear that this is a registration form to become an escort rather than for someone who wants to pay to be escorted. It includes details of his eye colour (blue), hair colour (blond), weight (89kg) and height (6 foot 4 inches). The comments section includes: University boat race squad. Hot-air balloonist. Studying for PhD at Christ's College. Capricorn. At the bottom is a row of five golden stars, which I assume to be the company's rating for their new golden boy.

I reduce the picture from the folder and move it up to the top corner of my screen where Cal stares back out at me, grinning with his perfect teeth and looking like a million dollars in his black bow tie, stud-fronted shirt and fashionable dinner jacket. Then I open the next folder. This takes a while to open and I realise with a sinking heart that it too will comprise photographs. Compromising photographs.

The top one shows a side-on view of a bed in a plush bedroom – an upmarket hotel, perhaps? It is definitely not *Nirvana*. Cal is naked on the bed. His powerful and well-tanned physique contrasts strikingly with the flabby white flesh of the middle-aged men in the other pictures. He could almost be from a different species. However, unlike them, he is not pictured with teenage girls, or even teenage boys. No, he has been photographed in the act of pleasuring a much older woman who is stretched out under him. But it isn't the sexual act, or the chasm between their ages, which is the most shocking thing about the picture. It is the look on Cal's face as he stares directly at the camera rather than the woman. He must know exactly where the hidden lens has been placed and his handsome features are disfigured by a look of profound self-loathing and a deep unhappiness.

CHAPTER FORTY-ONE

It takes me another two hours to go through the folders and files more methodically. Cal features in 25 different photographs with 20 different women. Most of them are in colour. Some of them feature the same hotel bedroom, some of them seem to be in private bedrooms and a couple are black-and-white and labelled as being on *Nirvana*. All of them display a significant age disparity between Cal and his partners. They also include initials which seem to cross refer to another folder that I don't have. Presumably it logs all of the female clients' names and details along with their own picture galleries and record of payments.

Ophelia does not feature in any more files other than her apparently blameless staff record. I keep a notebook at my elbow and jot down a list of all the male clients' names, addresses and occupations from the accompanying client registration documents. There are 30 in total, including the senior ranking police officer. Then I double check that I have opened and checked everything before pocketing the memory stick and switching the laptop off with a sigh of relief, mixed with fatigue. It has been a deeply unpleasant experience and I head for a much-needed shower.

I am dumbfounded. Why on earth would Cal stoop to this? He can't have needed the money. His father is obviously very wealthy and successful – and Cal seems to be the apple of his eye. Is he a sex addict of some kind? But his face in all of the pictures shows not the slightest hint of pleasure at what he is doing. The underpowered trickle of warm water isn't great, but my thoughts prompt me to linger as I try to soap myself clean. If only I could wash away what I have seen just as easily. And as I stand there, the water seeping down my head, face and body, I begin to form a theory.

I have just seen plenty of evidence that the Garden of Eden operation is a cover for prostitution involving children and the blackmail of male and female clients on an industrial scale. If Cal wasn't involved as a client, and there is nothing in his file to suggest that he was, there is only one reason I can think of for him to be doing what he has been doing. He was being blackmailed himself! The pictures certainly didn't suggest that he was a willing participant. But he must have set up the hidden cameras himself in order to capture the action – particularly in the private bedrooms – perhaps a wide-angle lens camera hidden inside a bag? And these pictures were presumably being used to blackmail some of the older women who were pictured in them. The ones with something to lose – careers, wealth, status, husbands, the love and respect of their children and grandchildren? They would have faced losing everything in exchange for a brief moment of pleasure with a ridiculously handsome young American after a pleasantly expensive dinner *a deux*.

I pull on a t-shirt and a pair of boxers and stretch out on my berth with just a sidelight on. As I lie there, I think about Ophelia. None of what I've discovered sheds any light on her connection to it all. What could possibly have led to her being throttled and dumped below Iffley Lock? Until now, all the connections led to Romaine. He knew Ophelia. He was connected to Garden of Eden and Ophelia worked for Garden of Eden. He had been on *Nirvana*. *Nirvana* was pinpointed in Ophelia's room at St Hugh's. It all joined up. But something wasn't right.

I sit up, grab my notebook again and begin sketching the diagram of a mind map. Now that I know what I know, don't all the same connections also apply to Cal? The circles begin to join up on the paper. Obviously, he knew Ophelia very well. He also worked for Garden of Eden. Ophelia worked for Garden of Eden and Cal had been on *Nirvana*, the boat named and located in Ophelia's room. Moreover, it seems that Cal had been helping Garden of Eden with their blackmail operation, possibly as a blackmail victim himself. I turn out the light and lie back with my head on my pillow but sleep is a remote prospect as the shocking photographs remain burned on my retina and my thoughts continue to swirl.

I think back to our visit to Ophelia's room and my discovery of the pad of Post-it notes in the wastepaper bin. The missing top sheet had clearly had *Nirvana* written on it. And Cal told us himself that he was the only person to visit the room after the last sighting of her and after the cleaners had been in. Did he see the Post-it notes on her desk that Sunday, rip off the top sheet and put the rest of the pad in the bin? I remember him saying that Ophelia could have done it, but Ophelia hadn't been seen in college for more than a week before her body was found. It was possible that she had slipped into her room after the cleaners had been in and that no one had seen her. He had suggested as much. Possible, but unlikely.

Other things come to mind as I begin to replay the events of the last few days. I remember Cal driving us to Iffley Lock for the impromptu prayer meeting. And only now does it strike me that he knew the precise way through the sprawling village and to the lane that led to the lock, even though the water was hidden from view by riverside houses at that point. He did not use his sat nav or ask any of us to look up the directions for him. He drove straight there, confidently and without any kind of reference. And yet he suggested otherwise. He told us that he wanted to see the location for himself and asked us to join him. Why would he dissemble like that?

I look at my watch: three a.m. I fetch a glass of water and resume my horizontal position in the dark. A memory of the painting called 'The Nightmare' by the Swiss-English painter Henry Fuseli springs to mind.

I know I don't look anything like the woman it depicts, bathed in white linen and stretched across a bed, her arms, neck and head hanging off the end of the mattress. But the really shocking thing about the painting is the apelike figure which crouches malevolently on her chest while a horse with glowing eyes and flared nostrils lurks devilishly in the background. I feel a nightmare scenario beginning to take shape in the darkness around me.

What if the statistics were right? What if the most probable scenario is that Ophelia was murdered by someone who knew her very well? What if it was Cal who had killed her? There. I have said it. And the more I turn the theory over in my mind, the more credibility it assumes. There is something else in the back of my mind. I am sure it dates back to our painful balloon debate. What is it? It vaguely struck me at the time, but now it feels important. I close my eyes and exhaustion begins to kick in. But as I turn my head to get comfortable it hits me. I sit up. It was something Cal said. I was telling the others about the parties on the houseboat. I am sure I had referred to it as the houseboat, time and time again, because that is what I thought it was. But Cal suddenly called it the barge. It was when he was upset with me. How would he know it was a barge? Of course, now I know he had already been on *Nirvana*, the former St Michael's college clubhouse barge.

But that didn't prove he killed Ophelia. His alibi is rock solid. He was away at the training camp when Ophelia went missing. She was texting him until the day before the body was found. And he didn't return to Oxford until after she had been pulled out of the water. Philpott's team must have looked into his movements and decided he could be ruled out.

But they had no idea about his connection to Garden of Eden – the same company that Ophelia had been working for. Wait. Wait a moment. I switch the bedside light on again and grab the notebook. Ophelia had been studying for a degree in Computer Sciences. Was it inconceivable that she had somehow accessed the same secret files that I had while she was working in their office? Presumably Marcie had them restricted or encrypted or whatever it was called? But Ophelia might just have been curious enough to wander around the more secret parts of her employer's digital network and archive. She almost certainly had the technical know-how. Would that explain her sudden resignation in early December after completing only a handful of shifts? It could certainly explain her lack of a reason.

'Did Ophelia see the CZH pictures????' I write in my notebook and underline it. How else would she know about *Nirvana*? The barge's name recurs time and time again under the blackmail photographs. Is that why she wrote it down on the Post-it note? She must have tracked down its location and marked it on the map in her room. It's horrifying to imagine her stumbling across the pictures. I imagine her shock at suddenly seeing her handsome and beloved boyfriend pictured *in flagrante delicto* with a score of other women. What would she have done? Perhaps she confronted Marcie and was then silenced by her thug, the arsonist I saw on the boat. Or she could have taken it all to the police. Or she could have walked out of her job and asked Cal for an explanation. Surely that would be the most likely scenario? And then, perhaps, something happened to her which prevented her from talking about it to anyone else, ever again?

CHAPTER FORTY-TWO

I eventually achieve a couple of hours sleep but I'm conscious of tossing and turning and I wake at six a.m. It will be another two hours before the first hint of grey light comes through the porthole above the bed. However, I know it will be useless to try and drop off again, so I shower, shave, swallow some toast and coffee and take Eddie over the bridge for a run around Strode Meadows. The good-natured little dog doesn't show any signs of begrudging his pre-dawn exercise in the dark. We're back on the boat by seven. I have used the past hour to stiffen my resolve about taking the next step.

I text Nina. I have decided that I must tell her everything, before anyone else. She will take it hard and, I have no doubt, act as lead counsel for the defence. That's fine. I don't mind being proven wrong. But I trust Nina's judgement and bravery when the chips are down and, if I'm right, she needs to get out of Cal's house as quickly as possible.

> Sorry it's early. Need to speak to you urgently ASAP.

I'm not expecting a reply for at least an hour or two, but one comes straight back.

> OK. Breakfast here? Anna's been staying overnight.

I don't want to meet her at Cal's place. It'll be too difficult to have the conversation that I am planning.

Let's meet at coffee shop, or by the canal.

No. Don't be silly. See you here soon.

I'll just have to try to detach her from Cal when I get there. I clamber back into my coat and hat, settle Eddie with a bowl of breakfast and head off immediately. There is a definite breeze this morning and I'm not surprised the balloon event has been called off. However, there is currently no sign of rain, just as the weather forecast promised, and I hope that when it arrives at midday it doesn't increase the river level too much.

I can see some lights are already on in the windows of some of the boathouses on the opposite bank as I approach. There is a slight mist on the water, the sky is brightening fast and a few hardy souls are already up and carrying sculls and oars to the river for early morning training sessions. A couple of the pedalo-style safety boats are zipping around on the river. They're waiting for the action to start and I see that one of them is being steered by the same young man who ferried me across before. I call across and raise my hand. He immediately makes his way over towards me.

'Hi,' he says, throwing me a small rope to keep the craft steady by the bank. 'You're Cal and Nina's friend, aren't you?'

'That's right. I'm Jack.' Shaking hands is too difficult across the small gap of water between us. 'I'm afraid I didn't catch your name before.'

'Chris. Christopher Fisher.'

'Have you seen Cal jog past this morning?'

'No. I don't think he's training this morning. He said something about flying his balloon over at Blenheim. Rather him than me.'

'Oh, I think his event has been cancelled, actually. Too windy,' I tell him. 'I thought Cal might have run down to Iffley after all. You said you shared a room with him at Caversham during the training camp, didn't you, or have I misremembered?'

'Yes, that's right, before I was injured. I think I might have been a bit too messy for him. Cal likes everything neat and tidy.'

'Yes,' I laugh falsely. 'That sounds like Cal. Were you all there the whole time? Or did any of you leave for a while?'

'No. We were in strict lockdown for the duration. In fact, we joked that we saw a lot more of each other for those twelve days than the average married couple. If I wasn't with Cal on the water, I was eating with him, training with him and sleeping with him. In the same room as him, I mean!' he laughs. 'He's an amazing guy, like I said. Wholly committed. One night he said he couldn't sleep so he actually went for a run. A run at midnight!' He shakes his head in amazement.

'You didn't go on the run with him?'

'No. No. He told me the following morning that he'd just gone jogging around the lakes until he felt sleepy.'

'Can you remember what night this was?'

'Umm...we arrived on the Wednesday and so it must have been about four or five days later – yes, it was Sunday night.' Suddenly, he frowns. 'Why d'you ask?'

'And how long was he out running?'

'I don't know. I went back to sleep and didn't wake up when he got back. But he was definitely there for breakfast on Monday morning because I teased him about it. Why d'you want to know?'

He is now looking at me suspiciously, but I can't think of a convincing lie on the spur of the moment. 'Oh, nothing important. Don't worry about it. I was just curious about how strict the training regime is.'

This seems to make him even more alarmed and he looks rapidly back at the boathouses and back. 'Why do you want to know about that?' He sounds genuinely panicked. 'You're not from the Other Place, are you?'

'The Other Place?' I am genuinely baffled. 'What do you mean?'

'From Cambridge. We've been told to look out for light blue spies. Why d'you want to know about our training regime?' Now he is starting to sound aggressive.

'No. No, of course I'm not. I was just interested. That's all. I'm on my way to Cal's house now actually.'

However, this seems to make the situation worse. 'Yeah?' he says challengingly. 'Well, I told you he was going ballooning. So, he isn't going to be there, is he?'

'As I said, I think it's been cancelled. Thanks for your help, Chris. See you around.'

As I walk away, I use my phone to establish that Caversham is a 27-mile drive from Oxford. So that would take about 40 minutes, possibly even less in a powerful car like Cal's and on deserted roads at night. He could have had at least an hour in the city, maybe more, and returned in plenty of time for breakfast at the camp with nobody the wiser. Did he meet Ophelia that night? Chris said his midnight run was on Sunday night/Monday morning and the last sighting of Ophelia at her college was the day before. She had resigned from Garden of Eden the day before that. Was this something Philpott and his team knew about? Somehow, I doubted it.

But there is something else nagging me now. If Cal had slipped out of camp and was somehow responsible for Ophelia's death in the early hours of that Monday morning, how come he had texts from her in the following days? The texts that put her time of death much later. Unless the texts hadn't come from her. Could he have been using her phone to send himself texts? I pull out my own phone as I walk briskly towards Jericho.

'Hugh? I'm sorry to ring you so early.'

'Jack? What is it? Is everything alright?'

'I need your medical knowledge,' I say. 'Ophelia's body was found in the Thames, tightly wrapped up in canvas and weighted down. Correct?'

'Well, that's what you told me, old chap.'

'Okay. So, is there any chance she could have been in the water for five to six days rather than just twenty-four hours? Would the pathologist have been able to definitively say that she'd only been in the water for a day and no longer?'

'I was never a pathologist, Jack.'

'I know. But you were a bloody good surgeon. Just give me an opinion. Please. It's important.'

'Alright, let's think about it. She was dead before she went into the water, wasn't she?'

'Yes. Strangled.'

'Okay, so there would have been no water in her lungs. And the water at this time of year is bloody cold – so that would have considerably slowed down any decomposition. I don't think that any remaining food in her stomach would make much difference. And there would have been little or no predation because of the canvas bag.'

'Predation?'

'Fish feeding on her. Not very likely in these rivers anyway.'

'What are you saying, Hugh?'

'I'm not an expert. But no. I don't think it would be easy to say exactly how long she had been in the water in these particular circumstances. Certainly not if the timeframe that we're talking about is between one and seven days.'

'So, she could have been dead and in the river for pretty well the whole week before her body was found?'

'Well, yes. Theoretically. What is all this, Jack?'

'You've been a great help, Hugh. I'll catch you later.'

Nina answers Cal's door and ushers me inside. Anna is buttering toast in the kitchen. They are already dressed in spite of the early hour and they are both looking at me curiously.

'Where's Cal?'

'He left twenty minutes ago. He called Ben and Simon and asked them to help him with the balloon again after all. They're all going to Blenheim.'

'But it's been postponed. It's too windy.'

Nina shrugs. 'He didn't think it was. He said he'd flown in worse conditions in the States. He said he fancied a solo flight anyway and that it would be the last chance to fly his balloon before the boat race. He didn't want to pass up the chance to see Blenheim from the air. Coffee, Jack?' She turns to get the mugs out.

'Sit down. Both of you. Please.' My tone is serious and she turns around, looks at me and then does as she's asked. Anna joins her aunt.

I sit down opposite her. Our knees are almost touching.

'Okay. There's no easy way to tell you this but I'm going to have to make it fast. Yesterday, I acquired some secret computer files from Garden of Eden.' Nina immediately frowns and opens her mouth to speak but I rush on. 'It doesn't matter how I got them for now. What matters is what's on them. Look for yourself.'

I hand them my phone and they scroll through an email I have sent to myself with some of the pictures attached, including those of Cal. They both look utterly shell-shocked and Anna covers her mouth with one hand. Nina has gone grey.

'I've done a lot of thinking. I believe Cal may have been blackmailed to do this. I don't know why. But I also believe Ophelia may have seen these pictures when she was working at Garden of Eden. There are hundreds of other pictures which show men sleeping with underage girls. Including Romaine. It's one huge prostitution and blackmail racket and that could be why Romaine killed himself. He didn't actually confess to killing Ophelia in his suicide note, as far as we know.'

Nina is shaking her head in disbelief and staring at the pictures on my phone. Anna is clearly struggling to take it all in.

'I think it's unlikely that Ophelia just stumbled across these pictures. She must have had a reason to get a job there and go looking. She was studying for a Computer Sciences degree. She must have found her way into their secret files and discovered the pictures of Cal and the references to Nirvana. I went on board *Nirvana* before it burnt down. There were secret cameras and a recording studio on board.'

Nina looks up at me. 'Why didn't you tell me? Anna gives a slightly guilty look.

I ignore her and press on. 'The pictures refer to *Nirvana* time and time again, every time the barge has been used as a location for a shot. That would explain why she had written 'Nirvana' on the top sheet of the Post-it notes and researched the boat's location. Cal was the only one who could have taken that Post-it note out of her room – when he supposedly went looking for her the first time. He must have dumped the rest of the pad in the bin and that's where I found it.'

'No,' says Nina. But I can tell that I'm getting through to her.

'There's something else,' I say, leaning forward and taking one of her hands. 'When we went to Iffley Lock with Cal and he said a prayer. Did you notice that he found his way there with no help at all? No sat nav. No map. No directions. He drove straight there. And it wasn't straightforward, was it? The river was hidden from the road. But he knew exactly how to get there and where to park. I'm sorry, but I believe that he'd been there before.'

There is a silence. Nina is the first to realise what I may be saying.

'You think he killed her and dumped her there?' she says in a horrified whisper.

'No!' says Anna, reaching out to hold Nina's other hand.

'No.' Nina sounds firm. 'Cal couldn't have killed her. If you had seen him grieving like I did you'd know he couldn't have done that.'

'And he's got an alibi,' says Anna. 'He was at the training camp the whole time.'

'Except once,' I say. 'He went out on his own for a run at midnight and his room-mate doesn't know when he came back. It would have given him the opportunity and the time to drive here from Caversham and back. I think he met Ophelia that night and something happened. Maybe she confronted him with those pictures. I think he must have dumped her body at Iffley Weir under cover of darkness and raced back to Caversham. That's why he knew his way there.'

'But she was texting him until the Friday before he came back,' says Nina. 'Until the sixteenth. When did he go for the run?'

I am relieved that she isn't angry. Not yet anyway. She seems to be genuinely perplexed and trying to work it all out.

'On the Sunday night/Monday morning – overnight between the 11th and the 12th. But he if he still had her phone, he could have been texting himself. He could have been pretending to be her.'

'What? How do you know he had her phone?'

'I don't have any proof of that,' I admit. 'But it's a possibility. She was his girlfriend. It's conceivable that he knew her phone access code. Or maybe he even used her finger to get into it then changed the settings. I'm sorry, Nina. I'm sorry to both of you. I didn't imagine I would find those pictures of him. I was just convinced that something very strange was going on at *Nirvana* and I was right about that.'

'Have you talked to anyone else about this?' asks Nina.

I suspect she is thinking of Jane. 'What? No. Well, apart from his friend Chris on the river at the clubhouse. I spoke to him this morning, on my way here. He shared a room with Cal at Caversham.'

'Cal had a call just before he changed his mind about flying this morning,' says Anna. She looks at Nina. 'You were in the bathroom. It must have been this Chris guy.'.

'And Chris must have told him that I'd been asking about Cal's midnight run during camp.'

'So what do we do now?' asks Anna in a whisper.

I look Nina squarely in the face. 'I wanted to tell you first. But I think we have to take this to the police now.'

'No!' says Nina. She sounds forceful but looks wretched. 'The pictures are horrible. Of course they are. But they don't prove Cal is a murderer.'

We all look at each other and there is silence until Anna breaks the impasse. 'Okay. We don't take this to the police yet. But let's have a look around and see if we can find anything else here. I suggest we split up.' This feels like a waste of time to me, but I don't want to overrule Nina immediately.

Anna heads upstairs. Nina trails into the sitting room shaking her head and muttering. I head for the garden. There is a large shed at the end of a straight path with a neat lawn on both sides. Inside, there is a range of exercise equipment and the lingering smell of sweat. There are dumbbells, an exercise bike and a gym mat facing a large mirror. A large squashy ball is on the floor and a punch bag is hanging from a rafter. There is also a plastic covered weight-lifting bench with a bar resting on upright struts above it. I sit on the bench and look around the room. The bar has large 25 kilogramme weights attached to both ends which reminds me of Philpott saying that two round weights were found with Ophelia's body. There is a rack of other weights nearby. I go closer to examine them. They go down in size from 20kg to 15kg to 10kg to 5kg to 2.5kg to the smallest, which is 1.25kg. I crouch to examine them more closely, picking them up one by one. They all seem to come from the same manufacturer, and they are all present and correct in their different sized slots on the rack. Then I see it. One of the 20kg weights has *'Property of Oriel'* painted on it in tiny lettering. I check the other 20kg weight. It has the same message on it. Then I closely check the other weights. None of the others have *'Property of Oriel'* painted on any of them.

Ophelia's body had been found in a bag with a circular weight at either end. What if Cal had used his own 20kg weights for this purpose and subsequently stolen a pair from Oriel's boathouse to replace them? Had the police missed this during their search? Cal could have easily replaced his weights on the days immediately after he returned from camp. I had seen the chaotic jumble of exercise equipment at the boathouse for myself and it would be easy enough not to notice their absence.

There is a shout from upstairs just as I am pushing open the back door of the house. I take the treads two at a time. Nina and Anna are in what I assume is the master bedroom. I can't stop myself quickly scanning it to see if Nina has been sharing it with Cal – but there are no obvious signs of her things. Nina and Anna have taken a large seascape off the wall and propped it on the floor, by the skirting board. The unfaded wall behind the painting is a darker colour than the surrounding paint and in the centre of the rectangle is a small safe. It looks identical to the electronic push-button type of safes that you see in most hotel bedrooms. We all stare at it.

'Any ideas?' I ask.

'They're usually 4-digit numbers,' says Nina quietly. 'But shouldn't we wait...'

'40-40,' says Anna immediately. 'I bet it's 40-40.'

'What?' Nina and I ask her simultaneously.

'It's the name of his father's religious cable channel in the States. It stands for forty days and forty nights in the wilderness, apparently. It's on that photograph of his father preaching. Remember?'

'Well, it's either that or a completely random pin number that no one could possibly guess,' I say. 'Be my guest.'

Anna moves forward and presses a button which says 'OPEN'. Then she presses 4-0-4-0. There is an immediate whirring and a beeping noise. The four digits turn into horizontal lines and the door springs open an inch. Anna moves forward to open it further but stops when I urgently tell her to wait. 'Don't touch it. Gloves?'

'Hang on.' Anna disappears and reappears a few moments later wearing a pair of yellow rubber washing-up gloves. She opens the door wide and we all peer inside, even Nina. Anna reaches in and pulls out a mobile phone, turning it over in both of her gloved hands. The phone case is decorated with tiny flowers and has the name Ophelia inscribed on it.

'He's got her phone!' says Anna.

'Oh my god,' says Nina looking at me in horror. 'He *could* have been sending himself those text messages.'

'Is there anything else in there?' I ask.

Anna moves closer and peers in, then extracts a small Bible. She opens it. A knot of black hair has been placed between the inside cover and the first page, which has 'Ophelia McVeigh, St Luke's Sunday School' written on it in childish handwriting.

'A pair of weights in Cal's gym has been replaced too,' I tell them. 'There were weights in the bag with the body at Iffley Lock. I'm prepared to guess that those ones weighed 20 kilogrammes, and that a couple are missing from Oriel College's boathouse at the moment.'

Nina is shaking her head in disbelief but I can tell her heart isn't in it any more. She had poured her sympathy and trust into this young man – and I have little doubt she has developed even deeper feelings for him too. It is a bitter pill for her to swallow. 'What *do* we do now?' she asks quietly.

Anna pulls off one of her gloves with a snap. 'That's easy,' she says firmly. Again, Nina and I both turn to look her at the same time. 'Now we call the police.'

CHAPTER FORTY-THREE

We return to the kitchen table and I get out my mobile. Nina and Anna watch me as I call Jane's number. She answers on the third ring.

'Jack?' She sounds sleepy. 'Ugh. What time is it?'

'Jane. I need you to get hold of Philpott. We're pretty sure we've got evidence that Cal killed Ophelia McVeigh.'

'What the hell?' She sounds fully awake now.

I skip over my night-time adventure on *Nirvana* and what I discovered there. That could wait. But I explain how Cal's alibi is far from watertight and tell her what we have discovered in his house. 'At the very least, he's got some serious questions to answer.'

'Where is he now?'

'He's taken his balloon to Blenheim. He left over half an hour ago. I think he knows I may have cracked his alibi this morning. He was supposed to be here and he changed his mind about flying at the last minute.'

'Stay there. Don't move. I'll speak to Philpott.' She hangs up abruptly.

Nina begins to make a pot of tea, but then she sits back down again and stares into space. Anna gets up to finish the job as the kettle boils. 'There has to be an innocent explanation,' Nina says to me. She still looks stunned. 'He was so upset by her death. He can't have been faking it.'

'His grief was probably genuine,' I say, trying to reassure her. 'But that doesn't necessarily mean he didn't kill her. Perhaps he did. And perhaps that made his grief even worse.'

We are sipping our tea in silence when a text arrives from Jane.

Stay there. We're coming to fetch you.

Twenty minutes later two orange and white police Range Rovers stop in the road outside Cal's house. Philpott has reacted fast and has even less time for niceties than usual.

'Show me,' he snaps. I take him out to the gym in the garden and point him towards the replacement weights. He shakes his head. 'Idiots,' he mutters to himself. I assume he's referring to the officers who searched Cal's home, and not me this time.

'They missed something else,' I tell him.

He sighs heavily. 'Show me.'

I take the detective upstairs, trailed by the three women. Nina shows him the safe and its contents and Jane transfers the phone, locket of hair and the Bible into three separate evidence bags. The broken veins on Philpott's cheeks are flushed a deep red. He doesn't seem to be having a very happy time.

'And he left for Blenheim when?'

'About an hour ago,' says Nina.

'Alright. All of you, in the car with DS Grey and me.'

He sends the driver of the first car to join two other officers in the second vehicle and places himself at the wheel while Jane climbs in alongside him. Nina, Anna and I shuffle onto the rear seat.

Jane is speaking on the police radio and she seems to be giving terse instructions to the control centre about scrambling the force's helicopter. When she has finished talking, Philpott glances back at me.

'Motive?'

'Only a theory,' I say.

'Go on.'

'Ophelia McVeigh wasn't the only one working for Garden of Eden.

Cal was too. But in a very different capacity.' I scroll through my mobile phone and pass it to Jane who looks at the pictures and then shows a couple to Philpott. 'He was some kind of escort for them – but he didn't need the money, so I suspect he was being blackmailed himself. I think Ophelia discovered those pictures and confronted him about them. Probably on the night that he went for his night-time run during the rowing training camp.'

'How did you get these pictures?' asks Jane.

I knew this question was going to come and have already decided that there is no ducking it. 'I broke into the house of the woman who owns Garden of Eden. Marcie Lopez – I think you interviewed her about Ophelia's work for the company? I downloaded files from her laptop and these photos were inside.'

'Jack!'

'Fuck,' mutters Philpott. 'The lawyers are going to love that.'

'I also broke into *Nirvana* before she was torched,' I add quickly. In for a penny, in for a pound. 'I discovered there was a secret recording studio on board. It was an underage prostitution and blackmail racket, organised by Garden of Eden. There are hundreds of pictures of young girls and boys having sex with older men on the files I have.'

There is silence in the car while the two police officers digest this new information. Philpott is driving very fast and the second police car is keeping pace behind us.

'Send someone out to pick the woman up,' growls Philpott to Jane. 'They'll have her home and business address in the case file.'

'There's something else,' I tell Philpott when Jane has finished with the radio. 'I think he may know I'm onto him. I think the guy on the safety boat who told me about his midnight run may have phoned him afterwards. He was his roommate at the training camp.'

'We spoke to the coach,' says Philpott. 'He was adamant that Hopper was in total lockdown throughout his time at the camp.'

'The coach probably didn't know about the midnight run.'

'So, the boy had possible motive, means *and* opportunity,' Philpott says.

'The ballooning had been cancelled today due to the weather. But Anna said he changed his mind after a call this morning – and that was just after I spoke to his roommate. I think he's realised he no longer has an alibi.'

'Well, he's not going to get far in a hot-air balloon,' says Jane. 'We've scrambled the chopper.'

Nevertheless, Philpott now accelerates and activates the siren and lights. The car behind follows suit. But after a couple of minutes he switches them off again.

'Tell them to be quiet,' he barks at Jane, who contacts the car behind, and they follow suit. He looks at Nina in the rear-view mirror. 'Try his phone. Just tell him to stay on the ground. Say you're on your way out in a taxi. Tell him to wait for you. Put it on speaker phone.'

Nina nods and takes out her phone. She looks at me and I try to give her a look of reassurance. She dials and then holds it flat in front of her mouth. The call connects.

'Hi? Nina? Is that you?'

'Hello Cal. I'm on my way out to see you take off. I'm in a taxi. Can you wait until we ... until I get there?' She shakes her head in annoyance at her slip.

'We're ready to go, Nina.' There is a short pause. 'Who is 'we'? Who else is with you?'

'Anna and Jack.' Nina's eyes fill and she gives another little hopeless shake of her head.

'Jack's with you? Put him on.' Then we hear him call out to his ground crew. 'Just a minute, guys, I just need to take this call.' I turn the phone's volume to maximum so that his voice is filling the interior of the large police vehicle.

'Hi Cal.'

'Hi Jack. I thought maybe you'd had enough of ballooning after last time?'

'Don't worry, I don't want another flight. I just wanted to see you take off – you know, for the article I'm writing,' I say, thinking quickly. 'Will you wait for us? It would really help me out.'

'Chris tells me you called by the boathouse this morning.'

'Yes, that's right. It was on my way.'

'He says you were interested in what happened at training camp?'

Philpott is drawing a circle in the air with his forefinger. He obviously wants me to keep him talking.

'He was obviously very impressed by your dedication.'

'Cut the bullshit, Jack. He said you seemed really keen on asking questions, about my night-time run amongst other things. You know, don't you?'

'Know what, Cal?' I say, in as puzzled a tone as I can manage. A sign flashes past announcing that the village of Woodstock, home of Blenheim Palace, is just a couple of miles away. Nina is gripping one of my arms tightly.

'I loved her, you know. Truly I did. But when I met Phi, they already had their hooks into me. They approached me in the street just after I got here. It was the Spanish woman, Lopez. She asked me to help her out with her business, told me I was just the good-looking type they needed. She was very flattering. I did a couple of bookings for her just for a laugh. Just dinner dates. Out of curiosity. I was lonely and single at the time. But then they invited me onto *Nirvana*, and they drugged me and took pictures of me with a young boy and a girl.' His voice is anguished. 'They were just kids.'

Nina has her hands over her face. I keep quiet, letting Cal talk on.

'They'd found out who my pa is. They threatened to post the pictures on his church website. But they didn't want money. They wanted me to turn tricks for them – with older women. Then they were blackmailing some of them with the pictures they took of me. I was trapped. Phi found one of their business cards at my place. She asked me about it – she was really suspicious and maybe I didn't lie well enough. So she got a job temping for them, without telling me, and she hacked into their locked files. I'd gone away to training camp and she phoned me to tell me what she'd found. She was disgusted. I pleaded with her. So yes, Jack, I slipped out of camp to see her at my house. But you know that, don't you? She said if I didn't stop, she'd tell my pa myself. What could I do? The shame would have killed him. I didn't know what to do.' He gives a racking sob. 'I have to go now.'

'Cal!' calls out Nina. But the phone is silent. He has hung up.

Philpott activates the sirens again and we are soon sweeping through an enormous stone entrance arch with a lake on our right-hand side. There is a bridge leading up to the vast ducal palace and I get a glimpse of the balloon's green fabric beyond it. 'There!' I point.

Philpott continues to race up to an avenue of trees, swings right across the front of the grand main building and then doubles back across the bridge between two lakes. The balloon and Cal's car are several fields away but the track we are on seems to lead directly to them. The balloon is fully inflated above the basket, but I can only see a single figure inside it. It is Cal. The two police cars are barely a hundred metres away when the balloon begins to move quickly away from the ground. The ground crew are turning their heads between our fast and noisy approach and Cal in the basket as he rises away from them.

Jane is talking on the radio, telling someone that the balloon is in flight and heading south-west. The breeze is pushing it away from us faster and faster now as it rises. Philpott swears and sets off in the same direction, accelerating away past the shocked faces of Cal's friends.

'Call him again,' shouts Philpott. 'Persuade him to come down.'

I am still holding Nina's phone, but she snatches it off me.

'Cal,' she shouts above the noise of the sirens. 'Please! You must come down. We can sort all this out.'

We can hear the balloon's burner firing and the roar of the wind on the speaker of Cal's phone, but he isn't saying anything.

'Cal! Cal! Speak to me, please,' shouts Nina urgently.

When Cal does start talking, his voice is low and calm by comparison. 'I didn't mean to kill her, Nina. I swear it. But she was hitting me and hitting me and crying and shouting and calling me names. She wanted me to go to the police. She said she would go to the police. But I couldn't let that happen – you understand, don't you? They'd have ruined my father if I'd gone to the police. They're ruthless, those people – the photos they took are so disgusting. She was hysterical. She wouldn't calm down and I just tried to stop her yelling. But it went too far. I choked her, Nina. I choked the life out of her. And then I panicked. I dumped her body in the water. And now I'm damned to hell and back.'

'No, Cal. You said it. You didn't mean to do it,' says Nina imploringly. 'Please! Just land the balloon. We can sort all this out. You were being blackmailed. Your father will understand.'

'Goodbye, Nina. You're a lovely person.'

'No stop Cal. How many times have you said the Lord's Prayer? How many times have you said, *I believe in ... the Forgiveness of the Sins*. You can be forgiven too.'

There is a moment of silence. Then we all hear Cal clearly above the wind noise. 'Let the words of my mouth, and the meditation of my heart: be always acceptable in thy sight, O Lord: my strength and my redeemer.'

'That's right,' says Nina urgently. 'That's right Cal. Your redeemer. God will give you redemption. Just come back down. Please.'

Philpott and Jane are craning their necks forward, scanning the sky at the top of the car's windscreen and trying to keep the balloon in sight. I have no idea how high it is now, two or three thousand feet? Then we hear the loud clatter of a helicopter above. The yellow and black craft roars over us like a giant hornet, low and fast, closing in on the balloon ahead. The pilot's voice is crackling over Jane's radio, but I can't make out what he is saying.

The road ahead takes a sharp turn to the right and stretches away into the distance, leading away from the balloon and the helicopter. Philpott screeches to a halt in the centre of the road and kills the sirens. We all clamber out onto the tarmac and crane our heads upwards. The helicopter is circling the balloon now and we can hear a voice over its loudspeaker, but the words are indistinct to us here on the ground. 'Tell them to back off,' Nina is shouting at Philpott. 'Please tell them to give him some space. I'm getting through to him.'

Her phone rings again. Philpott reaches out a hand for it, but she ignores him and accepts the call.

'Please tell my parents I'm sorry, Nina. Tell them I loved them.'

'Cal! No!'

But it is too late. He has cut the call and we watch, powerless, as the distant figure reaches with his arms and pulls himself upwards, so that he is balancing with both feet on the rim of the basket.

'NO! Cal!' screams Nina.

Seconds later, Cal lets go of the wires which hold the basket to the balloon and stretches out both his arms horizontally, as though he is mimicking Christ on the cross. He holds this position for a moment and then the dark figure is in the air, tumbling, turning and twisting for mere seconds before disappearing behind a line of trees on the horizon. Nina doesn't see this because I have already pulled her into my arms and burrowed her face into my chest.

CHAPTER FORTY-FOUR

Having presided over a flawed murder enquiry, Detective Chief Inspector Brian Philpott clearly decided that his future career depended on raising his energy levels. After hearing Cal's confession for himself, he threw his energies into bringing the rest of the people responsible for Ophelia McVeigh's death to justice.

Marcie Lopez and her laptop were picked up just as she was leaving her home that morning for the Garden of Eden office. Once the contents of her computer folders and files had been properly seized by the police and laid bare, they didn't need my illicitly downloaded files. Philpott worked alongside Jane Henry and an expanded team to take the necessary actions. Blackmail targets were spoken with – some with more discretion than others – and efforts were made to identify and safeguard as many of the underage escorts as possible.

It took two days of questioning before Lopez accepted her solicitor's advice and finally identified Finn Connolly as her partner in crime. By that time, he had disappeared from his apartment in Wapping where his new 4x4 Mercedes was already gathering a thin layer of dust in the building's underground car park. Police checks on his multiple bank accounts found that every penny had been withdrawn; his solicitor denied all knowledge of his whereabouts.

Finn Connolly had suspected that airports would be on alert for his passport, and so he had walked onto the Belfast ferry at Liverpool instead, intending to disappear into the countryside around Dublin, change his name and appearance and bring forward his plans to move into the property rental business. He knew he wouldn't need to show a passport for the trip, just some false ID which he had already prepared. Unfortunately for Connolly, one of the British police officers at the port happened to be a big fan of Ultimate Fighting Championship. He recognised the well-dressed man with his powerful physique as he strutted past a one-way observation mirror. He also remembered the nationwide alert that said Finn Connolly was wanted for questioning about a range of serious crimes. The police constable had seen Connolly on television, fighting in the cage at the height of his powers – he wasn't going to take any chances and called in reinforcements. But it still took him, five more burly officers and a taser to overpower the fighter after they smashed in the door of the cabin Connolly had booked to stay out of the way of the other passengers.

Jane came to *Jumping Jack Flash* to tell me about the man's arrest. I'd already confirmed that he was the same man with the gold tooth who I saw ferrying Romaine and the others to the party on board *Nirvana*, and the man who set fire to the barge.

'What about the senior officer you saw in the boat with Romaine that night?' I asked. I was being disingenuous. His name, rank, age and home address were one of many on the list I had systematically transferred into my notebook, just in case.

'Oh yes,' said Jane, taking a coffee from Nina with a nod of thanks. She had moved back onboard *Jumping Jack Flash* as soon as we'd returned from Blenheim. Cal's home was now secured while the police went over it with a much finer toothcomb than they had before.

'He's decided to take early retirement. Quite a sudden decision, apparently. And he isn't having a leaving do. I suspect he'll end up in the dock. And we're making pretty good progress on identifying the kids. I'm working closely with social services on all of the follow-up actions. It's going to keep us busy for quite some time.'

Hugh and I had watched the deteriorating weather conditions and taken a joint decision to move our boats onto East Street Moorings, a long stretch of much safer river moorings, immediately upstream of Osney Lock. We were allowed to stop there for the duration of an impending flood, and, for some reason, we were never visited again by the officious man from the Environment Agency. Hugh's wife was discharged from hospital and they had recently returned home to Gloucestershire. I still planned to help him to get *Raven* home; Nina was wondering whether to join us for the journey or remain on *Jumping Jack Flash*.

About a week after Cal's death, a young woman from a delivery company knocked at the boat's hatchway bearing a letter addressed to both Nina and me. I sliced it open. Inside was an thick single sheet of writing paper, a quarter filled with elegant handwriting:

The 40:40 Ministry, Tennessee

Dear Mr Jack Johnson and Mrs Angelina Wilde,

I am taking the liberty of contacting you after extensive conversations with the British authorities about my son's death. Caleb was a fine young man and my wife and I are distraught that Our Lord has chosen to take him from us in this way.

I am now coming to England to bring him home and my plane will be landing at London Oxford Airport on Monday February 2nd.

I would like to meet you both in order to finalise some arrangements and I have taken the liberty of booking lunch for the three of us at Le Manoir aux Quat'Saison at 1pm on the day of my arrival.

I look forward to seeing you there.

God Bless You,

The Reverend Eli S. Hopper

Nina takes the letter from me and reads it for herself. I watch her nervously. Anna has told me that Nina is still 'working through her feelings' for Cal, 'coming to terms' with his suicide and 'rationalising the part that I played' in what happened. I have been advised not to raise any of these issues with her until she is good and ready. As you may imagine, this has not created a free and easy atmosphere on board a cramped narrowboat where we are imprisoned by poor weather. Perhaps this visit by Cal's father is the catalyst we need?

'How do you feel about seeing him?' I ask tentatively.

She looks thoughtful. 'I wonder how much Philpott has told him?'

'Quite a lot, I think. Or he wouldn't be wanting to meet us for lunch tomorrow. Nina. Shouldn't we talk about all of this before we sit down with Cal's father?'

She leans forward, puts both elbows on the table, clenches both fists together and rests her chin on them. Her big black eyes stare into mine. She sighs. 'Okay. What do you want to know, Jack? What do you want to say?'

'I want to know if you blame me for what I did. I want to know if we're still friends and whether we still might be more than that one day. I want to know ... no. I want to say that if you and Cal had some kind of ... some kind of relationship going on, then it doesn't matter to me. My feelings for you are unchanged.'

She keeps her chin resting on her fists and the pose gives a particular intensity to her words. 'Okay. You're right. Let's do this. Do I blame you? My head says no, but my heart isn't so sure. I know you had good reasons for everything that you did, and you were proved right. But I'm not sure what truly motivated you. Were you really trying to save those kids? Or were you driven by your frustration at seeing me with Cal? I was trying to help him.'

'Yes. I have been miserable. As I said, in a sense I wish I had never trailed here after you. It's been a strange and upsetting time for me. But no, I liked Cal.'

'And that probably made it worse for you. Poor Jack,' says Nina softly. 'You say it doesn't matter if I had ... how did you phrase it? Some 'kind of relationship' with Cal.' She rubs both her eyes vigorously with the palms of her hands. 'Yes, I did, Jack. I had a relationship with him that involved long and heart-searching discussions into the dead of night. I had a relationship with him which involved him sobbing on my shoulder until it was soaked with his tears. I had a relationship where I tried to give him as much comfort as I could in the depths of his despair. Because I've been there too, in that deep, dark pit of grief. But our relationship wasn't what I thought it was.' She pauses before going on. 'I now realise that he only told me as much as he thought I needed to know. He never told me the whole truth and it was you who brought it all out into the open. But if what you're asking is a much more basic question ... if you're asking whether I slept with him, then the answer is no, Jack. No. I didn't sleep with Cal.'

'I'm sorry.' She is right. That's exactly what I wanted to know and I'm ashamed of myself.

'Sorry for wanting to know?' she says. 'Okay. In the spirit of full and open disclosure, if he'd asked me to sleep with him, I probably would have. But he didn't and that's the truth. Having seen those horrible pictures, I suspect he had come to see sex as something quite sordid and sinful.' She shrugs and smiles sadly. 'Perhaps I should ask you the same question about Jane?'

My heart is hammering so hard that I am certain she can hear it during the lengthy silence that follows. 'Yes.' I swallow hard. 'We slept together. Twice. It didn't mean anything. We were both lonely. But no excuses. I'm sorry.'

'And it was because you felt that I'd abandoned you?'

I nod, too choked-up and desolate to speak any more.

'It's been a bloody mad time, hasn't it?' she says. 'Come on. Rain or no rain, Eddie needs a walk.'

The atmosphere between us is much easier after this exchange. It is as though a fierce thunderstorm has swept through and defused the glowering static which preceded it. We potter companionably in the galley that evening, share a warming stew of beef cooked in beer and read our books quietly. Nina even pours herself a generous measure of single malt. It feels like life is returning to normal – whatever that means.

CHAPTER FORTY-FIVE

My phone rings as Nina and I are eating breakfast together. The voice is female, chirpy and American. 'Hello there. Am I speaking to Mr Jack Johnson?'

I switch the speaker on so Nina can hear. 'Yes, that's me.'

'Why hello, sir. I'm so sorry to call you this early your time. My name is Natasha and I work for the Reverend Eli S. Hopper of the 40:40 Ministry.'

'Right. Hello.'

'I'm just calling to check that you received the Reverend's letter and that you'll be joining him for lunch later today? His private jet lands at London Oxford Airport at midday UK time, so he'll be going directly to the restaurant.'

'Yes. That's fine. We'll see him there at one o'clock, Natasha.'

Nina and I take Eddie for a jog along the riverbank path, downstream to Iffley Lock where we pause, both silently remembering our little prayer meeting with Cal. As usual, Nina slows her pace to allow me to keep up, but I am still blowing hard by the time we return from Sandford. Three hours later, a taxi has delivered us to the front door of the posh restaurant and hotel at Great Milton, a few kilometres to the east of the city. Nina looks elegant in an all-white dress and black heels. She seems at home in the moneyed surroundings of the honey-stone manor house with its surrounding kitchen gardens. Young waiters flutter around us as we settle into seats at the bar and agree that yes, two flutes of champagne would be rather splendid, thank you very much.

'Stop staring, Jack,' she says, laughing. 'It's as if you've never been in a Michelin two-star restaurant before.'

'I haven't.'

The low murmur of conversation from the other guests pauses briefly when the loud American accent of Reverend Eli S. Hopper drifts through from the lobby before his impressive frame fills the doorway. I recognise the preacher from the photograph of him at his son's house and it is immediately obvious how Cal acquired his physique and good features. Cal's father is easily as tall as his son, 6ft 4 or 5 inches. He has a mane of thick silver hair above a Mount Rushmore carving of a face. His brow, nose, cheeks and chin could have been designed by central casting for the movie role of Moses. He bears down on us with an intent and serious look.

'Mrs Wilde. Mr Johnson.' He kisses Nina's hand and pumps mine. His grip is even stronger than Cal's. 'I do thank you for agreeing to meet me. Shall we go straight through? I'm told the table is ready.' His voice is a deep rich rumbling bass. A waiter insists upon carrying our drinks into the dining room for us and escorts us with them on a silver tray. My eyes are soon boggling at the price of the nine-course tasting menu, but the Reverend courteously directs us to a three-course meal 'solely in the interests of time, you understand.' He says that he will have still water with ice but makes sure we both have two glasses of a good Burgundy that the sommelier recommends.

'Thank you again for meeting me,' he says after bowing his head to say a silent grace to himself.

'I wish it could be in happier circumstances,' Nina replies.

'Caleb often rang me after he arrived in Oxford, so we heard all about his life here. But please, tell me something about how he was while you knew him.'

Nina takes the lead and talks about his sporting and academic prowess, his religious faith and his easy companionship. But Cal's father seems impatient and distracted. Finally, he interrupts. 'Yes. But after this girl's death. How did he seem to you then?'

'Grief stricken. My own husband was killed in Afghanistan not long ago, so I know. He seemed terribly affected by Ophelia's death. He called her Phi. It was very genuine. I think he loved her deeply – in spite of what happened.'

The Reverend nods his massive head. 'His mother and I are baffled that he never told us about Miss McVeigh.'

'He hadn't been seeing her for very long,' says Nina.

'He once said he thought you might fear he was being distracted from his commitment to rowing – and to his PhD,' I add.

The Reverend turns to look at me with a real intensity. 'I have paid a team of researchers to get to the bottom of what happened. The final report was delivered to me just as I got on the plane. I have read it three times from cover to cover above the Atlantic. The police have been very forthcoming and I know all about your role in revealing what my son did, Mr Johnson.'

I try to look back at him without flinching. 'I wouldn't do anything differently again, Reverend Hopper,' I say quietly. 'At least I don't think I would. Events seemed to move very quickly at the end.'

Waiters appear to take away the starters and fuss around with a silver crumber on the immaculate white linen cloth. Cal's father has his hands clasped together on the table and his eyes closed while they do this. I wonder if he is praying again. But as soon as they have gone, he looks at me again. 'My son sinned, and he paid the ultimate price,' he says simply. 'I don't blame you, Mr Johnson. I believe you followed your conscience and did what you thought needed to be done for the right reasons. There were other victims in this case. Child victims. And they had nothing to do with my son. And Miss Wilde, you provided my

Caleb with some degree of comfort and friendship when he was at his lowest ebb. My wife and I thank you for that.'

Three main dishes materialise at our elbows. They are beautifully presented but look small. I fear I may need to stop for some fish and chips on the way home. The Reverend takes a couple of mouthfuls in the American way, with a fork in his right hand, and then pushes the plate away.

'I will be direct with you both. I'm afraid I can't linger. I am due to see the university authorities later today and I hope to say a prayer at Christ Church cathedral. My plane is expecting me with Caleb for a four p.m. take-off. You are a journalist, I believe, Mr Johnson? I have read about your previous books and articles. Perhaps you are now thinking about writing about my son? Well, I am here to beg you not to do so. His mother and I shall have to live with the knowledge of what he did. But we have no desire to see it bandied across the world.'

'I have no plans to write about it, Reverend Hopper,' I say.

Nina gives me a little smile. Perhaps she has been worrying about this too, although she hasn't said anything.

'I am pleased to hear you say this, Mr Johnson. But I understand your finances are ... not all that they might be at present and so, perhaps you will be tempted to change your mind after I go home?'

'If I give you my word, I will keep it,' I say, drumming the fingers of one hand lightly on the tablecloth.

He holds both his huge palms towards me placatingly. 'I have no wish to offend you Mr Johnson. Nevertheless, it is a big story and I do not doubt your inside knowledge and pedigree would be attractive to a publisher. You will be financially worse off if you do not write about your role in exposing the scandal of what has gone on in this city among some of its leading citizens. And, of course, my son is now part of this terrible sequence of events.'

I shake my head again. 'As I said, I have no plans ...'

'No plans!' he says, suddenly banging the table with the palm of his hand. I only just manage to catch my wine glass from toppling. The restaurant falls silent for a few moments before the gentle hubbub of conversation resumes. For the first time the immense strain he is under is made obvious. 'No plans? I'm sorry, Mr Johnson, but these are weasel words. They are what big corporations say when someone catches them about to do something they don't yet want to be made public knowledge. An organisation or a man with "no plans" can easily change their mind without being accused of an outright lie. I want you to guarantee to me that you won't write a word about my son.' He reaches into the inside breast pocket of his suit jacket and removes a folded piece of paper. 'I'm sorry. I don't mean to upset you or doubt your word. But I need a written promise. Read this, Mr Johnson. It is a financial contract. You will be rewarded generously if you sign it. Think of it as compensation for what you might have earned.'

I scan the unfolded piece of A4 paper and give it to Nina. The Reverend extracts a gold fountain pen and holds it out to me.

'No,' I say, refusing to take the pen. 'I don't want your money. You don't need to do this Reverend Hopper. Tell him, Nina.'

'You can trust Jack,' she says, handing the paper back to him. But he immediately pushes my plate back and puts the paper and pen in front of me.

'Please, Mr Johnson. Sign it. Please sign it.'

Horrified, I see that a big fat tear is slipping down one of the deep vertical crags of his cheek.

Nina covers my right hand with her left and gives it a slight squeeze. 'Just sign it, Jack,' she whispers.

So, I do. He pockets it and stands. 'Thank you. I doubt I shall ever be truly happy again, but you have given me some small measure of comfort. Please stay and finish your lunch. There will be nothing to pay. Now, my car is waiting. I am going to prevail on the university's vice chancellor to create a professorship in Caleb's honour. It will be called the Caleb Hopper Oxford University Chair in International Terrorist Studies. And then I shall say a prayer for him and take my poor boy home.' He stands stiffly, shakes hands with each of us and then turns to stride out of the restaurant without a backwards glance.

'Phew,' I say after he has gone. I drain my glass of wine. 'I wasn't expecting that.'

'You did the right thing,' says Nina. 'I know how much you would have wanted to write that book.'

'Not about Cal,' I say. 'I promise.'

'I know, Jack. But about all the other stuff. The powerful men and the county lines criminals with their drugs and their child prostitutes. You hate injustice and cruelty like that, and you would have wanted to expose it.'

'He's got a cast iron contract that says I won't,' I say.

'Yes. And you've got £100,000 in compensation.'

'He didn't need to pay me anything.'

'I know that, Jack. But he wanted to be sure. It gave him some small measure of comfort. Taking the money was the kindest thing to do.'

'I suppose I could just write it up as a memoir. Just for myself. Although to be honest I think I just want to forget the whole thing.'

Nina's look suggests that she shares this feeling and I think she is about to say something to this effect. But instead, she asks what I will do with the money. 'I'll give some of it to the two county lines charities Jane told me about,' I say.

'Good call,' says Nina approvingly.

'But first, shall we look at the pudding menu?'

Eventually, we are respectfully bowed out of the restaurant and a taxi takes us back to *Jumping Jack Flash* on its new mooring. I am amazed that, despite the tiny portions, I feel as though I have had a good lunch. It must have been all that delicious bread that I ate at the start. We change out of our finery and go on a long walk with Eddie along the river, into the Botanic Gardens and through the city's streets, until we have completed an enormous three-hour circuit that brings us back to the boat. The sudden improvement in my bank balance prompts me to call in at an upmarket off-licence during our walk and invest a tidy sum in an eighteen-year-old bottle of Hakushu whisky from the pine forests and fast flowing mountain streams at the base of the Southern Japanese Alps. Nina is eyeing it as enthusiastically as me, but we force ourselves to wait until after some of yesterday's stew has been reheated and digested for our evening meal. Finally, I pour two generous measures of the pale gold liquid, which we smell, dilute and savour with due reverence. Nina is curled up with Eddie in the love seat and I am taking an enormous amount of comfort in the sight.

'Will you start looking for an apartment again now?' I ask.

She is stroking the brown hairless part of Eddie's prone belly and one of his legs is twitching automatically in response. 'No. I don't think so. I'm going to have a rethink. You were right. Anna does need a bit more space from her aunt. And I don't have very happy memories about this place now.'

'Nor me. I'd really like it if you gave me a hand to take *Raven* back with Hugh. It would be fun and he's good company.'

'Yes, alright,' she says cheerfully.

I rejoice silently and top up her glass as a reward. 'Excellent.'

I suddenly realise that I haven't told Nina about Will's brief appearance. They like each other. 'Talking of good company ...' I begin, and soon we are hooting and snorting with laughter at the trick that his jilted agent played on him and the image of him naked and shivering behind a napkin on my boat's roof. 'He did cheer me up enormously when I was quite blue,' I confess. 'And he also urged me to keep the faith with you.'

'Lovely Will,' she says, lowering her eyes to sip her whisky, but ignoring my comment about our relationship. 'I wish I'd seen him.'

We then spend an hour pouring over the maps and the relevant Pearson & Son guidebooks, working out our route to Hugh's permanent mooring in Gloucestershire and deciding on the best places to stop for the night.

'But it won't be a proper holiday, will it?' she says suddenly. 'And I do think we deserve one. Dreaming spires indeed! It's been more like a waking nightmare.'

'Where would you like to go?' I ask.

'I don't know. We'll have to sleep on it.'

'It has to be somewhere with canals?' I say firmly. 'Venice?'

'Or Amsterdam?'

'Aviero in Portugal? The Venetian Hotel in Las Vegas?'

We spend a happy hour huddled together searching the internet, looking at options and I'm in something of a daze as I shave and brush my teeth before bed. Nina will be sharing our journey to Gloucestershire and then she wants to go on a foreign holiday with me. I couldn't be happier. At least that's what I think. But I am to be proven wrong.

About half an hour later the door swings open and Nina pads towards me in a singlet that looks indecently short above her bare legs. Eddie is trotting faithfully at her heels. I look at her curiously. She must have forgotten her glass of water. But instead of going past me and into the galley, she reaches across and flicks off my little side lamp. The cabin is plunged into semi-darkness.

'You asked me a question yesterday and I didn't answer,' she says quietly.

'Oh yes?'

'You asked if we were still friends – and whether we might be more than that one day?'

'Uh huh.' I don't quite trust my voice at this moment.

I sense rather than see her pulling her top over her head. 'Well,' she whispers, holding the back of my head with one hand and bringing her mouth close to my ear. 'I think it's time to answer that one, don't you?'

I have dreamt of this moment from my very first meeting with Nina. It would be the easiest thing in the world now to turn my head, find her mouth with my own and pull her warm naked body close against mine. But instead, I find myself taking hold of her bare shoulders and gently holding her at bay. My voice is slightly strangled by the effort of what I say next.

'Not now, Nina. Not yet. I love you very much – you know that. But I want you to be sure that you love me just as much. This is too soon after ... after what's happened. Trust me. Please.'

She laughs softly, stands and retreats to the doorway. 'Who'd have thought it?' she says quietly. 'Jack Johnson's head ruling his heart for a change. All right, Jack – maybe not tonight, or next week. But it'll happen. We will happen one day. I promise you.'

The door swings closed behind her.

And beyond the boat, in the blackness of the cold and swirling flood water, the two river gods Thamus and Isis pause in their own lovemaking and laugh gently to themselves at the folly of mortals who dare to make plans.

Author's Note

Oxford Blues is the third book in the Johnson & Wilde crime mystery series. It has been said that there are essentially three different motives for murder: hatred, greed and lust. The killings in my debut novel, *Canal Pushers*, were motivated by the hatred of a sociopath for his mother and his workmates. In its sequel, *River Rats*, the crimes were motivated by the financial greed of unscrupulous property developers. The main theme of this book is love, lust and desire in its many and various guises.

Once again, my novel is inspired by real news stories – in this case the history of various police operations and investigations into county lines criminal activities in Oxford. Some of these are faithfully summarised when Detective Sergeant Jane Henry is being interviewed by Jack. Other than this, the plot is entirely the product of my imagination.

All of the book's characters are also entirely fictional, although Hugh Spencer's extraordinary service record mirrors that of the late Surgeon Captain Richard Jolly OBE RN Rtd. His bestselling account of the South Atlantic conflict, *The Red and Green Life Machine: A Diary of the Falklands Field Hospital*, was published in 1983 and I have drawn upon it as a tribute to his achievements.

As usual, I have tried to make the setting of the book as accurate as possible so that readers may revisit the location of the story on foot or even by boat should they wish to do so. Once again, I am grateful to Michael Pearson of J.M. Pearson & Son Ltd for reference to his company's excellent Canal Companion series of guidebooks and for the bespoke map at the front of the book showing the story's location.

However, I must stress that the precise location of the barge *Nirvana* has been invented, along with Strode Road, its bridge and the nearby Strode Meadows. No such barge called *Nirvana* exists and nor does St Michael's College, to whom my fictional barge is attributed. Its appearance and history is based on the beautiful floating college boathouses that preceded the brick-built boathouses now in place along the Isis. All of the events that are depicted taking place on board *Nirvana* are completely fictitious, as is the Oxford-based Garden of Eden escort agency.

Thank you once again to the excellent team at Orphans Publishing for continuing to support my waterways-based crime mysteries and particularly director Helen Bowden, senior editor Debbie Hatfield and their former publishing manager Joanna Narain. Their expertise and high standards match their values as a proud and independent publisher.

I am grateful to Dr Jerry Luke for his medical input, to Dr Mike Drayton for his psychological insights and to Alex Wade for his legal advice. Thanks also to David Birt, Kate, Guy and Rob Hinchley (rowing), Stuart Makemson (boating), Will Griffee (UFC) and to Eddie Duller, OBE, a former editor of the *Oxford Mail*.

My research trips to Oxford (which included a stay at the Landmark Trust's Old Parsonage at Iffley and also St Hugh's College) were made wholly enjoyable by the companionship of my wife Helen and our great friends David and Lynne Annetts and Tony and Joanna Burke. I'm very grateful to my friends Chris and Deb Palin for the generous and highly productive loan of their flat in Budapest as a writing retreat. Thanks also to Karl Rose, a supporter of the wonderful St Richard's Hospice in Worcester, whose donation won a charity auction prize to be named as the taxi driver in my story.

Oxford Blues was largely written during the coronavirus lockdowns of 2020 and so I must thank my wife Helen again and my daughter

Ella. It was nice for this author's regular routine of self-isolation to be relieved by their unexpected company and encouragement during the day.

Finally, thank you to my parents, John and Kay, to whom this book is dedicated. I love you very much and thank you for all of the love, support and life chances that you have given to me and all of your family.